DEATH UNLEASHED

ALSO BY STEVE McHUGH

The Hellequin Chronicles

Crimes Against Magic

Born of Hatred

With Silent Screams

Prison of Hope

Lies Ripped Open

Promise of Wrath

Scorched Shadows

Infamous Reign

The Avalon Chronicles

A Glimmer of Hope

A Flicker of Steel

A Thunder of War

The Rebellion Chronicles

Sorcery Reborn

DEATH UNLEASHED

THE REBELLION CHRONICLES

STEVE McHUGH

Published by 47North, Seattle

www.apub.com

ISBN-13: 9781542006170
ISBN-10: 1542006171

Cover design by @blacksheep-uk.com

Cover illustration by Larry Rostant

Printed in the United States of America

Joan McHugh. Baker of cakes, encourager of dreams, and hater of fuss. My nan. One in a billion.

LIST OF CHARACTERS

Nate's Story

Nate Garrett: Sorcerer and necromancer. In a relationship with Selene.

Selene: Dragon-kin. In a relationship with Nate.

Eos: Sister to Selene. Dusk walker.

Tommy Carpenter: Werewolf. Best friend of Nate Garrett. Married to Olivia. Father of Kasey.

Olivia Carpenter: Water elemental. Onetime head of Avalon's law enforcement. Wife to Tommy. Mother to Kasey.

Kasey (Kase) Carpenter: Half-werewolf, half–ice elemental. Daughter of Tommy and Olivia.

Remy Roax: Fox/man hybrid. Swears. A lot.

Sky (Mapiya): Necromancer. Adopted daughter of Hades and Persephone.

Zamek Merla: Royal prince. Norse dwarf. Alchemist. Searching for the rest of his people.

Masako: Jikininki. Ambiguous as to whose side she's actually on.

Mordred's Story

Mordred: Sorcerer. Video game enthusiast. In a relationship with Hel.

Hel: Necromancer. Leader of Helheim. In a relationship with Mordred.

Elaine Garlot: Sorcerer. Mordred's aunt. Onetime leader of Avalon, before she was overthrown by Arthur and Merlin.

Tarron: Shadow elf. One of the last of his kind. Searching for the rest of his people.

Lancelot: Sorcerer. Master swordsman. On the run from Arthur with Guinevere.

Guinevere: Sorcerer. On the run from Arthur with Lancelot.

Layla's Story

Layla Cassidy: Umbra. Able to manipulate metal.

Chloe Range-Taylor: Umbra. Able to absorb and discharge kinetic energy. Married to Piper.

Piper Range-Taylor: Umbra. Able to harden her skin to near-unbreakable levels. Married to Chloe.

Tego: Saber-tooth panther. Layla's pet.

Irkalla: Necromancer.

Ava Choi: Teenager. Shinigami. Thrown into a world she's not quite come to grips with.

Jinayca Konal: Norse dwarf. Alchemist.

The Rebellion

Hades: Necromancer. One of the leaders of the resistance. Married to Persephone.

Persephone: Earth elemental. One of the leaders of the resistance. Married to Hades.

Odin: Sorcerer. Father to Nate. Leader of Asgard.

Melinoe: Earth elemental. Daughter of Hades and Persephone. Sister to Sky.

Loki: Hodgepodge of different species. Father to Hel.

Valhalla

Rela: Valkyrie. Empress of Valhalla.

Brynhildr: Valkyrie. Mother to Nate. Leader of the rebellion in Valhalla against Rela and her forces.

Orfeda: Dwarven queen.

Snagnar: Dwarven king.

Avalon

Arthur: Sorcerer. Leader of Avalon. Not a nice guy.

Hera: Sorcerer. In control of London.

War: Sorcerer. Hera's weapon sent to assassinate those who displease her.

Gawain: Sorcerer. Brother to Mordred. Partially responsible for Arthur's rise to power.

Merlin: Sorcerer. Father of Mordred. Brainwashed by Gawain to help Arthur but now doing so of his own free will.

Licinius: Sorcerer. Assistant to Hera.

Miscellaneous

Hope: Once known as Pandora.

Rasputin: Sorcerer. Onetime employee of Hera.

Eleanor Owino: Prime minister of the UK.

Prologue

Nate Garrett

December 1916
Saint Petersburg

For someone who could use fire magic to keep warm, I was still bloody freezing.

I'd been sitting on the frozen ground under a large tree for the better part of an hour. I was wrapped up warmly in a big dark-brown coat and thick trousers and carried several books that helped keep the cold out, but I still didn't want to be here. While my fire magic kept me warm, I couldn't use too much of it for fear that someone would see, and I'd have to explain why steam was rising from all around me.

The Malaya Nevka River was a stone's throw away, its icy top a crust on the frozen water beneath it. Any human who fell in would die in moments. Even a sorcerer like me would certainly remember the time without any fondness.

I sighed, ignoring the suspicious glance from the man who walked past me. It was early in the morning, and the only people out right now were those working and those up to something bad. I definitely looked like I belonged in the second camp.

Stretching, I walked toward the bank of the river, hoping I hadn't been sent here for no reason.

Two decades ago, I'd left Avalon when it had become apparent to me that it was built on corruption and that even Merlin—a man I'd once considered a father figure—was capable of evil but had convinced himself he was doing the right thing. The murders he'd ordered committed in the name of keeping Arthur alive in his coma still haunted me.

I'd left Avalon and done very little else since. I'd just been beginning to figure out what I was meant to do next when Hades had offered me a job. Come to Saint Petersburg, help him with someone who wanted to escape Hera's grasp, and maybe it would help me discover what I should do with my life. So far, it had only helped me realize that Russia was a mess. Economically, socially—everything was heading toward disaster. I'd been in Russia for a few months arranging everything, and the longer I'd spent in the company of workers and commoners, the angrier I'd seen them become.

The ice thirty feet back from the bank broke, and a gloved hand reached out to find purchase on the frozen surface. A second later, the hand vanished back beneath, then remerged ten feet farther toward me as it smashed through again. This time a second hand appeared, grabbing hold of part of the fractured ice, but the hands slipped and fell back into the dark water.

"Just *swim* to the bank," I said, probably slightly louder than needed.

Either he heard my instruction or he decided the bank was the best idea anyway, as less than a minute later the cold, wet man dragged himself out of the water and onto the mud. He was taller than my own five nine by a few inches but slighter in frame than I was—gaunt, almost. His looming presence was frankly . . . disconcerting.

I walked down to him, helped him to his feet, and practically dragged him up the bank before dropping him on the grass behind a stone wall.

"What if they see me?" he asked in Russian, his voice trembling from the cold.

"They think you're dead," I told him, speaking his own language. "At least, I hope they do."

"They poisoned, beat, stabbed, and shot me, before throwing me into a frozen river," he said. "I very nearly *was* dead."

"Well, if they don't think it now, they never will," I told him. "Why didn't you just pretend to die after the poisoning?"

"Didn't realize I *was* poisoned until it was too late; by that point they'd stabbed me. I pretended to die then, but apparently they needed to shoot me first. Have you ever been shot? It hurts like the fires of hell."

"Yes, I've been shot," I said. "Now, to the world, Rasputin is dead, and in his place is . . . actually, I have no idea. Call yourself Fred if you want."

"I will call myself whatever you wish so long as you take me from Hera's grasp."

"That's why I'm here."

"How are we leaving?"

"We have a carriage to take us to Finland, where we'll be getting on a boat to England, where we'll be changing to another boat to America. Once in New York, we'll . . . well, I'll explain that later."

I took Rasputin to the nearby carriage, where its driver nodded a greeting.

"Any trouble?" I asked him.

He shook his head. "Clothes are inside."

"Get changed," I told Rasputin. "You're wearing fine clothing, and despite them being saturated and covered in mud, it's a bad idea for where we're going."

Rasputin nodded and removed his coat, revealing the orange glyphs lit up over his arms. Fire magic keeping him warm and dry: it was why he hadn't died in the river. Being a sorcerer certainly had its advantages, although Rasputin was quite low on the power levels when it came to our kind. He was manipulative, cunning, and shrewd but not powerful. He used fire and air magic, like me, although I'd gone to great pains to explain to him that should he cross me, I would kill him.

I climbed in the carriage just as Rasputin was pulling on a shirt, showing the scar on his stomach where a silver knife had been used to try to kill him a few years earlier.

"Hera sent you here to steer the czar and his family toward actions that benefited her," I said as the carriage set off. "Like keeping Europe from descending into war."

Rasputin nodded. "Didn't work out so well. The war is a mistake. I actually agree with Hera on that."

"Me too," I said. "It's a waste of time, money, resources, and, more importantly, people. Lives thrown away because of pettiness and politics. But once the war started, Hera changed her position, using you to get information about the Russians' military plans. She saw an opportunity and didn't care how many lives were sacrificed to benefit her."

"I know what I've done," Rasputin snapped. "Hera craves power over all else. She might not have wanted the war initially, but once it happened, she was happy to use it to her own ends. She constantly switches sides, playing them off one another, to ensure that whoever wins, she's on their side. I cannot work for her any longer."

"Hera has started rumors that you and the czar are members of a pro-German group. That you're encouraging the czar to make a separate peace treaty with Europe. A lot of people want your head."

"As I discovered," Rasputin said. "Thank you for arranging my death, by the way."

"It took me a couple of weeks to put the idea in a few heads that your death would be better for Russia," I said. "Funny, they didn't take much convincing. They *really* don't like you! I may have suggested some suitable methods; ensuring you were disposed of in the right manner was important. Last thing we'd want is them cutting your head off or using silver." Decapitation could kill us, just as it would any human, and silver hurt like hell.

"Well, I'm glad you helped."

"Rasputin, the drunken debaucher who influenced a czar and his wife," I said with a smile. "Hera has clearly finished her use of you. You made a good decision to seek Hades's aid."

"Hera is a monster," he said. "She lies and betrays everyone. There's no one she wouldn't sacrifice should it aid her. Her own family is terrified of her."

"I've met her on several occasions," I said. "Never been someone I liked. Why work for her all these years if that's how you felt?"

"Being on Hera's list of enemies is a good way to seek an early grave. Once you're in her grasp, getting out is not as easy as walking away."

Rasputin coughed and spat out the open window, closing it afterward. "What happens once we've reached our destination?"

"You will tell your interviewers everything. And I do mean *everything*. Hera's plans, plots, schemes, why she wants the czars to fall. You'll leave nothing out, and in return you will be rehomed somewhere safe with a new identity. You will never refer to yourself as Rasputin again; you will learn a language that isn't Russian. I don't care which one. You will always need to look over your shoulder, because if Hera should discover you *didn't* die . . ."

Rasputin sighed and nodded. We both knew what Hera was capable of.

We were in the carriage for over an hour before we stopped unexpectedly, and voices could be heard from outside. There was a bang on the carriage roof. "Stay here," I told Rasputin before opening the door and stepping outside, wrapping my long dark coat around me as I crunched through the fresh snow to the front of the carriage. I looked up at the driver and nodded that it was okay.

"Gentlemen," I said, paying attention to the three men for the first time. "How can we help you on this cold night?"

The three men were all slightly taller than me, and all wore thick coats that had seen better days. One held a wooden club, one a rusty sword, and the final one a scythe. Although two of them, from their clothing, appeared to be farmers, one of them wore an old military uniform. Things could go very badly, very quickly.

"We want all of your valuables, and whoever is in the carriage can cough up as well," the man in the uniform shouted. "Now, or we start hurting people."

He was obviously the leader, which made sense considering he'd had the training to fight. He looked more assured of himself, while the other two appeared outright terrified.

I reached into the large pocket inside my coat and grabbed the smallest of three leather money pouches, throwing it to the man who was closest to me, completely shutting out the leader. The expression on his face told me that he knew what I'd done. No matter what else happened, he would not let that lie.

"There's enough in here for six months' wages," the man closest to me said, the awe in his voice easy to hear.

"All silver," I assured them, turning to the leader. "I assume a good soldier like yourself knows of somewhere to exchange it?"

The two farmers looked at their leader in horror.

"He knows you deserted," the man in the middle of the three said to the leader.

"I don't care if you deserted," I said. "Look, I'm in a hurry, and I need to leave. It's a matter of life and death. Please take your money, go home, and feed your families."

"We should," the man with the money pouch said.

The leader took a step toward me, pointing his dagger at me the whole time. "I think I'm going to take that nice coat and those nice boots, and then I'm going to *kill* you."

"We don't need to do that," the middle man pleaded with him. "We have money for food. That's all we need."

"I *need* something more," the leader said. "I *need* to show this rich asshole that he can't spend his whole life looking down on us, letting us die for his kind."

"I'm not who you think I am," I said. "And I'm sorry for your loss, but you don't want to do this."

The leader took two steps toward me before I sidestepped him, grabbed him by the wrist with one hand, swept out his legs, and threw him into the snow. I picked up the dagger and threw it into the trees at the side of the road.

I looked over at the two remaining men. "Either of you try, I'll kill you," I said. "Go home."

The leader roared, thrusting himself up from the ground and charging at me, but he met my elbow with his jaw and got a fist to his stomach, which sent him back to the ground. I placed a dagger of fire against his throat.

"As I said, I do not have *time* for this," I said. The two other men ran off into the woods as the leader's eyes opened wide with shock and fear.

"I tried to be nice, I tried to just get you to go, but you want something I can't give you. And if you try again, I *will* kill you."

I moved back to the coach and opened the door. We were on our way a moment later.

"Why didn't you just use magic?" Rasputin asked. "Why not kill them?"

"Because they were desperate men who have been pushed to a breaking point by poverty. The leader wanted some kind of retribution for what he'd been through, and besides, I get the feeling this place is going to see a lot more death in the future."

"Not just here if we don't stop Hera," Rasputin said, smoothing his beard. "She will unleash War on this world if she isn't stopped."

"Other than the war in Europe?" I asked.

Rasputin shook his head and looked about to say something but sighed instead. "No, my friend," he said after several seconds. "Her War is something else entirely. It's to be feared like nothing you've ever seen."

Chapter One

Nate Garrett

Realm of Asgard

For the first time in my sixteen hundred years of life, I was a father. And it was simultaneously the most awesome and most terrifying thing I'd ever been part of.

I'd had what most would describe as a tumultuous few years. I'd died, murdered by a friend of mine because I'd asked him to—it was a long story, but I'd obviously come back to life. I'd lost all of my magic for two years and, when it had returned to me, destroyed a large part of a forest in Oregon. I'd been forced to kill my half brother. Admittedly, it was because he was a massively psychotic dick who believed that by killing his mother he would bring about the end of the world, but even so, it was a lot to go through.

None of that even came close to the fear I'd felt when Selene had told me that she was pregnant with our child.

Being over sixteen hundred years old had done little to ease the worry about how I was going to help bring up the little bundle of joy in this crazy-ass world. I'd been about to have a child for the first time. I'd been a lot of things over the centuries but never a parental figure. Hell, I'd been pretty sure I couldn't even have children; magic did a lot to remove a person's fertility.

My daughter was now two weeks old, and Selene and I still hadn't settled on a name. At least officially.

I sat on a grassy hill overlooking the building where Selene had given birth. Or at least the remains of the building. It turned out that when dragon-kin gave birth, they could lose control over their power. Giant spikes of ice had torn through the brick-and-glass building, all but destroying the roof and one side of the top floor.

Thankfully, no one had been injured, and once the baby had been born, it had taken Selene only a few hours to regain her strength. I looked down at the tiny, helpless baby who was my daughter. She was in a red-and-silver pram that Zamek had made for her. Being one of the Norse dwarves, he was an alchemist of exceptional talent, and the pram was comfortable inside and also looked a bit like it could be used as a small mobile tank should need arise. I was pretty sure it was completely bulletproof for a start, which wasn't something I'd ever expected a child of mine to need, but here we were.

My daughter was currently fast asleep, and I'd been told to take her away from the long house that was Odin's—my father's—seat of power until summoned. There was to be a party. A party that I had suggested was a bad idea for several reasons. Mostly because outside the hundreds-of-feet-high wall that separated the city of Gladsheim from the rest of the realm was the army of Avalon.

They'd been steadily marching toward the city for a few months, and then, just before they'd reached the enormous forest of the realm, they'd stopped. No one knew why, and though my father had sent scouts to find out, none of them had returned. We were in a state of impasse. No one wanted to go out there and prepare to fight, and no one wanted to just wait around either.

"So you're still here," Tommy said as he took a seat beside me on the hill. He wasn't a tall man, but he was broad and muscular. His long brown hair was tied back in a ponytail, and he had a bushy graying beard.

Tommy was my best friend. I'd known him for centuries, ever since he'd been turned into a werewolf during the Hundred Years' War between England and France. He was probably one of the most powerful of his kind.

"I've been told to stay away until someone comes to collect me," I told him as he looked in on my daughter.

"Zamek did a good job," Tommy said, admiring the pram. "It's a little imposing, though. Are you planning on using it as a tiny war chariot?"

"Well, there's an impending war," I said, looking up at the griffins flying high above. They'd been more than happy to come help if it meant killing people who worked for Arthur. Half-lion, half-eagle, and more than capable of tearing a man clean in half in a multitude of ways, they were exceptional allies. "That's if Avalon ever move again. Something is going on. I can't imagine Arthur is staying there for the scenery."

Centuries before Arthur had been born, one of the seven devils, Asmodeus, had tried to conquer all of the realms but had eventually been defeated. Asmodeus had been captured and executed, but that hadn't stopped his blood and spirit from being used in the rituals that had given birth to Arthur. Arthur was his own man, but more than a little of him was that thousands-of-years-old devil. At one point, Asmodeus had been considered the most powerful being in existence. Arthur wanted that power back, he wanted that control back, and most of all, he wanted to finish what Asmodeus had started all those millennia ago. To rule over all. And to destroy anyone who dared oppose him.

"Avalon are staying put, and so are we," Tommy said, scratching his beard with one hand. "Olivia is still here with Daniel, who, despite being only three months old, is now walking and talking."

Werewolf children aged quickly. The first year of a werewolf child was roughly the same as the first five years for a human infant. Being half-werewolf and half-elemental, it wasn't clear exactly what Daniel Carpenter would become, but right now he was a handful.

"People are still being evacuated," I said. "Daniel will be among them at some point, if that's what you're worried about."

"I know. And I know he's probably safer here with Olivia and me for now, but there's still the worry of, you know, impending battle." He looked back in the pram. "You got a name yet?"

"Yes," I told him. "Or at least we have a first name. We haven't figured out what else to call her. We have ideas but haven't settled on anything. Apparently, we're meant to come up with the full name before the party."

"Ah, a good old naming party," Tommy said with a small laugh.

"Apparently, it's important," I said. "At least, Odin thinks so."

"How's that going? You and your dad, I mean."

"It's weird," I said. "He's been the doting grandfather, and I've spent a few months getting to know him. The first time we met, he cried. I hadn't been expecting the outburst of emotion."

"He wears his heart on his sleeve," Tommy said.

I nodded. "That he does."

"You know, he's coming on a mission with me."

I turned to look at him. "Are you serious?"

Tommy nodded. "We've gotten word of some kind of experiment factory in Kilnhurst, Montana."

The name did not bring back good memories. "Kilnhurst? That's not exactly a name I expected to hear again. We wiped that place off the map for being a town of pretty much pure evil."

"Apparently evil doesn't know when to stay dead," Tommy told me with a sigh.

Kilnhurst was a town that in the 1870s had decided to throw its lot in with a lich, who had then gone on to murder countless people while promising the inhabitants a life of riches and safety. Eventually, anyone there had been either murdered by the lich, turned into a ghoul, or killed by me, Hades, and his soldiers. A lot of good people had died to stop the lich and its followers. I had very little interest in seeing such depravity take root again.

"And Odin is going with you?" I asked.

"He suggested it. He wants to show people he's pulling his weight, and with Hades, Olivia, and the others taking control of different parts of Asgard, I think he's feeling like he needs to do something. Possibly punch someone. Which sounds like you."

I couldn't help but smile. "Valid point."

"So, you planning on going to Valhalla to meet your mum?"

I shrugged. "Men aren't allowed to travel to Valhalla. I guess the ball is in her court. If she even knows I'm alive and here. Basically, I have no idea."

My mum, Brynhildr, had given me up to Merlin when I was only a child. She hadn't wanted to, but my mere existence was cause for a whole lot of people to want me dead, and that was something neither my mother nor my father had felt they could protect me from. Merlin, in theory, could. It hadn't worked out as anyone had planned, but I understood why my mum had given me up.

It had taken centuries before I'd even known who either of my parents were, and now that I did, it felt weird planning to meet them. They were, for all intents and purposes, strangers to me. Odin had certainly tried his hardest to change that, but I hoped that I'd get to meet my mum too. Unfortunately, as much as I wanted to just go there, if I set foot in Valhalla, there was a pretty good chance I'd be arrested, killed, or something worse I hadn't considered.

I spotted Selene striding toward us, with three Asgard soldiers a respectful distance behind. She wore black leather armor with purple runes that occasionally glimmered as the sunlight struck them. As dragon-kin, Selene was able to roar ice, using it both as a weapon and for defense. She'd once saved my life with a shield of the stuff. Selene was in her human form, but though she had given birth a couple of weeks earlier, her skin continued to glow silver, which was the color of her scales when she was in her dragon-kin form.

The dragon-kin were mostly humanoid in appearance, but they had two thick wings, silver scales, and razor-sharp talons on their hands and feet, and their faces took on a sort of half-human, half-dragon appearance.

"Nate, Tommy," Selene said as she joined us.

Tommy got up and hugged Selene. "How are things?"

"I'm tired," Selene said with a slight sigh. "I can't take our daughter through the realm gate because people aren't sure what will happen when the child of a dragon-kin and a sorcerer goes through one. I think Leonardo and Antonio were concerned she may cause it to explode. But people said she might cause the building to explode when she was born, and I managed that myself."

"You worried?" Tommy asked.

Selene shook her head. "Not really. I'm a warrior. If that horde comes through this city, they'd better have brought a fucking Death Star with them. People are always going on about mama bears, but they don't have shit on mama dragon-kin."

Tommy laughed. I wasn't sure if it was because of the bear thing or because Selene had mentioned Star Wars. He was, in the words of his adult daughter, a fanboy.

"Eos still here?" I asked.

Selene bent down and kissed me on the lips. "She is. She's preparing to go through the realm gate that Leonardo, Antonio, Zamek, and Jinayca are currently modifying somehow. I told Eos that she could take the bundle of joy through to Shadow Falls while I stay here to defend this realm."

I said nothing. I agreed with her completely, but the last time I'd tried to vocalize my agreement, she'd found that I was a good target for her frustrations. She'd apologized immediately after, not that I felt she'd needed to. I got needing to vent, and I got that she wasn't particularly venting *because* of me, more *at* me.

"Smart man," Selene said and kissed me again.

"You're going to be here fighting?" Tommy asked.

Selene's head snapped back toward my friend. "And if I am?"

Tommy held his hands up. "Whoa, just asking. I'm all for powerful people to help kick ass."

Selene's hard expression melted. "Sorry, I keep being told that I'm a mother now and should be making doilies or something. I see no reason that I can't be a mother and still kick the shit out of Avalon."

"Olivia, Persephone, and many others seem to do okay," Tommy said. "I'm sure you'll be fine. People are just worried at the moment, and a new baby in all this just makes people more worried. Someone said a similar thing to Olivia, and she knocked them out. End of people asking her to stay home."

"Have I ever told you I like your wife?" Selene said.

Tommy smiled. "Everyone likes Olivia. Except the people she knocks out—they're probably not big fans."

I chuckled and wondered if that was the way Selene was going to have to start dealing with people.

"Your dad is here," Tommy said.

I craned my neck to look past him. Sure enough, Odin was marching toward us. Forty or so soldiers followed him, and even from this distance, I could tell that he'd rather they weren't there.

"Son," Odin said as he reached us, the soldiers trying to look inconspicuous at the bottom of the hill. His long silver hair was pulled back into a ponytail, and he wore a black leather eye patch over one eye. His rune-scribed armor was a mixture of black and silver leather, and he wore a long blue cloak that stopped short of trailing along the ground.

"Did you bring your friends?" I asked.

"Smart-ass," he said back. "This is your friend's fault."

"My friend?" I asked. "Diana is in charge of getting the population of this city who weren't soldiers or guards into fighting shape. This is a job you agreed to give her. She is making sure that your people, a lot of whom were farmers, fishermen, and generally just not very well trained to fight in combat, won't die at the first sign of trouble."

"But she has them follow me *everywhere*."

"You are their king," Selene said. "And Avalon isn't exactly against using assassins to get to their enemies."

"That's not why she's done it, though," Tommy said. "You were rude to the woman she loves."

"I *apologized*," Odin said defensively.

"Which is why you have the forty soldiers following you around, and you're not recovering from having your arms ripped off," I said.

Odin sighed. "How long do you think she'll have these people follow me?"

"A few days more," Selene said. "Or you could go and apologize again."

"I am the king," Odin said, puffing out his chest. "I do not apologize twice."

"I heard she's teaching them how to play musical instruments while they march," Tommy said.

Odin sagged. "I will find them both and apologize again."

"And this time, don't make comments about Medusa's snakes," Selene said.

"I was very drunk," Odin said.

"How does that make it better?" I asked.

"It doesn't?" Odin said thoughtfully.

"Good answer," Tommy said, clapping Odin on the back.

"Slight change of subject," I said. "But does anyone know what's actually happening to the realm gate?"

"They're making it bigger," Odin said. "Taking over the buildings on either side of the temple. Honestly, I wasn't sure it could be done, but Zamek and Jinayca have been a revelation. Without the Norse dwarves, it would take three times as long to get everyone out of here. Unfortunately, they have to make the realm gate bigger in Shadow Falls, too, so it's taking a while. If anything is off, people could get hurt."

I got to my feet. "I assume we're wanted at whatever party you're throwing."

"Hades told me there's a custom about wetting the baby's head. I think we should do that."

I'd learned that while it took a huge amount of alcohol to get sorcerers like Odin and me drunk, that same rule didn't apply when the alcohol was as strong as whiskey and still served in pint glasses. It was illegal to give to humans because it would literally kill them. When I'd first arrived in Asgard, Odin had thrown a party to celebrate our reunion. I'd had two pints of the fifty-proof citrus-flavored beer and had to stop. Odin had been on his seventh when he'd insulted Medusa. I wasn't entirely sure what he'd said, but I was pretty sure that Medusa's punching him in the face was a bad sign.

I pushed the pram while walking back to the longhouse-style building at the far end of the city. It was called the Bright House. The building was three times the size of a normal longhouse, and there had been additional work done to build onto the sides, essentially making it look a bit like a palace without the pomp and ceremony. Several hundred feet behind it lay the cliffs that adorned the side of the city. The walls stretched around the foot of the cliffs, ensuring that no one could climb them to drop down on the city, not that it would be my first way to get inside.

The cliff face was about nine hundred feet tall at its highest point, and apparently the realm gate Odin had mentioned was at the top, inside some old tomb. Thankfully it didn't stretch far enough back at that height to be a threat to any of the buildings that were this close.

Six guards stood outside; they stepped aside as we reached them. Odin's "punishment guard" stayed with them.

The interior was lit up with hundreds of candles held on black steel candelabras hanging above a table. It was fifty feet long and could have easily seated a hundred people. Dozens of people stood around it, most with drinks in hand. I recognized the majority of them; Hades and Persephone nodded a greeting to me that I returned.

Wooden staircases—one on either side of the hall—went up to the floor above, with guards standing at the bottom, and more guards stood in front of large wooden doors on both sides of the room. There was a large cheer at our entrance.

"So this is where you want to announce the name of our daughter?" Selene asked, picking up our baby, who was now awake from the noise.

"Have you decided on anything?" Odin asked as people began to talk among themselves.

"Let us go feed her, and we'll report back," I said.

Odin nodded.

Selene and I took our daughter upstairs to one of the many guest rooms.

"So your dad is excited," Selene said as she began to feed our child.

I nodded and sat next to her on the queen-size bed. "I think he wants to make up for not really being allowed to celebrate my birth. I get it must be difficult for him. He's been trying hard to be a dad to a fully grown man who doesn't need one. He finds it weird. I find it weird."

I lay back on the bed.

"This has been a hard few weeks for you," Selene said, placing her hand on my knee.

"The impending battle, the new baby, the meeting my dad for the first time," I said. "It's all been a lot to take in. I sit with her at night while you sleep, and it's just me and her, and the world is quiet, and I wish it could stay that way. I wish I could tell her that the world will get better."

"I love you, Nathan Garrett," Selene said, turning her head to look at me.

I smiled. "I love you too. We need to name her. I know we've talked about it, but we do need to actually settle on something. I still think Gruntar the Destroyer is our best bet," I said.

"How about Sally?" Selene asked.

"Sally the Destroyer?" I asked.

"I feel you're fixating on the Destroyer part."

"Well, she has to destroy something," I said with a smile before kissing Selene on the lips.

"I think she'll be destroying stuff with or without the word in her name."

We discussed it for half an hour until our daughter had had her fill. I left Selene to change her and put her back to sleep. I wasn't sure if it was the same for human babies, but ours ate, slept, and pooped, not necessarily in that order. She barely cried, even for night feeds. When she woke up, she just lay there and stared. I'd told Tommy after a few days, and he'd promptly told me to fuck off.

Selene joined me a few minutes later, just as a crowd of people began to make their way toward me and were intercepted by Tommy, Olivia, and their eldest child, Kase, the latter of whom held a large mug of beer. Despite Olivia's being hundreds of years older than her daughter, the pair didn't look dissimilar in age. Both had dark skin, both had long dark hair—although Olivia's had streaks of white in it—and both were incredibly intelligent and powerful.

"So have you two picked a name?" Tommy asked Selene and me.

"There are bets on it," Olivia said.

"I bet it's something really ancient and foreboding," Kase said as Daniel ran past with several of his friends to go play.

"Foreboding?" Selene asked. "This isn't Star Wars."

"Is it Leia?" Tommy asked, his eyes suddenly wide.

"No, Tommy," I said. "No, it isn't."

"You going to put us all out of our misery, then?" Kase asked.

"Quiet," Odin shouted from the head of the building. "My son and Selene have come to tell us the name of the child."

Selene and I made our way up to where Odin stood.

"Ladies and gents," I said.

"Meet Astrid Winter Garrett," Selene finished.

There were lots of people speaking and cheering all at once after that, and thankfully Astrid remained asleep the whole time.

Chapter Two

Nate Garrett

After several hours of revelry, I headed outside and found a wooden bench far enough away from the longhouse, where I took a seat and waited for the ringing in my ears to stop.

One of the guards came over to me, his silver armor gleaming as the moonlight hit it. "Can I help you, sir?"

I shook my head. "I'm okay. Just needed some air."

He nodded and walked off toward the closest tram station.

The city of Gladsheim was about the same size as Birmingham, so walking from where I sat at one end to the realm gate temple at the opposite end would have taken hours before Leonardo had installed a tram system identical to the one in Shadow Falls. But in Asgard the tramline consisted of three lines sitting alongside one another, meaning it was three times as efficient. They were powered by the same small purple crystals, too, so in the darkness the trams held a sort of ethereal glow in the distance.

The trams went in one direction, making a full lap of the city, and each tram stopped off at different locations and went every ten minutes. It was well organized and certainly made travel a much easier proposition. Hopefully that meant moving troops would be easier too.

I watched the guard walk away and turned as Odin strolled toward me. "Can I take a seat?" he asked.

I motioned for him to join me.

"You left your own party," he said.

"I left *your* party," I corrected. "I'm not good around lots of people."

"I didn't know," he said softly.

"I know—it's fine," I told him. "I just needed some air."

"I'm still awkward around you," Odin said with a sigh. "I don't know how to be a father to a sixteen-hundred-year-old man who is probably one of the most powerful beings on any realm. Can you shoot a bow and arrow?"

I laughed. "Yes. I can ride a bike and shave too."

"Swim?"

"Yep, that too."

"I am a great warrior," he said without any sort of bragging. "And as you may have noticed, I show my emotions. You are my son. I loved you from the moment you were born. Your mother and I . . . well, there was no love between us, but we both loved you. I had to lie about being your father, had to hide it from everyone. That hurt more than I can ever put into words. I didn't even know if you were still alive. And all this time you were in danger, and I couldn't help."

"You don't need to explain yourself," I said. "I do understand."

"I need you to know that I couldn't protect Thor, your brother; I couldn't stop Baldr from killing him. I wanted you to meet Thor. You'd have liked him. He was a stubborn pain in my ass too. And I can't stop you from going to war here, but I do blame myself for the path you're on. It's a hard life you've led. And I am sorry for that."

I looked over at the cliffs. "So this realm gate you were talking about," I said.

"Ah," Odin said with a smile. "Come with me. I'll show you."

We walked past the longhouse, where I spotted Loki and Medusa in conversation. The pair noticed us and waved, and even Odin waved back.

"I said sorry," he told me. "Diana promised to stop having the soldiers follow me around. I apologized to Medusa too. I have to admit there was a time long ago when I would have just let the animosity fester. I guess that's not the most mature way of dealing with things."

"We all have to grow up eventually," I said as we passed a set of barracks. Several soldiers stood to attention to let us onto the path snaking up the cliff face.

It took Odin and me the better part of half an hour to walk to the top, and while the views over the city were spectacular, even at night, more than once I wished we'd never started. By the time we reached our destination, I forgot about the walk and just stared off across the realm in awe.

"This is incredible," I said. The moonlight bounced off mountains in the distance, close to where it was believed that Avalon had decamped its forces. No scout had been able to get close enough to confirm.

"They're moving toward us," Odin said.

"I heard drums yesterday," I said. "And saw plumes of smoke."

"They found the realm gate in the mountains; it's how they've managed to get people here."

"There's a realm gate in the mountains?" I asked.

"Apparently so, yes," Odin said. "I didn't know it existed until Zamek told me. It's how they're getting in and out of the realm, but we can't do anything about it because if we send anyone, they'll be killed.

"The evacuation is still ongoing in the city. Zamek and his team have assured me that the realm gate will be fully operational today. We'll be able to evacuate ten times as many as we could before. Thank you for helping with that."

"I'm not going to stand by and do nothing," I said. "Is this why you brought me up here?"

Odin shook his head. "That is," he said, pointing to the realm gate that sat in the middle of the large clearing.

"So this is a realm gate." I looked around. "No dwarves or guardians to operate it. This works with my blood, right?"

"It was a gift from the dwarves when you were born. It only activates when the blood of my kin touches it, and it only goes to one place. Munster."

"Yeah, about that—Munster is a big place," I said.

"Ah, it's an island just off the coast by the name of Little Skellig. It's officially closed to anyone else, but there's a helipad and small dock with a boat there. You get there, and you can pretty easily make your way to the mainland. Your daughter, Astrid, will one day be able to use this realm gate to travel between here and the Earth realm."

The realm gate was a beautiful thing. A mixture of wood and stone, each realm gate glowed a different color when activated.

"Why did you choose the name?" Odin asked.

I turned back to him. "Selene chose Astrid. She wanted her to have a Norse name. I didn't know my heritage until a few years ago, and she wanted to make sure that Astrid does. Winter because Selene is a dragon-kin linked to the moon, so, you know, ice. And Garrett because it's my surname."

Odin opened his mouth.

"I know, Woden," I said. "But my name is Nathaniel Garrett. I didn't even know the Woden bit until a few months ago. I can't just start double-barreling my name. I am your son; I don't need a name to tell me that."

My father smiled. "I brought you here not just to see the sights and the realm gate but because I'm going on a mission in the morning."

"Tommy told me. Apparently you want to keep busy."

"Tommy originally asked for you to take part," he said. "I told him not to ask you."

I waited for an explanation.

"Hades told me about what you two went through in Kilnhurst all those years ago," Odin began. "I thought it best to see it with new eyes."

"You thought I'd turn up, see something I didn't like, and burn the whole place to the ground?" I asked.

"The thought crossed my mind," Odin said.

"Any way this is a setup?"

"By whom?" Odin asked. "We got the information from Atlas, and he's been pretty good with his info for years now, ever since he joined Hera's organization. If she's involved in the rebuilding of Kilnhurst, it can't be for anything good. Besides, if it is a setup, Tommy and I are more than capable of taking care of whatever comes along."

"And also, if Hera is involved in Kilnhurst and she's doing something awful, then I might go after her."

"Also a thought that had crossed my mind," Odin agreed. "She's in charge of Avalon while Arthur is out there waiting to kill us. Hera has been waiting for you to raise your head so she can go after you. I would rather not have you aim yourself at her without good reason."

"The reason is she's a monster."

"She's always been a monster," Odin said. "Killing her now, without anyone in place to take over control, would be a disaster.

As much as she deserves to die for all the horror she's inflicted on so many, she controls the UK government. She controls London. And she will not give them up without a fight that will cost lives."

"I'm okay with staying here for now," I said, looking back across the landscape to where the Avalon forces were. "Sooner or later they're going to be here, and Arthur is going to have his reckoning. If I don't need to leave, I think it's better I don't. Besides, Astrid and Selene are here, and I'm helping with the evacuation. Right now, they're more important than sticking my head out of a hole so that Hera can take a shot."

Odin was quiet for a moment. "Frigg is in Shadow Falls," he said softly. "I want to see her before I go on the mission."

"There's no change in her condition?" Baldr had tried to murder her with a venom-coated blade, and she'd been placed in a coma for several hundred years as a result.

Odin shook his head. "Without an antidote, I doubt there ever will be. I miss her, Nate. My life feels like it's empty without her in it, and then Thor was murdered, and everything went to shit. I'm sorry about the party; it's just I wanted to show off you, Selene, and Astrid. I wanted to feel like I still had family . . . and hope."

"No need to apologize," I said.

"I wanted it to be a citywide party," he said. "But that was probably unworkable, considering so many have evacuated. My kingdom feels like a ghost town. I needed to feel normal. I wanted others to feel normal. To know that there's something worth fighting for when Arthur arrives and tries to kill us all."

"Why not go see Frigg before your mission?" I asked. "You have time."

Odin hugged me. "Thank you," he said. "I think I will."

Odin and I sat next to the realm gate and talked for a while longer, until he left to go to Shadow Falls to see his wife. I remained up there until the dawn cast beautiful reds and purples across the sky. Black smoke billowed up from the distance. I didn't know what Avalon's horde was doing, but I knew it wasn't good.

Eventually, I descended the long pathway back into the city and walked the mile to where Selene, Astrid, and I were staying. The house sat close to the massive lake that was at the rear of the city, and I quietly tried the door handle and found it unlocked. Selene was sitting on the large sofa inside.

"She's asleep upstairs," Selene said. "How are you?"

"Tired," I told her. "Odin wanted to talk."

"Still not used to calling him your dad?"

"I flicker between the two," I said, sitting beside her. She put her head on my shoulder. "Is that weird?"

"You haven't known him long, so probably not," she said, kissing me on the cheek. "I came back here after you left. As nice as it was to have a party, now feels like a weird time."

"I know. It was a strange thing to have, but on the positive side, we finally picked a middle and last name for Astrid, which is good."

"Odin dotes on her."

"He said he wanted to show us all off," I said thoughtfully. "He's gone to see Frigg now. He misses her a lot more than he lets most people know."

"It must be hard for him," Selene said. "He had to have Frigg shipped to the Earth realm just to keep her safe, and now even there isn't safe. Thor is dead, so is Baldr, and then you turn up with your own small family, and he looks at that and sees that it's not quite so shit. My dad is having difficulties too."

Hyperion was one of the Titans of old, who had waged war against Zeus and the Olympians. Like Selene, he was a dragon-kin, one of the most powerful I'd ever met. We'd had a strained relationship for many reasons over the years, but since Selene and

I had rekindled our love a few years before Arthur and his goons had turned the world to shit, we'd gotten better.

I opened my eyes to find myself lying on the sofa with no Selene in sight. A dark-gray blanket had been placed over me. There was a moment of panic before she appeared, walking down the stairs with Astrid in her arms.

"You fell asleep," Selene said. "So I left you alone. We need to talk about this one."

"What about her?" I asked as Selene passed Astrid to me. She was awake, staring up at me with light-blue eyes that I assumed were a part of her dragon-kin blood.

"I'm taking her to Shadow Falls tomorrow," Selene said. "I know we talked about it, but Olivia is taking Daniel, and they are literally the last children in Asgard at the moment."

"Okay," I said. "I think that's a good idea. Arthur isn't going to wait forever. And we only kept her back because I wanted to spend time with her."

"Also because we thought that maybe we shouldn't be jumping the queue of people trying to evacuate."

"That too," I said with a smile. "Are you coming back here?"

Selene nodded. "Warrior, remember? My sister is taking her."

Smoke billowed up under the doorframe until it formed a woman.

"Eos," I said as she hugged me.

Eos looked a lot like Selene, but her skin was slightly darker and her hair cut shorter. She was the only one of her siblings who wasn't a dragon-kin but a dusk walker—someone who could manipulate shadows and use them to move around, a little like my own shadow magic, although I'd never been able to turn into smoke.

"It's good to see you," Eos said. She motioned for Astrid, and I passed her over. "It's good to see you too, troublemaker."

"Thank you for doing this," I said.

"I get some serious auntie time," Eos said with a smile. "My son brought his young children to Shadow Falls, so it can be like a big family reunion. How's fatherhood?"

"It's good," I told her.

"Astrid is going to have Nate wrapped around her little finger," Selene said with a laugh.

"Yes, she is," Eos said. She looked over at me. "Mate, you're absolutely fucked."

"I'm okay with it," I told her, kissing Astrid on the head. "You all have plans for the morning?"

"Afternoon," Eos said with a smile.

"You were asleep for four hours," Selene said. "I assume you needed it."

I nodded. "I feel better. I'll feel even better knowing that Astrid is safe."

"She will be," Eos said. "Avalon don't even know how to get into Shadow Falls anymore. We'll be safe there."

I placed a hand on Astrid's head and sighed. I was going to really miss her. "I'll see you all tonight, though, yes, before you leave tomorrow?"

Selene hugged me. "Of course. I'm not going to let our daughter go through to another realm without us saying goodbye."

"Do all new dads feel this utterly helpless? The need to protect, the constant worrying about everything to do with her?"

"Yes," Eos said. "The good ones, anyway."

I spent the rest of the day at the realm gate temple, helping people evacuate. Leonardo and Antonio had finished the changes and gone through to the Shadow Falls side to ensure that things were done properly. Leonardo was an incredibly gifted alchemist, but I imagined his version of "properly" and everyone else's were wildly different. Hopefully Antonio could ensure he didn't piss anyone off.

I spent some time walking around the city, checking to make sure that no one was staying behind out of stubbornness or some desire to defend their home. It took a few hours, but I was happy for the walk, to stretch my legs and clear my mind.

As night fell, I used the tram to travel back to my accommodations. The tram gave incredible views of the city, but any hustle and bustle that had once existed was long gone. There were still shops open, but they served the military now. It would take a few more days to get everyone who had lived in the city through to Shadow Falls, and I hoped that one day they'd be able to return. *Prepare for the worst* was something I'd heard over and over again, but I wasn't sure many civilians actually knew just how bad this could get.

I got off the tram and made my way home to find Selene inside with Elaine Garlot. Elaine was Mordred's aunt and the onetime ruler of Avalon. She'd done a good job of keeping Arthur's allies in check while the man himself had been in a coma for a thousand years, but this was back when no one had known Arthur was a psychopath. When Arthur had woken up and the truth had come out, anyone trying to keep Avalon from sliding into evil had either been killed or had run. Elaine had had a lucky escape, but Arthur and his most ardent supporters would not stop until she was dead.

"What's wrong?" I asked.

"We've been trying to find you," Selene said.

"I was at the realm gate, and then I went for a walk. What happened?"

"It's Odin and Tommy," Elaine said. "They've both been hurt badly. We're not sure that they're going to make it."

Chapter Three

Nate Garrett

My father and best friend were dying.

The hospital was a blur. People spoke to me, but I couldn't have told you who, or what they said.

I was guided through empty corridors while people tried to either get out of the way or say sorry. Nothing stuck. Everything went in one ear and out the other. Right until I saw Odin.

Odin in a coma in a bed, doctors around him, examining his unmoving body. That broke me. Everything rushed in like a nuclear shock wave. And I crashed forward against the glass partition that separated me from the room he was in.

"Nate," Hades said from beside me. He was over six feet tall, with a bald head and several days of stubble growth. He'd been one of the people in charge of the rebellion against Avalon since its inception several years earlier. He was probably the most powerful necromancer on the planet and one of the few people I knew Merlin feared.

I looked around and took in everything for the first time.

"What the hell is going on?" I asked. "Where's Tommy?"

"Here," Tommy said from a doorway behind me. He looked fragile and weak, but he was on his feet.

I stepped toward him, and he fell forward. I caught him before he hit the floor.

"They're all dead," Tommy whispered, his voice breaking. "I got him back, but . . . I'm so sorry."

I looked back across the corridor through the window at where my dad was as Kase ran in and dropped to her knees next to Tommy, burying her face in his neck.

Kase helped Tommy to his feet and propped him up against the wall as Olivia arrived.

"What happened?" Olivia asked. Her voice was hard. She saw Tommy, hurt and weak, and her face crumpled as she went to him. She held Tommy and Kase against her, and I turned away. They didn't need any intrusion in their moment.

My brain swirled, and I took a deep breath and felt Selene's hand slip into mine, squeezing it slightly.

"Thank you," I whispered to her.

"What happened?" Selene asked. "Is Odin going to live?"

Hades pressed a button on a speaker at the side of the glass. "Lucifer, could you come here?"

One of the doctors with Odin nodded and left the room. Lucifer was one of the oldest beings I'd ever met. He'd been created using similar methods to the ones that had been used when I'd been conceived and born, although he was thousands of years older than me. Lucifer was a short, bald man with a white beard. He was a powerful sorcerer but had long since lost any desire to fight and turned his attention to healing.

"I'm so sorry," Lucifer said. "Odin is alive but in a coma. He was attacked, along with the rest of his team, but he and Tommy were the only survivors. It looks like they were both infected with a poison similar to the one used on Frigg but considerably more potent."

I turned to Tommy. I knew that he was powerful and that his healing might actually be the strongest I'd ever seen, with the exception of Baldr's, but the fact that he was even standing up while Odin was in a coma spoke volumes as to his power.

I reached over and placed a hand on Tommy's chest. "What happened?"

"It was a trap," Tommy said. "They were waiting for us. Everyone died. We arrived at a bar in Carver Creek and met up with a bartender, who told us that our contact had gone on to Kilnhurst. We made our way there, but it didn't take long before we were ambushed in the town by . . . something. This . . . monster, he had these creatures with him. They just kept coming." Tommy wobbled slightly, and Olivia helped steady him. "The one in charge, he had these knives. One of them cut me, and I've never felt pain like it. It was as if my entire body was covered in lava. My healing is maxed out."

"What?" Olivia asked.

"I didn't even know that was possible," I said, looking back at Lucifer.

"Tommy's ability to heal is the only thing keeping him alive," Lucifer said. "His strength will return in time; frankly I'm amazed he's even walking, but his healing is doing everything it can to kill the venom that was used on him. He still has his powers, but I fear that his body has reached its limit. He will not be able to turn into a werewolf, nor a wolf, not while he's in such a condition. Odin was not so lucky."

"He took one in the chest," Tommy said. "I couldn't move fast enough to stop it. I'm sorry."

I squeezed Tommy's shoulder. "You have nothing to be sorry for," I assured him. "Will my dad live?"

"At the moment, he's stable," Lucifer said. "But it's not good. Odin might actually be one of the strongest people I've ever met, but while the pathogen, or whatever it is, is similar to Frigg's, it's similar in the same way that a Ferrari is similar to a Ford Model T. It's not naturally occurring; I can tell you that. It's also self-replicating, and as soon as you find a cure, it completely changes, making healing Odin next to impossible. His own body is fighting the poison's attack, but the second we find a way to slow it down or his body heals it, the pathogen just changes to something else, rendering our work useless. With Frigg, we managed to slow it down and stabilize her, but with Odin, we can't do either because it's just so much quicker to adapt. We even tried to use runes to slow it down—nothing. We need a cure. And we need it soon."

"Is it contagious?" Olivia asked.

Lucifer shook his head. "It doesn't appear to be, no."

Tommy wobbled again, and Kase and Olivia moved him back into his room as Persephone arrived. She kissed her husband, Hades, on the cheek and placed a hand on my shoulder, squeezing slightly. I reached up and squeezed her hand. Her long dark hair flowed freely over slender shoulders. A diamond clip in the shape of a butterfly sat just above one ear, which was pierced several times.

"I'm sorry," she whispered. "We will fix this."

"Nate," Tommy called out. "We'll get a cure. I have your back."

"No, Tommy," I said. "Not this time. This time you need to heal. You need to fight the war inside you."

"I *need* to do something," he almost snapped.

"You *need* to sit down, Dad," Kase snapped back.

"Please," I said. "Just stay here and heal. You won't be any help dead, and at least here you can help prepare troops."

Tommy stared at me, and I knew that he was hurt more than just physically, but I couldn't risk him getting killed. I *wouldn't* risk him being killed. Not just because he was my best friend, not just because when I had gone to a dark place all those centuries ago, he had been the one to bring me back, but because Olivia didn't deserve to lose her husband. Daniel and Kase didn't deserve to lose their father.

"Heal," I said, closing the door and turning back to Lucifer. "How long?" I asked.

"Five days. Seven at most."

"I want details on everything that Tommy was dealing with," I said, keeping my voice steady. "I want names, I want to know where he was going and why, and then I'm going to go find out who did this and get a cure."

"Nate, you can't just—" Hades began.

"Do not finish that sentence," I said. "I can do an awful lot." Lightning crackled as it jumped between my fingers. "My best friend and dad were sent to a trap. Odin is dying, and Tommy has been taken to the brink of what he can do to keep himself alive. And I will burn everything standing between me and the cure."

Hades opened his mouth, but Persephone motioned for him to be quiet. I didn't want to lose my temper at anyone who didn't deserve it, but I could feel the anger and hate bubbling up inside me. Better to release it on someone who deserved it.

"I'm going to see my dad," I said, opening the door and walking into the hospital room as the half dozen doctors looked up at me.

"It's okay," Lucifer said from the door. "We'll keep working on him, Nate."

I nodded and looked down at Odin as tears filled my eyes. "I've only just found you," I said as everyone left the room. "All of this time not caring who you were, I finally find you, and now this. It doesn't feel fair."

The door behind me opened, and Selene stood beside me. "I will help keep Tommy from doing anything stupid," she said. "I'll make sure Olivia sends him to Shadow Falls when she can. If he changes . . ." She stopped talking and looked away.

"It'll tear his body apart, which is already trying to keep itself together," I said softly.

Selene turned and hugged me. "Find the cure," she whispered. "Find the cure and bring it back here."

"I will," I promised as my emotions bubbled over, and I wept.

"And find who did this and *end* them." She pulled away from me. "You hear me? Scorch these fuckers from the face of the earth. The only way I want to hear their names is whispered in fear."

I left the room. "Lucifer, any way you can wait for Tommy to completely heal and use his blood to create an antidote?"

"I don't know," Lucifer said. "We have no idea how long it'll be before Tommy is fully healed, although I am hopeful that he will be. But werewolf powers are considerably different from your father's. There's no way of knowing if they're compatible."

"Thank you," I said and walked across the corridor to where Tommy was currently looking very angry as he sat on a hospital bed. "I'll find them," I told him. "I'll be back here, and we'll get you healed so you can go back to telling me how happy you are that you found an adult-size stormtrooper costume, you big geek."

Tommy smiled. "Nate, I don't know who the big guy was, but *do not* underestimate him. Nor his . . . creature friends. I don't want you to be put in a bed next to your dad."

"Heal," I said. "Then we'll stop Arthur together."

"One last thing," he said, wincing as he moved. "Masako was my contact in Montana."

The name was familiar, but I didn't think I'd met her. "She's a jikininki, yes?"

Jikininki were humans who had died and returned. They fed on the flesh of the living and were strong, durable, and more than a little creepy. They also tended to not differentiate between friend and foe should their hunger overtake them.

Tommy nodded. "She contacted me, told me she had information on bad shit going down in Montana."

"Dad, please lie down," Kase said.

"In a second," Tommy told her with a warm smile. "I need to tell Nate."

Olivia motioned for Tommy to get on with it, but I could see that she was as concerned as her daughter. "I didn't find out anything about the experiments, but I didn't find Masako either. If she's still there, she's in trouble. Big trouble."

"I'll keep an eye out for her," I promised.

I left the room and closed the door behind me. "I need a team to come with me. Tell them to meet me at the realm gate in Montana in a few hours."

"Nate, if someone could do this to Odin," Hades said, "you need to be more than careful."

I followed Hades out of the hospital as Persephone caught us up. "You need to know why your father and Tommy took their team to Montana," Hades said.

"The experiments," I said.

"Not just that," Persephone told me. "They went there because we had a lead on Atlas from Masako."

"Tommy told me about her," I said. "What happened to Atlas?"

"Atlas vanished a month ago," Hades said. "His last report was that Hera was in command of the Earth realm until his return. Apparently, Arthur plans to join the battle here, along with a large number of his supporters. Atlas was a big help to us during his time in Avalon."

"So Montana is where Atlas was last heard from; Masako tracked him there and then discovered a whole lot of awful experiments, attempted to get help from us, and it all went horribly wrong. That about sum it up?"

Hades nodded.

"Where was she meeting Tommy?" I asked.

"A small town north of Helena called Carver Creek. It's close to Helena National Forest."

I stared at Hades for a few seconds. "Tommy said they were going into Kilnhurst. A place we both know very well, considering we destroyed it for being a town of pure evil. Anyone know how a town that we destroyed is back up and running?"

Hades nodded again. "They turned it into a prison city in the 1940s."

"They what?" I shouted.

"It's currently not on any maps," Persephone said. "Anywhere. Makes me think that maybe Avalon don't want something found there."

"Any chance Masako set up our people?" I asked.

"We can't rule it out," Persephone said.

We reached the nearest tram and all took a seat.

"What was Atlas doing before he vanished?" I asked.

"He was feeding us intel on Hera's activities," Hades said. "His last correspondence said something about how because you screwed Avalon out of using legal means to get the power they wanted, they were going to try and take it. We assume that once they deal with us here, the Earth realm is next."

"Anything else?"

"Hera is still looking for you. She still wants you dead," Persephone said.

"Some things never change," I said. "So what's stopping me from walking into London, straight into her offices, and turning them into several hundred tons of rubble?"

"You know what," Hades said softly.

I nodded. I knew that civilians would be killed. That Hera used them as a sort of bulletproof vest, surrounding her tower with human businesses so that getting to her meant hurting others. "And London is a powder keg at the moment."

"That too," Persephone said. "Riots in the streets, protests—the Inter-species Task Force has been brought in to keep the peace. The ITF might as well be called the secret police at this point. Dissent is stamped out. People the world over know what Avalon is now. They've seen the films. But Avalon are, at the moment, keeping a lid on it."

"What about the prime minister?" I asked.

"The UK government still has a few Avalon sympathizers there, but Avalon effectively rule from the shadows. The PM's family was taken from her and driven to Chequers for 'safekeeping.'"

"She does what they want, and they don't die? That it?" I asked.

Hades nodded. "The youngest prime minister in history, and she's effectively a prisoner in her own country. She's been in charge for over three years now, got elected just before Arthur turned it all to shit, and I've been hearing rumors that she's been looking for a way out that doesn't involve murder on the streets of London in response."

"So going after Hera is out at the moment," I said. "If she's behind Tommy's attack, though, it might be the only way."

"Cross that bridge if, or when, you come to it," Persephone said.

The tram stopped, and we all exited as the sounds of drums could be heard in the distance. "Avalon?" I asked.

"They're not going to wait forever," Hades said. "Sooner or later they'll attack. I don't know why they haven't yet, to be honest."

From somewhere in the distance over the wall, the sound of drumming continued. It got louder as we made our way through the city to the realm gate temple. More and more people had stopped what they were doing to listen.

"Fear," I said. "That's what Arthur wants. He wants you all afraid of him."

"He doing that, you think?" Hades asked.

I nodded. "Air magic used to amplify and move around sound. There might only be one drummer a mile away, and it sounds like a hundred right next to you. They're preparing for what comes next."

"We'll be ready," Persephone said.

We stopped outside the temple. "I'll meet the team in Carver Creek."

"Don't die," Hades said.

"I'm going to get that cure and bring it back. Anyone who creates a weapon like that has the cure. Otherwise, what's to stop someone getting accidentally infected? I'll find who made this shit and make sure they tell me how to cure it. No matter what it takes."

"Don't lose yourself," Persephone said as we all walked into the temple. "Don't become that person."

I nodded. Tommy had brought me back from the brink the last time I'd lost control after surrendering to my grief and rage. I'd allowed myself to become judge, jury, and executioner to anyone I felt didn't deserve to live while people I loved had died. Persephone had seen what I'd done all those centuries ago. Seen the destruction and death I'd created.

Thunder rolled across the sky high above us, and both Hades and Persephone looked up, concerned.

"It's not me," I said as Zamek walked into the temple.

The Norse dwarf had once been a prince of his people, before they'd been betrayed and scattered to the realms. He was one of the few people who could change the realm gate destinations at a whim.

"I'm coming with you," he said. He wore a double-headed battle-ax on his back, and two smaller hatchet-like weapons hung from his belt, along with various knives and probably other weapons hidden about his person. He might have been just under five feet in height, but he was broad and strong. And like all dwarves, he was a master alchemist.

"Fair enough," I said as Zamek activated the realm gate, the destination runes changing as he needed them to.

"I'm coming too," Kase said, entering the temple. "I ran here; it was quicker than taking the tram. My parents know I'm helping you. They weren't exactly happy, but I'm an adult, so I get to do what I need to in order to protect those I love. It would be wise not to argue."

"Wouldn't dream of it," I said.

Zamek, Kase, and I walked toward the realm gate.

"Send the others on," I called to Hades and Persephone before stepping through the realm gate.

It was time to hunt.

Chapter Four

Layla Cassidy

Realm of Asgard

Layla had been preparing for a mission when she'd been informed that Tommy and Odin had been hurt. Tommy had been like a father to her, which, considering how awful her own father had been, was about the highest praise she could give. The possibility that someone had hurt him made her want to hurt someone in return.

She rushed to the hospital and soon found where Tommy was staying, and she flung his door open and stepped inside, expecting to see the worst. She'd been told only that he was seriously hurt, so to see him sitting up in bed was a bit of a surprise.

Olivia sat in a chair next to him.

"You're a lot less hurt than I was led to believe," Layla said.

"Ummm, I'm sorry?" Tommy said.

"No, that's not what I meant," Layla stammered. "Damn it. I thought you were near death."

"No," Tommy said. "Although my healing is all screwed up. It's Odin who came off worse."

"Is he . . . ," she began, not wanting to finish that sentence. What could kill Odin? She'd met him several times and liked him. He was somewhat larger than life and always willing to talk and laugh.

"He's in a coma," Olivia said. "In the room opposite."

Layla left Tommy's room and knocked on the door, where a large window looked into a room with Odin in a bed, hooked up to machines.

Lucifer opened the door. "Layla," he said, stepping aside so she could enter.

Layla stared at Odin, who was covered in bright-red runes.

"Nate went to find the cure," Lucifer said. "Hopefully he'll be okay."

Layla nodded but didn't risk saying anything. She stared at her metal arm, watching as small parts of it moved around as if it were alive. She clenched a fist and sighed. "I'm meant to be going to Valhalla," she said. "I was getting ready. I didn't even know he was going on a mission."

"We felt it best to keep the number of people who knew limited," Olivia said from the doorway. "And you are preparing to go to Valhalla."

"I just . . . do I still need to go?"

Olivia nodded. "What you're doing is important. We need the Valkyries' help if we hope to defeat Avalon."

"How many know about this?" Layla asked.

"A few," Olivia said. "News has gone to those who you're going with. We didn't want them to come back to find Odin in here. Chloe and her wife took it hard. I got the feeling that they both thought a lot of Odin. Irkalla broke a wall."

"He's a good man," Layla said. "He treats everyone the same. Always has. Is Tommy going to be okay?"

Olivia nodded. "We think so, yes. Tommy needs to rest and heal. And you need to go to Valhalla."

"He is in the best possible care," Lucifer said. "They both are."

"Where is Kase?" Layla asked. "Does she know?"

"Kase has gone to find out who did this with Nate. There was a slight disagreement about her involvement. She has her mother's temper and her father's need to do the right thing."

"She'll be okay," Layla said. "Kase is stone-cold badass."

Olivia smiled. "Yes, that is one way of putting it. Go to Valhalla; help out there; keep busy. It's better than just waiting for news."

"Where are Chloe and Piper now?" Layla asked.

"There's a garden at the rear of the hospital—it's been pretty much destroyed with the number of troops coming and going, but that's the direction they went."

"Thank you," Layla said. "You need anything, let me know. This realm or another, I'll come running."

Olivia hugged her. "Thank you."

Layla stuck her head around the door of Tommy's room. "Take care of yourself."

"You got a second?" Tommy asked.

Layla looked back at Olivia, who shrugged, so Layla stepped into the room. "What is it?"

"I just wanted you to know that I'm proud of you," Tommy said. "You've come a long way in only a few years, and you've managed to do it while gaining the respect and admiration of nearly everyone you work with. Just in case I don't get to tell you later."

"Don't talk like that," Layla said, feeling upset.

"No, not because I'll die, you idiot," Tommy said with a laugh. "I'm sure I'll heal this, but when the evacuation is done, I'm being taken to Shadow Falls. I apparently have no choice in this."

"No, you don't," Olivia shouted from the corridor.

Layla walked over and hugged Tommy. "Just get better," she said. "If that means resting in Shadow Falls, then do it. Whatever happens here, we're going to need your help. Miss the battle to win the war."

"You sound like Hades," Tommy grumbled.

"I will take that as a compliment," Layla told him. "Will Odin make it?"

"If there's a cure and Nate can get it back here in time, Lucifer thinks so, yes. Without one, no. He will never regain consciousness. Apparently, I got lucky. I don't feel very lucky, though."

"I'm sorry for the people you lost."

"They were good," Tommy said. "They will be missed. Now, go to Valhalla. We need that help."

Layla nodded and left Tommy, saying her goodbyes to Olivia and Lucifer before stopping by Odin for one last moment. "Come back to us," she whispered.

Layla left the hospital soon after, using the rear exit and finding Piper and Chloe sitting on a wooden bench by the remains of a trampled garden. They'd only gotten married a few months earlier and had been immediately thrown into defending Asgard.

"You two okay?" Layla asked.

Piper kissed her wife on the cheek before getting up and hugging Layla. Piper was from a small town in northern Wisconsin that Layla couldn't remember the name of. Layla knew there was a large college nearby and that Piper didn't really like to talk about her childhood growing up there, so Layla didn't push.

Piper pushed strands of her dark-red hair behind one ear. "Chloe is going with you to Valhalla, yes?"

Layla nodded. "She was meant to be, but that really depends on her."

Chloe turned back to Piper and Layla. It was obvious she'd been crying, and Layla immediately hugged her.

"It's just a lot, you know?" Chloe said. "How many people are we going to lose to these monsters? And yes, I'm coming. I'm hoping there will be something to punch."

"Irkalla broke a wall," Piper said.

"I heard," Layla told her. "That sounds like Irkalla. Any idea where she is?"

"At the realm gate," Chloe said. "Ava and Jinayca are coming too."

"Ava?" Layla asked. "But she's only sixteen." Layla had spent some time with Ava over the last few months and found herself enjoying being the teacher to the teenager. They had wildly different powers, but both had come from being human with no knowledge of the world they now found themselves in.

"Irkalla is certain she'll be helpful," Piper said. "And apparently this is supposed to be a nice, safe mission. You're going to negotiate help, after all."

"Irkalla isn't the negotiating type," Layla said.

"That's what I thought too," Chloe said.

"I've been reading up on this Empress Rela person," Piper said. "There's something not quite right about her. Too many missing details about her life. Although maybe that's because no one has been in the realm for centuries."

"Are we being distrustful of our allies already?" Layla asked. "We haven't even gotten there yet."

"I think given the current climate, a little distrust is a good thing," Piper said.

Layla left Chloe and Piper to say their goodbyes to each other and waited for the former at the front of the hospital. A large sabertooth panther padded over to her and licked her hand.

"Hey, Tego," Layla said, scratching the massive animal behind one ear. Tego still wore the specially designed leather armor that had been made for her during the battle of Helheim a year earlier.

The thought made Layla pause and remember the friends that she'd lost during and before the battle. And now another one was looming. *How many until this is done?* Layla sighed, and Tego rubbed her nose against Layla's palm.

"Thanks," Layla said to the panther as Chloe joined her.

The three of them made their way to the realm gate temple, where Ava and Irkalla were waiting. Irkalla was tall and athletic, with olive skin and long dark hair. Few people managed to make the leather armor look good on them, but somehow Irkalla was one of those people. Layla had once thought that if anyone ever needed a physical description of elegance, Irkalla was about as close as you could get.

Ava was several inches shorter than Irkalla and gave the impression that she'd rather be kicking a soccer ball around in shorts and a T-shirt than wearing the leather armor she found herself in. She'd cut her dark-brown hair to shoulder length since arriving in Asgard with her grandmother, sister, and young nephew, all of whom were now safely in Shadow Falls. Ava's powers were not shared by her family.

Ava removed a dagger from her belt. "They gave me a weapon," she said gleefully. "I didn't ask for one; I just got given it."

Layla wasn't sure about giving an enthusiastic teen a knife—but she'd keep an eye on her rather than argue about it now.

Once inside the temple, Layla looked around at the team assembled there. They looked like a group of women who would be the last you'd see if you pissed them off.

"Jinayca," Layla said, embracing the Norse dwarf. "It's good to see you again." She was a gaunt woman who Layla knew had been through hardships that most could only have nightmares about. Her jet-black hair was tied up with dozens of colored bows, and colorful bangles adorned her wrists. They'd met several months previously and found that they got on well.

"I've designed some different armor for your cat." Jinayca pointed to the side of the temple, where there was a huge metal-and-leather set of armor that had a seat in it.

"You want me to ride her like a horse?" Layla asked.

"She's big enough, fast enough, and I'm betting a lot more capable of taking care of herself than a horse."

Tego padded over to the armor and sniffed it. She snorted derisively.

"You want me to ride you like Battle Cat?" Layla asked.

"What's Battle Cat?" Jinayca asked her.

"It's a character from an old cartoon from the 1980s," Layla said. "I wasn't even born at the time, but I used to have a boyfriend who was obsessed with all things *He-Man*."

Jinayca stared at Layla for a few seconds. "Humans are weird."

"No argument from me," Layla told her. "If Tego is okay with it, then we'll go to war together."

Tego purred.

While Jinayca walked up to the realm gate and activated it, Layla set about putting the new armor on Tego. The massive cat remained still while it was all fitted into place, and when it was done, she looked even more terrifying than she had in her normal armor.

"Holy shit," Layla said, scratching the massive animal behind her ear when she was finished. "You look like a tank."

Tego moved her head to look at her. The helmet that shielded the top of her skull had four large spikes on it. Layla figured they probably weren't needed, considering Tego's entire mouth consisted of large spikes, but she didn't want to say anything.

"It's a good thing," Layla said. "You sure you're okay with this?"

Tego pawed at the ground.

A few seconds later, they'd all traveled through and found themselves in a large manicured garden with tall trees surrounding the whole place. The sky above was bright and cloudless, although flickers of red and yellow lightning could be seen in the far distance.

Six women stood on the grass before the group. All wore silver-and-red armor, a lot of which was metal, and it gleamed in the sunlight. They carried spears and gave the impression that they were not afraid to use them. One moved forward to meet the group.

"Welcome to Valhalla," the Valkyrie said, without even slightly sounding like she meant it. "I am the Third Consul. If you do anything to jeopardize our empress, I will not hesitate to execute you."

"She sounds nice," Chloe whispered to Layla.

They were led through the palace grounds with the huge building looming over everything around it. Layla found the palace magnificent to look at. There were four spires, one at each corner, and each had at least one Valkyrie guard on it. More walked the ramparts high above the group. The front doors of the palace were a dark wood, and more guards stood outside. Layla found herself drawn to the many stained glass windows, which appeared to depict various battles of the Valkyries.

The palace grounds were as vast and intricate as the building itself, and Layla spotted that both Ava and Irkalla had opted to go sit on a nearby bench. The Valkyries didn't seem to care much either way, and Layla found herself wondering what mischief the pair was up to. If there was one thing Irkalla was good at, it was finding trouble.

"I'll catch you up," Layla said. "Just want to check that Ava is okay."

The Valkyrie in charge shrugged and continued to walk on, while Chloe rolled her eyes in Irkalla's direction.

"What's going on?" Layla asked Irkalla as Tego rubbed her head against her hand.

"Ava was feeling unwell," Irkalla said.

Ava coughed the worst fake cough in the history of anything.

"Why are you here?" Layla asked Ava suspiciously. "The actual reason, not whatever Irkalla told you to say."

"You suggest that I would have the child lie?" Irkalla asked.

Layla stared at her for a few seconds.

"Yes, okay, I would have the child lie," Irkalla admitted.

"The *child*," Ava said tersely, "is right here."

Irkalla nodded. "Apologies. Both for calling you a child—at sixteen I was married and killing my enemies—and for having you lie."

Layla waited for an answer.

"Ava is a fairly unique person," Irkalla said. "You know she can commune with the spirit of her shinigami."

"Yes," Layla said. "I've known for a while."

"I've been talking to it," Ava said as Layla sat beside her. "It turns out they can do more than just show me future death. They can show me where a particular spirit is."

"What spirit?" Layla asked.

Irkalla looked around, making sure that their Valkyrie guard wasn't within hearing distance. "Zeus," she whispered.

Layla stared at the pair for a moment. "Okay, before we get to the why and what the hell, how about you explain about this tracking power."

"It doesn't work on the Earth realm," Ava said. "I don't really know why—maybe the population is too big—but in the other realms it's like the shinigami's power increases. And so I can find the spirits of the dead. So long as the body is in the same realm as the spirit."

"And you've been practicing this?" Layla asked.

"She's gotten good at it," Irkalla said. "We took her to Helheim and had her track the spirits of the known deceased."

"Sounds like fun," Layla said, when in reality it sounded anything but. "So why are you looking here for Zeus?"

"After Hera killed him, this is where his body was taken," Irkalla said.

"So why are you looking for Zeus?" Layla asked again, feeling a little concerned about the number of Valkyries who were still walking around the palace grounds and could overhear her.

"It's to do with Nate," Irkalla said. "We've been trying to keep this information from him and Mordred."

Layla looked up at the sky as the first drops of rain fell. "Explain faster."

"There were seven of them," Irkalla said. "Seven people created to be weapons. Nate and Mordred were two, a third died, but the last four vanished. We have no idea who they are or where they are. Until six weeks ago, when Atlas informed us that Hera was looking into one of them. A girl. The daughter of Zeus and . . . we don't know the other person involved."

"You're here to find Zeus's body and ask him where his daughter is?" Layla asked.

"Pretty much," Irkalla said. "If Hera finds this woman and she's as powerful as Nate or Mordred, she'll either try to get her on her side or—"

"Kill her and anyone who tries to protect her," Ava finished.

"And you think Zeus's spirit has the location?" Layla asked.

Irkalla nodded. "I can communicate with it; we just have to find it. Someone as powerful as Zeus is going to have a spirit that hangs around for centuries and retains a lot of memories. And spirits tend to go where the body is unless it's cremated, so Zeus's spirit is in this realm. Somewhere."

"It's not a small realm," Layla said. "It's not something you're going to find in an afternoon."

"We have to try," Ava said.

Layla nodded. "Yeah, I guess you do. So how are you going to get the Valkyries to let you stay and search?"

"We'd hoped that we'd be able to figure something out," Irkalla said.

"You don't have a plan, do you?" Layla asked.

"Not so much, no," Irkalla admitted. "Hades and Persephone asked us just to look into it. We come here, try to get a reading, and then figure it out from there. Getting the support is the most important thing, but if we can pinpoint Zeus, we can work on them letting Ava and me stay and find him."

"I'm going to go see the empress," Layla said. "You do your thing."

Ava smiled. "That's the plan."

"Tego, stay with Ava and Irkalla," Layla said. "Try to keep them out of trouble."

Tego snorted.

Layla jogged after the rest of the group and caught them up just before they reached the palace itself.

"Your friends are not joining us?" the head Valkyrie said.

Layla shook her head. "Ava, the youngest one . . . it's her first time through a realm gate. Made her queasy."

The Valkyrie nodded in a show of solidarity for Ava's illness. The first time anyone went through a realm gate was not a good experience, and most were quite ill afterward. It quickly became second nature, but anyone who'd been through a realm gate felt a pang of sympathy for those who had just taken their first journey. The fact that this wasn't even close to being Ava's first time was hopefully something that wouldn't be discovered.

"There was no guardian at the realm gate," Layla said conversationally as the Valkyrie opened the huge wooden double doors to the palace.

"Are there dwarves here, by chance?" Jinayca asked one of the Valkyries as the group was led inside the palace.

The question was ignored.

"Why aren't men allowed here?" Layla asked.

"We have men here," the Third Consul said. "There are nearly a hundred thousand people who live in this realm. Approximately five thousand of them are human males."

"I didn't know that," Layla admitted. "I'd heard that this was a realm only for women."

"Men cannot enter this realm without express permission from the empress," the Valkyrie said as the group walked down a large marble-floored hallway. Dozens of large mirrors adorned each side of the hallway, and torches lit up the area, the light bouncing off the reflective surfaces.

"Men used to be allowed here," another Valkyrie said. "But they had to prove themselves as great warriors first. It was where those who had committed great acts of bravery or war were allowed to come. But that was before Empress Rela's mother banned all males from entering the realm."

"And Empress Rela's thoughts on it?" Jinayca asked.

"I think Empress Rela has more important matters to consider currently," the Third Consul said.

Eventually they reached a set of double doors, which the guards opened.

"Empress Rela," one of the guards announced as they walked into the throne room that looked like Rela's own personal shrine of self-adulation. There were pictures of her on the walls, statues of her in marble and gold. A dozen guards lined each wall, wearing dark-red leather armor, the runes on them a light purple in color.

The group all walked toward the golden throne, which sat at the top of a set of five steps. The woman upon the throne wore a silk dress that spilled out over the sides. She stood and walked down the steps toward the group, her heeled boots clicking on the floor with every step.

She would have been a few inches taller than Layla even without the boots, and she smiled, looking down on the group in the way that some people did when they thought they had an advantage. Layla wasn't really sure what the advantage was yet, but she got the feeling it wasn't going to be long before she found out.

"Your Imperial Majesty," Jinayca said, bowing her head a little, followed quickly by Chloe and Layla.

"I know why you are here," Rela said. "We will dine together tomorrow morning, where we will discuss the reason for your visit. Any alliance with you is something that I can only really decide upon getting a feel for the kind of people I'll be aligning my Valkyries with. You understand, yes?"

Layla didn't.

"Of course," Jinayca said.

"In the meantime, please feel free to explore the grounds. But do stay away from the village to the north, by the Great Lake. It's . . . host to humans who would consider so many powerful beings to be a threat."

"Thank you for taking time to see us," Jinayca said. "We look forward to tomorrow morning."

"Third Consul, please show them out," Rela said with a wave of her hand.

The Third Consul looked happy to do just that, and Jinayca, Chloe, and Layla were soon back outside.

"Do not make trouble," the Third Consul said. "You would not like what happens."

Layla took a deep breath and let it out slowly as the three of them were left alone. "Anyone else get the feeling something weird is happening here?" she asked.

"The second I got here," Jinayca said.

"Let's find Irkalla and Ava and see what trouble they've managed to get into," Chloe said with a smile.

Layla looked back toward the palace as the three of them walked away.

Chapter Five

Layla Cassidy

Realm of Valhalla

Layla spent the rest of the afternoon trying to ignore the two heavily armed Valkyries who followed her and her team around wherever they went. They kept to the palace grounds, as requested, but eventually split up to look around and hopefully figure out what was making them all feel so uneasy.

Layla found herself sitting on a stone bench on top of a hill that overlooked the city of Fólkvangr, according to the large sign at the city entrance. Population just over twenty-five thousand. It stretched out toward the ocean, where several large ships were docked in the bay.

"It's a beautiful view," Layla said to the Valkyrie that had been following her.

"Thank you," the Valkyrie said from behind.

"I'm Layla," she said.

"I am not permitted to give you my name," the Valkyrie told her. "You may call me Valkyrie, or palace guard, if you must."

"You're not allowed to give me your name?" Layla asked, confused. "What do you think will happen when you do?"

"That's not for me to say," the Valkyrie said. She was a few inches taller than Layla, with a deep tan. She wore silver-and-black metal armor and a matching helmet, but her arms were bare and muscular. The spear in the guard's hand was not for show. Layla knew that if it came to it, the Valkyrie would try to kill her. She just hoped it wouldn't come to it.

"Can you tell me who ordered you to do such a thing?"

"First Consul," the Valkyrie said.

"And you work for her?"

The Valkyrie nodded.

"We're not here to hurt anyone," Layla said. "We're just here to ask for help."

"Not for me to decide," the Valkyrie answered.

"Is there anything you can decide for yourself?" Layla snapped.

The Valkyrie looked taken aback by Layla's irritation but quickly recovered and turned to leave.

"I'm sorry," Layla said. "It's been a really long day, and now I'm going to be here longer than I'd expected."

"This must all be very strange to you," the Valkyrie said. "Being told where you can and can't go, having to wait for the empress to talk to you."

"I've met royalty before," Layla said. "I've been made to wait before too. Neither of those are new things. But I'd hoped we would be done and dusted by now. Asgard is about to be attacked by who knows how many people from Avalon. Arthur won't just kill us all and be done with it. You either submit or you die. So what happens when he comes here?"

"We will stop him or die," the Valkyrie said. "We will not submit to Arthur. Our empress would not allow such an affront."

"I hope it doesn't come to that," Layla said. "It's a beautiful village. Do the humans deal with your kind often?"

"We Valkyries are their protectors," the Valkyrie said, sounding happier to be on a topic she was allowed to discuss. "They are used to spending time around us, but they are not used to outsiders. I think they would be suspicious and/or overly enthusiastic to see you."

"Either way we cause a commotion, yes?"

The Valkyrie nodded.

A few hours passed while Layla tried to talk to the Valkyrie about anything that might put her at ease, but as soon as the conversation went back to anything to do with why they were there or the empress, she shut down.

Eventually, Layla walked back through the gardens to meet up with the others, each of whom had their own shadow.

"This is fun," Irkalla said, making no effort to keep her displeasure from the tall Valkyrie close to her.

The Third Consul came back to the group. "We will take you to your lodgings," she said. "Follow me."

"Are we in the palace?" Chloe asked.

"No," the Third Consul said. "There are building works being carried out. It's not safe for strangers to be wandering around unaccompanied."

"We can wander around unaccompanied?" Irkalla asked.

"The guest building is large enough to house a dozen people," the Third Consul said without taking the bait. "You should be able to only have your own shadows for company for a while."

Layla spotted the grin that spread over Irkalla's face. She was enjoying herself a lot more than she probably should have been.

The guest building was magnificent. It was like a smaller version of the main palace, with its own spires and stained glass windows. The Third Consul stopped outside the blue door and turned to the group. "You will stay in this building tonight. You *will not* leave. Guards will patrol, and I cannot guarantee your safety should you wander the grounds unaccompanied."

"Don't leave, or we get stabbed," Chloe said. "I think we can manage that."

The Third Consul opened the door and beckoned the entire group inside. The room was tastefully decorated and reminded Layla of a log cabin, complete with comfortable-looking seating and a lit fireplace. A staircase went up from the side of the room, and there were three doors inside the room itself, which was about twice the size of her first flat when she was at university.

"What a fucking asshole," Irkalla said the second the door was closed, although Layla was pretty sure that it wasn't soundproof.

Tego walked off to the fireplace and lay down, making Layla smile. It didn't matter that Tego was bigger than a fully grown tiger; she was still a cat at heart.

"Which one?" Chloe asked. "I wanted to get back to Asgard, not stay in whatever the hell weirdness is happening here."

"I think we can assume this room will have ears," Jinayca said. "You can do a lot with runes." She withdrew a piece of chalk from her pocket and drew a large circle around the group before spending ten minutes drawing a collection of complex-looking runes.

"We can talk now," Jinayca said after placing her hands inside the circle, creating a hiss of power as it snapped shut. The runes pulsed yellow and green.

"What did everyone find?" Irkalla asked.

"The nearby city is massive," Layla started. "Thousands of people. And all of them rely on the Valkyries. Something is weird, though. I asked the Valkyrie if she'd heard about the rebellion, meaning Avalon and Asgard, and she reacted like I'd asked her something horrific."

"You think there's another rebellion going on here?" Irkalla asked.

Layla shrugged. "All I know is that I don't trust Rela or her Third Consul."

"Me neither," Ava said. "Bad stuff happened here. There are a lot of dead bodies around the palace grounds. I think they were slaves. I can't tell how long ago, though, because there are so many runes around the place; I think they disrupt my power."

"And Zeus?" Layla asked.

Irkalla had to spend a few minutes explaining the situation to Chloe.

"So?" Chloe asked. "Did you find him?"

"He's in this realm," Ava said. "But there's, like, a barrier of power around the gardens. It makes it hard to pinpoint anything. There's definitely power coming from around this place, though."

"So we need to check later tonight," Irkalla said.

"I am shocked—shocked—that Irkalla suggests doing something dangerous," Chloe said sarcastically.

"You love it," Irkalla said with a grin.

"I studied the realm gate," Jinayca said. "There are no guardians here. The runes on the gate are slightly different when there are. Either they found another way, or there are dwarves. And I don't see any dwarves walking around, do you?"

"You think they're prisoners?" Layla asked.

"I can only guess, but possibly. Either that, or they're kept out of the way when not needed. But someone had to open the realm gate from here to let us know that Rela wanted to talk."

"So we have a few mysteries," Chloe said. "There are large barracks to the east of the palace. Officially it's undergoing renovation, but I'm not so sure. The way the Valkyrie glanced over before asking made me think she was worried about it."

"We should all get some rest until tonight," Irkalla said.

"I'll go with you," Layla told her. "If all five of us go, it's going to cause issues should anyone come knocking."

"You okay with going walkabout?" Irkalla asked Ava.

Ava nodded. "This place gives me the creeps."

"Tego," Layla said, and the big cat padded over toward them. "Keep Jinayca and Chloe company."

The cat nodded and turned to walk back to the fireplace.

"I feel so much safer," Jinayca mocked and received a slap around her head with Tego's tail in response.

They all got a few hours' sleep, with the group taking it in shifts.

Layla met Irkalla and Ava in a library room at the far end of the building on the ground floor.

"Is it always so clandestine working with the rebellion?" Ava asked.

"Sometimes we just punch people in daylight," Irkalla said. "Depends on the mood."

"Let's go find a ghost," Layla said.

Irkalla tried the window, but it was locked. Layla manipulated the metal to unlock it, allowing all three of them to escape the building with ease.

"It's this way," Ava said, pointing off toward a large patch of land to the far side of the palace.

The three of them set off in the darkness.

"You found anything?" Layla asked after they'd been following Ava for ten minutes, who appeared to be in some kind of trance.

Ava stopped by a large tree that towered over them, its branches hanging low. What looked like acorns littered the ground.

"What is this?" Irkalla asked, touching the bark of the tree and moving her hand away. "I think Zeus is under here. It's hard to tell with the interference from the runes."

Ava nodded. "The tree is born from his remains. Holy shit, that's some serious power."

"I imagine there was something on his body when he died," Irkalla said. "Even dead, a sorcerer as powerful as Zeus is going to have some residual energy."

"Hence the acorns?" Layla asked, picking one up. The moonlight was bright enough that she could make out that they were red in color. "You sure this is Zeus?"

Ava nodded, although she didn't look convinced.

Irkalla took a seat beneath the tree. "I'll try talking to him."

Layla spotted three Valkyries headed their way. "Oh shit," Layla said. "I'll distract them."

"You were told to stay inside," one of the Valkyries said. The second and third stayed back, one holding a bow in her hands, while the third kept her hand on her sheathed sword.

"My friend here had a vision of something terrible happening," Layla said. "We didn't want to disturb your empress until we knew what we were dealing with. The runes disturb her power, so we took a walk. We made no effort to conceal ourselves." Okay, that last part was a lie, but Layla was pretty sure they didn't need to know that.

"You will come with us," the Valkyrie closest to Layla said. She took a step forward, and an arrow slammed into her chest, piercing the metal armor that she wore. The Valkyrie's eyes went wide from shock as a second arrow hit her in the throat, followed by two more that killed the archer Valkyrie.

Ava practically threw Irkalla onto the ground, the older woman still in a trance as she tried to communicate with whatever spirit was under the tree.

The remaining Valkyrie drew her sword. "You dare," she shouted.

"Not me," Layla said, who'd already thrown herself to the ground. She caused the metal in the Valkyrie's sword to dissolve, which stung like hell, as there was silver in the blade.

Another arrow took the Valkyrie in the eye, and she fell just as Layla rolled to her feet and ran over to the tree.

"This isn't great," Layla said.

"Can you feel any metal coming toward us?" Irkalla asked.

Layla reached out but felt nothing, just as she looked up to see an arrow being pointed at her from a few feet away. The female archer wore leather armor, and while Layla tried to manipulate any metal she could sense, a second woman appeared.

"I wouldn't," the second woman said to Layla. "I know what you're trying to do; I saw the Valkyrie's sword, and I'm pretty sure you'll find it difficult to stop an arrow that isn't metal. That's what you can do, yes?"

Layla nodded; she'd decided that it was probably wise to cooperate with the people aiming deadly weapons at them. "I don't know what's going on here, but we're not involved."

"We'll see," the woman said. She wore black leather armor and had dark hair cut just above shoulder length. A scar ran from her forehead around her eye to her cheek.

"Spear," the woman said, obviously noticing that Layla was looking at it. "Get up."

Everyone did as they were told while four more archers arrived, all pointing arrows at them.

"I think you're going to need more than arrows," Layla said.

"These are rune scribed," the woman told her. "The runes mean that they pass through magic as if it wasn't there. Probably why you can't manipulate it. You tried, yes?"

Layla nodded. Didn't seem much point in trying to suggest otherwise.

"We need to leave," the woman said. "And you're coming with us."

"Okay, look, we're not from here," Ava said. "And we're just here to try and get your empress to help us fight Avalon, who are going to murder everyone in Asgard if we don't stop them."

The woman looked confused for a moment. "You can explain yourselves once we're somewhere safe."

"Our friend is talking to a spirit," Layla said. "She can't be moved."

The woman placed the tip of a short sword against Layla's throat. "Wake her up, or leave her here. I don't care."

"Did we not just establish that I can control metal?" Layla snapped.

The sword moved from her throat.

Ava touched Irkalla on the forehead, and the latter opened her eyes and yelled. "What the fucking hell?" she started, before noticing the armed women looking her over. "Hey, who are you fuckers?"

"Try not to swear at the armed people threatening us," Layla said, noticing the dozen more women who'd arrived. "They want us to go with them."

Irkalla got to her feet and looked around her. "My name is Irkalla," she said. "You are?"

"Impatient," the woman said. "Move."

"We have friends still on the palace grounds," Ava said.

"Move," the woman said again, leaving no doubt as to what would happen if they decided to fight back.

All four of them began to walk in the direction that the woman had indicated, with several of the women hanging back to ensure they weren't followed. Eventually they reached several carriages. Each carriage was pulled by two large horses. Ava, Irkalla, and Layla were all put in one carriage, with Irkalla and Layla next to one another.

"You want to tell us what's going on?" Layla asked once they'd ridden far enough that the palace was a distant blip on the horizon.

"You say you're here to form an alliance with the empress and her Valkyries," the scarred woman said.

"True," Irkalla said.

"We will see," the woman said.

There was very little talking for the rest of the ride, until they reached the outskirts of a forest and rode through a narrow pathway, where branches occasionally flicked into the open windows of the carriage.

It was comfortable, but Layla took no enjoyment from the journey. She got the feeling that these people weren't there to hurt them, because they could have done that earlier, and while they were threatening and more than capable of causing them great pain, they'd mostly just ignored them.

"So, your name?" Layla asked as the carriage stopped.

The woman pushed open the door and stepped outside into a clearing lit up by torchlight. An owl hooted high above them in the darkness of the trees.

Layla craned her neck to look up at the city that sat above them, built among the trees as far as she could see. "Tommy would make an Ewok joke," Irkalla said.

"What is an Ewok?" one of the archers asked.

"Small furry creature," Irkalla said.

"Like a dwarf?" another archer asked, clearly confused.

Layla shook her head. "No, nothing like a dwarf. Smaller and hairier . . . this is a weird conversation to be having with kidnappers."

"You are prisoners of war," the scarred woman said.

"We're not at war with you," Irkalla told her.

"That we know of," Ava said. "We seem to be at war with a lot of people these days."

"Deal with the carriages," the scarred woman commanded.

"How do you stay hidden?" Layla asked.

"No more questions," the woman snapped, before she led everyone to a wooden lift that took them all high up into the trees.

"This doesn't feel great," Layla whispered to Irkalla.

"If this turns bad, get ready to run," Irkalla whispered back.

Layla nodded. She worried about Chloe, Jinayca, and Tego, still at the palace grounds, and hoped that whatever happened next, they managed to escape from the Valkyries, who would surely blame them for the deaths of their comrades.

The lift stopped, and the scarred woman led her prisoners along wooden paths that wound between the massive trunks and branches of the trees. Layla looked down from one and couldn't see the ground through the thick leaves, but she knew she was several hundred feet in the air and was immediately glad she wasn't afraid of heights.

There were dozens more people up in the tree city, the majority of which appeared to be female, although Layla spotted the occasional male. She kept all questions to herself as they were taken past a row of huts and told to stand outside the largest one while the scarred woman went inside.

"Ever get the feeling you're being watched?" Ava asked.

"I don't think they're trying to hide it," Irkalla said, looking around at the dozens of people who were staring at them.

Layla fought the urge to wave just as the wooden door to the hut opened and the scarred woman exited. "My name is Kara," she said. "I have been informed that my not introducing myself could be considered rude. Apparently, this is bad."

Layla and Irkalla exchanged a confused glance.

"Okay," Layla said. "What's going on?"

"I told her to apologize," another woman said as she left the hut. "Kara is an excellent warrior and Valkyrie but not always so good with the people side of things."

"I prefer to stab my problems away," Kara said with a smile that was much more terrifying than Layla assumed the Valkyrie meant.

"We have friends back at the palace," Irkalla said. "So we either need to go get them, or you need to tell us what the hell is going on."

"I'm sorry for your friends," the newcomer said. She was a few inches taller than Layla, with short auburn hair. Dozens of deep scars covered one of her muscular arms, and she caught Layla's gaze at the four claw marks that ran from her shoulder to her elbow.

"I didn't mean to stare," Layla said, raising her metal arm. "We all have our wounds."

"It's fine," she said. "Werewolf was wearing a silver claw for some reason—didn't really get time to ask him, seeing how I beat him to death with it."

"Who are you, and what is going on here?" Irkalla asked.

"My name is Brynhildr," she said. "And I'm the leader of the Valkyrie resistance."

Layla stared at the woman for several seconds, until she and Irkalla uttered the same thing at once. "You're Nate's mother?"

Chapter Six

Mordred

Realm of Asgard

Mordred stood atop the Great Wall of Asgard, looking out over the landscape. The drums were becoming louder now, and there were great plumes of black smoke billowing up from the Avalon camps.

"You look upset," Hel said as she stood beside Mordred, linking her fingers with his.

"Tommy is in hospital," Mordred said. "My light magic did absolutely nothing to help heal him. Odin is in a coma, and once again my light magic was worthless in helping. Nate has gone to the Earth realm to . . . I assume murder everyone in his way in his effort to find a cure. But more than that, Avalon are just *sitting* there. I preferred it when they were marching toward us. It was something to look forward to."

"Look forward to?" Hel asked.

"Okay, maybe not *forward* to, but at least I knew what I'd be doing about now. Fighting for my life against overwhelming odds. I'd planned for it. I do not like waiting."

"Patience is not one of your strong points," Hel admitted.

Mordred turned to her and smiled. "I was hoping our time alone would have been longer."

"Damn hordes coming over here and spoiling our romance," Hel said, resting her head against Mordred's arm.

"Fuckers," Mordred said with a smile of his own. He sighed. "Arthur is in there somewhere. Probably Merlin and Gawain too."

"Your father and brother chose their path a long time ago."

Mordred nodded. "I know. But Merlin never chose to be led down this path. He was corrupted by Gawain and Arthur. I'd always hoped there would be a spark of good left in him. Somewhere." He started humming the theme tune to *Zelda*. He'd tried to branch out into different tunes from different video games, but he always found himself coming back to the same few.

"Nervous?" Hel asked.

Mordred shook his head. "I love you."

Hel held Mordred's gaze. "I know. I love you too. You know this will be okay, right? We're going to win."

"No," Mordred said softly. "I don't know that. I know that I will fight for those I love, I know I will continue to fight until I have nothing left in me, but I don't know we'll win. I thought we'd have won several times over by now."

"We stopped Avalon in Helheim," Hel said.

Mordred nodded. "I know. And it was a beautiful victory, but this . . . this feels different. These walls aren't going to stop Avalon. And to think otherwise is naive at best. The runes within their construction will only work for so long, and then we'll have a war inside the city to contend with. The wall is too long to defend every part of it with the numbers we need. This whole place is going to turn into Helm's Deep, but I don't think Gandalf and the Riders of Rohan will be coming to our rescue."

"You have seen those films way too many times," Hel said with a smile.

"No such thing," Mordred said.

Hel looked over the battlements. "It's a long way down. Maybe we can bottleneck Avalon, force them to come through only a part of the wall. Give us time."

Mordred nodded. "We need to figure out what they're waiting for."

"Odin sent scouts before," Hel said. "You want to go scout yourself, don't you?"

Mordred grinned. "It's a great idea."

"No, it isn't. It's a terrible idea. But for some reason your terrible ideas seem to work out, so I say go talk to Hades. I'm coming with you, though, because there's no way I'm waiting to find out what stupid thing you decided to do."

Mordred kissed Hel on the lips. "You get me."

"Someone has to," she said with a roll of her eyes.

Mordred caught sight of Diana and Medusa walking through the streets hand in hand. "I'm glad they found happiness," he said.

Hel followed his gaze. "They're good people. They deserve it."

Mordred nodded.

"You deserve it too," Hel said. "I figured I'd say that, you know, before you say anything stupid."

"It is one of my many talents," Mordred said.

The pair left the ramparts as the guard changed. There were hundreds of soldiers standing upon the wall at any one time, but Mordred didn't feel any safer with them or the wall. He'd feel safer if Avalon were done. If Arthur were dead. If he didn't have the overriding belief that no matter what happened in the coming days, he would have to finally confront his father. Killing Gawain was never going to be an issue. Gawain was an asshole who deserved to have been shot at birth. But Merlin was different. He wasn't sure he could kill Merlin, not after discovering that he'd been dragged into the darkness that had consumed him. As much as he said aloud that Merlin's soul was done for, that he was too corrupt to be saved, deep down in his heart Mordred knew that if he could be saved, anyone could. Even Merlin.

Despite Hel's company, Mordred found himself lost in his own thoughts as they made their way through the city to the Bright House, where they found Elaine Garlot waiting outside.

"Oh, nephew of mine, I was wondering when you'd come by," Elaine said.

Mordred paused. "What's wrong? I mean now, because so far it feels like there's a lot that's going wrong."

"We need to have a chat," Elaine said.

Mordred's eyes narrowed. "What do you need me to do?"

Elaine pushed open the door, revealing the Bright House's long table, where four people were seated. All of them looked up and stared at Mordred and Hel as they entered the building.

"Oh yeah, this bodes well," Mordred said.

"We need to talk," Hades said as Mordred took a seat next to Persephone.

"Lucifer," Mordred said. "Persephone, Hades, Olivia, and Loki. I am honored to be in your company."

"Liar," Elaine said, taking a seat opposite Mordred.

Mordred smiled. "Okay, my aunt has a point; I'd rather be anywhere else. Morgan gets to go off and fight in other realms, and I'm beginning to wish I'd gone with her."

"We need to talk to you about Arthur," Loki said.

"Dad, a heads-up would have been good," Hel said, sounding slightly irritated.

"Honestly, you're right," Loki said. "But right now, we needed to ensure that no one overheard anything about this plan. Especially with Tommy and Odin hurt."

"So, Arthur," Mordred said. "He's a massive bellend. What else do we need to talk about?"

"Excalibur," Elaine said.

Mordred shrugged. "No idea where it is. No one knows where it is—that's the whole bloody point. Some people think that it was given to Zeus; some people think it was thrown into the sea. All anyone really knows is that Arthur wants it. And he wants it badly."

"Do you know why?" Olivia asked.

Mordred shrugged again. "Because he's a bellend? Because he collects swords? Because he likes shiny things? Who knows?"

"It's one of half a dozen weapons that Arthur had made for him," Hades said. "Many are lost in time. Caliburn is destroyed. The sword of peace—"

"I destroyed Clarent," Mordred interrupted. "I used it to stab Arthur—it's what put him in a coma for so long. But once it did its job, it broke."

"Carnwennan," Loki said.

"The dagger of shadows is in my father's possession, last I heard," Mordred said.

"Pridwen," Persephone said.

"No idea," Mordred said. "But there's only one left, and it's the one I'd be most worried about. Rhongomiant. Arthur's spear. It's designed to lessen the effect of magic on the user, and it makes him more powerful. Thank you, Merlin, for that one."

"Only Rhongomiant, Carnwennan, and Excalibur are known to still exist," Hades said. "Excalibur has two main attributes. One is to do something similar to the spear. Increases the power of the wielder and decreases the power that magic has over whoever holds it."

"And the second thing?" Hel asked when no one spoke for several seconds.

"It's why I don't want to touch it," Mordred said with a sigh. "It removes everything from a person. My father wanted a weapon that meant that no matter how powerful the opponent, whoever went up against Arthur while he held that sword, Arthur would have to be beaten on skill alone. It projects a fifty-foot-diameter area around the wielder that makes all power inside it impossible. But it also strips away any lies or misinformation. The people inside the barrier can only tell the truth. They can't hide behind any facades or coping mechanisms that they might have built up for themselves. It's just them. Pure."

"And you fear that everything you've built for yourself to cope with what happened to you would come crashing down?" Elaine asked.

Mordred nodded slowly. "My brain was torn apart and put back together again, over and over, for a century. I was a monster. And now I am not. I am unsure exactly which Mordred will turn up if I wield the sword and activate the power it contains."

"You're a good man," Hel said softly, placing her hand on Mordred's.

"That doesn't much matter when you pick up Excalibur," Mordred said. "To activate its power, to allow yourself to bond with the weapon, is to accept who you are. Arthur wants it, I assume, because if anyone else gets it, they can use it on him to strip away his lies and deceit. They can use it to force him to fight on skill alone and to tell the truth. Neither of those things appeal to him."

"We know," Hades said. "We know what Excalibur does. And we know why it was made."

"Cool," Mordred said. "What does that have to do with . . ." He paused. "No. No, I'm not. No."

"It was made for you," Persephone said.

"No," Mordred said, slightly more forcefully. "It was made for the king of Avalon."

"Which was meant to be you," Elaine said firmly.

"I don't want to be the king of anything," Mordred snapped. "I want to be as far away from that as possible. I never even fucking wanted it when my own father sent me to the dwarven realm to get my fucking mind ripped out for a hundred years. I didn't want it when Arthur, Gawain, Hera, and countless others took fucking turns destroying me. Breaking me. Making me into their goddamn monster. I am not a fucking king."

There was silence for several seconds, and Mordred looked up at the ceiling and sighed. "Why do you think it was made for me?"

"Because that's what I was told," Hades said. "The dwarves made that sword. A lot of us were worried at the time. There had been weapons like yourself and Nate created in a sort of magical arms race, and many were concerned that whoever held Excalibur would use it to do awful things. So a number of people, including myself, petitioned the dwarves to ensure that only one of the weapons like yourselves could wield it."

"Give it to Nate, then," Mordred almost snapped.

"We both know why we can't do that," Elaine said. "I love Nate like a son, but he was never meant to be king. A good king isn't someone with the most power; a good king is someone who wants to do right. Even when it's hard. A good king has seen the face of evil and stepped back from its shadow."

"Sounds like Nate to me," Mordred said.

"Excalibur was made for *you*," Loki said. "Specifically you. We think that Arthur found out and had Merlin send you to the dwarven realm because he knew it was meant to be yours. He knew that you could end him before this all started."

"I am not a king," Mordred said. "I can't be responsible for all these people. I just . . . I just can't. Some days I'm barely responsible for myself."

"We need your help," Elaine said. "Because only one person knows where Excalibur really is."

Mordred looked around the room. "Who?"

"Guinevere," Elaine said.

Mordred sighed and placed his forehead against the table. "Bollocks," he said, his voice muffled.

"Arthur's ex-wife?" Hel asked. "The one who was shagging Lancelot?"

Elaine nodded. "The same one. Arthur found out about the affair, and they escaped Camelot before he could get to them, but Guinevere took a little insurance with her."

"Excalibur?" Mordred asked without moving. "Please don't make me deal with these people."

"You don't like them?" Hel asked.

"Lancelot is a prick," Mordred said. "I liked Guinevere. Besides, it doesn't matter, because no one knows where they are."

"Scotland," Elaine said. "They're near my house there."

"The ruined house that Arthur's allies tore apart when they kidnapped you?" Mordred asked. "Why would you send them there?"

"They live about a mile away in the middle of nowhere with enough security around them to tell them if anyone is coming," Elaine said.

"And why, pray tell, do you need my help?" Mordred asked.

Olivia sighed. "Guinevere said she'll tell us who she gave the sword to all those centuries ago but that you had to be there."

"Why?" Mordred asked.

"No idea," Persephone said.

"Is this some kind of really awful practical joke?" Mordred asked.

"I really wish it was," Loki told him. "But no. Unfortunately not. Guinevere wants you there, so we need you to go find the sword."

"I'm not being king," Mordred said, his tone hard. "I'll go get the damn thing, and then you can pick another sucker from a long list of . . . well, give it to Nate. Nate can be king."

Everyone stared at Mordred for a few seconds.

Mordred sighed. "I hate you all. Why now? Why after all these centuries is Excalibur suddenly important? I don't mean to stop Arthur; I mean important enough that Guinevere and Lancelot come to you for help, Elaine?"

"Guinevere contacted me," Elaine said. "She's noticed more and more Avalon agents searching for her. Heard more rumors of something going on. And we started to hear more chatter about Excalibur too. Arthur has his people actively searching for it."

"Of course he does," Mordred said. "Any chance my brother is involved?"

"Gawain has been awfully quiet for a while now," Olivia admitted.

"That's just awesome," Mordred said with a thumbs-up.

"We'll discuss it further when you're back," Hades said. "The important thing is getting the sword away from Arthur. If he finds it first, then we can't use it to strip away his lies, and he can use it to increase his power."

"Yeah, I get the need to ensure the old bag of dicks doesn't get it, but damn, this sucks," Mordred said, getting to his feet. "Are there any guards or things we need to worry about with Guinevere and the massive twat that is Lancelot?"

"When you said you don't like Lancelot, you meant you *really* don't like him," Hel said.

"Can't bloody stand him," Mordred said. "I wanted to believe that Arthur was good, was the best of us. All of us were told that Guinevere and Lancelot were traitors, that they were sneaking around behind Arthur's back, that they had tried to kill him before they ran. The whole thing was bollocks, but Arthur, Merlin, and the paladins were convincing at the time. I should have guessed it was bullshit when Gawain swore to hunt them down and kill them both for their treachery so as to restore the honor of Camelot. Gawain never gave a shit about honor in his entire life."

"And you don't like Lancelot because . . . ?" Loki asked.

"A lot of different reasons," Mordred said, leaving the building.

As he stood outside, taking a few deep breaths, the ground started to shake beneath his feet, forcing Mordred to put his hand on a nearby tree to keep upright.

The Bright House doors opened, and those inside flooded out. "Was that you?" Elaine asked.

"Nope. Earthquake?" Mordred guessed.

"Not in Asgard," Loki said. "Not naturally occurring ones, anyway."

"I get the feeling that whatever Arthur and Avalon are doing out there is coming to a head," Persephone said. "Go to Earth and get Excalibur sorted."

"And if I can piss off Lancelot in the process, I think we all win," Mordred said as he strolled away with Hel beside him.

"I don't think you can kill him," Hel said.

"Oh, just wait. You haven't met him yet."

Chapter Seven

NATE GARRETT

Montana, United States, Earth Realm

I'd been doing everything I could to keep my anger in check. In Asgard people had repeatedly asked me if I was okay, reminded me not to lose control, to lose my temper, and I'd assured them I was fine. I would go to the Earth realm, find the cure for Tommy, Odin, and Frigg, and return. I felt bad that in all of the running around, I'd barely thought about Frigg. She'd been hit with the same stuff as my dad, only a less potent version, centuries ago. If there was a cure for Odin, then there was a cure for Frigg too. At least, I hoped so.

Arriving in the realm gate temple in a cave in Montana was easy enough. I changed into more appropriate attire: a pair of blue jeans, a black T-shirt, and a red hoodie.

The three of us left the cave in a dark-green Ford four-wheel drive and drove the forty-five minutes in silence until we reached Carver Creek, which pretty much consisted of a large bar, a diner, a small church, and a dozen houses farther down the main road.

There were several motorbikes outside the bar, so I stopped the Ford outside the church, and we all climbed out.

"You think this is Avalon territory?" Zamek asked, looking around, one hand on the hilt of an ax.

Kase nodded. "My dad went here. I can smell that his trail leads off, though. He said he went to talk to the barman, who told him that Masako had been here."

"Let's go ask the barman, then," I said. "You two look around, see if you can find anything useful."

Kase looked over at the bar. "Lot of bikes out front."

"I won't pick a fight," I said, walking off just as the radio in the car went off and Zamek grabbed it.

"Backup is here," he shouted to me.

I gave him the thumbs-up and continued on to the bar. It was a single-story building with a wooden door that looked like it had seen better days. Several of the windows had been covered over on the inside, and the whole place had the air of the kind of biker joint where a fight would break out at the drop of a hat.

I pushed the door open and, ignoring the smell of stale beer and sweat, stepped into the gloomy bar. It was all one room, with a pool table at the far end—five men around it, all playing or talking—a jukebox with two men standing in front of it, and a dozen circular wooden tables, four of which were occupied by a combination of men and women. There were fourteen people in total in the bar; maybe eight of them looked like threats, and the rest just appeared to be there for a drink. Those at the pool table stopped and watched me walk to the long bar, take a seat on one of the red leather-topped stools, and beckon over the closest bartender.

"You new?" he asked. He looked to be in his midthirties and was wearing a Motörhead T-shirt that had long since faded from black to a sort of blocky gray. He was bald, with tattoos on his skull and on pretty much every other part of his body I could see that wasn't his face. One of his knuckles, each of which looked like they'd landed their fair share of punches, had a small bullet tattooed on it.

"In general?" I asked him.

"You a smart-ass?" he asked.

I nodded. "Pretty much. You got bourbon?"

The man removed a bottle of brown liquid that had no label on it and poured me a single measure.

I knocked it back in one shot, feeling the burn as it went down. It wasn't bad, considering it had probably been made in someone's bathroom. I removed ten dollars from my pocket and placed the bill on the counter. "That enough for another?"

The bartender looked a little surprised but poured a second glass. "It's called Envy," he said.

"Good name," I told him, knocking it back. "It's got a kick."

"So you passing through?" the bartender asked, putting the bottle of moonshine away.

I nodded. "Looking for a friend of mine who came here recently on her way through."

"This friend have a name?" the bartender asked.

"Masako," I said.

You could have heard a pin drop in the silence that followed.

"Don't know her," the bartender said tightly.

"Shame. I was hoping she might put me in contact with the people who tried to murder my friend and killed some people he was working with."

More silence.

"You're not human," the bartender said with a smirk as several people hurried out of the bar.

I shook my head. "Nope. Just have a few questions for you."

The bartender picked up my glass and placed it behind him. "We don't serve your kind."

"You have no idea what *my* kind is. I'm going to assume that you guys work for Avalon, yes? I'm not exactly sure what you do, but I know that you set up people I care about. People who died or got hurt really bad." I looked in the mirror behind the bartender. Nine people stood behind me. I'd been off by one. I was okay with that. Two held pool cues, and more than one had a knife in their hand.

"The pool cues aren't going to be a lot of use," I said.

"Leave, and we'll pretend this didn't happen," the bartender said.

"I'm guessing I leave here, and your friends follow to deal with me outside? You weren't expecting me, so you didn't put runes on the floor. I can see the scuff marks where something was rubbed out. Just over where that large bloke with the overalls is standing." I turned to him and waved. He took a step back.

"I noticed it when I walked in," I said. "You didn't quite get rid of it. Were you told to remove all evidence of Tommy Carpenter having come here? I imagine when they told you to remove all evidence, they didn't mean to get rid of runes that would save your lives. I'm going to guess there's a second one under the bar. If you try to touch it, you die."

The bartender placed his hands on top of the bar. "Who are you?"

"My name is Nate Garrett," I said, getting down off my stool. "I'm here because you set up my friends. You sent them off toward Kilnhurst, where they were ambushed. You're going to tell me what attacked them, and you're going to tell me if Masako was part of the plot."

"I have no idea what you're talking about," the bartender said. "But it doesn't matter, because you're going to die in here."

"Nothing says *I'm innocent* like threatening to kill someone," I told him.

The sound of a round being chambered echoed behind me, and an instant later tendrils of shadow exploded out of the floor and walls, each one slamming into a different person, piercing their flesh, and impaling them on the floor, walls, or ceiling.

The screams were deafening for a second as I continued to look only at the bartender and the horror on his face, but more shadows burst free until there was only silence. A shotgun went off, hitting the bar near me, and only then did I turn to the culprit, and with a flick of my hand, he vanished up into the darkness on the ceiling. The wraith inside my shadow realm would feed, making me stronger.

I looked back at the bartender. His eyes were wide with fear as he looked behind me at the carnage I'd brought into his bar.

"Masako," I said again. "Where is she?"

The bartender began to back away, toward the door at the far end of the bar, which quietly opened. Kase stepped inside. She stood still as the bartender continued to walk backward toward her, and when he was a few feet away, she let loose a low growl.

There's something in the deep recesses of the human psyche that remembers being hunted. The bartender froze solid, and his entire body began to shake as Kase moved closer. She laid a hand on his shoulder, her nails growing in length, her hand changing into a combination of hand and paw. The bartender cried out in fear and passed out, falling back toward Kase, who caught him.

"What the ever-loving fuck?" a voice asked as someone entered the bar.

I turned to see Remy standing in the doorway. "I've seen some weird shit in my life," he continued. "I mean, I *am* some weird shit, but . . ." He motioned to the people pinned to the walls and ceiling by shadows.

I removed the shadows, allowing the bodies to fall to the floor.

"That was fucked up," Remy said as Zamek and Sky entered the bar. "I thought you promised not to go all dark, Nate."

I looked away. "Bring the bartender," I said. "I have questions for him."

"Do you *bollocks*," Remy said, climbing up on a chair so that we were nose to nose. "You're not questioning him. I'm not entirely sure how much of him you'd leave. Same with Kase. We need answers right now, not vengeance. Can you tell me that you'd leave him in one piece to question?"

I opened my mouth to answer and closed it before shaking my head.

"I want the antidote too," Remy said. "I want to find the people who did this and hurt them, but we need answers."

I sighed.

Kase picked up the unconscious bartender and threw him over one shoulder, carried him around to us, and placed him on the table.

"Can you still see blood curse marks?" Remy asked.

I shook my head. "Since mine have gone, I can't see them on anyone else."

"So there's a chance that he's been blood cursed and we all die because his brain explodes with some kind of disease?" Remy asked.

Zamek used the blood sample on the barroom floor to draw runes on the bartender's chest, which turned black.

"He definitely has a blood curse mark," Zamek said. "No idea what it does, but judging from how quickly it turned color, I'd say nothing good."

"And now he's on fire," Remy said, doing absolutely nothing to put out the small fire that had started on the bartender's chest.

"Ah, well, that can't be good," Sky said as I used my air magic to blow the fire out.

"No, spontaneous combustion is usually a bad thing," Zamek said. "I'll change my original diagnosis. Whatever curse was put on him, it's fucking huge. Like, the kind of thing that you used to have on those sorcerers who killed themselves with their own magic a few years ago. I wouldn't go messing around in his brain, and I certainly wouldn't try to get information out of his spirit."

Sky slapped the bartender across the face. "The rest of you, out. Me and the bartender are going to have a chat."

We all did as we were told. Sky's tone suggested that there would be no argument, and frankly I was still a little bit unsure whether I could question him without tearing him in half.

"You okay now?" Remy asked me when we were outside.

I nodded. "I would have torn his spirit apart," I said.

"And then you'd be dead or a drooling wreck," Zamek pointed out.

"He's sort of the second one already," Remy said, making everyone laugh.

"You find anything else in town?" I asked Zamek and Kase, making a point to ignore Remy.

"Nothing," Kase said with a shake of her head.

"Some bodies in the church," Zamek said. "They'd been looted and just thrown into a pit under it. I get the feeling the bartender and his friends liked to rob people."

Sky left the bar. "He's told us what we already knew," she said. "That they went north to Kilnhurst. I've tied up our bartender friend, and he's going to come with us."

"Why?" I asked.

"He said he'd show us exactly how to get there in exchange for Kase not tearing his head off and using it as a football," Sky said with a smile. "Oh, and he's terrified of you, Nate. Apparently, living shadows springing out of the ground was a new one to him."

"Good. Hopefully that fear will keep him in check," I said.

Zamek went back into the bar and returned a moment later with the bartender.

"I take you there, and you let me go?" the bartender said.

"Maybe," Kase said, letting a growl leave her throat. "But if you lie to us, you die. Hard."

The bartender swallowed and nodded before climbing into the rear passenger seat of a Ford identical to the one we'd taken when we'd arrived. Zamek and Kase sat on either side of him, while Remy joined me in the second car.

"We'll follow," I said.

"Don't throw Remy out of the car," Kase called out as they pulled away.

I started the car up, and Remy stared at me as we followed.

"What's wrong?" I asked.

"Just wondering how much you're keeping your shit together so you don't turn into a nuclear bomb."

"I'm fine," I said.

"No, you're not, and you're a terrible liar," Remy told me.

"No, I'm not," I admitted. "But I'll be fine enough to do what I need to do."

"Oh, well, *now* I feel better," Remy said sarcastically.

"Fine," I snapped before taking a breath. "Sorry. You're right—I'm not okay. I'm barely keeping my temper in check. I'm scared that it would be really easy to just tear everything apart until I got the answers I wanted and deal with the consequences afterward. But that might not get me the cure. And so I'm doing everything I can to not turn into the Hulk and smash the shit out of everything."

"Nate smash later," Remy said, mimicking the Hulk's voice. "Doesn't really have the same ring to it."

A smile touched my lips, but it quickly faded. "I'm trying very hard to focus on one thing at a time. And I was focused on being a father, which, I'd like to add, is fucking terrifying. And then

Tommy and my dad got hurt, and all of that emotional shit inside of me just shifted to needing to hurt the people who tried to take them away from those who love them. From their family."

"You mean all of us, don't you?"

I nodded. "We're a family, Remy. We're a fucking weird family, but I think families of friendship and love are sometimes better than those born only of blood and some weird obligation because you're related. Someone hurt my family. *Our* family. And that shit will be met with biblical levels of vengeance."

"You're damn fucking right it will," Remy said. "But even so, just remember, Nate—someone hurt my family too. And Sky's, and Kase's, and Zamek's, and everyone else's back in Asgard and in Shadow Falls and on the Earth realm. You're not the only one hurting here. Remember that. You have people to lean on, just as people will need to lean on you. Your father is dying, and Kase's father is so hurt that he can't even turn into his werewolf form without putting his body at risk of just giving up. I know what you're going through sucks, but imagine how Kase feels right now too."

"I never thought that my pain was greater," I said, feeling like shit for possibly making Kase feel even worse.

"I know," Remy said. "And Kase knows too. I'm just saying. You're angry and want to hurt the people responsible, but she's got to be feeling exactly the same, except she's a werewolf, and that shit is hard to keep in check at the best of times. If she loses control of the beast inside of her, we're all fucked."

I sighed. "I thought about it. I figured she'd keep it together. I was being a selfish prick."

"No, you were being someone who was hurt and wanted to lash out. Thankfully, I'm here to tell you how to not be a selfish prick and stop you before you start to forget your friends. Which, if I remember correctly, happened once before, and it wasn't a good time for anyone."

"You're a smart little foxman," I said.

"The motherfucking smartest," Remy said with a grin as I stopped the car behind the one in front. I got out and walked over to the other Ford as the rear passenger door opened and Kase climbed out.

"Hey," I said to her. "I'm sorry. I was thinking about how it all hit me and not about how it hit everyone else. That was really dickish of me."

She looked at me for a second and hugged me. "It's okay," she said. "I was too lost in my own mind to notice."

Sky got out of the car and dragged the bartender out. "You said stop, so here we are."

I stared down the hill at the nearby town. The sun was still up, but Kilnhurst looked as creepy as it had over a hundred years ago. The town had gotten considerably larger than when I'd last been here, with hundreds of buildings where once had stood only ruin and destruction.

"That's the prison," the bartender said, pointing off into the distance at a gray mass a few miles away.

"Kilnhurst," I said. "We burned this place to the ground last time we were here."

"It appears to have sprung up like a phoenix," Remy said. "A really shit phoenix."

"Whatever hurt my dad is down there," Kase said, her voice determined. "Let's go find them."

Sky stood beside me as everyone else got back into the cars. She'd been the only one here with me the last time I'd been in Montana. She'd seen the horrors that had taken place.

"I don't know who decided to build on the ashes we left, but I'm guessing Avalon are involved," Sky said.

I nodded. "They were behind the lich and what he was doing there. I'm pretty sure of that. You have any ideas what's currently in there?"

Sky shook her head. "Whatever it is, it can't be good. It took out Tommy, Odin, and their whole team. We haven't even found the bodies of most of them. Something in there can take out a team of highly trained people, including two of the most powerful beings I've ever met."

"You wondering what they'll do to us if they can take out Odin and Tommy?"

Sky nodded. "I don't want to go in there unprepared and overconfident."

"Odin and Tommy's team was ambushed. We have more information than they had. We know there's something awful in there. We know that it isn't to be underestimated."

"That's why we brought guns," Sky said, opening the trunk of one of the vehicles and removing a blanket to reveal several cases. She opened one that contained an MP5 and passed it to me. "No fucking about. We get in, we kill everything that moves, we find what we need, and we get out."

I loaded the MP5 with silver rounds. "Happy to."

Chapter Eight

Nate Garrett

We drove slowly down the hill and along the deserted road to Kilnhurst. The closer we got, the more we saw how overrun the buildings were, how old everything looked. We stopped by the sign proudly showing that Kilnhurst had a population of 888 people and got out of our respective cars.

"I have scents," Kase said. "My dad is one of them. They came through here."

"This place has been abandoned for years," Sky said. She looked over at the bartender. "You want to explain this?"

"I thought you knew," he pleaded. "I thought everyone knew. No one comes here. No one has come here since the fifties."

"It looks like that *Fallout* game Mordred likes," Remy said. "All old houses and cars just abandoned. Like a nuclear bomb went off and people just ran."

"If I see a single super mutant, I will not be happy," Kase said.

"Why did everyone leave?" I asked, looking at a partially rusted light-green Chevrolet Bel Air.

"Don't take me in there," the bartender pleaded, dropping to his knees. "Please. No one who goes in there comes out. No one."

"Bullshit," Sky snapped. She held an MP5 identical to the one she'd given me. Zamek had refused a gun, preferring his axes, and Remy had obviously brought his own pistols and swords. Kase had taken an MP5, too, although I knew she wasn't a big fan of guns. Neither was I, truth be told, but that didn't stop me from killing people with them.

Kase stepped past the billboard into the city limits and then back out again. "See? Nothing happened."

"Don't fucking taunt me," the bartender snapped. "There are things in there. A man comes to the bar once a month. He pays ten thousand dollars in cash to send people up here."

"What man?"

"I don't know," the bartender said. "A really fucking scary man."

"And who do you send up here?" Zamek asked.

"Anyone—just people coming through looking for the old town," he said. "It's a tourist thing. They make out that it's out of bounds, that the whole place is dangerous, and then it's advertised online by people who say they've been here and that it's a really cool place, but you need to be careful because of the cops and stuff."

"Thrill seekers come here?" Kase asked.

The bartender nodded. "It's like those people who go to Chernobyl but enter illegally to look around without a guide. Except this place was supposedly abandoned because of a mass breakout."

"Was it?" Remy asked him.

He nodded.

"That rings true with what research Tommy and his people did," Sky said. "There was a bunch of stuff online about how the prison failed and dozens of mass murderers got out and overpowered the guards. They escaped into the city and slaughtered people while they were evacuating. Apparently, the National Guard was called in, and it all went horribly wrong. People come here to search for clues as to what happened to the murderers who escaped."

"Is that true?" I asked.

"I don't know," the bartender said. "I don't know what happened. I know that people lived here and now no one does."

"Clearly Avalon didn't want to let go of the place," Remy said.

"This must have been a pet project for someone high up," Sky said. "Even before Arthur took control, before we knew what he was, before everything went to shit, it wouldn't have been hard for someone with power to keep knowledge of this place out of our hands."

"No one came here for decades," the bartender said. "It's only been the last few years that we were told to tell people about it. Before then, I don't know what happened here."

"Let's go find out," I said, dragging the bartender to his feet and pushing him forward.

"Please, don't," he begged. "Please. The man that deals with us, he warned us all to stay away. That we would die if we came looking. He scares me. Scares everyone. He killed the priest that lived in town. He just tore his head clean off."

"Why?" Remy asked.

"The priest didn't know what we were doing, and when he found out, he was less than happy about it. Threatened to tell the FBI. The man killed him, told us to dump any bodies in the church that we needed to. We had a quota of people to send up here; anyone over that we were to kill and get rid of."

"A quota?" I asked.

"They only want young, fit, healthy people," the bartender said. "A few arrived with parents or were older travelers just stopping on their way through. We drugged them, dealt with those not needed, and brought the others here. If we didn't kill them, we would have been found out. They had to die."

Kase stopped walking, spun toward the bartender, and punched him hard enough in the stomach to lift him off his feet. She spun back to face the way she'd been walking and continued on as if nothing had happened while the bartender tried not to throw up his own lungs.

"I'd get up," Sky said absentmindedly as she walked past him. "You don't want to see what happens to you if you decide to piss her off any more than she already is."

The bartender got back to his feet and turned to run but found Remy standing behind him. "I know," Remy said. "I'm just a three-foot foxman." He smiled, showing his sharp teeth. "But I'll hurt you. Get walking."

With nowhere else to turn, the bartender started walking into the city. He stopped crying after a few hundred feet as we stopped beside the wrecks of two old cars, and Sky passed around canteens of water, making sure to give none to the bartender.

"Why am I even here?" he almost shouted.

"Because you deserve to see what you caused," Sky said. "Also, because we figured you might be useful at some point. We can change that, if you'd prefer to die now?" She drew a dagger from her belt.

"No," the man almost shouted. "I'm good."

Sky winked at him and turned to me. "I don't like this place. A lot of old spirits hover around; can you feel them?"

I nodded. My necromancy was nowhere near as powerful as hers, but a lot of people had died fighting in the city.

"I thought I might feel some of those who died when we were last here, but there's nothing," I said.

"I know," Sky agreed, not looking happy about it. "Something really bad happened here. Something worse than just a bunch of prisoners escaping and killing folk. Something . . . Old Testament. Fire, brimstone, death, all the fun stuff."

Once everyone had finished their water, we continued on deeper into the city, past practically falling-apart buildings or overgrown vegetation that had burst through the concrete street. It was its own little postapocalyptic corner of the country. Something most people didn't even know existed, and those who did either were dead or were going to wish they were.

As the sun began to set, the bartender's mood became increasingly paranoid and erratic. "We need to leave," he said for the hundredth time in only a few minutes.

"If there's something in here, that's not a bad idea," Zamek said as we reached a crossroads. "We can always hole up in one of the high floors of a building, see if we can barricade ourselves in and keep safe for the night."

"Anyone else noticed that not a single animal lives here?" Remy asked. "No birds flying overhead, no noise, nothing. I've been to places like this before. They're not the kind of places you want to be out in at night."

"Agreed," I said, although I was far from happy about it. Time was of the essence.

Kase's expression changed from determined to resigned as common sense prevailed. "Okay," she said softly.

"We can't find a cure if we spend all of our time running from something," Sky said. "First light, we head off to the prison. Hopefully we can figure out where your dad and his team were hit and go from there."

Kase nodded.

"You still have your dad's scent, yes?" I asked.

She nodded again. "It's strong enough to pick it up again once we get up in the morning. He wasn't fighting here. He was just walking with his team. There's no fear or worry in the scent. Just Dad."

"We'll find the cure," I promised as something made a sound that resulted in the hairs on the back of my neck standing up.

"What the hell was that?" I asked, looking around at the deserted streets.

It was somewhere between a low growl and a howl. And it didn't sound like it belonged to something friendly.

The sound continued again, this time for longer, although it was impossible to pinpoint exactly where it came from.

"That building there," Sky said, pointing farther down one of the roads. "Looks semidefensible."

No one disagreed, and we ran to the building, which had long since lost the large front window, although the sign above suggested it was some kind of office.

We entered and made our way through the ruins of what had once been someone's place of work. Kase and Remy sniffed every few feet until we reached a set of stairs that led to the floor above.

"There's nothing in here," Kase said, making me feel a little better, until the noise from outside was heard again.

We ran up the stairs to the floor above and quickly searched it before continuing on to the third floor and following the same procedure. The fourth floor was the first one where we discovered signs of life, although the skeletal corpses had long since stopped being anything close to alive.

We piled up the remains of office furniture in the stairwell of the fourth floor and ascended to the fifth, where another quick search found yet more office furniture and little else. Another barricade was made in the stairwell, and I used the last flight of stairs to go up onto the flat roof, which was empty and had high brick sides all around. I looked over the edges of the building as the sun finally finished setting, and the noises in the city below grew in size and frequency.

I went back inside and found everyone in a large office room at the front of the building. One of the floor-to-ceiling glass windows was missing, and another was cracked, but there were enough remaining to keep out the worst of the cold wind.

We moved all of the wooden remains to one side of the room and settled down for the evening. It would be a while before the sun rose again, and those of us who weren't human would be able to survive the freezing temperatures without too many problems, but the bartender would be uncomfortable at best.

Sky and Zamek took their backpacks off and passed around several pouches of food. None of it looked particularly appetizing, although the jerky they had was surprisingly tasty. We decided to take shifts for lookout, just in case whatever was out there could smell us or tried to find us.

There was a shriek in the darkness outside, and I moved to the far end of the room, crouching down beside Kase, who was staring outside with steely determination on her face.

"You see anything?" I asked.

She shook her head. "The cold wind is screwing around with my sense of smell, but there's definitely something down there."

I closed my eyes and allowed my fire magic to change my vision to thermal. When I opened them, the world was awash with orange, yellow, and red heat signatures. Several things crawled over the rubble down below, running in and out of buildings, darting into alleyways. They looked human in size, although they moved oddly, as if they were occasionally being pushed along.

"Ghouls?" Sky said as she crouched beside me, her voice telling me everything I needed to know about her thoughts on that.

"No," I said. "Not ghouls."

"What then?" Kase asked.

"I don't know," I said, looking farther down the street and seeing several more creatures chase what appeared to be a deer. The creatures got close enough to the deer that they swiped at its legs but then immediately backed off as the deer ran farther toward the three creatures waiting in the mouth of the alleyway. When the deer was close enough, one of the creatures pounced on the animal, grabbing it around the throat and bringing it down so that the monsters could feast.

"They hunt in a pack," I said. "They killed a deer."

"We saw no animals earlier," Kase said.

"I guess they chased it in from outside the city limits, probably hounding it for the better part of a mile. It looked like they were playing before they took it down."

"You think they used to be human?" Zamek asked.

I nodded and looked beyond him to the bartender. "Do you know what these things are?" I asked.

The bartender shook his head. "About a year ago one of the men in the bar asked the big guy what went on up here. He was brought here to be shown. No one ever saw him again."

"You think those things attacked my dad?" Kase asked.

"Your dad said that there were creatures with a person leading them," I said. "But killing a deer is one thing; taking down a seven-foot, three-hundred-pound beast-form werewolf is another. Especially with Odin there."

A scream sounded from the top of the street, close to where we'd been when we'd first heard the creatures. I ran up to the roof for a clearer view, with Sky and Kase behind me.

Crouching down by the edge of the roof, we watched over the brick wall as a horse and carriage were stopped at the crossroads.

"I can see horses," Kase said.

A person was being dragged out of the carriage by someone who could only have been described as gargantuan. "Tommy said he faced a huge monster," I said, feeling the anger grow inside me. I looked through the scope in my MP5. I could take a shot, but I didn't know what would happen with the packs of creatures if I did, so I lowered the rifle.

The huge newcomer threw the passenger out behind him before he dragged out two more people. One of them kicked him in the face, and he grabbed their legs and threw them behind him;

the person tumbled through the air before hitting the ground and coming to a stop.

There was another scream as a fourth person was dragged out of the large carriage and dropped to the ground. Then the man climbed up on top and rode away, farther into the town, leaving the four people in the crossroads.

I looked back down toward the pack of . . . whatever they were and saw them move up the road toward the newcomers, three of whom ran, while the fourth—the one who had been thrown—barely moved.

"We need to help them," Sky said, getting to her feet.

"It's too late," I told her as several shapes ran out of the alley closest to the three who were moving and tore them apart. The fourth, more injured person was descended upon by the same pack who had killed the deer, and the person's screams echoed all around the night.

"Nate?" Sky asked as I closed my eyes.

"I don't know what those things are," I said. "But whoever that large guy in the coach was, he left them live food."

"What the hell is happening in this place?" Sky asked.

"I don't know," I said. "Nothing good."

"They smell like death," Kase said. "I caught a whiff when they ran past. They smell like decay and death, but I don't think they're dead. They're not reanimated or zombies."

"And we've established they're not ghouls," Sky said. "What creatures hunt like that and smell like death?"

I shook my head. "No idea."

"And what about that large guy?" Kase said. "I could see him in the darkness. He was . . . the same size as my dad when my dad turns into his wolf-beast form. He took the road that leads toward the prison."

"I guess tomorrow we'll be looking to find him and ask him a few questions," Sky said.

"You think he'll answer them?" I asked.

Sky shrugged. "Never said he had much of a choice. Big or not, everyone feels pain." She paused for a second. "Even lich."

"He wasn't a lich," I said. "And these aren't ghouls."

"I know," Sky said. "I just like to remind myself." She got up and went back inside, while Kase and I remained on the roof.

"She's scared of liches, yes?" Kase asked when she was certain we were alone.

"Not scared as such," I said. "We fought a lich here over a century ago, and it wasn't much fun. And then she helped kill that one who hunted your mum a few years back. I think she'd had her fill of the evil monsters."

Kase nodded. "I remember. I had nightmares after for a long time. You killed it, though."

"Technically your mother and Sky killed it; I just hurt it a whole bunch. Everyone has a thing that they don't really want to go up against again. For Sky it's the lich."

"And for you?" Kase asked.

"Friends who have betrayed me," I said. "Had more than my fair share of those in the past. Arthur being the most recent. Would rather not go through that again."

"You think you can kill Arthur?" Kase asked.

"I don't know," I said honestly.

I gestured for Kase to be quiet when I noticed the pack of creatures walking back along the road in front of the building we were in. Six in total, none of which appeared to be in any hurry. The one in the rear was the largest of them, and it stopped, sniffing the air. It looked around and then turned to the building we were in.

Don't you fucking dare.

It raised one arm toward the building and let out an ear-piercing shriek. We'd been found.

Chapter Nine

Nate Garrett

Kase and I sprinted back down the stairs, taking them three at a time. Sky, Zamek, and Remy were all by the broken window, hidden in the shadows but looking down on the creatures.

"They found us," Zamek said.

"How?" Remy asked.

"Scent," Sky said. "I imagine, anyway. They probably only got a whiff because they walked past at the right time. Just unlucky on our part."

From the tone of her voice, Sky didn't believe that any more than I did, but we didn't really have time to try to figure out the truth.

"Everyone to the roof," I said. "If those things come in here, I'd rather not fight inside the building. We can move from roof to roof; they're pretty close together."

"Why don't you stand and fight?" the bartender said. "They won't stop. And you have guns."

"Because we don't know what these things are," Sky said. "We don't know how to kill them or what they're tracking. We start shooting at them, it could bring down a thousand more, so unless you have information we need, I'd suggest you shut up."

The bartender fell silent.

"Roof," Remy said.

No one argued, and we ran to the roof and closed the metal door behind us. I melted the frame to the door, hopefully giving us time to get some distance between us and the creatures, and was about to cross to the other roof when I stopped.

"Zamek," I called. "Can you put a rune on this roof? One made to take a lot of power."

Zamek smiled, immediately getting where I was going with my suggestion. I could have drawn the rune myself, but Zamek was considerably more talented at them and was able to make runes that took a lot more power.

He removed a piece of white chalk from his pocket and drew the rune on the door, leaving a small gap on the bottom. "This will link itself with your power," Zamek said. "It'll take a lot, so be aware of that."

I thanked him and placed my hands on the rune. I gasped as it closed and began to absorb my power, taking more and more out of me as the white outline of the rune turned to a deep orange. Eventually, it flashed once, and I stepped away, took a moment to catch my breath, and ran after the rest of the team, jumping the five-foot-wide gap between buildings to reach them. We'd moved across another two roofs when I heard the sounds of banging on the metal door. We stopped three roofs away from where we'd been and moved behind a brick wall.

A second later the explosion from the creatures forcing open the metal door tore through the night. I looked around the corner of the wall to see that almost the entire top floor of the building we'd just escaped was missing. Rubble cascaded down over the ruined building, and I spotted more than one body amid the carnage.

"We can go this way," Sky said, pointing over to a metal-framed bridge that linked a roof farther along to one on the other side of the street.

"They'll keep coming," the bartender said.

"How do you know?" Kase asked. "What are they?"

The bartender sighed. "I used to bring deer and rabbits up here for the man who came to our bar. He told me about these creatures, told me not to come at night. That they hunted at night. He bragged about it. Bragged about how they could hunt magic."

Everyone looked at me.

"They smelled my magic use up on the roof?" I asked.

"Yes," the bartender said. "I don't know how or why, but I know that they were created to hunt magic. Or they were created to do something else, and it went wrong. Either way, it's you they won't stop hunting. Every time you use your magic, it's like a damn beacon."

"And you didn't think to tell us earlier?" Kase shouted.

"I'd hoped I would be able to get away," he admitted.

"And we all die in the process?" Zamek asked.

"Bullets," I said. "Do they work?"

"I don't know," the bartender said. "Honestly, I swear. I don't know anything else about them."

"And where are you going?" Remy asked as I started to move away.

"I'll keep these things busy," I said.

"You're going to use yourself as bait?" Sky asked, with the slight sigh of someone who had spent far too many days and nights seeing me do something stupid.

I nodded. "I'll draw them away." I looked over at the bartender. "How many of them are there?"

"I don't know, hundreds in the city," he said. "Maybe more."

"He clearly knows more than he let on," I said. "Find out everything."

Remy cracked his knuckles and smiled at the bartender, who visibly shrank away.

Another shriek sounded from the street below. "Go," I said. "I'll find you in the morning."

"How are you going to get their attention?" Zamek asked.

I glanced over at the burning building. "Looks like magic hurts them." I looked over the wall and spotted four more of the creatures below; they were climbing up the wall toward us. I created a dagger of fire in my hand and threw it at the nearest creature. It caught the thing in the shoulder and knocked it from the wall, but apart from screaming at me in pain and anger, it was barely slowed down. Apparently, it needed a lot more magic to kill them.

"Take care," Kase said.

I turned, grinning, before I stepped off the roof and used my air magic to drop to the ground with enough force that it blasted the creature I'd hit earlier, causing it to spin away from me until it slammed into an old car.

I reapplied my thermal vision and spotted six more of the creatures at the end of the street, coming toward where I stood. The three on the wall dropped off onto the ground.

I put two rounds into each of the three in quick succession, and they paused but kept coming. *That's just terrific,* I thought to myself. Magic could hurt them, though, so it wasn't all bad.

With a slight adjustment of my power, I changed my sight to night vision and got a good look at the creatures for the first time. They looked human . . . well, humanish. They were lithe, with longer arms and legs than a human; their heads were completely bald; and when they opened their mouths, they were like snakes—all unhinged jaws and razor-sharp teeth. Someone had taken humans and turned them into these things. They reminded me of ghouls but were more animal in appearance, as if someone had mixed ghouls with wolves or lions. Whatever they now were, they were no longer human.

I moved away from the creatures slowly, keeping them in sight. They followed me, keeping pace and never getting too close. The one I'd hurt with magic had a slight limp as it began to move on all fours, but it showed no other signs of discomfort.

I looked behind them as the other group got closer. I wanted them all to be as close to me as possible, to give them no reason to go looking for the rest of the team. I was pretty sure I was going to be able to take them all, but I wondered just how many more of these things there really were inside the city.

I kept the creatures in front of me as I walked back along the road, making sure not to trip over any detritus, until I was about thirty feet from where I'd dropped. The pack of creatures from farther up the road had joined with the four that had been climbing the side of the building, but none of them seemed to be in a hurry to attack.

"You like to attack from the back," I said. I instinctively threw a powerful blast of air behind me and heard the cry of something as it was thrown back. "Better luck next time."

I poured fire out of my hands, creating a wall of flame that stretched from one side of the street to the other between me and the pack of creatures. The wall raged twenty feet high and would at least give them all something to think about before they could get to me. I turned and ran down the street, finding the injured creature that had tried to sneak up on me. It was on its front, its rear legs twisted in unnatural positions. I assumed it had struck the nearby car and broken most of the bones in the bottom half of its body from the force. The creature was already healing, the bones snapping back into place, causing it to cry out in pain.

I drove a blade of fire into the back of the creature's skull, killing it, as the screams of its pack reached my ears. I looked up the street in horror as the creatures jumped into the wall of flame, allowing themselves to be burned before they landed on the other side, their bodies charred but already healing. Magic would kill them, but it would need to be more than just a wall of fire.

I continued on, using my thermal vision to ensure that the pack was following me and that there was nothing else about to jump out at me from one of the many alleyways in the town.

Entering a dilapidated building, I blasted rubble away from the stairwell before taking it up two at a time. The sounds of the pack were still close, but I wasn't concerned. I burst through the door to the roof, ran across it, and jumped over to the next building, which had partially caved in, allowing me to almost slide all the way to street level.

The detour had the desired effect, as I saw the pack emerge onto the roof of the first building and let out a shriek of rage as they realized I'd gotten away. I glanced at my watch; it was only midnight, and there was still a long way to go until morning. I needed to keep the pack busy until we were far enough away from the rest of the team that none of them were likely to try to find other targets.

I sprinted down a dark alleyway and out the other side, where I found myself in a partially destroyed street. A quick look down the alleyway showed nothing pursuing me, but a howl in the distance told me that the creatures were still on my trail.

The road had only one way out, as the other end had long since sunk into the ground, leaving a massive crater of mud, muck, and water that probably gave you a disease just from looking at it. There was no way to jump over the hundred-foot gap, and climbing around it would take forever, even with magical assistance. The best way out was to go up the road, which would take me closer toward the crossroads than I wanted to be, but needs must.

I'd started to run up the road when I spotted an overgrown park. Vaulting over the metal fence, I threw a ball of fire behind me, which exploded. I hadn't seen any of the creatures for a few minutes, but the second the ball exploded, I changed back to thermal vision and spotted them piling out of the alleyway, scrambling over one another in an effort to get to the magic first.

Switching back to night vision, I turned and ran into the park, keeping to the pathway. I didn't want to get turned around in what appeared to be a sizable piece of land, and a few hundred feet into the park, I changed my vision back to thermal to check out if I had any followers. Behind me were my pursuers. They were close to where I'd entered the park but weren't coming any farther. I quickly looked around and spotted half a dozen shapes moving through the park toward me. They were larger than those that had been on my trail, and I got the immediate feeling that I'd just stepped into somewhere I shouldn't have.

I glanced over at the smaller creatures, who snarled and hissed but made no effort to come closer.

My night vision showed me the oncoming creatures. They were well over twice the size of those that had been chasing me, and I wondered if I'd made a very large mistake.

The six larger creatures stopped a hundred feet from me and pawed at the ground. Unlike those that had chased me, they didn't look like they'd once been human; they looked like they'd once been cave trolls or something close to it. All muscle and strength. I imagined that any one of them could kill me given the chance.

I ran back toward the pack of smaller creatures, and the larger ones roared and followed me. The smaller creatures, clearly unsure as to whether to go for me or make their escape, scattered, allowing me to jump back over the fence and sprint up the road. They ran after me just as the larger ones burst through the metal fence like it was made of kindling.

I stopped at the end of the street, a few hundred feet from the battle that ensued between the two sets of creatures. Half of the smaller ones swarmed over one of the larger, tearing into it as the other larger ones tried to swipe at the remaining smaller creatures.

One of the smaller ones spotted me and ran toward me, a snarling mass of ferocity. It launched itself at my head, but I stepped to the side and connected with a blade of lightning, removing its head midleap as its brethren took down the largest of the six creatures from the park, but not before the remains of several of their kin were smeared all over the street.

I continued on, moving away from the carnage and farther from my friends, hoping that they wouldn't encounter any of these creatures. I stopped half a dozen streets away.

The alley led toward the front of the park, and there were few buildings to use as cover.

I looked around and caught sight of a metal cross that someone had set at the entrance to the park. Something hung from the cross, moving slightly in the wind.

I ran over and found the metal was slick with blood, and silver-covered handcuffs were hung from both ends of the horizontal portion of the cross. An arm dangled from one of the cuffs. It had been ripped free by something, although the rest of the body was nowhere to be found.

The blood beneath the cross was probably several days old, and I wondered if whoever had been unfortunate enough to be hung from the cross had been taken into the park or killed by the smaller creatures and dragged into the city.

I scanned the ground, looking for more blood, and discovered a considerable amount leading away to a nearby building. The structure itself was in good condition compared to everything around it.

I tried the door and found that the metal handle had rusted away but that the door itself was blocked from behind. I placed my hand against the wood as a roar sounded through the night. A quick glance over my shoulder showed me the remaining large creatures—four in total—running through the park. There were no smaller creatures in sight, so I assumed they'd lost their short-lived battle.

I switched off all magic and shoved against the door with my shoulder. It gave an inch. Another shove, another inch. After the fourth shove, I'd moved it enough to be able to slip through the gap and into what looked like a museum for the city park. There were various pictures on the walls of the animals that lived in the state of Montana, as well as a fully grown stuffed grizzly bear at the far end of the room that had certainly seen better days.

I pushed all of the debris—much of which was covered in blood—back behind the door just as a snort sounded from outside. The windows were all boarded up, but I could still see through the slats as a massive creature walked past.

I probably should have killed it, but with four of them out there, there was no telling just how dangerous they would be as a pack.

I moved deeper into the building, which was larger than I'd expected. Stairs led up to a balcony that looked down on where I stood, the cases and contents of the museum attractions long since stolen or destroyed. There was blood on the debris, and I followed it to a door stained with even more blood.

When I pushed open the door, I saw steps that went down into a dimly lit basement. The steps, too, were slick with blood. Maybe one of Tommy's team had made it this far? Who else could have survived long enough to barricade themselves in?

I moved slowly down the stairs to the basement, where there was a makeshift bed, a small cooker, and several hundred bottles of water. Beside the water lay a woman, the bloody remains of one arm across her chest. She pointed a gun at me.

"I assume you're Masako?" I asked her, as the description we'd been given matched the disheveled woman before me.

The recognition on her face told me I was right, and she lowered the gun. "What happened to you?" I asked, moving over to look at her injured arm.

"One of those big bastards ripped me off the cross," she said, her voice barely above a whisper.

Her arm from the forearm down was gone; in its place was a ragged stump.

"Why didn't it eat you?" I asked. "Sorry, but how'd you get away?"

"Turns out they didn't like the taste," Masako said. "I guess someone who is already dead doesn't taste as nice as fresh meat. Those things still out there?"

I nodded again.

"You with Tommy? I tried to get ahold of him."

"Tommy got hurt coming here," I said. "He got attacked by those things, I think, and someone in charge of them. I'm here to try and find a way to help him and my dad."

The shock and concern on her face couldn't have been faked. "Oh no . . . damn it. Who the hell are you, then?"

"Nate Garrett," I said.

She started to laugh. "*The* Nate Garrett? Tommy spoke about you."

I nodded. "Pleased to meet you. Why didn't those things come in here after you?"

"No scent," Masako said. "I assume they gave up a while ago."

"One of the bonuses of being dead?" I asked.

She winked at me.

"Which means now they have my scent, and I'm probably somewhat tastier," I said, realization dawning on me.

"I would assume so, yes. So just how fucked are we?"

A huge crash from above answered that for me.

Chapter Ten

Layla Cassidy

Realm of Valhalla

Layla, Irkalla, and Ava were taken into a large building high in the treetops. They sat near a fire, though Layla personally thought this was probably not the best place to have an open flame, and Brynhildr explained to them what was happening.

The upshot of it all was that Empress Rela was not a good person. There was certainly more to it, but to Layla, that appeared to be the gist of the problem. Rela was evil, in league with Avalon, and looking into how she could consolidate her power by murdering everyone who disagreed with her. This had been going on for the better part of two hundred years.

"So she started murdering the day after she came to power?" Irkalla asked. "Because I'd have thought there would have been warnings leading up to her killing her enemies."

"We had no inkling of how power would change her," one of the guards in the room snapped.

Brynhildr placed a hand on her soldier's leg, calming her. They were all sitting on cushions on the rug-covered floor.

"Rela's mother took over from me," Brynhildr said.

"Why'd you let her?" Layla asked.

"I had no choice," she said. "I had a child, and he would have been in grave danger had I brought him here, so I left to go to the Earth realm, where it turned out he was still in grave danger. I gave him to Merlin to look after and returned here, but over time the queen grew resentful of my continued existence. And instead of living a long and quiet life, I had to fight a war. A war that lasted nearly a thousand years and cost the lives of countless souls."

"This place doesn't look ravaged by war," Ava said.

"The north, toward the mountain ranges, is where the fighting was heaviest," Brynhildr said. "Rela was part of the rebellion that overthrew her mother, but once she was in charge, things took a drastic turn. She massacred large numbers of the rebellion, and few of us managed to escape with our lives. We've been fighting when we can, but mostly we live and hide in the forest."

"You got onto the palace grounds easily enough," Irkalla said.

"We have people inside the palace guard who alert us to newcomers. We stay in the forest and watch for the most part. We have tried to mount a fight against Rela, but she uses the town as a threat. If we fight her, she'll kill them all."

"She's certainly been taking tips from Hera, then," Irkalla said.

"Hera and Rela were working together, and Hera's people started to encroach within our realm."

"Hera does like her fingers in as many pies as possible," Irkalla said. "Last intelligence put her in London on the Earth realm. Asgard is about to be under siege from Avalon."

"Led by Arthur," Ava said.

"How long have you been here?" Layla asked.

"A century," Brynhildr said. "Give or take."

"Our friends are with Rela," Layla said, getting to her feet. "We aim to go retrieve them."

"To be fair, we haven't seen anything to suggest that they're in danger," Ava said.

"She makes a valid point," Irkalla said.

"You think we're lying?" the guard snapped.

Ava shook her head but kept her gaze leveled at Brynhildr. "No, I mean she might well be a monster, but she's been quite nice to us. Weird, sure, but not overly hostile. Our friends might not need rescuing. We might be able to go back and find out what's happening without having to pick a fight. I know that must be strange for you all."

Irkalla smirked. "The smart-ass has a point."

"We go back and pretend that nothing happened?" Layla asked. "Or we could tell them that we were kidnapped by a bunch of rebels. See what happens from there."

"I have a question," Ava said. "Why are you here? You say that you're not strong enough to fight, but this place looks set to house thousands of people. It's massive. You want to free your realm, but you can't because you don't have the numbers, so what's your end-game? To sit here and wait until they die of old age?"

"I cannot say at the moment," Brynhildr said with a slight smile. "I do not yet know if you are on our side."

"So you're all sitting here waiting for something and being a pain in the ass to Rela in the meantime," Irkalla said. "But you can't go start a fight because, A, you don't have the numbers; B, she'd massacre an entire city just to prove a point that she's the one with the power; and C, you can't get to the realm gate to leave and get reinforcements. Sounds like a bit of a stalemate."

Brynhildr nodded but said nothing else.

"I have a plan," Layla said after no one else had spoken for several seconds. "I go back alone, say I managed to escape from the rebels and that you two are still here."

"You'll say you escaped the rebellion?" Brynhildr asked.

"Sure—my team is injured," Layla said. "You used silver weapons, took us hostage before we could fight back. Make you all out to be some kind of mythical assassins."

"That's not far off what they think of us now," Brynhildr said grimly. "I've heard the stories. Rela has her people terrified of us and not looking at what she's doing."

"Tyrants are always good at misdirection," Irkalla said. "Blaming others for the problems that they had a hand in causing. It's easier to have a faceless enemy to fight against than believe that your own government—the very people who are meant to protect you—are responsible for the horrors being perpetrated."

"That sounds like the voice of experience," Brynhildr said.

"More than once," Irkalla told her. "You sure you can do this, Layla?"

Layla nodded. "Not a lot of choice. We need to know where Chloe, Jinayca, and Tego are, and we need to make sure that Rela doesn't execute them or use them as hostages to get what she wants. I get to the palace, ask for help, hopefully get a little more information about what the hell is going on in that palace that means we're not allowed to walk around unguarded, and maybe you guys could jump the guards that come with me and get some intelligence."

"You could tell them that there are lots of rebels here," Ava said. "Just waiting to start a war. You know, lay it on thick and all that."

Layla smiled. "That could work. But I don't want to make Rela afraid. Scared people do stupid things."

"How many of you are there?" Irkalla asked.

"Thousands," Brynhildr said.

"Bollocks," Irkalla said. "I've seen a few hundred at most."

"The majority of them are not here," the guard said, sounding irritated that Brynhildr's answer had been questioned.

"Okay, so this isn't your big base?" Ava asked, looking around.

"No, this was built centuries ago during the rebellion. Rela ordered it destroyed after, but those carrying out the orders were working for us. She doesn't know we're here, and she doesn't send people into the forest to search for us."

"Why?" Layla asked.

"There are reasons," Brynhildr said. "We'll discuss those at a later date too."

"This whole cagey thing is fine and all, but it doesn't help anyone," Irkalla said.

"I'm not going to put my people in danger," Brynhildr said, showing irritation for the first time.

"I trust her," Ava said to Layla and Irkalla.

"Me too," Irkalla said.

Layla nodded. "I very much doubt the mother of Nathan Garrett would be anything other than honest with us," she said.

Brynhildr's eyes lit up as she smiled. "That was my son, yes. Do you know him? Is he well?"

"He's fine," Ava said. "I like him. He's nice to me; he helped me figure out what I am."

"Where is he?" Brynhildr asked, and for the first time her voice held a note of desperation.

"Earth realm," Layla said. "Murdering his way through whoever hurt his best friend and put Odin in a coma."

It was Brynhildr's turn to look confused. "Odin is in a coma? What the hell happened?"

"I'll explain it all while Layla goes back," Irkalla said. "You're going to have a lot more questions."

"It means if this all goes well, you'll be able to see Nate soon enough," Layla said.

Brynhildr smiled again and wiped away a tear. "It has been a long time since I last saw him. It would be good to get to know the man he's become."

The guard beside Brynhildr placed a hand on her shoulder to show support.

"Do you think your friends are safe?" Brynhildr asked eventually.

"Jinayca and Chloe can take care of themselves," Irkalla said.

"And the first person to try and harm Tego is going to lose an arm," Ava said.

"Who's Tego?" Brynhildr asked.

"The saber-tooth panther that I sort of adopted," Layla said. "She's not exactly the type to allow people to threaten her or her friends."

Brynhildr raised an eyebrow in question. "Interesting."

"You're going to have to punch me," Layla said.

Without warning, Brynhildr punched her in the jaw hard enough to knock her to the ground. Layla spat blood onto the floor. "Ouch," she said.

"Need another?" Irkalla asked.

Layla got back to her feet and rubbed her jaw. She tapped the side of her face by her eye. "I'll have started healing up by the time I get back, but the bruises should still be there."

Brynhildr punched Layla again.

"Can you stop that now?" Ava asked. "It's, like, super weird."

"Yeah, I'm good too," Layla said. "Goddamn, that hurt."

Irkalla and Ava told Layla to stay safe, and Brynhildr took Layla onto the lift, back to the forest floor.

"I'll be back as soon as I can," Layla said as one of Brynhildr's Valkyrie rebels brought a horse out of the woods.

Brynhildr removed a dagger from her belt and ran the blade over her hand, held it on the blood for a few seconds, and passed it to Layla. "A bloody dagger should do the trick. Valkyrie blood, too, just in case they test it."

Layla stared at the dagger before taking it, sheathing it, and shaking Brynhildr's hand, wiping the blood on her armor. "Make it look good," Layla said.

"When you're back, we'll talk more about what happens next. About where the rest of our people are." Brynhildr sighed. "There's more going on than just Rela being a tyrant."

"Prepare for whatever comes next," Layla said. "I'll be back as soon as I can."

"If they don't believe you, they'll arrest you," Brynhildr said. "If you're not back here by next dawn, we're coming for you. We will send someone to the village. There's an old stable there, near the exit. A black X is on the wall. The owner is a friend. If you can't leave immediately, go there and wait. We will find you."

Layla nodded and rode away as fast as she was comfortable. She'd never ridden a horse until a few years ago, but apart from Earth and that one time with Zamek that she'd rather not think about, she'd never been to a realm that had cars, so learning how to ride horses had been a necessity.

By the time she'd reached the outskirts of the palace, there were dozens of mounted guards around, and several of them intercepted her path, pointing spears in her direction.

One of the Valkyries—the Third Consul who had shown them around earlier—took the reins of Layla's horse in her hand. "You are under arrest."

"For what?" Layla demanded. "I've done nothing wrong. I was abducted, along with two of my friends, and just managed to escape." She removed the sheathed dagger and passed it to the Valkyrie. "I stabbed one of them, but one of my friends is hurt, and she needs medical attention. They have silver in their weapons, and she was stabbed in the initial attack."

The Third Consul was clearly skeptical, even as she drew the dagger and saw the dried blood on the blade.

"I will accompany you," she said. "Just to make sure you aren't *abducted* again."

Layla bit her tongue instead of telling her where she could stick her *sarcasm* and continued on for a short ride to a building at the far end of the palace grounds.

The one-story brick building had large wooden doors at the front and was divided into three, with windows on each part.

They dismounted, and Layla was led to the side of the building and down a corridor. The first three rooms along it contained beds and appeared to be sleeping quarters for guards or soldiers. The final door revealed a set of stone stairs that led down beneath the ground. The hairs on the back of Layla's neck stood up. If the Valkyries thought to take her down there and hurt her, they would find themselves facing off against someone a lot more powerful than they imagined.

The steps were lit by the same types of crystals in abundance in Shadow Falls. Once at the bottom, the Valkyrie unlocked a metal door with a set of keys and led Layla into a large open room with half a dozen doors on each side and another door directly opposite the entrance. The whole place smelled of sweat and blood, and Layla wondered how many people had been tortured down here.

"Where are my friends?" Layla asked.

"They were brought to the dungeons in this old guardhouse," one of the Valkyries said. "We didn't know if they were working with the rebels or not, so we thought it prudent to put them somewhere safe for everyone."

Layla had to admit it was a fair point, but she didn't like it one bit. "Somewhere safe" could just as easily have been a room in the palace with a lock or basically anywhere that wasn't a dungeon.

The group walked through the brick-floor room, and Layla noticed several buckets full of water and large patches of wet brick. There were four large brick pillars in the room, too, and more than one of them had been stained with red. Bad things happened here, and Layla's anger stirred inside her.

"We'll wait here," the Third Consul said. "Go and ensure that her friends are ready to receive her. I'll keep her company."

The three Valkyries shared an expression of confusion but nodded and left through the door opposite the entrance.

"You understand why they had to be brought to the guardhouse?" the Third Consul said.

"I understand that you did what you thought was best," Layla said. "But my other friends are still in the hands of these rebels, and I'd like to go after them and rescue them from their clutches."

"The rebels will have already murdered them and feasted on their flesh," the Third Consul said with the barest hint of a smile tugging on her lips. "While you're here, I guess I should retrieve your pet."

"My pet?" Layla asked.

The Third Consul unlocked a door behind her and stepped into a large cell. Tego was dragged out by a metal chain connected to a studded collar around her large neck.

"She didn't want to go easy," the Third Consul said. "So she had to be convinced."

Blood caked Tego's fur, and the large cat barely moved from the spot.

"What did you *do* to her?" Layla demanded, doing everything in her power to keep her fury in check.

"Shock collar," the Third Consul said. "They're quite good for keeping the more . . . vicious of our guests in line."

"Remove it," Layla said through clenched teeth.

"Excuse me?" the Third Consul asked with a slight chuckle. "Who are you to give me orders?"

Layla reached out with her power and took control of the metal studs inside the Third Consul's armor, lifting the larger Valkyrie from the floor and smashing her into the wall with enough force to cause brick to explode.

"Remove it," Layla seethed. "Now."

The look of shock and fear on the face of the Valkyrie as she was held six feet off the ground by Layla's power was quickly overridden by anger. "You fucking whelp," the Valkyrie shouted. "How *dare* you."

Layla tore the metal out of one of the cell doors and wrapped it around the Valkyrie, squeezing it tight. She went to Tego and smoothed her hand down the back of the panther's neck. "I'm sorry they did this," she said softly. The panther rubbed her huge head against Layla's leg in reply.

"There are runes on this," Layla said to the Valkyrie. "I assume whatever they do, it isn't good. Where is the key to this . . . thing?"

With her arms pinned to her sides, the Valkyrie was unable to do anything but nod to a nearby hook on the wall, where several keys were kept. Layla removed the bundle and tried them one at a time on the shock collar until it clicked open. Layla flung it across the room in disgust.

Tego licked Layla's hand.

"You hurt my friend," Layla said. "You did it for *fun*. There was nothing you could have gotten out of Tego, and some of those wounds look fresh. You tortured her."

"She's an animal," the Third Consul said. "She's—"

Layla wrapped metal around the Consul's mouth. "Be quiet," she said softly as the door opened and the three Valkyries reentered the room.

"Have you had enough time to teach the human a lesson?" one of them asked with an unpleasant laugh.

Layla stepped out from behind one of the four large brick pillars. "My friends," she said. "Where are they?"

"What did you do with the Third Consul?" one of them demanded, lowering her spear toward Layla, who continued to advance toward them.

"Your weapons are made of steel," Layla said with a fierce smile. "You might find that a problem."

She darted toward the spear wielder, using her power to force the tip of the spear aside, and moved on toward the second Valkyrie, who had drawn a short sword. Layla wrapped her power around it and flung it out of the Valkyrie's grip into the throat of the comrade standing beside her.

Layla kicked the Valkyrie in the chest, sending her back toward the open door, before using her power to take control of the spear user's metal armor, turning it into a hundred spikes that ripped into her, dropping her to the floor in agony.

"I assume I'll need silver to kill you," Layla said, extending her metal arm into a blade. "Just so happens I have some right here. Don't make this worse."

The Valkyrie she'd kicked charged at her, a blade of translucent energy appearing in her hand from nowhere. Layla tried to avoid it, but the Valkyrie blasted her in the chest with pure necromantic power, sending Layla flying through the room. She landed on the floor with a painful jarring that caused her to lose control of the metal surrounding the Third Consul, who dropped to the floor and shrugged off her leather armor.

"Let's see how you do now," the Third Consul said with a sneer as Tego avoided a swipe with a soul weapon in the shape of an ax.

Layla rolled her shoulders. "You should have been nicer," she said as Tego stood beside her and roared.

Chapter Eleven

Layla Cassidy

Layla hadn't wanted to come here and kill anyone. She had been determined to get her friends and try to figure out a way out of the mess they'd found themselves in while working out whether to help the rebels.

Considering she'd almost decapitated one Valkyrie and tried to crush a second, a peaceful resolution was probably out the window.

The Third Consul rushed Layla, trying to catch her with her spirit ax, but Layla easily avoided the blow and punched the Consul in the mouth for good measure. She spotted another Valkyrie busy drawing runes on the floor and darted toward her, avoiding the spear of the guard protecting her. Layla drove a knee into the side of the Valkyrie's head, snapping it aside with considerable force, and then launched herself over the stunned Valkyrie as Tego drove into the other, forcing the now-prone woman to try to block the razor-sharp teeth of a pissed-off saber-tooth panther.

Layla got back to her feet and used her sword arm to cut through the brick on the floor, destroying whatever rune they'd been planning to use.

The Valkyrie with the sword through her neck made a slight movement, and Layla looked down at her. "Get up and die," she said. "No fucking around now. You started this shit."

"And we will end it," the Third Consul shouted, throwing a dagger at Tego, who couldn't move in time to stop it from piercing the back of her leg, causing the panther to howl in pain.

"Silver," the Third Consul said. "Bet it hurts."

Layla dragged the blade free and absorbed the metal into her arm. She noticed movement from the corner of her eye and struck out with her arm, extending it to three times its normal length and slamming it into the eye of the Valkyrie who'd been writing the rune.

Layla retracted her arm but let it hang down beside her like a whip. She sprinted toward the Third Consul, flicking the whip toward her, but changed it at the last second as the Consul moved to avoid it. The newly formed sword drove up into the Third Consul's chest. Layla twisted the blade, and the Consul screamed in pain.

"I told you," Layla whispered. "I told you what would happen."

"We should have killed your friends," the Consul said as her blood poured over Layla's arm.

Layla removed the blade from the Consul's chest and stood before her. "I was going to tell you to stay here in case my friends were hurt, but screw it." Layla removed the Consul's head with a swipe and turned back to the two Valkyries, one barely moving and the other with a mass of panther standing on top of her.

"Don't play with your food," Layla said, and as she stepped past the third Valkyrie, a sword still in her neck, she heard the unmistakable crunch of Tego crushing the skull of her prey.

Layla walked through the door, down the corridor beyond, and into a second room almost identical in size and shape to the one she'd just left. She tore the metal doors off their hinges, throwing them at the far wall as her friends staggered out of their cells.

Most appeared to be okay, but Jinayca moved gingerly and had to sit down, holding her bloody side. "One of the bastards nicked me," she said.

"We'll carry you," Chloe said. Chloe had the appearance of someone who had been treated less than pleasantly by their captors.

"The Third Consul is dead," Layla said.

"Good. She was a bitch," Chloe said, rubbing her hands. A sorcerer's band sat on one wrist.

"We'll find the keys," Layla said, and sure enough, they weren't hard to track down. Soon everyone had the bands off, and people started to heal again.

"Doesn't matter how many times I see those things; I still hate them," Chloe said.

"So how do we get out of this place without attracting a lot of attention?" Jinayca asked as they went back to the room with the dead Valkyries.

"This one is still alive," Chloe said, crouching over the seriously injured Valkyrie.

"I imagine that sword in her neck hurts," Jinayca said without pity.

"Good," Chloe snapped. "These people were less-than-perfect hosts. That Empress Rela needs a sharp kick too. I volunteer to do the kicking," she said, raising her hand.

"Tego is hurt," Jinayca said, crouching down beside the large feline and stroking her face.

"The person who hurt her is now dead," Layla told her. She knelt beside the still-conscious Valkyrie. "You've lost a lot of blood. Probably hurts like hell."

The Valkyrie stared at Layla with pure malevolence in her eyes.

"We came here peacefully," Layla said. "We came to secure allies in the war against Avalon. But your empress is working *with* Avalon. She's working with Hera on something, and I'm not sure what it is, but I'm going to find out. And then I'm going to bring this entire fucking palace down around her smug head. She should have taken the offer to help us."

"Where are Irkalla and Ava?" Chloe asked.

"With the rebels," Layla told her. "Rebels that are being led by Brynhildr."

"Nate's mum is leading the rebels against Rela?" Chloe asked and burst out laughing. "Why doesn't it surprise me that *his* mum would be doing that?"

"Stay here until we've left," Jinayca told the injured Valkyrie. "I don't think it would be wise for you to stand up with that sword in your neck. It might not be silver, but I'm thinking decapitation will do the trick just as well."

"Okay, so how do we get out of here without fighting through the throng of pissed-off Valkyries?" Layla asked.

"Nice use of the word *throng*," Chloe said.

"I thought you'd appreciate it," Layla replied with a smile.

Layla took the stairs first, making sure that there were no guards in the building above, and when she found it empty, she called for everyone else. Tego took up the rear, moving with a slight limp. Layla wasn't often actually glad she'd killed someone, but the Third Consul was certainly one of the exceptions.

Layla gathered everyone in the room with the exit. "Okay, it's some distance from here to the palace itself, but we're still on palace grounds, so there will be guards. Even if Irkalla and Ava weren't still in the realm, we have no chance of getting to the realm gate and using it to escape, so we're stuck here. Unfortunately, we're also on the exact opposite side of the palace grounds to where I entered. I'm not entirely sure of the best way out of here."

"Through the city," Jinayca said. "It's crowded, and there are enough alleyways that we can split up if we need to."

"Brynhildr said that there's a stable with a black X on the side wall," Layla said. "We're to go there and wait until dawn."

"Then that's the plan," Jinayca said.

"We can't hide Tego, though," Chloe said. "She sort of stands out."

"She's right," Layla said to the panther. "The silver you got hit with is going to take you longer to heal, and I don't want to put you in more danger. But you can't stay here either."

Tego pushed Layla aside and strode to the front of the room, standing by the doors as if daring everyone to even try to stop her.

"She's a stubborn cat," Chloe said.

"Yes," Layla said with a proud smile. "Yes, she is."

"There are woodlands to the east of here," Jinayca said.

"And several hundred feet between us and them," Chloe said.

"If you have a better idea, I'm all for it," Layla told her.

"I don't," Chloe admitted. "I'm just making everyone aware that we have zero good options."

"That's a hell of an inspiring speech," Jinayca said. "We're not exactly without capability to defend ourselves, so let's go before anyone comes looking."

Layla pushed open the door and looked outside. No one was close enough to be a threat, and it didn't take long for everyone to leave the guardhouse and run around to the far side of it, using it as cover from anyone looking out the palace windows down on the surrounding lands.

The palace grounds had an abundance of hedges and trees, which made for perfect cover for the group as they moved through them. They put enough distance between each member of the team that they were never clumped together for long periods, and apart from the occasional Valkyrie who needed to be avoided, there were no immediate threats.

"Anyone else find it odd how sparse the guard is?" Jinayca asked as the team crouched behind the remains of a large white stone wall.

"I've been thinking the same thing," Layla said. "I expected more guards considering Rela has a rebellion problem."

"And an us problem," Chloe said.

"So where is everyone?" Jinayca asked.

"Did they mark you back in the cells?" Layla asked.

Everyone shook their heads.

"They roughed us up a bit, but even the torture wasn't the worst I'd ever endured," Chloe said. "Which is probably a damning indictment of my life in some way, but there it is."

"The only one of us they really hurt was Tego," Jinayca said. "They didn't even ask questions. It was a bit odd."

"Same here," Chloe said.

"So they either knew that none of you were involved with the rebels," Layla surmised, "in which case, why keep you locked up? Or they wanted you to run so they can track us."

Everyone looked around.

Tego took a long sniff of the air and let out a low growl.

"We're being tracked," Layla said as she spotted movement a few hundred yards away behind one of the buildings. "They're using the buildings as cover."

"We need to hurry," Jinayca said.

The group hurried up, almost flat-out running when they reached the edge of the palace grounds. They quickly scaled the thirty-foot-high stone wall separating the palace from the start of the city and dropped down onto the slope beyond.

It took a while for them to find a spot on the fast-flowing river that didn't look deep and dangerous, but eventually they forded it. Layla was hoping for a way for them to get dry and take a few minutes' respite, so when they found an empty house, they piled inside to wait for the sun to set. The interior of the house was sparse, but it had been hot all day, and the building had retained much of the heat. A small blessing in what had been a pretty crappy time.

As the sun set, the temperature dropped by a dozen degrees, but the team waited it out until the moon was high in the sky. Only then did they venture out into the city, moving silently between alleyways to avoid the patrols they heard walking around the city streets.

It took several hours for them to make their way through the city, but eventually they reached the outskirts. They paused, hiding behind the wall of a house, looking to the city exit, which was right next to a guardhouse. Several guards walked in and out of the guard building every few minutes. There was very little chance of getting to the exit without being spotted.

Layla stared past the guardhouse, and her gaze fell to the stable beside it. A black X sat on the wall. "That's where Brynhildr said to go," Layla said. "She didn't mention the guardhouse, though."

"How long do we have?" Chloe asked.

Jinayca looked up at the sky. "Five hours. If we're lucky."

Layla continued to watch the door of the guardhouse, trying to spot a way to get past the guards without having to involve the rest of the town in their escape, until she spotted a woman at the top-floor window looking out. Layla stood up and walked around the wall.

"What are you doing?" Chloe half whispered.

"It's fine," Layla said, continuing on as everyone else looked confused.

Layla was halfway to the door when it opened and Irkalla stepped out. "What are you doing here?" Layla asked.

"Brynhildr said that someone would be waiting for you," Irkalla said. "We were meant to be in the stables, but the guards were already in here. Apparently they're not Valkyries and aren't exactly big fans of Rela."

Everyone entered the guard building, where several Valkyrie rebels were sitting. One of them looked over, her eyes bulging, as Tego entered the building.

"She's had a hard day," Layla said to the Valkyrie as she eyed the saber-tooth panther.

"I have never seen her kind," the Valkyrie said.

"Blood elves tortured her from birth," Layla said. "Forced her to undergo experiments. Made her smart. Made her more dangerous."

"And you saved her?" the Valkyrie asked.

Layla nodded. "I had help."

Brynhildr descended the stairs, thanking the guards, who had entered the room.

"You have the guards on your side?" Layla asked her.

"A lot of the town considers Rela to be their protector," Brynhildr said. "They're mostly human, and Rela likes to cultivate this notion that she's a benevolent leader. But some aren't human, or they've had the details of Rela's mother passed down, remember that she was a tyrant. She dealt only in pain and suffering. Rela deals only in smiles while she stabs you in the back. She's no less a tyrant, just one who learned from her mother's mistakes. The people of this city have felt Rela's wrath when she doesn't get her own way. People go missing; people are involved in . . . accidents. They wanted something better, but they just got the same thing, only with a nicer smile."

"So just how many are on your side?" Layla asked.

"The guards here and maybe twenty percent of the population," Brynhildr said. "Not enough to cause a rebellion. Not enough to stop Rela from slaughtering them."

"You think she would?" Chloe asked. "Just straight up murder everyone here?"

Brynhildr nodded. "She had two dozen executed the last time the rebels killed two of her people. Those she killed were innocent, and they were murdered far away from the town to ensure that they could spread the rumor that the rebels had done it."

"If Rela feels that power begin to slip, she'll kill everyone on her way out," Jinayca said.

Everyone turned to look at her.

"It's been done by tyrants before," Irkalla said.

After the introductions were concluded, everyone except Tego moved to a basement, where a dozen more Valkyries were waiting for them.

"You called us here," one of the Valkyries said to Brynhildr.

"This is the Second Consul," Brynhildr said, introducing her and her companions to everyone.

"Do you have a real name?" Irkalla asked.

"Skost," she said.

"You no longer have a Third Consul," Layla said. "I figured you should know."

"Did you kill her?" Skost asked.

Layla nodded. She saw no point in continuing as allies with the death of someone who could have been Skost's friend hanging over them. Better to get everything out in the open.

"She was a cruel woman," Skost said with a shrug. "Few will mourn her passing."

"Did she die hard?" another Valkyrie asked.

"She hurt my friend Tego," Layla said. "She didn't die having fun."

"That'll do," the Valkyrie said with a nod of her head.

"You said you have more people to aid you in this fight," Layla said. "I think now is a good time for everyone to lay their cards on the table."

Brynhildr nodded. "Rela is doing some kind of archaeological dig at the mountains in the north. No idea why, but she's using slaves to do it. A fact that the dwarves appear to be ignoring."

Jinayca stood. "My people are here?"

Skost nodded. "They've been here for centuries. A great number of them were brought here, although I don't know how or by whom. Rela's mother used them as slave labor, although they were all meant to be freed once Rela took control."

"You sound like that might not be the case," Layla said.

"I do not know," Skost said. "I made my dislike of slavery known when we were fighting Rela's mother, so they have made sure to keep me far away from the mountains. I do not know what happens there."

"We've been breaking the slaves free for centuries," Brynhildr said. "There's a city to the west of here where several thousand dwarves live in peace, and we've brought the slaves to them as they're freed. I didn't mention them before because . . . well, to be honest, I didn't know how much I could trust you, and I promised them that I wouldn't lead Rela to their doorstep. It's where most of the rebels live too."

"Why aren't the dwarves trying to free these people?" Jinayca asked.

"The politics of the dwarves are not exactly fast moving," Brynhildr said. "The queen offered her support, but the king opposes it. That's how it's been for decades now. We've helped where we can, and there are dwarves who have helped free a great many of their enslaved brethren, but . . ."

"But what?" Jinayca asked, clearly angry.

"We believe that forces within the dwarven hierarchy are working with Rela," Skost said. "Rela leaves them alone, and they promise to do the same. Even as high up as I am, I'm not permitted to know the details. Only the empress, her most trusted advisers, and her First Consul have any information regarding their deal, but I've seen carriages coming and going under the cover of night."

"And what is happening in the palace?" Ava asked. "We weren't allowed to stay in it."

"Dwarves are adding runes all around the building," Skost said. "No idea what they do. I am considered a high-ranking member of the military, but not high enough, apparently."

Layla was pretty sure that Jinayca would have killed Rela there and then given the chance. Jinayca took a deep breath and slowly exhaled. "My kin will be saved."

"How long has this dig been going on?" Irkalla asked.

"A few hundred years," Brynhildr said. "There are entire slave villages up there."

"So why did Rela contact us to come here and discuss a pact of help?" Layla asked. "What's her angle here?"

"That I do know," Skost said. "She makes friends with you and offers you her help, and then during the upcoming war in Asgard, she switches sides. Thousands of Valkyries suddenly attacking exposed areas of your people would cause mass panic. It would be a massacre."

"This sounds like a Hera plan," Irkalla said.

"Hera has been at the palace several times over the last year," Skost confirmed. "She arrives with a group of people, and they all travel north to the dig. Before that she would come once a decade, if that."

"They've been digging for centuries," Ava said. "And there's been a stalemate for centuries, too, so why all of a sudden are dwarves putting runes on the palace? And now Hera is turning up a lot. What happened to change things?"

"They found something," Layla and Irkalla said in unison.

"But what did they find?" Chloe asked.

"Umm, I think I might know," Ava said. "You remember when we found what we thought was Zeus's body under that tree, and

Irkalla tried to link with it, but the Valkyries came, and then the rebels came, and everything sort of moved quickly? Well, I didn't mention at the time that it wasn't Zeus under there. It didn't feel like that was a thing we needed to worry about, seeing as we were trying not to die at the time."

"Zeus isn't buried under a tree," Skost said. "That was a bodyguard of his. It was done to throw off the scent, so to speak."

"That would have been helpful to know beforehand," Ava muttered to herself.

"Do you know where he is?" Layla asked her.

Skost shook her head. "No one does. He was taken here after he died, but I have no idea what happened to his body. I remember hearing that some of the dwarves had a hand in his burial, but that's more of an old tale than anything with evidence."

"So back to how I might know," Ava said, interjecting herself. "If Hera's really that interested in what they found, any possibility that it's Zeus they're looking for? Could he have something they need? Information, a weapon, something, anything?"

"It's certainly possible," Skost said. "Hera loved and hated Zeus in equal measure. And she does seem to be very interested in whatever they found there."

"Can we find out where Zeus is buried for sure?" Irkalla said. "He might be the only clue to finding his daughter before Hera does."

"Ah," Brynhildr said. "If Zeus knows where one of his children is and that child escaped Hera's wrath, then yes, she would be very keen to find his spirit."

"This is all just a guess, though," Ava said.

"Whatever Rela is having her slaves do there can't be good," Jinayca said.

"Even if it doesn't involve Zeus, it's worth looking into," Layla said. "And if it does involve Zeus, it could help us. Either way, we might be able to stop Hera from doing something awful before it starts."

"So we head to the dwarves," Irkalla said. "We find out what they know and hopefully figure out a way to stop Hera or Rela. Preferably both."

"Avalon forces are coming in a day," Skost said. "They will have reinforcements."

"We definitely need the help, then," Brynhildr said. "My people have been waiting for battle. Maybe this is it."

"If we can convince the dwarves to aid us," Skost said.

"I will help with that," Jinayca said determinedly.

"Everyone, rest," Irkalla said. "Tomorrow the shit is going to hit the fan."

Skost shrugged. "I don't understand that."

"However bad it is now, it's about to get worse," Layla told her.

Skost nodded. "Oh yeah, that I understand. Rela will not go easy. Nor will those who follow her. I shall try to get as many of my sisters who disagree with her as I can to lay down their arms. I do not want this to become a bloodbath. On either side."

"Agreed," Layla said. "But anyone who stands next to Rela has made their choice."

Skost nodded sadly.

Layla went back upstairs and lay down next to Tego. "Looks like the river washed all of that blood off," Layla said.

Tego purred.

"We go to war soon. I think. We came here for peace, and we'll be leaving covered in blood."

Tego pushed her muzzle into Layla's hand.

"When this is all done, I want to do something that doesn't involve battles," Layla said. "Maybe a nice desk job."

Tego snorted.

"Good answer."

Chapter Twelve

Mordred

Scotland, Earth Realm

It was quite the journey from Asgard to Shadow Falls, where one of the many dwarves who lived there helped change the realm gate to go to England. Bath, to be more precise.

The guardian at the realm gate temple there was more than a little surprised to see people, seeing as how she'd been there for the better part of a hundred years and no one had turned up. Apparently, most people had forgotten the realm gate there existed. Mordred certainly had. The nearby village where the guardian lived had a small airfield used for light aircraft. The hangar contained a helicopter, which Elaine assured everyone she could fly.

While Elaine flew the helicopter, Mordred and Hel sat in the back. Hel had wanted to bring more people, but Elaine had said that they'd need as few as possible. Guinevere and Lancelot were already jumpy, and the situation didn't need to be made worse.

The helicopter landed near where Elaine's home had once sat. It had been mostly ransacked and destroyed by Avalon when she'd been kidnapped a few years ago. The windows were all broken, the roof had a hole in it, and the door was in about five hundred pieces and scattered over what had once been Elaine's front garden. Two years of Scottish weather had managed to pretty much ruin anything inside that the elements could get to.

Elaine sighed as she picked up a book and opened it, finding the pages destroyed. "I liked this book," she said, putting it back down on the table.

Mordred started to whistle "Prelude" from *Final Fantasy VII*, and everyone turned to look at him.

"What's wrong?" Hel asked.

"Who said anything was wrong?" Mordred asked. "I happen to like that song."

"You save that one for when there's something bothering you," Elaine said.

"Just want to get a move on," Mordred said. "I know you want to look at the old place, Elaine, but I'm anxious about seeing Guinevere and Lancelot, and time is just making it worse."

"All of this is ruined anyway," Elaine said. "I liked this chair." She pushed the chair with her foot, and a flood of water poured out of the bottom.

Mordred patted Elaine's shoulder sympathetically. "Shall we leave before we end up swimming out?"

Elaine nodded. "It's a bit of a walk to where they are."

They left the house. Mordred looked across the open land to the nearby mountains. He'd always loved Scotland, and being at Elaine's home made him feel like he might actually be able to find a place of his own one day. Somewhere he could settle down and just rest.

Hel placed her hand on the back of Mordred's neck and kissed him on the cheek. "It's nice, isn't it?" she said.

Mordred nodded. In the distance, three deer ran across the grassy expanse before vanishing from view in the woodlands nearby.

"So what can we expect from Guinevere?" Hel asked.

Mordred shook his head. "I don't know. She *was* a nice person. Although she and Morgan did not get along—at all. Mostly because Morgan thought that Guinevere was conspiring with Merlin to alienate her from everyone. But it was Merlin doing that, and it probably saved Morgan's life. Merlin started to realize what Arthur, Gawain, and the others who were helping them were. But it was too late. He got Nate away, sent him to China for a century just to remove him from Arthur's influence. I think he was trying to do something similar with Morgan, especially after I'd returned from my time in my brother's trap. Guinevere was gone by then, which was probably for the best."

"And Lancelot?" Hel asked.

"We have issues," Mordred said, unwilling to talk more on the subject.

"Try not to punch him," Hel said with a smile.

Mordred didn't share her humor. "No promises."

They continued across the heath toward the mountains. It took them an hour over rough terrain to get there, but Mordred was glad not to be in a helicopter trying to find a place to land, not to mention that Guinevere and Lancelot were somewhere that wasn't easy to get to. It would be a short mission if they got to the pair and found that Avalon had gotten there first.

They reached the mouth of a cave soon after, and Mordred looked back across the landscape to the house in the distance. It was a good location to see anyone coming from the road, which snaked away from the whole area a few miles away. Elaine was never one to give up strategic importance, even in picking somewhere to live.

The mouth of the cave was practically invisible to anyone who wasn't a few feet away, as the rock hung over it like a melted candle, forcing anyone going inside to practically bend in half to get under it.

Once inside, Elaine placed her hand on the cave wall, and the whole place lit up as if someone had switched on the Christmas lights in a high street.

The group walked deeper into the cave. Soon a set of stairs carved into the stone itself led them down.

"This has been here awhile," Hel said. "I mean the renovations, not the cave itself; I assume that's been here longer."

"I found the cave about a hundred years ago," Elaine said. "I had some people move it around a bit. It was my go-to place should I need it. Unfortunately, when I was taken, I didn't have any warning. But it was the perfect place to put people running from Avalon."

At the bottom of the stairs, the cave opened up, and three soldiers stood to attention. Each soldier carried an SMG, a sidearm revolver, and a sword.

"Ma'am," one of them said to Elaine.

"I'm here to see our guests," Elaine told her.

"They've been waiting for you," she said.

"Thank you," Elaine told her, turning back to the rest of the group. "I had a few people from Asgard come here to watch them. These three used to be part of my personal guard when I ruled Avalon."

Elaine led them to the rear of the large cavern, through a large steel door, and into a hallway beyond. It was as if someone had built a house underground. Several doors led off the hallway, and Elaine opened the farthest one from the entrance, revealing a large room. Two identical doors stood at one side, and the rest of the room held comfortable-looking furniture and a TV that hung on the wall.

A woman got up from the sofa and walked across the collection of rugs to greet Elaine with a hug.

"Guinevere," Elaine said with a smile full of genuine warmth.

Guinevere had been considered a great beauty when she'd been married to Arthur, and in Mordred's mind it was easy to see why.

She was curvaceous, with long dark hair that finished at her waist and an easy smile that had always been able to disarm even the most stonehearted. In another lifetime she could have graced the cover of a hundred magazines.

"Mordred," Guinevere said, crossing over to him and hugging him. "It's been so long."

"Pretty much," Mordred said, noting the bags of white powder—he assumed it wasn't sugar—piled high next to the table. One of them was open, and lines had been made on the wooden coffee table. "Where is Lancelot?"

"In his bedroom," she said, her smile faltering for the first time. "Please don't hurt him."

Mordred looked over at the bedroom door and considered Guinevere's words for about two seconds before walking over and banging on it.

Lancelot opened it and came face-to-face with Mordred for the first time in over a thousand years.

Mordred had to admit that time had done little to diminish Lancelot's looks. He was a beautiful man with long brown hair, the beginnings of a beard, and—in Morgan's words—cheekbones you could camp on. His eyes were piercing blue, but Mordred had found the man behind them to be someone who never lived up to the lofty ideals he liked to pretend he believed in. A few years earlier, Mordred had finally seen the *Beauty and the Beast* Disney film, and he had been convinced that they'd modeled Gaston on Lancelot. A man with incredible charisma that hid an ego almost too big to be contained in one person and absolutely nothing of value behind his muscular body and model looks.

Lancelot's hand dropped to his sword hilt. Mordred followed it with his eyes and looked back up at Lancelot with a sharklike smile. "Please do," Mordred whispered.

Lancelot removed his hand with a pout.

Mordred turned and walked away, content that his memory of Lancelot and the man himself were meeting up, as he'd expected them to.

"Lancelot," Guinevere said. "We have guests."

Mordred recognized a look of disappointment on Hel's face. She'd expected better from the two fugitives.

"Where did the drugs come from?" Elaine asked.

"Oh, you know," Guinevere said. "We had to bring some with us."

"This was all in the large bag you had?" Elaine almost snapped.

"They help take the edge off," Guinevere said, throwing herself backward on the sofa. "Makes everything much easier to bear."

"Cocaine?" Hel asked.

"Oh dear, no," Guinevere said with a wave of her hand. "That doesn't even touch the sides."

"What is it?" Elaine asked, picking up one of the bags and sniffing it. "Smells strange."

"It's ground-up cave troll bone," Guinevere said with an empty smile. "We have a coven of witches who make it. Make lots of pills and things, too, but this is the good stuff. No long-term side effects, and seeing how I'm not human, I can take a whole bag on Monday and be good until the weekend with no cravings. It's glorious."

"You buy from a drug-dealing witches' coven?" Mordred asked.

"Oh yes," Guinevere said. "You see, here's the thing we didn't realize when we ran away from Arthur. We have to *keep* running. The second one of his cronies finds us, we get brought back to him and Abaddon, and Arthur gets to watch as his pet devil flays us alive."

"Abaddon is dead," Elaine said. "Or at least missing, presumed no longer a problem."

"Well, there are still other problems I need help to cope with," Guinevere said, looking over at Lancelot, who turned and walked back into his bedroom, closing the door behind him. "Turns out he's a fucking prick." She leaned over the sofa toward the door. "Aren't you, dear? A fucking prick?"

The door flew open again, and Lancelot stormed out. "You're not exactly a barrel of laughs, you evil bitch."

"Okay, I think we're done reliving an episode of one of those god-awful talk shows," Mordred said. "Both of you get dressed. Be fast."

"That's all right," Guinevere said with a laugh. "Being fast is Lancelot's specialty."

"Okay, this is *really* awkward," Hel said as Guinevere walked over to the second door in the room and stepped inside.

"They *hate* each other," Mordred said. "I don't remember that bit."

"Yes," Elaine said with a sigh. "Yes, they do."

"That would have been nice to know," Mordred said.

"Honestly, some days they get on okay," Elaine said. "And some days—okay, most days—they don't. From what I understand, Lancelot spends most of his time getting drunk, going into towns, and paying to have sex with anything that will have him, while Guinevere uses drugs but does pretty much the same thing. They have a toxic relationship that neither of them can get out of, because they're both terrified that if they do, they'll get grabbed, and the other will give them up. We've tried separating them a few times, but they refuse to be apart for long. I'm not sure how they've managed to survive for a thousand years on the run."

"How long have you known about this?" Hel asked.

"I've known where they are for centuries," Elaine said, "but never had any contact with them. I just let them be. Actually, meeting up with them a few months ago was a bit of a surprise. I was hoping they'd be able to sort their shit out once here, but it turns out they can't."

"She's snorting cave troll bone," Mordred said. "That is . . . not great."

"I thought you were going to punch Lancelot," Hel said to Mordred.

"Considered it," Mordred admitted.

"Why don't you like him?" Hel asked.

"Lots of reasons," Mordred said vaguely. "He's a dick, for one."

"There's more to it than that," Hel said.

Mordred nodded. "Lancelot was the warrior we all wanted to be. He was quick with a sword and able to get any woman he wanted. When we were kids, he was our damn hero. Then we grew into adults, and we learned that he was also a bully and liked to lord his abilities over everyone. He'd tell people that he'd slept with their wives or their betrothed, just to see the defeat in their eyes, because he knew that they wouldn't fight him. A blacksmith stood up to him once after Lancelot kept making lurid comments about his wife. It ended in a fight that Lancelot won easily. He beat that man nearly to death, and he enjoyed every second of it."

Lancelot left his room. "Mordred telling you about how much of an asshole I am?"

"Yes," Mordred said. "And that you are a coward who only fights people he thinks he can beat. And a bully. And frankly just—as Remy would say—a cockwomble. You care only about yourself; you always have done. You only ran with Guinevere because you knew once Arthur discovered you were having an affair with his wife, he'd actually be able to kill you. Easily."

Lancelot shrugged, his hand hovering over his sword hilt again. "I guess this is the time for us to sort this out."

"If you put your hand on your sword, I'll kill you," Mordred said calmly. "No games, no fucking about—I will end your fucking life and move on with mine as if nothing had happened."

"You think my son would have been happy with that?" Lancelot asked. "Galahad loved me."

"Galahad hated you," Mordred corrected. "He knew who you were. And now he's dead because Arthur's people killed him while he tried to protect the people of Shadow Falls from their invasion. Your son died a hero. An actual hero, not one who needs to make up stories about how awesome they are."

"I always knew he would get into a fight he couldn't win," Lancelot said.

Mordred took a step toward Lancelot. "If you say anything bad about my friend, I will rip your face off. And I mean that literally."

"Mordred," Elaine said. "Not here. Not now."

"I'm fine," Mordred said, his tone hard as iron. "I'm just letting Lancelot know where he stands. Galahad was my friend, and he died a hero. You are an asshole who will die forgotten and alone. Don't compare yourself; you can't hope to live up to him. You're alive because Galahad hoped that one day you'd live up to your stories." He turned away from Lancelot. "I'll meet you all outside."

Hel was the first to join him. "So this isn't going brilliantly."

Mordred sighed. "I still don't understand why Guinevere needs me here. She could just tell us where the sword is, and we could go get it."

"Because I need assurances," Guinevere said as the rest of the group left the cave. "I need to know that once I tell you where Excalibur is, you will ensure I am kept safe."

"You knew where that fucking sword was all this time?" Lancelot snapped. "You told me that these people were coming to move us somewhere safer."

"Technically, they are," Guinevere said with a snarl.

"Why am I here?" Mordred asked. "Specifically me."

"I know where the sword is," Guinevere said. "I know *who* has it. But only you can get it."

"Why only me?" Mordred asked. He looked over to Elaine. "Did you know about this?"

Elaine shook her head. "No. I knew her requirement was you be here, but that's it. Guinevere, I'd advise you to hurry up and explain."

"When Lancelot and I escaped, I took the sword. I told Lancelot it was something my father had given me and had deep sentimental meaning. And seeing how the sword was wrapped up at all times, he never asked. Also, he doesn't really pay attention to anything that doesn't specifically involve him."

"I don't think now is the time to argue more," Hel said before Lancelot could retaliate.

"So I gave the sword to Zeus in return for safe passage, and he gave it back after, telling me that his one condition to help was for me to return the sword to its rightful owner."

"And that is?" Mordred asked.

"You," Guinevere said. "You're the rightful owner. But you were, you know, evil and shit, and that would have been a bad idea, so Zeus advised me to give it to the next best person."

"If you're pausing for dramatic effect, I'm going to be really irritated," Mordred said after a few seconds.

"The Lady of the Lake," Guinevere said with a smile. "Smart, eh?"

"No one has seen her in centuries," Elaine said. "There's a rumor that Merlin had her killed."

"I heard that one too," Guinevere said. "But that's who I gave it to."

"And why am I here?" Mordred asked.

"Because she told me that only you could come reclaim the sword," Guinevere said.

Mordred sighed. "Yay, me."

"So where do we need to go?" Hel asked.

"Llyn Ogwen," Guinevere said.

"Snowdonia?" Mordred said. "Why would she stay there? That's the exact spot where Merlin said the sword was thrown after Arthur gallantly died after the Battle of Camlann, which never bloody happened, by the way."

"Which bit?" Hel asked.

"Any of it. The battle, the sword throwing. Merlin just wanted a cool story to show how badass Arthur was and how everyone loved him and hated me. The whole thing is bullshit of the highest order." Mordred rubbed his eyes. "Why would the Lady of the Lake stay in the one place that Merlin said the sword was thrown?"

"Because, like you said, Merlin made it up," Guinevere said with a smile. "Hide in plain sight and all that."

It started to rain, which Mordred felt was pretty apt, considering how he was feeling.

"Is any of the story true?" Hel asked.

"It's a real place; that's about it," Mordred said. "Sir Bedivere was there at one point. He tried to kill me there. I was evil at the time, so I'll let it slide. He started to see Arthur for what he truly was, and he searched me out, but I was a bit of a mess, and it didn't end well."

"Did you kill him?" Hel asked.

"No, he escaped," Mordred told her. "I haven't heard from him since."

"You're thinking this is a bad idea," Elaine said as they reached the helicopter.

"I'm thinking that there's more to this than the Lady of the Lake sitting in a fucking puddle for a thousand years to wait for me."

"I guess we'll go find out," Hel said, climbing aboard as Lancelot and Guinevere strapped themselves in, leaving most of their belongings behind—something Guinevere was less than happy about. Mordred climbed on board with the uneasy feeling of a man who was about to have a much worse day than the shitty one he'd already envisaged.

Chapter Thirteen

Nate Garrett

Montana, United States, Earth Realm

"I'm going to need you to stay here," I told Masako as we reached the top of the stairs. She was using my shoulder as a support, although judging from the pain on her face, she wasn't having a good time of it.

"No problem," she said, taking a seat at the top of the stairs. "If you could grab me some food, I'll heal faster, be less of a burden."

"Jikininki eat flesh, yes?" I asked.

Masako nodded. "I'd prefer a liver, heart, or brain if you can get it. More nutrients."

"Great, so I need to go kill one of those mutated cave trolls," I said with a slight sigh. "Just once I'd like a day to be easy." The crashing sound from above me signaled that it was going to be anything but.

"I'll wait for you," Masako said with a thumbs-up.

"Any idea if magic has an effect on these things?"

"Nope. Best of luck."

"And bullets?" I asked.

"Oh, none," Masako said. "I emptied a magazine into one of them. It did nothing."

I pushed open the door as a nearby wall exploded and one of the cave troll creatures crashed through. It saw me and roared. Twelve feet tall and a mass of muscle, a cave troll wasn't much fun to deal with at the best of times. But this had been twisted into something that only just resembled a cave troll.

It roared again, showing me the secondary row of tiny piranha-like teeth that sat behind its normal teeth. They were new. As was the long black tongue it used to lick its entire face.

I readied a sphere of air in my hand, spinning it faster and faster as it grew in size before pouring fire magic into it.

The troll looked down at my hands and charged forward. I dodged and drove the sphere into its rib cage before detonating the magic. The troll was thrown back through the maelstrom of magic, which tore through the building like a bomb, completely removing the exterior wall in front of me and all but melting the metal fence beyond. The troll landed fifty feet away, its entire side now a mass of exploded bone and muscle. Apparently magic could hurt them. Good to know.

I knocked on the door behind me. "Food will be here shortly."

I walked through the room and stepped over the ruined wall to the park outside, where there was a smattering of snow. There were two more trolls bounding through the park toward me, but I had enough time to create a sword of lightning, plunge it through the throat of the dead troll, and expand the blade to decapitate the creature. I used air magic to toss the head back into the building; it hit the door with a thud. I saw the door open and Masako almost pounce on the head with the eagerness of someone who hadn't eaten in months, and I turned away, back to the two oncoming trolls. I really didn't want to watch a jikininki feed.

The two trolls closed in on me, and I shot a bolt of lightning at the one closest, taking the creature in the chest, and then threw it back with a blast of air. The second troll continued on, building up speed as it moved toward me like an unstoppable mass of death.

"I've been waiting for this moment," I said with a smile and blasted it in the face with fire, which forced the creature to throw itself to the side and try to bury its face in the loose dirt in an effort to put out the flames.

Creating a sphere of fire and air in my hand, I smashed it into the back of the creature's skull and jumped away as the magic detonated, removing the troll's head and several meters of dirt beneath it. The soil began to rain down over the park as the surviving cave troll staggered to its feet, only to be met with my soul weapon in the shape of a jian piercing its heart. The troll let out a gasp before a whip of fire removed its head.

"Why a jian?" Masako asked from behind me.

I turned to see her licking her fingers clean of blood.

"When I was younger, Merlin sent me to China to keep me from Arthur's grasp. I spent a lot of time with several families, but one in particular—the father of whom was a blacksmith—became very dear to me. When I left, he gave me the sword as a gift. It's probably destroyed now, seeing how everything else I owned was destroyed by Arthur, but when I discovered I could use necromancy, I found that my soul weapons were a jian and battle-ax. I guess subconsciously they were the weapons that meant the most to me."

"I'm feeling much better, by the way," Masako said with a smile. "Thanks for the food."

"There's some more scattered around if you need it."

Masako stretched. "No, I'm good. My body is healing, so I won't complain. Good thing you found me," she said. "I'd probably be dead otherwise. Well, deader. The little ones don't like the sunlight, so I think we have time to get through the city before we have to deal with them again."

"Tommy said you used to work for Nergal," I said after we'd been running for a while.

"We had a falling-out," she said. "And by 'falling-out,' I mean he was an asshole. I escaped him but also escaped Tommy and his people arresting me. Unfortunately, Tommy tracked me down. He offered me a deal to work with him in exchange for him not throwing me to Hades and his people and telling them to find a pit for me."

"I think you made the right decision," I told her.

"I think I should have hidden better." She grinned. "I'm sorry to hear about Tommy and your father. How long does Odin have?"

"A few days," I said, the hurt from those words making them taste bitter. "I'm hoping that whoever poisoned him has a cure. It seems like the kind of thing you'd make sure to develop a cure for."

"If there is one, then the prison is the best place to look."

"What information did you discover that you were going to give Tommy?"

"I found Atlas. He's in the prison," Masako said.

"He okay?"

"No," Masako said. "Not even slightly." She stopped walking. "Look, I don't know what happened to him, but whatever that bastard in charge in there is doing, these things are *his* creation. It's like he wants to create some kind of weapon. He has pits in there full of blood with runes around them."

You have to be fucking kidding me.

"You saw the runes?" I asked.

She nodded. "Can't read them, though."

I picked up a stick and drew one on the loose snow and dirt. "Anything like this?"

"How do you know that?" Masako asked as I kicked the rune away.

"They were used to create me and Mordred and the devils . . . and about a hundred other people over the centuries who went insane and murdered everyone around them before being put down. The Four Horsemen—they were created using these runes. It's a blood magic ritual. You get enough blood in a pool and have people make a baby, and that baby grows up to be a monster. Sometimes they get it right, and they grow up to be me or Mordred or Lucifer."

"There was no baby making going on that I saw," Masako said. "Only adults in there."

"You sure?"

Masako raised an eyebrow. "Yes, I'm sure. I got caught snooping around and ran for it but got grabbed by those troll bastards before I could get free of the city. This whole place is a mass of fucked up. You know that everyone who was here was murdered by escaped killers?"

"They didn't get free?" I asked.

"Hell no, someone blocked all of the exits and allowed these killers to have free rein over the entire town. But these killers weren't like the normal human serial murderers you read about in the news; these were . . . something else. The prison was used as a place to try and create bioweapons. Humans who were extra durable or had exceptionally loose morals about killing. They got free and killed everyone, and whoever was in charge did not want that getting out, so they let everyone die and went in to mop it up after."

The entire population of a town did not disappear without someone somewhere asking questions. Except . . .

"Avalon made sure that no one asked questions, I assume."

"Bingo," Masako said. "And this was before Arthur returned to make it extra-special evil. I think this was Ares's pet project. They erased it all after it went to shit. Probably had people going around to relatives who asked too many questions."

"Ares is dead," I said.

"So I heard. Well done on that front, by the way. The world is better off with him gone."

"Ares answered to Hera," I said.

"If Ares was here, his mother knew about it. She's not exactly the kind of person who likes to be surprised. She would have known what he was doing."

There was a howl in the distance. "There are more of those things?" I asked.

"Dozens, hundreds—I have no idea how many," Masako said. "They live in the basements of ruined buildings. I think most of them were the people who escaped the killing spree in town by running into the prison. Not sure what was worse."

The pair of us moved through the city in silence after that, occasionally waiting when we heard the sounds of the creatures around us. I knew they'd be able to track me, as I'd used my magic, but I hoped to at least find somewhere to keep safe until morning. Masako was healed, but she still wasn't a hundred percent.

We were near the center of town when Masako started to cough, causing her to spit blood all over the snow-covered street.

"You're not good, are you?" I asked. "I mean, apart from the fact that you've lost your arm."

She shook her head. "That troll brain healed me enough to move, but I got bitten by one of the little ones before that bastard in charge strapped me to the cross, and I think because I'm already dead, whatever they did has screwed around with my body. Losing my arm hasn't helped."

"You're dying." It wasn't a question.

She nodded. "Again." She laughed, which turned into another cough, this one longer, forcing her to her knees.

I helped her to her feet and half carried her into the nearest building.

"I don't smell any creatures," Masako said as we stepped inside. "They have a distinct aroma."

I carried her up a flight of stairs and lowered her to the floor in what had once been a bedroom, the windows giving a good view of the street in front of the house. She lifted her shirt to look at a wound on her stomach, which was oozing pink. I looked at the stump of her arm, and that at least wasn't any worse than when I'd first seen it.

"You came here alone?" I asked.

Masako winced as she lowered her shirt. "Yeah, I figured I'd be in and out with the info on Atlas that Tommy wanted. It didn't work out as I'd planned."

I sat down next to Masako. "You need to rest," I told her.

"You want me to sleep while there are creatures hunting us out there?"

I nodded. "But not here—we need to find my friends. They might be able to heal you."

Masako shook her head. "I can feel my body dying, Nate. I had a good run."

I racked my brain to think of any runes that might be able to help her, but I came up with nothing. Even healing runes wouldn't help heal someone who had already died and come back to life once.

"I'm sorry," I said.

"You find out who hurt Tommy, and you get him healed," Masako said, her eyes dropping closed before she forced herself awake again.

I waited until Masako was asleep and kept an eye on the street outside. I hadn't used magic since killing the trolls, so hopefully the time and distance between that event and now would make me harder to track.

I didn't know how long Masako had, but she was right: moving her through the city was a bad idea. I hoped that we'd find something inside the prison that could help her as well as those back in Asgard.

Eventually I drifted off to sleep, my dreams marked with my friends dying and me being helpless to do anything to stop it. I woke as the first rays of light came through the dirt-smeared window.

I stood and stretched. It had been a cold night, and the inability to use my magic had ensured it had stayed that way, but my coat was thick and warm, and I was thankful for the wool socks and well-made boots.

I rolled over and found that Masako was gone.

I got to my feet and looked out of the window. It had snowed again during the night, but there were no fresh footprints.

"Masako," I shouted, looking through each of the rooms in turn before heading downstairs. I found her outside in the back garden, sitting on the remains of a wooden bench. Her eyes were closed, and seeing as she didn't need to breathe, I wasn't sure if she'd died in the night.

"We need to get going," I said to Masako, who stirred and cried out in pain.

I took a look at the wound and saw that the purple-and-pink oozing was gone, but the flesh around the wound had turned black and green. I looked up at her eyes and saw that they were the same color. Shit.

"Told you so," Masako said with a smile.

"I have no idea what's happening," I said. "I could try the runes anyway; they might do something."

"No," Masako said. "I've had dwarven healing runes put on me before; they're worse than this. They rot me from the inside out."

"I don't have a lot of other options, Masako," I said.

She nodded. "Leave me here."

I didn't answer.

"You know it makes sense, Nate," she said. "You don't have time to argue. I have my gun, so I can keep myself defended as I need to. You go get the cure, come back for me."

We both knew that she had no intention of waiting for me to return.

"You sure?" I asked.

She nodded. "I like it out here. I like nature, and despite the horrors that happened in this city, there are moments of beauty. I wanted to see the sunrise."

"How was it?"

"Stunning," she said with a smile. "Really, Nate. Go. Save your friend. Save the world. Help Atlas if you can, but if not, end him; he wouldn't want to be someone else's tool. And be careful of that man in charge. There's something not right about him."

I placed my hand on hers, squeezing slightly. "I'll be back for you."

Masako nodded. "I know." She lifted the gun in her hand. "But these are silver bullets. Just in case."

I left Masako and used the nearby fence to vault into the garden next door. I was two gardens away when the gunshot rang out. I stopped walking and turned back for just a moment to where I'd left Masako, then ran on to find my friends.

Chapter Fourteen

Nate Garrett

It was much easier to get through the city without the constant concern of the creatures jumping out at me every few feet. I ran on toward the prison, hoping that at some point Kase or Remy would pick up my scent and find me.

I found them first.

They were all standing next to what had once been a petrol station, the pumps gone, the signs rusted away.

"You all look rested," I said.

"We're good," Remy said. "Our bartender friend is not. He tried to escape; then he tried to stab Kase."

I looked over at the bartender, who was cradling his clearly broken arm.

"I drew some runes on it to ease the pain," Zamek said. "Still hurts, though, I imagine."

"Good," Kase said. "You okay, Nate?"

I told them all about what I'd gone through in the night.

"Masako is dead?" Remy asked.

"Tommy spoke well of her," Sky said. "Mostly, anyway. He called her a pain in the ass, but that's what he calls most people he likes, so I assume he liked her too."

"We need to get to the prison," I said. "I have no idea what we're going to find, but I have a feeling that our bartender friend will be able to point us in the right direction."

"And if I don't want to?" he snapped.

Kase growled, and the man stepped back.

"You have two options," I told him. "One: you're able to get us into the prison, and we let you go. And two: you can't, and you die here."

"I can get you into the prison," he said.

"See? You give a little; you take a little," I said, slapping him on the back. "Oh, and if you fuck with us again, I'm going to nail you to the floor and let those things have their fun. Okay?"

His eyes widened in fear, and he nodded quickly.

"Good man," I said, pushing him forward.

The prison loomed in the distance, and with no other way of getting there, we had to walk.

No one was particularly in the mood for chatting in the few hours it took to get there, but once we arrived, it was pretty clear that the prison had a large security problem. One of its outer walls had a thirty-foot hole in it.

"Well, I guess we can go straight in," Remy said.

"What happened?" Sky asked.

"It fell down," the bartender said. "I don't know. It's old."

There were carriage and horse tracks that led through the hole in the wall and back toward the town. "These look fresh," I said.

"And there's blood here," Sky said, closer to the prison. "Human blood. Not a lot, but I'm guessing it belonged to those poor bastards from last night."

"These are some big horses," Zamek said, placing his hand on one hoofprint. "Even bigger than a warhorse."

"Another mutant?" Kase asked. "I'm beginning to sense a theme here."

We stepped through the hole in the wall, the bartender squirming in Kase's grasp.

"You said get you in the prison. Well, you're in," he snapped.

"I know this is semantics," Remy said. "But 'inside' means *inside*, not in the place inmates used to go do exercise. Actually *inside* the main building."

"I think I found the horses," Kase said, pointing across the courtyard to a set of wooden stables that certainly hadn't been there when the place was open for business.

We went over to the stables, opened one of the shutter windows, and found the black horses inside their pens, eating. They were huge creatures.

"Unless horses have started to evolve and not told anyone," Zamek said, "they appear to have tusks."

"You ever hear of anything like this?" Kase asked no one in particular.

"No," nearly everyone said almost in unison.

"Once," Zamek said. "Or at least I heard about something like this."

"You going to tell us?" Remy asked. "Or are we just meant to guess? Because I'm assuming it had something to do with blood magic fuckery."

"Remy would be correct," Zamek said.

"Yay, me, I guess," Remy said with a slight shrug.

"Well, before the dwarves were betrayed and almost destroyed, there were rumors that the ancient dwarves conducted experiments on the animals in the realm of Nidavellir. I read several scrolls from scholars who theorized that their experiments with animals and blood magic were the reason for so many species in the realm being much larger and more aggressive than elsewhere."

"The spiders?" Remy asked with a shiver.

"I hated those things," I said.

"For one, yes," Zamek said. "We're talking tens of thousands of years before I was even born, but the blood magic ritual twisted the animals in new ways."

"Any chance it was a similar ritual to the one that helped create me?" I asked.

"Maybe," Zamek said. "The ancient dwarves weren't exactly big fans of leaving instructions, so there aren't any depictions of which runes they used, but I would certainly say it's possible."

"We should get inside before anyone spots us," Sky said as we made our way around the exercise yard, through another destroyed wall, and over to what would have been the car park near the front entrance to the prison.

I pushed the barman in front of me. "If we open this door, are we all going to be killed or something?"

"No. It's the only way in and out of the main prison block," he said. "The only way I know of, anyway."

Remy ran up to the door and, after turning the handle, pushed it open with his foot. Nothing exploded. He put his head inside the prison.

"It's a reception area," he said as we all caught him up. "Nothing in there. Smells like something bad happened, though."

"Bad how?" Sky asked.

Kase opened the door, stepped inside, and took a deep breath. "People died in here a long time ago. Still smells weird, but there's no fresh kills here." She sniffed again. "No one has been through here recently, but there are a lot of scents outside and around the door. I think those horse things were brought past here at night; I imagine this is where they all set off from."

"You think you can go back out there and get a sniff of any recent trails?" I asked. "See if we can't figure out what exit the humans were taken from last night."

Kase ran out of the prison, with Remy following. Two noses were always better than one.

The rest of us closed the door and dragged the bartender back outside. "Is there another way in?" I asked.

"Not that I know of," he said. "I haven't been here in a year at least. And the last time I was here, I came through the front. That was where I was told to meet him. I was only allowed in the little reception room just beyond the front desk, and I stayed there until I was told to leave."

"Seeing how you've lied repeatedly, really makes it difficult to believe you," Sky said.

"You two go see what Kase and Remy have found," I said to Sky and Zamek. "I'll have a chat with our friend here."

Both ran off without a word, and I led the barman back into the waiting room and sat him down on a tatty old chair.

"I really don't know anything," he said, nervous and scared.

I nodded. "I believe you. I don't think the people behind this would tell you anything you didn't need to know; I don't think you are worthy of the knowledge. I think you've taken us as far as you can, and you've lived up to your end of the bargain, so you can go or stay in here; I don't really care."

The barman tentatively got to his feet. "I don't want to stay in here," he said. "But if I start walking now, I'll never make it through the city before nightfall."

I nodded. "I know."

The realization of his position dawned on him. "So I either stay here and risk being killed in the night or run back to Carver Creek and definitely get killed in the night."

"I never said you had good options. But you lived up to your end of the deal, so now I will."

"Let me come with you," he said hopefully.

"Why? You have nothing I need."

"I can help fight the things in here. The monsters. The man who runs this place created them. I know him; I can talk to him."

"We're not here to talk," I said.

"Come on. You can't just leave me here. You need me."

I shook my head. "I really don't."

"Leaving me here would be cruel!" he shouted.

I grabbed him by the scruff of his neck and slammed him up against the wall. "You sent my friend and father here to die. You sent their team here *to die*! If you think I'm the good guy in this scenario, you have sorely misunderstood who you're dealing with. The only reason I haven't torn you in half is because I'm trying very hard to keep my temper in check, to not go off and kill every fucking thing in my path to finding that cure. Because if I do that, I might lose the cure and, with it, my dad." I pulled him closer until our faces were only an inch apart. "If you think leaving you alive is cruel, I assure you I can show you *real* cruelty."

I ignited a blade of fire in one hand and held it to his face as he tried to squirm away. Shadows ripped out of the ground, keeping him in place, and he made a whimpering noise. I removed the magical shadows and fire before pushing the bartender back onto the chair.

"Stay, go—I don't care," I said. "But if I ever see you again, I'll kill you."

I took a step toward the door and paused.

"It would be better if you'd just kill me now," the bartender said.

I turned back to him. "I know. That's why you're alive." I left the prison with the bartender cursing my name and returned to the rest of the team.

As I got closer, I saw that they'd found a pair of double doors next to a large set of steel shutters, leading to what I assumed had been a loading bay.

"These doors were used recently," Kase said.

"Did you kill him?" Remy asked.

I shook my head. "He can stay here or run back to the city."

"Whatever option—the chances he'll be eaten are high," Zamek said.

"Good," Kase said, almost tearing the entire door out of the frame and tossing it aside.

"I guess we're no longer bothering with stealth," Sky said.

Kase smiled. "I want the fuckers to come get me. Or at least try. It would give me an excuse to let a bit of frustration out."

Kase went in first, and the rest followed into a loading area. An old 1950s-style truck sat in the center of the bay, next to a much newer Range Rover.

Zamek went over to the older truck and checked it out, which meant smashing one of the windows to get inside. "It's working fine," he said. "Lots of runes in here, though."

"What do they do?" Sky asked.

"Power dampeners, ones to make you weak, that kind of thing. They're old, though; some have all but worn away, so I'm guessing this isn't used regularly as a transport. It's in good condition, though."

"So we could use it to leave once we're done here?" I asked.

Zamek nodded. "Keys are over there."

I followed where Zamek was pointing to a wooden key hanger at the side of the room. There were two sets, and I grabbed both and tossed the older ones to Zamek while I used the Range Rover keys to open the car and take a look inside.

The older truck came to life almost immediately, and Zamek quickly switched it off. "We've got fuel and water, and this thing is good to go if we need it."

"This one too," I said, searching the back seats and boot. "No weapons, though."

I climbed into the driver's seat and pressed the starter button without depressing the clutch so that it didn't start the engine but let me check the gauges on the dashboard. "This car is the cleanest I've ever been in. I would expect it to have just come off the forecourt, except there are a few thousand miles on it. Someone loves this car."

"Are we going or what?" Kase asked from the door that led farther into the prison.

I switched off the ignition, got out of the car, and put the keys in my pocket, just in case.

"How's things?" I asked Kase when I reached her.

"Impatient," she said. "How are you so calm?"

"Oh, I'm not."

It took us half an hour to make our way through the prison, but we found nothing that any of us would consider a threat.

"This place is a prison for rats and moss," Remy said after we'd exited a flight of stairs next to another security door. Beyond that had been a prison staff room, where the most dangerous thing had been the possibility of tetanus from the remains of the furniture.

"Any chance there's a map somewhere in this bloody place?" Zamek asked.

"If you were an evil bastard conducting experiments on people, would you go upstairs or underground?" Sky asked.

"Underground," everyone said in unison.

The staircase to the underground section of the prison was easy to find, and the thick metal door that barred our way was covered in runes that had been drawn in blood. It took Zamek about a minute to disarm them, and he pushed open the door, which squeaked as the bottom rubbed against the tiled floor beyond.

"That was whisper quiet," Remy said when the door was open enough for us all to walk through. "No one could *possibly* have heard it."

On the wall in front of the door was a map. It showed the mazelike structure of the underground part of the prison.

"There are two sides," Sky said. "Dozens of rooms, and it's not exactly a setup that makes for easy navigation, but there's a part at the opposite end to here where the two halves join up together."

I looked at the map where Sky was tapping, and the room she pointed to looked to be much larger than any of the others.

"If you were an evil shitbag hell bent on creating monsters, wouldn't you want the largest room?" Remy asked.

"I would," Zamek said. "And that gives you the chance to escape if anyone comes."

"So long as they don't come from both sides," Kase said.

"Which is exactly what we're going to do," Sky said.

"I'll take the left," I said.

"I'll go with Nate," Remy said. "He needs a nose."

"Zamek and Kase can come with me," Sky said. "We'll meet up there."

"That's a lot of rooms to check on the way," Zamek said.

"Hopefully we'll find something useful," I said, setting off down the corridor. The fluorescent lighting wasn't quite powerful enough to light up everything, leaving parts of the corridor lingering in shadows.

Remy reached the first door before me and pushed it open with one hand while the other rested on the hilt of one of his swords.

The room was empty.

"Smells like piss," Remy said.

"It hasn't been uninhabited for long," I said, stepping inside and looking around the small cell. The mattress had been torn to shreds and the metal bed frame pulled apart. Pieces of the frame had been stabbed into the walls, and blood stained the tips, as well as the floor. A drain sat in the middle of the room.

"Nate, did someone jab those metal spikes into that wall and then impale themselves on them?" Remy asked, his tone suggesting he already knew the answer and would rather he were wrong.

We continued on, checking room after room but finding nothing beyond devices of torture and evidence of imprisonment. We followed the twisty corridor as we moved farther away from the entrance, and the more we walked, the less comfortable I felt. We were in someone else's domain, and that meant they had the upper hand.

We'd been searching for what felt like hours but had probably only been a fraction of that time when the corridor opened out in a large room with two doors on either side and the continuation of the corridor on the opposite side to where Remy and I had entered.

Remy moved over to one side of the room, and I took the other, each of us pushing open a door at the same time.

I gasped. I couldn't help it. The room contained dozens of jars of a translucent purple liquid. The jars were stacked floor to ceiling on wooden shelves, and in the middle of the room was a large steel desk. Each jar contained a small animal or a part of a larger one. There were the remains of foxes, wolves, deer, and horses, and more than one contained a human head.

"That is some *nasty* Frankenstein shit," Remy said from the doorway. "My two rooms had empty jars stacked up."

"So someone is planning on continuing this?" I said. "What is the purple liquid?" I tapped a jar with a human foot in it, and the foot moved, causing me to jump back.

"Did that fucking thing just wiggle its toes?" Remy asked. "It fucking moved!"

We checked the remaining room and found the same setup as the first. The only difference was several files piled up on the desk.

I picked up one of the manila folders, opened it, and read a report detailing the procedure that had been carried out on those who had been brought in here.

"This is all old," I said. "Ares signed this."

"So these are Ares's . . . what? Trophies? Snacks?"

I shrugged. "No idea. Maybe. There's a lot of notes about trying to create a creature that would match those of ancient Greek myth."

"He wanted to create his own chimera?" Remy asked.

"Sounds like it. At least a bit, yeah." I flicked through the rest of the papers. "The rest is just circle-jerking bullshit. Ares loved himself; no one understood his genius; he'd show everyone, including Hera. Looks like Hera paid for all this."

"I'm not sure if it's been brought up again, but Hera has a really screwed-up family," Remy said.

"No kidding," I told him, dropping the file back on the desk. "Some of these jars go back hundreds of years. Looks like there are crystals in the fluid that give a mild current to whatever he puts in, making it spasm with any kind of movement to the jar."

"He created his own little horror show," Remy said, looking around the room. "I'm *really* glad he's dead."

"So who took over the family business?" I asked. "All of these are old, but there's still someone carrying on the experiments."

"Hera?"

"She's in London," I said. "I checked before we came. If she knew I was here, she'd probably be trying to drop a nuke on us."

"Don't even joke," Remy said, leaving the room.

I followed him out and farther down the corridor, where the lights above flickered on and off, giving the whole place an even creepier vibe than it already had.

Remy was a dozen feet in front of me, walking past a cell, when the door exploded open and something big rushed out, grabbing hold of Remy and slamming him into the ground. A blast of air hit me in the chest, throwing me back down the corridor. I used my air magic to turn myself and land on my feet as a second blast of air was thrown at me, smashing all of the lights in the corridor. I raised a shield of my own air, and the blast harmlessly dissipated over it.

A large man walked out of the darkness, carrying a struggling Remy by the neck in one hand. The man was easily six and a half feet tall and was barrel chested. He held Remy up by his head as Remy snarled and went for one of his swords, but the man was fast and disarmed him.

I rushed forward and stopped when the man put the tip of the sword to Remy's throat. "Don't," he said. "Actually, I don't care." He plunged the sword into Remy's throat and threw my friend at me like he was a tennis ball.

"Let's have some fun," the mystery man said, rushing back into the darkness, and I cradled Remy's body.

Chapter Fifteen

Nate Garrett

I removed the sword from Remy's throat and dropped it beside him with a clatter. There was no point searching for a pulse; it was clear he was dead, and there was nothing I could do.

Walking over to the room where light met darkness, I used my fire magic to look where the man had vanished. He was down there somewhere. He'd murdered my friend. I was going to find him and kill him.

A cough from behind me got my attention, and I turned to see Remy sitting up. "Fucking hell, that shit never gets any easier," he said, spitting blood onto the floor. "Seven lives left, Nate. Anyone makes a cat joke, and I will hurt them."

"Stay here," I said. "I'm going after him."

"Nate, there's something off about him," Remy said, wincing as he got to his feet. "He killed me here, in the light. He could have done it in the corridor. He wanted the spectacle. I think he wants you to go after him."

"You going to be okay?" I asked.

Remy nodded. "He moved quicker than I could react. I tried to teleport away, but there were runes on his gloves; they stopped me from doing anything. If he's running down that way, the others will have no idea that he's heading in their direction."

Remy walked over to me.

"You're not staying, are you?" I asked.

Remy sheathed his sword. "Nope. Fucker killed me, so I'm going to stab him in his eyes, go home, cure Odin, and have a big cup of tea. It's the gentlemanly thing to do."

I gave him a grin, stepped into the darkness with my night vision activated, and walked down the corridor for a few steps before stopping and sending out a pulse of air magic to try to pinpoint where the assailant might be. But the magic only told me there was nothing in the immediate vicinity, and farther down the corridor it cut out.

I continued on until I reached the point my magic had stopped. It was at the edge of a large room, similar to the one where Remy and I had found the jars, and it was lit up, showing the many runes carved on the walls. The continuation of the corridor was bathed in darkness, and there were only two doors inside the room. A spiral staircase was situated in one corner, and the fact that it wasn't on the map led me to believe that it was a new addition to get from the basement to the prison above.

One of the doors opened, and the large man stepped out into the light. "Nathan Garrett," he said, his accent nondescript. He shrugged off a large dark-gray coat and placed it over the back of a wooden chair. Like Remy had said, he wore black leather gloves with red runes painted on them.

"How very *Fullmetal*," I said, tapping my hands.

He looked down at the gloves. "Ah, yes, I like to take every advantage I can get, and these ensure anyone I grab with them is momentarily powerless. Doesn't last long, but not long is all I need."

I stepped into the light while Remy remained in the darkness of the corridor. "Who are you?" I asked.

"War," he said, running a hand over his bald head.

"Is that the first or second name?" I asked him, making sure to keep distance between us.

"It's all the name I need, Mr. Garrett."

"War?" I asked. "Like the Horseman?"

"Well, I think that was the intent. Just like you were created to be Death, and Mordred was to be Conquest. We are siblings . . . of a kind."

The shock on my face must have been easy to read.

"Didn't expect that, did you?" he asked with a laugh.

"Are you telling me that the seven of us who survived the rituals were *literally* created to be the new Horsemen?" I asked.

"You didn't know?" War asked. "Eight horse . . . people. Four men, four women. Not all of us were meant to survive, but only one died, so they got stuck with seven Horsemen. Death, Conquest, War, Pestilence, Famine, Spirit, and Judgement. They had to come up with a few new ones, obviously. Although Famine didn't last long. And I had to kill Spirit when he refused to join us. Now it's three men and two women. And when you and Mordred are dead and Hera finally finds Zeus's bastard, it'll just be me and one other. And they're no threat to anyone, so I don't much care what they do."

"Why are you telling me this?"

"I'd hoped to bring you over to my side," he said. "Hera doesn't want that. She wants your head on a pike, but we are brothers, so this is the only chance you get to live to see tomorrow."

I shook my head. "We're not brothers. We just happened to be created in the same way. Otherwise, we have nothing in common at all. You're an evil sack of shit. You tried to murder my friend. Where is the rest of his team, and where is the cure?"

War started to laugh. "His team died at my hands, and their bodies were given over to my experiments for nourishment," he said. "Tommy was a nice surprise. I was meant to just kill all but one and use that one to bring you here. Didn't expect it to be Tommy, though. I bet his werewolf healing is just destroying him right now."

I clenched my fists and took a step forward. "Where is the cure?"

War smiled. "You really never heard of me before?"

The change in conversation threw me. "What?" I asked. "Rasputin mentioned a War. But if he elaborated, it wasn't to me."

"Hera had me in hiding for years because she thought you might know. You specifically. She didn't want you to come after me, try to find out what I really was. I think she thought if you discovered me, you'd ask questions about yourself."

"Where is the cure?"

War sighed. "I'm not even sure there is a cure. If there is, though, I certainly don't have one. Maybe Hera knows. Or Rasputin. Or Atlas. Or maybe there is no cure, and this is all for nothing."

"Where is Atlas?" I asked.

"Around. You'll meet him soon enough. I just wanted to talk to you first. Without your rat friend."

"He's a fox, you contemptible prick," I snapped.

War's expression darkened. "I see we will get nowhere."

I cracked my knuckles and rolled my shoulders. "Guess you'll just have to get your ass kicked."

War removed one glove and slammed his hand onto a nearby piece of wall. Several runes in the room flashed, and a purple barrier appeared between the room and the beginning of the corridor.

"Nate?" Remy shouted.

"Go get the others," I said without looking over at him. "I'll be fine."

"You'll be dead before they get here," War said.

I shrugged. "You'd be surprised at how many people have said that who aren't here anymore."

The wall beside War exploded, showering the room in dust and brick. I raised a shield of dense air as Atlas charged through the wall and collided with my shield, throwing me back across the room into the wall behind me.

I hit the wall hard, but the shield held as Atlas stood in the center of the room and roared at me. He was well over seven feet tall and weighed probably over four hundred pounds of pure muscle. His head had been shaved. His half-giant side allowed him to retain his bulk all of the time and grow to twice his normal size, but it wasn't the giant side of his powers I was worried about.

He wore a dark trench coat, which he tore away as War ran to ascend the spiral staircase. I sprinted past Atlas, avoiding his charge, which ended with him slamming into one of the purple barriers and yelling in anger. I was halfway up the stairs when he turned and charged again, smashing into the staircase and tearing the metal railings apart in an effort to get to me as I took the steps two at a time.

Atlas's hand narrowly missed my foot as I pulled myself through the hatch and discovered I was just outside the prison building, close to where I'd left the bartender.

War was nowhere to be seen, but my respite was brief, as the ground beneath my feet was ripped asunder and Atlas pulled his enormous frame out of the hole in the ground he'd created. Now fourteen feet tall, he roared, and in the daylight I could see that his skin was blotchy and tinged purple, his face contorted in rage and hate. Scars adorned his massive chest and arms, and his eyes held nothing of the man he used to be.

"Atlas, I know we were never friends, but we're on the same side, so you need to snap out of whatever was done to you," I said, hoping there was some part of him that remembered the man he used to be.

Atlas took a step toward me, and I blasted him in the chest with a torrent of air that threw him back into the prison with enough force to punch through the outer wall.

A stream of water hit me in the back, knocking me to the ground, and my hastily thrown-up shield of fire turned it into steam. War charged through the steam, his skin blistering from the heat, although that didn't seem to bother him as he slammed into me, picked me up, and attempted to throw me to the ground.

Limpet-like, I wrapped my legs around his arm and neck, wrenching back on his arm until the elbow joint popped. I kicked him in the face and released my grip, dropped to the ground, and rolled away. After slamming a sphere of air and fire into his chest, I detonated the magic, throwing him back toward the outer ring of wall that surrounded the prison.

The sound of Atlas returning caught my attention. I quickly sank into the shadows at my feet, using the shadow realm to come up behind where Atlas had been. He turned midrun, trying to keep his momentum and charge back at me, but I unleashed my pure magic.

Pure magic had only offensive properties and could be used solely by those who were born in similar circumstances to my own. Atlas threw himself aside as the gray magic smashed into his arm, spinning him in place, but it hit War full on. The wall behind him was turned to rubble as the pure magic punched through.

I pulled back, surveying the devastation I'd caused. There was a gouge in the earth where the magic had hit, and Atlas crawled away, blood pouring from the jagged wound where he'd once had an arm.

War stood in front of the ruined wall, which continued to collapse behind him. He brushed rubble off his shoulders.

"How?" I asked.

"You can't use pure magic on someone who can also use it," War shouted. "I guess no one mentioned that to you."

I had to admit that it hadn't come up. The number of people who could use pure magic in all of the realms could be counted on two hands, so it wasn't like it was usually an issue.

"Get up," War told Atlas, who tried to obey. He staggered around and eventually collapsed back against the wall, bringing more of it down on top of him.

Before Atlas could recover, I charged at War, avoided his punch, and connected with an air magic–wrapped fist to his jaw, knocking him back. He threw a second punch, but I blocked it and caught him in the side of the head, snapping it aside. He danced away through the hole in the wall, and I followed, hoping to finish him before he could do any more damage.

I closed the distance between us, created a blade of lightning in one hand, and swung it up toward War's face. But he met it with a blade of air, pushing it aside and causing the ground beneath my feet to erupt, throwing me back.

Being able to use both earth magic and air magic was impossible. They were opposite elements.

"Surprised?" he asked as I got to my feet. He punched me in the jaw, knocking me to the ground, and I felt every piece of power I had access to vanish in an instant. He tapped the back of one hand in triumph.

My pause allowed War to follow up his attack with a kick to my ribs. He picked me up by the back of my neck and threw me forward onto the cold, hard ground.

"You were *stupid* to come here," he said, punching me in the jaw as I moved to stand. "Every hit will remove your power for a few seconds. I got the idea from Atlas. He's a siphon, you know, able to stop powers being used within a certain distance around him."

There was a rumble as Atlas emerged from the remains of the wall, tossing aside huge pieces like they were made of papier-mâché.

"Atlas will have to finish you," War said. "It's a real shame I can't stick around. I have a fight to prepare for. I'm going to help lead Avalon to victory. Honestly, though, I thought you'd be tougher than this."

"Give me a minute," I said as War punched me again, knocking me back down to the ground.

"You don't deserve your magic," he said before walking back toward the hole in the wall just as the bartender ran through it. The bartender paused for a second, and War encased him in rock. The sound of his body being crushed as War turned the rock into a ball before discarding it made me feel slightly sorry for his victim.

I got back to my feet just as Atlas towered over me. He threw a punch, which I narrowly avoided, launching myself back and rolling away, trying to put some distance between us until my magic returned. While he was in this large state, he couldn't use his siphon powers, which was at least something.

The crack of a gun being fired rent the air, and Atlas stepped back, his hand going to his chest where the bullet had hit. Four more shots, and I turned to see Masako casually walking toward us, firing the whole time. With only one hand, she emptied her gun, ejected the magazine, and continued firing, riddling Atlas's body with silver bullets. When she'd emptied the gun for a second time, she charged forward, easily avoiding the swipe of a kneeling Atlas and jumping onto his face. Her talon-like fingers sank into the flesh of his scalp. He grabbed hold of her and threw her free, but that also tore a large part of his face off.

My magic returned, and a bolt of lightning leaped from my fingertips and smashed into Atlas's head. He'd always wanted a fight with me, and I'd always known that one on one, he'd beat me. But throw magic into the mix, and Atlas was just a large, strong man.

And being large and strong did very little to protect against a bolt of lightning to the skull.

Atlas rocked back but didn't fall as Masako moved around him and launched herself up onto his back. She climbed up, grabbed hold of his neck, and tore out a big chunk, spraying blood all over the ground.

I ran toward him and drove a blade of fire into his side, causing him to scream in pain and giving Masako the time to attack the wound she'd caused on his neck. It didn't take long for a blood-drenched Atlas to drop to his knees.

"I'm sorry it had to be like this," I said to Atlas, who I was pretty sure didn't even understand where he was, let alone what was being said. The old Atlas was long gone. This facsimile in his place was just a monster.

I drove a blade of lightning into his eye, exploding the magic inside his head. Masako jumped off Atlas and landed softly on the ground as he crashed beside us and died.

"I thought you died," I said.

"I tried to kill myself," she told me. "But I couldn't. I fired in the air and then just sat there and waited to die. I don't think I have long, but apparently I had long enough to find one of your trucks and drive it here. It ran out of fuel about a mile back."

I crouched down beside Atlas, searching his trousers for anything that might give me a clue to how he'd ended up this way, but the cry of pain from Masako made me look up. Masako was being held in the air by War. He had hold of the back of her skull, and as I got to my feet, he crushed her head and tossed her body aside as he continued on toward me.

I stood. The sky above me darkened, and thunder rolled all around us. War paused and looked up as a bolt of lightning streaked down from above to touch my raised hand and travel through my body. The lightning mixed with the magic inside me and exited through my other hand, burning it beyond recognition in the process as the incredible power left me. It smashed into the shield of rock that War quickly created, completely destroying it and leaving nothing but rubble at War's feet.

For the first time, I saw fear on War's face as I walked toward him. I picked up speed until I was in a full sprint and collided with War, slamming a sphere of lightning into his chest with my good hand and detonating it.

War was thrown back into the prison grounds, bounced along the hard ground, and came to a stop next to the Range Rover I'd seen earlier.

I flexed the fingers on my charred hand. The muscle was already working to repair itself, but in the meantime it hurt like hell. I channeled the pain back into my anger.

War got to his feet and exhaled before taking a step toward me. The ground erupted beneath my feet, and a torrent of fire burst out from where I'd been standing, but I was already running toward War, who looked slightly to the side of me and threw a ball of fiery rock at whatever he'd seen. I turned quickly, using my air magic to deflect his attack into the wall of the prison and away from Kase and Remy, who had emerged from the basement.

The Range Rover's engine roared to life, and War was off before anyone could do anything to stop him. I ran back to Masako, but it was too late.

"From the time I spent with her, she'd have preferred to go down fighting," Kase said.

I reached out with my necromancy, found her spirit, and absorbed it to boost my power. With it, I took her memories. They were not all pleasant, and more than one made me feel ill, but when it was done, I opened my eyes to find myself surrounded by friends as I knelt on the ground.

"Are you okay? You learn anything?" Sky asked. She looked around at the destruction of the fight.

I nodded. "I'm good," I said, getting to my feet. "Just stuff about her life. She was genuinely trying to make amends by coming here and working with Tommy."

I moved to Atlas and reached out for his spirit, too, absorbing it like I had Masako's. I'd been concerned about doing it, as I wasn't sure if his spirit had been corrupted by blood magic, but I took it slow, making sure that I found no curse marks on him before allowing the process to be completed.

I opened my eyes and looked up at everyone. There was a car roof above my head. "How long was I out?"

"An hour," Zamek said from beside me.

"There was a lot to take in," I told him, sitting up and then immediately lying back down again. "Atlas was thousands of years old. I saw the Titan Wars through his eyes; I saw so much anger and need to prove himself in battle. It's all sloshing around in my head, but there were two things I got. One, Hera is in Brutus's old building in London. She's been trying to figure out how to get to me. That's what Atlas was looking into when they caught him. A big chunk of his memories were taken when he was turned into that . . . thing."

"And the second thing?" Kase asked.

"We need to see Rasputin," I said. "He really should have listened to my warning."

Chapter Sixteen

Layla Cassidy

Realm of Valhalla

They left the town before daylight broke. Jinayca, Brynhildr, Tego, Ava, and Layla were all going to see the realm's dwarves. One of Brynhildr's people drove the carriage, allowing everyone else to sit in the back. Layla was told that it would take several hours to get there, but the dwarves were close to the mountains, where Empress Rela and her people were digging, so they would meet the rebellion there. The others went with Kara to the woodland city to start gathering the rebels.

Layla hadn't wanted Ava to come with them, but she couldn't very well send a sixteen-year-old girl off to start a war, and seeing as how they couldn't send her back through the realm gate, it seemed like the most sensible option in a long list of bad choices.

"Are we really going to fight the Valkyries?" Ava asked after they'd been riding in the back of the carriage for some time.

Layla looked outside at Tego, who bounded through the high grass of the plains as if having the time of her life. "Looks like it," Layla said to Ava.

"The palace guards will have discovered what you did by now," Brynhildr said. "Security will be increased. I assume this all got a lot more complicated than you expected."

Ava nodded. "I miss my sister. I miss my gran. I hope they're okay."

"They're in Shadow Falls," Layla said. "If the worst happens and the fighting starts in Asgard, Shadow Falls is the safest place to be."

"I'm not a fighter," Ava said, looking down at the ground. "I mean, I took lessons and stuff. My dad wanted me to learn, and I've been getting more lessons since joining you guys, but I'm not Wonder Woman."

"No one expects you to be," Jinayca said warmly.

"I just . . . I want to do my part," Ava said. "But . . . but . . . I'm . . . I'm scared. And all of you fight all the time, and you go to war and you kick ass, and I'm just a kid. I want to play on my PlayStation; I want to go to the mall; I want to eat shitty food and watch awful trashy movies. Going to war was not on the list of things I wanted to be doing at sixteen."

"I know," Layla said. "I wasn't as young as you when I collided with this world, and it was still a lot to take in. I can't imagine how hard it must be for you."

"I've got to be honest," Ava said. "I didn't think this was how my life was going to turn out."

"Welcome to the club," Layla said. "Fighting gods and their minions wasn't exactly on the curriculum at school."

"Actually, gods were at mine," Ava said. "But that was because Arthur had taken over so much and we were told we had to learn about them." Ava sighed. "I miss my friends. I wonder if they even know what's happening in their own country. Avalon spent so much time squashing any kind of knowledge—I hope they're safe now that it's all come out. Now that people see Avalon for what they really are."

Brynhildr reached over and squeezed Ava's hand. "When this is done, when we win, we will do all of those things you want to do. We will gorge ourselves on bad food and watch whatever movies are. I have a lot of catching up to do with the Earth realm, so if you'll have me, I'd like you to teach me the ropes."

Ava smiled and nodded. "I can do that."

Layla looked back out of the carriage as Tego sprinted after a large deerlike creature and took it down just beside some woods. The last Layla saw was Tego vanishing into the darkness of the woods with the creature in her mouth.

"At least someone is having a good time," Jinayca said with a smile.

"She doesn't get to go hunting often," Layla said. "Not much to hunt in Asgard inside the city."

Layla was grateful that the carriage was comfortable, and she dozed, dreaming about war and fighting.

The plains and woods eventually led to marshes and a large lake with a bridge. Once they were over the bridge, the landscape changed again, this time into a mass of gray stone as far as Layla could see. Mountains eventually loomed up around them as the carriage began to climb up the pass.

Layla stopped looking at that point and tried very hard not to think about having to travel between mountain ranges and how high they might or might not be. She wasn't bothered about the heights, but that didn't mean she wanted to watch the landscape fly by at speed while they were teetering over some ravine.

The sun was still high in the sky when the carriage eventually stopped and Brynhildr opened the door, stepped outside, and beckoned for them to follow her.

Layla was last, and as she climbed down from the carriage and looked over at the bustling city built into the side of the mountain, she remembered the last dwarven city she'd been in.

"No matter how far apart dwarves are, they build very similar structures," she said.

"My people have long memories," Jinayca replied. "Wherever we are, we can always make it feel like home."

Many of the dwarves waved hello to Brynhildr as they walked through the town toward a hole in the mountain that an ocean liner could have sailed through. Several dwarves stopped and stared at Jinayca, and Layla noticed some huddled whispering as they walked by.

"Were you well known by the dwarves?" Layla asked Jinayca.

"Not famous or anything," she said with a smile. "It wasn't until after we lost our home that I became a leader. I was an elder back in our home, but I imagine most of these people wouldn't have had much day-to-day involvement with what the elders did. I think the whispers and pointing are more down to newcomers arriving than me specifically."

"Any chance those in charge will remember you?" Ava asked.

Jinayca shrugged. "That really depends who is in charge. Which is also the answer to whether or not we receive a warm welcome."

"Did you ruffle feathers?" Ava asked with a smile.

Jinayca smiled back. "I was known to stand my ground when necessary."

The group continued through the town until they entered the opening in the mountain. Layla blinked at the sudden change in light, and when her eyes had adjusted, she looked up at the high tower in the center of the mountain. It was deep red and gray in color, and with at least two hundred stories, it wouldn't have looked out of place next to a skyscraper. Every ten stories, there was a large ring around the tower, with bridges connecting to places higher up in the mountain.

"What is it with dwarves and towers in mountains?" she asked Jinayca.

"We're short, and we like a view," Jinayca said.

The interior of the mountain looked like an ant nest, with dozens of tunnels winding through the stone. The smell of baking reached Layla's nose, and she turned to watch a cart being driven into the mountain and over to a large lift at the side.

"Are there lifts inside the tower?" Layla asked. There had been in the last dwarven city she'd been to, but she had no way of knowing if all dwarven architecture was the same.

"I hope so," Ava said, her expression one of complete awe. "Because I'm *not* walking up there."

They caught up with Brynhildr and entered the tower, but Layla paused. "You think Tego is okay? I don't want her to enter the village and terrify the locals . . . or worse."

"I've put word out to those living there," Brynhildr said. "They don't have saber-tooth panthers in Valhalla, so she'll be easy to spot. They'll leave her be until we return."

Layla just hoped that Tego returned the favor.

The interior of the tower was even more lavish than the exterior. The walls were the same dark red and gray, but statues of gold and silver stood all around the first floor. Tapestries hung on the walls of corridors; one of them was at least a hundred feet long and depicted a battle between the dwarves and their mortal enemies, the blood elves.

At the end of the corridor were several large lifts. Everyone climbed onto one, and Brynhildr pulled a lever, which started the ascent.

"I haven't seen any guards," Layla said. "I expected guards."

"The entrance floor is free of them," Brynhildr explained. "There are floors beneath it that serve as crypts, so the first floor is seen as a welcome to both the dead and the living."

"We did that in Nidavellir," Jinayca said. "It's a very old tradition."

Layla had noticed that Jinayca had been constantly looking around at everything since arriving at the dwarven town and almost had to force herself to keep walking instead of stopping to gaze at the statues and tapestries. She placed her hand on Jinayca's shoulder, and the dwarven elder put her own hand over Layla's, squeezing slightly. "I am fine," Jinayca said without turning around. "My people have been scattered to the winds, it seems, and made prisoners or slaves wherever they ended up. There is still the problem of the dwarves you saw as prisoners of Surtr. They will need to be found and freed."

Surtr had been a flame giant who had tried to merge two realms as a way to destroy the giants he hated. Layla and her friends had stopped it from happening, but he'd gone to Asgard instead. Layla hadn't seen him since, but when she did, there was still a level of retribution that needed to be meted out for what he'd done and the lives he'd taken.

"I promise they will," Layla said. She meant every word too. She hadn't forgotten what she'd seen in Jotunheim. She hadn't forgotten Surtr's words. He would face a reckoning.

The lift stopped. They'd covered a huge distance in a short time. Layla walked over to the exit and looked out over the bridge at a large golden arch above a tunnel. The bridge was forty feet wide, and there were railings on each side to stop people from falling off and plummeting hundreds of feet, but even so, Layla felt a sudden pang of vertigo and discovered her feet wouldn't move.

"It's very high up," Brynhildr said. "But you get used to it."

"It's not so much the height," Layla said. "It's the fact that patches of the bridge are transparent."

"Is that safe?" Ava asked.

"Yes," Brynhildr said as she strode across the bridge with Jinayca behind her, stopping every few feet to look over the side, which made Layla even more nervous.

Layla took a deep breath and walked across the bridge with her head held high. After a few steps, she felt a hand slide into hers as Ava caught up with her. "Just . . . this is weird," Ava said by way of explanation.

The group followed Brynhildr, who was talking to two guards, one of whom was staring at Jinayca.

The guard eventually walked over, removed her silver helmet, her long dark hair falling out of the bun that it had been placed in, and held out a hand in greeting. "You're Jinayca Konal. An elder, yes?"

Jinayca nodded.

"You knew my mother and father," the young dwarf said with a smile. "They spoke fondly of you."

Layla and Ava left Jinayca to talk to the guard and followed Brynhildr into the tunnel, where even more intricate decorations could be found.

At the end was a large set of metal doors. Two more guards opened the doors, allowing the group to walk into a huge room with mirrored sides. The room had a golden-and-silver roof, which depicted several dwarves overcoming a group of giants, and pillars of marble. There were several places to sit and presumably wait for the opposite set of doors to be opened.

Brynhildr took a seat, so Ava and Layla followed suit. Jinayca arrived a few minutes later.

"Why are we sitting out here?" Jinayca asked everyone.

"Waiting," Brynhildr said.

"Fuck that," Jinayca snapped, marching across the floor and shoving open the double doors by herself. Shouting quickly followed from whoever was inside the room beyond.

"I guess we're not waiting," Ava said, getting to her feet and hurrying after Jinayca.

Layla sighed and walked after them with Brynhildr beside her.

"She's not one to sit around, is she?" Brynhildr asked.

Layla shook her head.

Jinayca was already shouting at a guard inside the room, who stood in front of a male and female dwarf sitting on thrones. There were a dozen more guards dotted around the room, as well as more than one dwarf, whom Layla assumed to be advisers or at the very least people of importance. One of them, an elderly male, strode over to Jinayca and pointed a finger in her face as he shouted about how she had no right and how there was important business going on that was almost certainly not for the ears of some old maid.

She broke his finger.

A lot happened after that. The guards all drew weapons, and Jinayca removed a battle-ax and buried it in the steps that led up to the king and queen. The queen got to her feet, and silence fell inside the room. Her long red-and-orange robes flowed behind her like flames as she moved. Her hair was plaited with gems that glinted as the sunlight struck them.

It was only then that Layla noticed the dozens of dwarves at the edges of the room, in the shadows between the huge windows that looked out of the mountain and across the realm of Valhalla.

The queen crouched in front of the ax, examining it. "Jinayca?" she asked.

"Yes," Jinayca said. "Some of you might have known me as Elder Konal."

"I thought she said she'd barely be remembered," Layla whispered.

"I think she exaggerated," Ava said.

The dwarf whose finger Jinayca had broken paled significantly. He scrambled back from her, cradling his hand, but said nothing.

"You were left in Nidavellir," the king said.

"And you are?" Jinayca asked.

"I am *your* king," the dwarf said, getting to his feet.

"Not *my* king," Jinayca said. "I've been listening to stories about how the king here has known about the trouble with the Valkyries for centuries. About how he refuses to do anything to help. About how he has forbidden anyone to leave this realm to search for more of his kind. You are *no* king."

"I was the only heir," the queen said, completely ignoring her beetroot-colored king. "When we fled Nidavellir, I was but a child. My parents were never found. My brothers and sisters died getting us here, or if not, there has been no trace of them. Only one of my brothers arrived here with me, and he became king but died in a hunting accident a few decades later. I am the last of the royal line of my house. I was asked to take the throne."

"I saw *Game of Thrones*," Ava whispered, causing Layla to smile, as clearly they were thinking the same thing.

"And the one calling himself king?" Jinayca asked, nodding at the fuming dwarf.

"I am from one of the great houses of dwarven history," he snapped.

Jinayca looked around the room. "Are you *bollocks*. I've seen the markings on the soldiers in the tapestry; you're from a lesser house. You would have had maybe two seats on the council. You were rich, and so you were afforded certain privileges, but you mistake your own history if you believe you were anything other than mediocre."

"That is *my* king," the queen snapped. "It matters little who we were before the fall of our lands; it only matters who we are now."

Jinayca bowed her head slightly. "My apologies. I am angry because we were searching in Nidavellir for centuries. We have taken back our home realm. We have expelled the blood elves. And we have found thousands of our own people, who have gone back to their home. But we are not done. There are thousands more adrift in realms, and I had only hoped that wherever those dwarves were, they'd have been searching for us with everything they have."

"Our home is returned?" the queen asked, a smile on her face.

"This is Layla Cassidy," Jinayca said, motioning to Layla, who hadn't prepared herself for being involved in the conversation. She made a small waving motion. "She helped us take back our home."

"Layla," the queen said with a smile. She crossed the floor and took Layla's hands in hers. "Thank you."

"I didn't do it alone," Layla said. "There was a lot of help. Zamek was there."

At the mention of his name, the queen's eyes opened wide. "My brother is alive?"

Layla nodded. "He's fighting with us to stop Avalon. He's a great warrior, my liege."

"He always was," the queen said. "You may call me Orfeda. A friend of Zamek's is a friend of my people."

Layla noticed the expression of concern that passed between the king and the man with the broken finger. She did not like it one bit.

"We need your help," Brynhildr said. "We need your help to get to the Red Mountains to the north. You are aware of the slaves there. Well, whatever they've spent all this time searching for, they found. Hera is coming to help Rela, and whatever that means, it's bad for everyone."

"I am aware of the slaves, yes," the queen said.

"And yet they are still there," Jinayca said, her tone hard, disapproving.

"We do not have the numbers to wage war against the Valkyries," Queen Orfeda said. "Not without agreement from all the members of the council. The Valkyries are not dwarves, so the council is hesitant to involve ourselves."

Jinayca looked around the room accusingly.

"I do what I can," Queen Orfeda said. "I help who I can. I wish I could do more."

"I'm Ava Choi, and I'm really new to all this," Ava said. "But isn't stopping your people from being in chains worth fighting for?"

"We will talk in more detail," Queen Orfeda said. "Everyone leave; I wish to talk to the newcomers and decide on a strategy."

"My queen," the king said, placing a hand on her shoulder. "You can't possibly believe these . . . interlopers."

"Snagnar," Orfeda said. "Do not presume to tell me what I should and shouldn't believe. You are my king, but you are not my master."

Snagnar bowed his head and left the room along with most of the other occupants.

"Are you two married?" Ava asked.

Orfeda shook her head.

"Good. He's a dick," Layla said, more to herself than to anyone else.

"Dwarven royalty don't have to marry one another," Jinayca said. "They don't even have to have children together. They often take other lovers and have their children. It's a political thing, not a love thing."

"I have two children," Orfeda said. "Neither are Snagnar's. I believe that upsets him, as he has been unable to have children himself, despite an awful lot of trying."

"Do you trust him?" Brynhildr asked.

Orfeda nodded. "He genuinely wants to do what's best for our people. His father, the man whose finger you broke, wants to do what's best for him. He is the one that will not allow the council to agree to action against Rela. I've been having teams of dwarves rescue my people when they can, but if the council discovered that, it could make things difficult for those who follow me here. I might trust Snagnar, but I do not trust his family."

"They're working with Hera," Layla said. "At the very least with Rela."

"You have proof?" Orfeda said.

Layla shrugged. "Not so much, no."

"Then without proof, I cannot make accusations against their name. I am sorry for that. However, I believe I know what Rela and her allies are searching for."

"Zeus's spirit?" Layla asked.

Orfeda shook her head. "Not quite. Judgement. They're searching for Judgement."

"What's a Judgement?" Layla asked.

"She is not a what but a who," Orfeda said. "And she's been living in the Red Mountains for hundreds of years."

"She's Zeus's daughter, isn't she?" Irkalla asked.

Orfeda nodded.

"Hera's coming to kill another of Zeus's children," Brynhildr said. "We can't let that happen."

Orfeda laughed. "You haven't met Judgement, have you?"

Everyone shook their heads, but judging from the expression on Orfeda's face, Layla began to wonder whether she should feel a lot sorrier for Rela and her people than for Judgement.

Chapter Seventeen

Mordred

Llyn Ogwen, Wales, Earth Realm

Mordred hadn't killed Lancelot yet, which frankly he considered to be either a complete miracle or a sign of deep personal growth, although he wasn't sure which one he actually preferred.

They'd taken the helicopter to a large field a half-hour walk from the lake itself, and the slight drizzle of rain that they'd left behind in Scotland was a full-on downpour by the time they reached Wales.

"Good Welsh weather, this," Mordred said, genuinely feeling at home, while others in the group grumbled about the lack of waterproof coats. He'd loved the country as a child and had many happy memories of the place. And a lot that weren't so happy, but he did his best to ignore those for a moment.

"You've been awfully quiet the whole journey," Elaine said from beside Mordred.

"Lots going on," Mordred said, tapping his skull.

"Not even a video game hum," Elaine said.

Mordred hummed a little bit of "Zelda."

"That's sort of missing my point," Elaine said with a smile. "Why are you angry?"

"Who said I was angry?"

"Mordred." Elaine's tone suggested that playtime was over and she wanted an answer.

Mordred sighed. "It's been a long few days. A lot has happened, and I'm a bit tired."

"Why do you hate Lancelot?"

Mordred cracked his knuckles and sped up, but Elaine was soon right beside him.

"I don't think running away is going to get you out of this," Elaine said.

"I think I told you," Mordred said.

"No, you gave us perfectly valid reasons as to why you think he's a dick. But you *really* hate him. I saw the look on your face when he almost went for his sword. You would have killed him right there and then."

Mordred had wondered whether or not he was going to have to tell anyone. He started to hum the battle theme to *Final Fantasy XI*. "Later," he said softly. "Please."

Elaine nodded. "This isn't over, nephew of mine."

Mordred sighed. "Yeah, I've met you before."

He climbed over a stone fence that had long since fallen into disrepair and walked down the mud-slick slope behind it, hoping he didn't fall on his ass and embarrass himself. He smiled. That would have put the cherry on the icing.

At the bottom of the slope was a small wooden hut next to a short pier. The water looked cold and dark, and Mordred remembered the times he'd swum in it or just sat and stared at it, wondering whether or not he would ever be the man he was meant to be.

"So where do we go now?" Hel asked.

"We wait for darkness," Guinevere said. "I don't think she comes out before then."

"I assume by 'she,' you mean the Lady of the Lake, yes?" Hel asked.

Guinevere nodded. "When I was last here, her name was Nineve," she said. "She was a kind woman who helped me when I needed it. And apparently someone had her murdered for daring to stand up for what was right."

"We met once or twice. She always seemed kind. How is she going to appear here, then?" Mordred asked. "Is she a zombie or a spirit?"

"There has always been a Lady of the Lake," Guinevere said. "And there will always be one."

"Do you know this one's name?" Elaine asked.

Guinevere shook her head.

"So you can't actually be sure that anyone is here, right?" Lancelot asked. "We could all be here completely wasting our time on this little quest."

"We might as well get comfortable, then," Elaine said, pushing open the unlocked cabin door.

"Looks pretty comfortable," Hel said, peering inside at the sofa, two chairs, floor-to-ceiling bookshelves, large heater, and small stove. "Wonder who lives here."

"And why it was left unlocked," Mordred said. "Any chance we're expected?"

Guinevere shrugged. "I have no idea. Nineve said she would know when the time was right to return the sword. Maybe this is that time."

Lancelot was first through the door, practically throwing himself onto one of the chairs. "Any chance someone could make me some food?" he asked.

Mordred placed a hand on Hel's shoulder before she lost her temper. "He's not worth the hassle, trust me."

After half an hour of everyone sitting inside the hut, even with the heater on, Mordred felt that he'd rather stand in the cold and wet than spend another second with Lancelot's overpowering smugness.

"I'm going to get some air," he said, opening the door and stepping out into the driving rain. He wrapped himself in a shield of air to keep dry and walked to the end of the pier.

"You feel like talking?" Elaine asked from behind him.

"Not really," Mordred said.

"Hel fell asleep," she said.

"She's pretty good at managing to do that no matter where she is," Mordred said with a smile.

"You really love her, don't you?"

Mordred nodded. "I didn't think I deserved to be happy. But I was wrong. And stupid for thinking it."

"Are kids in the cards?"

Mordred shrugged. "I think that's a conversation for future Mordred to have."

Elaine laughed as she stood beside Mordred and looked out over the settling dusk. "You want to talk about Lancelot now?"

"He knew," Mordred said quietly. "He knew what Arthur really was."

When there was no answer, Mordred risked looking over at Elaine, who stood dumbfounded.

"I know what you're thinking," Mordred said. "*Ah, Mordred has lost his fucking mind again.* Well, I haven't. Unlike the rest of us, Lancelot fought beside Arthur in a lot of battles with Gawain. Gawain and Lancelot were instrumental in the creation of the paladins, Arthur's own personal squad of psychopaths. Lancelot knew what Arthur really was, and not only did he keep that information to himself, he also actively participated in and organized missions to remove people who were a threat. Not a threat like they were evil—that's what Merlin used Nate for—I just mean outspoken.

"When Lancelot started shagging his king's wife, he still stood beside Arthur and helped him do whatever he needed. It wasn't until he knew that Arthur had discovered where Guinevere and Lancelot were going on their nights alone that Lancelot ran. He didn't run because he'd discovered Arthur was evil and knew they were both in danger, no matter what bullshit he spouts. He ran because he's afraid of Arthur and wanted to save his own skin. He knew that if he went to me or Nate or even Galahad, it would eventually come out what Arthur was and what Lancelot did for him, and then you've got Lancelot as a war criminal. And that's his life—and, more importantly, his legacy—over."

"You really believe that?" Elaine asked after several seconds of silence.

"A few hundred years ago, I killed a paladin. Some jumped-up little prick who decided to break me out of the prison I was in just so he could murder me and say he was a hero. I kept him alive for a very long time, and he told me a lot. When Lancelot had run, the paladin had found a lot of communication between him and Arthur that he'd been ordered to destroy. Well, this idiot had decided that instead of destroying it, he'd keep it, just in case."

"You still have those documents?" Elaine asked.

Mordred nodded. "Lancelot was instrumental in Arthur gaining the power he had before I put him in a coma."

"You think Guinevere knows?"

Mordred shrugged. "No idea. I think at the time, she thought that Arthur was nothing but the great man he pretended to be. I think she didn't realize that marriage to him meant weeks alone, and I think over time she saw a side of him that she was scared of. But no, I don't think she really knew what he was. In the beginning, Lancelot was charged with keeping her company, ensuring that she didn't hear anything she wasn't supposed to. I'm pretty sure he explained anything away as her own memory playing tricks."

"He gaslighted her?" Elaine asked, the anger in her voice easy to hear.

Mordred nodded. "Pretty sure of that, yes. Certainly the idea I got from the last time I spoke to her. Every time Guinevere believed something bad was happening, Lancelot or Arthur or Gawain or Merlin would convince her that it was her own mind playing tricks. That it was her own brain at fault. She was never cruel or mean; she just believed what she was told. And I think that's what would have gotten her killed if Lancelot hadn't started sleeping with her."

"Why did Lancelot take her with him?" Elaine asked.

"He needed a hostage," Mordred said. "She was there to be an insurance policy should Arthur come after him."

"You think Guinevere knows that now and that's why she hates him?"

"It could just be that he's a prizewinning bag of dicks," Mordred said. "But Guinevere isn't stupid, or wasn't when I knew her, so I'd say it's possible she figured it out."

"And Guinevere took Excalibur," Elaine said.

"Yes, she did," Mordred said. "She knew how important it was to Arthur to keep hold of it. I don't think Arthur hunted her because he loved her and wanted her back or for retribution for her affair. He wanted Excalibur, and he wanted her dead because she took something he needed."

"And Lancelot?"

"Ah, well, his is a betrayal Arthur can't allow to go unpunished. He was one of the big boys in Arthur's group, one of the inner circle, and he shagged Arthur's wife. That needs punishing."

"If Lancelot had known about the sword?" Elaine asked.

"He'd have used it as a bargaining tool to stop Arthur from killing him."

There was clapping from the hut. "You all think so little of me, don't you?" Lancelot said.

Mordred looked back at him. "Yeah, pretty much."

A darkness flickered across Lancelot's pristine face, and he stormed over to Mordred, who didn't move an inch.

"You have *no* idea what I went through," Lancelot seethed.

"I don't care," Mordred told him. "I don't care what you went through or what a harsh life you've had. I don't care that you've been on the run for so long or that Arthur wants you dead. I. Don't. Care. If it were up to me, you'd still be in a dank cave somewhere."

"Look here, you little pissant . . . ," Lancelot said.

"That's it?" Mordred asked as Guinevere and Hel joined them on the pier. "A pissant? That's the best you can do? Well, now I feel bad for you."

"You are not worth my time," Lancelot snapped.

"And you, sir, are a hoofwanking cocksplat," Mordred said with a large smile.

Hel placed a hand over her mouth to stop herself from laughing, but Guinevere didn't bother and just howled with laughter.

"Cocksplat," she said, pointing at Lancelot. "That's your new nickname."

"Fuck you, whore," Lancelot said, his voice full of rage.

Mordred was going to punch him for that, but Elaine got there first. She grabbed Lancelot by the throat, kicked out his legs, and slammed him down hard onto the wooden pier.

"If you ever call her that in my presence again," Elaine said, her hand squeezing around his throat, "I. Will. End. You. Do you understand?"

Lancelot nodded furiously, and Elaine released him. She looked over to Guinevere. "And you, stop winding him up. You're both fucking adults; act like it for ten goddamn minutes."

Guinevere nodded an agreement. "Apologies," she said. "To all of you."

Hel shrugged and walked over to Mordred. "You good?" she asked.

Mordred nodded. "You sleep well?"

Hel smiled. "If I could only have one superpower, it would be the sleeping thing. It's just amazing."

Mordred kissed her on the lips and then turned to the lake when the sounds of splashing caught his attention.

"She's coming," Guinevere said. "Hopefully."

The water of the lake parted, revealing a set of stairs that led down to a large golden door in the lake floor. A woman walked up the stairs, her hands spread out on either side of her, controlling the water.

"The Lady of the Lake," Mordred whispered.

"That's pretty damn badass," Hel said.

The woman had fair skin and long dark hair that stretched to her waist, and she wore a shimmering blue-and-white dress that appeared to be made entirely of water.

"How did you do that?" Hel asked the woman as she stepped barefoot onto the pier.

"I'm a water elemental," the woman said, her accent firmly placing her as Welsh.

"No, with the dress," Hel said. "How is the water not . . . you know, water color?"

"Ah, it's some dye," she said. "I have a lot of time to myself these days, so I try to make new clothing out of the water itself. Wearing actual clothes feels too confining."

"You live under the lake?" Mordred asked.

"I am the lake," she said. "Well, partially the lake."

"I'm sorry," Mordred said. "I didn't ask your name. You're not the Lady of the Lake I last met."

"My mother died long ago," she said sadly. "She was betrayed by someone she trusted."

"Merlin? My father," Mordred said.

The woman nodded. "My name is Viv."

"It's a pleasure," Mordred said. He leaned toward her and whispered, "What happens now?"

"We walk down into the cave I live in," she said, "and then you undertake the trials."

"What?" Mordred began, but Viv placed a finger against his lips.

"Answers when we're not out in the open," Viv said. She looked past Mordred to Guinevere. "My mother spoke fondly of you."

"She was a good person," Guinevere said.

"That she was," Viv said.

Everyone followed her down the steps, which, despite how they'd only recently been uncovered from masses of water, weren't slippery.

Viv stopped in front of the golden door and touched it a few times in different places. There was a colossal cracking sound, and the door rolled to the side.

"Hurry now," Viv said to everyone. "Unless you want to go swimming."

The group moved into the darkness beyond the door and remained there while Viv stepped inside, and the door closed behind them. There was a sound like something smashing into the door; it echoed around the group, and then there was silence.

"Welcome to my home," Viv said.

Purple lights ignited all along a long staircase that continued down into the depths.

"It's a few minutes' walk," Viv said. "It's not much fun coming up, though, unfortunately."

No one spoke as they followed Viv down the staircase. Finally they reached a large, cavernous corridor with three arches at one end.

Mordred stood before the three archways and looked though each one. One was a library, the second was some kind of living area with a sofa, a bed, and various pieces of furniture, and the last one was in darkness.

"You'll go there in a moment," Viv said. "Everyone who isn't Mordred, please go into the living room. There's no television here, but there are books. Thousands upon thousands of books."

"How do you live down here?" Mordred asked as everyone else walked away. Hel kissed him and told him to be safe.

"I don't," she said. "Not really. I usually live in the waters above and go into the towns when I need company. This is sort of my hideaway. It's where I come to rest and recharge."

Mordred followed her into the library. "My word, that's impressive," he whispered, looking up at the thirty-foot-high shelves, each one teeming with books.

"I think I have about half a million at this point," Viv said, motioning for Mordred to take a seat at a large golden wooden table. "I started reading graphic novels a few years ago, and I've been devouring any I can find."

"I've read a few," Mordred said with a smile. "I don't understand what I'm meant to do here."

"Ah," Viv said. "I am not a full water elemental. I'm obviously a lot of one, but like my mother before me, I am more than I seem. My mother was many things—she was a summoner, an elemental, an illusionist—and while I have a little of all of those, my father was a summoner. I gained his abilities as well as my mother's."

"Who was your father?"

Viv shrugged. "No idea. It's unimportant. He didn't want to stick around, and Mum didn't particularly want him to. I've done okay without him."

"Sorry," Mordred said. "Sometimes I just say things without thinking."

"You have no need to apologize to me, Mordred," Viv said softly. "It might be me apologizing to you when this is all done."

"When what is all done?"

"The trials aren't your usual test of skill or strength. You can take no weapons with you, so if you have any, leave them on the table here."

All the weapons that Mordred had taken with him from Asgard were still on the helicopter. He hadn't seen the point in bringing them with him. "Do I have to spell the word *Jehovah* in tiles on the floor?"

Viv stared at him.

"It's from *Indiana Jones and the Last Crusade*," Mordred said. "It's a film."

"Ah, I haven't seen that one. No, nothing like that."

"Damn it," Mordred said. "I figured that was as prepared as I needed to be."

"Sorry," Viv said and laughed. "See, I told you I'd end up apologizing." Her face became more serious. "Do you know how summoners work?"

"You open portals to other realms that allow huge creatures through," Mordred said. "I've met my fair share."

"That's not all we do," Viv said. "We also open portals without the need for a realm gate. The monster thing is helpful and all, but it's not all we are. We cannot go through the portal, but someone else can."

"You're sending me through a portal?" Mordred said.

"Yes," Viv told him. "To a realm of illusion. A realm where my grandmother was born. While there, you will undergo the trials to ensure that you are fit to carry the sword. You will either come back with Excalibur or die. There's no middle ground here, Mordred."

"Here's your shield; come back with it or on it," Mordred said.

"You don't get a shield," Viv said. "Do you need a shield?"

"It's just a figure of speech," Mordred said.

Viv's eyes lit up. "I don't get to spend a lot of time with people who have figures of speech. Fish aren't known for their metaphors."

"You talk to fish?"

"You don't?"

Mordred couldn't figure out if Viv's smile was one of mockery or not, so he just shook his head. "So, this portal. What happens when I get there? Any help would be good."

"You will complete the trial. I have no idea what the trial is, apart from what I've told you. It's not of strength or skill. My mother created it to ensure that only you could retrieve the sword and that you could only do it when ready. Are you ready?"

"I bloody well hope so," Mordred said.

Viv clapped her hands together and led Mordred out of the library and under the archway into darkness. She stood under the arch, the light from outside framing her. "I hope you are the person my mother believed you to be."

"Me too," Mordred said, and the room lit up bright white and flashed, blinding him. He blinked repeatedly and dropped to his knees.

A feeling of sickness exploded inside him, and he thought he was going to vomit, but suddenly everything stopped.

He uncovered his eyes cautiously and looked around the foreign landscape. The grass was bright purple, the trees a mixture of orange and yellow, the leaves bright red. He sat back and breathed out as a leviathan—a giant sea dragon—burst forth from dark-green water. It stood a hundred feet over Mordred and looked down on him. The creature's belly was white, while its back was dark gray, giving it, in Mordred's mind, a color scheme similar to a great white shark. That did little to dampen Mordred's concern.

"Nice terrifying beast," Mordred said.

The leviathan sank back into the water until only its head was showing. "Mordred," it said, its voice booming all around.

"Hi," Mordred said. "Please don't try to eat me."

The leviathan let out a noise that might have been a laugh but also might have been a snort. "Welcome to your trial, Mordred. Welcome to what I imagine will be your hell."

Chapter Eighteen

Mordred

Realm of Illusion

"You're not exactly selling it to me," Mordred told the leviathan. "What even is this place?"

"It's the realm between realms," the leviathan said. "It's where the sea monsters live. We might end up in other realms—there are certainly enough summoners to create portals—but we come from here."

"I have questions," Mordred said. "Do I have time to ask them?"

"Time is different in this realm," the leviathan said. "You are only the second humanoid to come here. I am interested in what you have to ask."

"Who was the other humanoid?"

"Nineve came here several times. She is buried here, taken to the sea and allowed to dissipate into the oceans."

Mordred recognized what sounded like sadness in the leviathan's voice. "I'm sorry for her death."

"Thank you. Summoners are not permitted to travel through their own portals, but she came here through her mother's. It was how she created the trials."

"What are they? Sorry, before you answer that, do you have a name?"

"They call me Gray Scales. Leviathan names are somewhat literal."

"So you all speak English?"

Gray Scales laughed, and Mordred was sure that the ground shook beneath him. "You come here through the portal, and your perception changes. There is no human language here; it's all placed in your head to understand."

"Telepathy?"

"Of a kind, yes. It's how summoners and us communicate in your world too."

"So what is this test, then?"

"Trial," Gray Scales said. "I did mention it was going to be hell for you, yes?"

"Yeah, that came up," Mordred said without emotion. "What do I have to do?"

"The trial is both an illusion and real," Gray Scales said. "It's born of illusion magic. This whole realm is riddled with it. What's real and what isn't is hard to say here. Beneath the oceans are the only places safe from it."

"Does that mean that you might not be real?"

Gray Scales lifted out of the water and stopped with his head a few meters from Mordred's. He reached one massive taloned hand out of the ocean and moved it toward Mordred. The hand was the size of a bus, and each jet-black claw looked sharp enough to tear through steel. Mordred didn't move a muscle. The talon came close and lightly tapped Mordred on the nose.

"That felt pretty real," Mordred said, rubbing his nose and finding a small cut along the bridge.

"See," Gray Scale said, sinking back beneath the waves.

"So where do I go?"

Gray Scale motioned behind Mordred, who turned to look at the large cave. "A cave, seriously?"

"It's as good a place as any," Gray Scale said. "There are runes in there. Nineve placed them inside, along with what you seek."

"The runes would ensure that whatever magic Nineve placed inside stayed there, I assume?"

"I am a leviathan," Gray Scale said. "I can't even draw a rune, let alone understand one."

The ground moved again.

"What is happening here?" Mordred asked.

"Karkinos is waking up," Gray Scale said. "He does not like humanoids much. Bad experience with one in particular."

"What happens when he wakes?" Mordred asked.

"He probably won't notice you, as small as you are to him. He'll walk a short distance and sit down somewhere else. Presumably feed on some of the smaller fish. I do not think it wise to wait around."

"You said he won't notice me."

"I said probably," Gray Scale said.

Karkinos the giant crab, Mordred thought. He sighed. He knew the story of Herakles killing Karkinos as one of his labors. He knew that Karkinos had been a minion of Hera's. That didn't necessarily make it evil, but Mordred didn't want to wait around to find out either.

"How do I get back?" Mordred asked.

"I don't know," Gray Scale said. "I was never told that."

"That is superb," Mordred said with a thumbs-up.

"I like you, little sorcerer." Gray Scale laughed. "I hope you don't go mad and die."

"Very kind of you," Mordred said as Gray Scale slipped his head beneath the ocean and vanished from view.

Mordred got to his feet and set off toward the cave, but another rumble of the ground knocked him to his knees. "Just keep still for five minutes," he whispered when the shaking stopped, and he began to run toward his destination.

The cave in question was basically a giant crack in a boulder that was probably the same size as a house. Moss had grown up from the ground to cover a large portion of the boulder. Mordred squeezed through the crack and found himself in a cavern that looked much bigger on the inside than it could possibly have been on the outside.

"Hello, Mordred," a voice said, floating through the dimness of the cavern. There were dozens of torches lit up with the same purple glow that had been inside Viv's home in Wales.

Bright red and orange runes glowed on the walls, and Mordred was pretty sure that touching them would do something bad, so he made sure not to be anywhere near either side of the cavern. It wasn't a particularly difficult thing to achieve, considering its size, but it always paid to be careful.

In the center of the cavern were two chairs facing one another. One was empty, and in the other sat a woman made entirely of water. "Nineve, I assume," he said.

Nineve nodded that she was.

"I'm pretty sure you're meant to be dead," Mordred said.

"I am," she replied.

"You're a spirit?"

Nineve motioned for Mordred to take a seat. "I am one with the ocean of this realm," she said softly. "Elementals don't really die when their bodies are allowed to go back to their element. Their spirit lives on, merging with the element itself. I am lucky to have so much water to merge with."

"Congratulations," Mordred said, not really sure what else he was meant to say.

"I've waited to see you for a long time," Nineve said.

"I really don't want that sword," Mordred said.

"That's why it has to be you," Nineve said. "No one who wants power should be allowed to obtain it."

"I'm not sure that's how it works," Mordred said.

"Maybe that's how it *should* work."

Mordred shrugged. "So I have to do something hellish to get Excalibur, yes?"

Nineve nodded. "I need to make sure that you are the person I always believed you could be. That Elaine always believed you could be. I know what you were, Mordred. I know the dark path that you strode down for so long. I know that only when you have conquered that darkness will you truly be whole."

"I conquered it over ten years ago," Mordred said. "I'm not that man anymore."

"You say that, but you don't *believe* that."

Mordred had a thought. "How did you know that I would come back here? That I would need to find Excalibur?"

"Partially because I knew that when Arthur awoke, he would hunt this sword down, and he should never be allowed to obtain it again. Partially because I knew that one day you would return to us. Also because the Fates wrote a lot of prophecies over the centuries—the original Fates, I mean. And one of them concerns you."

"I learned long ago that prophecies are never all that accurate," Mordred said. "They can say one thing but miss a whole lot of the little bits. One word here or there could turn the whole meaning of the prophecy. I don't put much stock in them."

"Neither did I," Nineve said. "But then I read them. 'The hero shall arise once again, but the evil he hid from others will come forth and bring great ruin and death to the realms.'"

"Arthur?" Mordred asked.

Nineve nodded. "Could be any one of a hundred people, I guess, but this one ends with, 'and with his War, the knights of the round will either bow to their king or die by his sword.'"

"Okay, definitely Arthur," Mordred said. "Why hasn't anyone read these and told the world?"

"Merlin had them destroyed," Nineve said. "I have the only copy left. Or had, I guess."

"Any other tidbits you can remember?"

"'The rightful king shall fall to darkness. Conquest and blood shall be his currency.'"

"Me, I guess?"

Nineve nodded. "You were born to be one of the Horsemen. A new breed of Horsemen of the Apocalypse. A weapon to be used just in case. You were born to be the new Conquest. And blood . . . well, you were addicted to blood magic, yes?"

"How do you know that?"

"I had a large library of books that no one else had. Elaine used to come and sit with me."

"She knew about these prophecies?"

Nineve nodded. "She told me she would not tell you. I made her promise. Things had to be allowed to unfold at their own pace."

Mordred wasn't entirely sure he wanted to know, but he asked anyway. "Any more about me?"

"'And the king shall rise from the darkness, and he shall reclaim what was his, but if he is not ready, if he cannot defeat the darkness inside of him, all will be destroyed.'"

"Cool," Mordred said. "It's not exactly catchy, is it?"

"That's the very last prophecy," Nineve said. "We don't know what happens next."

"I go home and have a nice cup of tea?"

"I really hope that's how this ends," Nineve said sadly. "Goodbye, Mordred. Good luck."

Nineve's body vanished, leaving a puddle of water on and around the chair.

"Still not the weirdest thing to happen today," Mordred said.

The lights flickered out one at a time.

"It's getting weirder," Mordred said as the last light extinguished, leaving him in darkness.

"You really think you're going to win?" a familiar voice asked in the darkness.

Mordred took a deep breath. He now knew why Gray Scale had said this would be his hell; he knew why people kept acting as if this trial was exceptionally difficult.

"I'm not in the mood for games," Mordred said.

The lights reignited, and a copy of Mordred stood in the middle of the room.

"How very original," Mordred said to his standing copy. "I'm not going to call you Mordred; I will get confused. I'm going to call you Bacchus, because I'm pretty sure I'm absolutely off my tits at this point if I'm seeing you. Hi, Bacchus, you're looking well."

"You think that humor will win this for you?" Bacchus asked.

"You're the evil me, yes?" Mordred asked. "The one who murdered and committed atrocities for a thousand years. Well, you can fuck off."

Bacchus laughed. "Did you think it would be that easy? Did you think that I would just let you win? I am part of you, Mordred. I was a part of you for longer than you've been without me."

"I. Am. Not. You." Mordred spoke while staring at the version of him in the middle of the room, each word full of the anger he felt bubbling inside him. "You died."

Bacchus sat down opposite Mordred. "Do you remember the first time you escaped the dwarf realm? Do you remember what you did to that farmer? You slaughtered him like an animal."

"I was an animal," Mordred said softly. "That's all I was. Merlin, Gawain, Arthur, Hera, Baldr, and countless others broke me. They wanted to turn me into their weapon. They wanted me to go out and murder their enemies. My friends."

"You escaped before the brainwashing was complete, but you just wanted to murder Arthur and everyone who worked with him instead. Including Nate. Including Elaine. How many people did you kill who were your friends? Hundreds?"

"I know who I murdered," Mordred said. "I live with their deaths every day."

"Liar," Bacchus screamed. "You buried their memories deep down inside you so you don't have to deal with them. You're terrified that I'm going to come back up. That I'm going to have you murder your loved ones again. You live in fear of that happening. You haven't dealt with what you were; you've just suppressed it. You know I'm there. You know I'm just waiting. Just waiting to feel their blood on my hands."

Mordred leaped to his feet and threw a punch at Bacchus, who vanished from view. Mordred collided with the chair and fell to the floor in a heap as Bacchus appeared behind him and laughed.

"Did I touch a nerve?" Bacchus asked. "You murdered men, women, anyone in your way. You slaughtered them all like cattle."

"I was a monster," Mordred said. "I know this. I do not wish to be so again."

"And you think that Excalibur will help you?" Bacchus laughed. "Excalibur will strip away the man you've created for yourself, and the world, those you love, will see you for what you really are. A monster. A cruel and vicious murderer of the innocent."

"That wasn't me," Mordred screamed at him. "I was never that man. I never wanted to kill innocent people. I never wanted to hurt people."

"But you did."

"Because people like my father broke my goddamn mind," Mordred shouted.

"Broke it or set it free?" Bacchus asked.

Mordred rushed Bacchus, who punched Mordred in the face, knocking him to the ground. "You're weak," Bacchus said with a chuckle. "Weak and pathetic. You hold that sword, and I will come out again. Maybe I should let you have it, let you take it to Asgard. Let Hel see the kind of man you are when your lies are stripped away. Do you think she will like that, to see the real you?"

"No," Mordred whispered.

"So pathetic," Bacchus said. "You never deserved happiness; you never deserved anything. I deserve power and respect. I command it. People feared me because I was strong. No one fears you. No one respects you. You are nothing without me. I gave you everything. I *was* everything."

"No," Mordred whispered again, this time looking up at Bacchus. "You were the monster that was poured inside my brain. The monster that was removed with a bullet when Nate killed me. You are dead. You are gone."

Mordred got to his feet as a parade of dead walked between Bacchus and him, each one a life Mordred had taken. Each one someone Mordred remembered. Each one innocent.

"I remember all of you," Mordred said when the crowd of dead threatened to overwhelm him. "I am sorry. I know it was me in body, but that was not me in mind. That was not the man I am today, nor was it the man I was before I was torn asunder. I wish I could do more to make amends. I wish I could give you back the lives I took from you, but I can't. The man who took them is dead, and I hope that gives you some peace."

Several of the dead vanished.

"You can't stop what you are, Mordred," Bacchus said. "Those people might have cracked your mind like an egg, but what was inside was always the real you. The murderer. The villain."

"I am not a good guy," Mordred said. "I never suggested I was. I do not want to be king. I do not want to wield Excalibur, but I try every single day to be a better man than I was the day before. I will never stop trying. I will never stop seeking retribution for what I did. Every life I save, every person I help, is a drop in the bucket for all those I hurt, and I have to live with that every day. I accept what I did. I accept what I was."

"Still with the lies," Bacchus said. "You still think that I'm down there, don't you?"

Mordred glanced down at his now-naked torso as darkness slithered out of his chest, covering his body.

"It scares me that you might be," Mordred said. "It scares me that Excalibur might reveal that I truly am the monster I was for so long. But I have to try to stop Arthur. I have to try to stop Avalon. I have to do these things because no matter what happens to me, I cannot hide from what is happening to everyone around me. I cannot shy away from the fight that's coming. I am not you, Bacchus. I am not that man anymore."

More of the dead began to vanish.

Bacchus rushed Mordred, who batted away his weak strike and punched him in the jaw, knocking him to the cavern floor.

"You have no power here," Mordred said. "I have let you keep a piece of me for too long. I cannot live in fear of your return. I cannot allow myself to hold back against Arthur and his minions."

The dead began to vanish at a faster rate.

"But you're still scared," Bacchus said, his lip split open from Mordred's punch.

Mordred nodded. "I am. I am scared that I might use that sword and enjoy it a little too much. I'm scared that I'll use the sword and it won't help. But those are things I can fix. Those are things I can have a measure of control over. Just like you. I had no control over you for a thousand years, and now I control everything about you."

Bacchus got to his feet as the last of the dead vanished. "I am the darkness in your heart," he seethed. "You can't kill me."

Mordred drove a blade of light into Bacchus's heart. "Wanna bet?"

Bacchus vanished from view, and Mordred dropped to his knees and wept. He wept for all those lives he'd taken; he wept for all the lost time he'd spent hurting people instead of helping them. He wept for the past and the future, the uncertainty that was to come. But most of all, he wept in relief. Tears spilled down his face at the relief of knowing that he could defeat any evil inside him, that he wasn't destined to become the thing he feared and hated the most.

"You have come a long way," Nineve said from behind Mordred.

"I'd have preferred it if I'd just had to pick the right cup," Mordred told her.

"I don't understand the reference," Nineve said.

Mordred laughed. "Your daughter said the same thing."

"Are you okay?"

Mordred nodded. "Maybe. I don't know. I don't know what happens next; I don't know how to get home; I don't know how to get off this crab. I'm a little freaked out that I'm on top of a giant crab."

"You are a good man, Mordred," Nineve said. "It's about time you believed it too. You were made not just to be a weapon or a deterrent but also to kill Arthur."

"What?" Mordred asked.

"The Horsemen were designed to ensure that should the previous devils ever appear, you would be their equal in power. You were literally born to kill Arthur."

The cave vanished, and Mordred found himself ankle deep in clear water. In front of him a crab the size of the Wembley Stadium walked across the ocean. It snatched up what looked like a large fish and started to eat before continuing on.

"How did we get here?" Mordred asked.

"This is the shallows," Nineve said. "The crab is one of the few places where you can put a cave."

"Neither of those answer my question."

"Maybe it doesn't need answering," Nineve said slyly.

"This whole place is really quite strange," Mordred said.

"You get used to it," Nineve said. "Or not. It's hard to say."

"So why am I here?"

Nineve pointed behind Mordred. In a stone a few feet away was Excalibur.

"You're really going to make me pull it out of a stone?" Mordred asked.

"It's traditional," Nineve said. "Also, only you can remove it. I wanted to put it somewhere no one else could get it. So I took it to a realm no one can get to and put it in a rune-marked rock no one can break. It's probably the most secure place in any realm."

"This isn't a real realm, is it?"

"Oh, it is," Nineve said. "Very real."

"I didn't like my meeting with Bacchus," Mordred said.

"You weren't meant to," Nineve told him.

"I thought he would have offered me power, but he didn't."

"That would have been the moment the illusion broke," Nineve said. "The darkness in you didn't want to offer you power; it wanted to replace you. You knew this."

Mordred nodded. "I did. The old me wasn't about power; it was about retribution and pain. It was about only those things. Power was just a side effect."

"You fell in love once. You had a child."

Mordred nodded again. "I did. Both were taken from me in one way or another, due to my actions. Bacchus didn't show me either of them."

"Because that was a time when the hold on your heart was weakest."

Mordred placed his hand on the hilt of Excalibur. "How do I get back home?"

"Draw the sword, and all will be revealed."

Mordred took a deep breath and drew Excalibur from the rock. He held it aloft and turned to Nineve, who passed him a blue-and-gold sheath. "Good luck, King Mordred."

"Not king," Mordred said. "Just Mordred."

Nineve clicked her fingers, and the world went white. The last words that Mordred heard were, "We'll see."

Chapter Nineteen

Nate Garrett

British Columbia, Canada, Earth Realm

The drive from Kilnhurst to our destination at Lake Louise in British Columbia had taken the better part of a day, and while I'd sat there and digested the memories of both Masako and Atlas, it hadn't seemed like anyone else was all that talkative. Even Remy, who usually couldn't be silenced with superglue and a roll of gaffer tape, had been quiet. A quiet Remy concerned me. Unfortunately, after absorbing all of the information in my head, and with my body adjusting to the vast amounts of power it had taken from the spirits, I'd needed to sleep, so I'd drifted off for several hours.

I woke up as we reached the outskirts of what used to be the town of Claresholm and was now a giant ruin. Avalon forces had taken the city nearly a year ago and decimated it, along with the several other towns in Canada where Hades had been influential. Avalon had left it a ghost town on purpose, never allowing anyone to come back here. From what I'd heard, Avalon had arrived at Calgary and Edmonton and told those in charge that they now fell under Avalon control. Claresholm had been used as an example to ensure that everyone else bowed as necessary. Avalon had gone through Canada and done similar things in any towns where they'd decided dissidents could be lurking.

"The city was on fire for months," Sky said from the front seat.

"It wasn't the most fun thing ever," Remy said.

Kase drove, while Zamek sat in the rear seat of the seven-seat four-wheel drive, leaving just Remy and me in the middle seats.

"You okay?" I asked him.

"Glorious," Remy said with a wink.

"Remy, no bullshit," I said. "What's wrong? And don't say nothing, because even I'm capable of figuring out that *something* is wrong."

"He won't say," Zamek said. "We've been asking. He just says he'll be okay. He is being stubborn."

"Or maybe I really *will* be okay," Remy said. He paused for a second and then sighed. "I change powers every time I die."

"Seriously?" Kase asked.

Remy nodded. "I spent a year learning how it works. Every time I die, I get a different set of powers. Unfortunately, I have no way of knowing what powers they are or how they work. It took me centuries to even learn that I had extra powers at all, and now I'm back to square one. No turning human. No vanishing in a puff of smoke. So yes, I'm a bit irritated about it. Frankly, this fucking well sucks massive balls."

"Nice image," Sky said.

"I could use more adjectives if you'd like," Remy replied. "Also, I'm a bit pissed off that War caught me. I was of no use, and I almost got Nate killed because of it."

"I think you're being too hard on yourself," I said. "I think the past few days have been hard on everyone. Don't worry, Remy. It's fine."

"And I liked Masako," Remy continued. "She was weird. I sort of gravitate toward weird people. I mean, look who I'm sharing a car with."

"Point taken, sweary Robin Hood," Sky said with a smile.

"You were Robin Hood?" Zamek asked. "The thief?"

Remy rolled his eyes.

"It's a film," Sky explained. "A cartoon fox based on the old myth."

"Ah," Zamek said. "Yes, that would look quite a lot like Remy. Does Robin Hood in the film also tell people to fuck off or call them cockwombles a lot?"

Sky laughed so hard she had to wind the window down to get some air.

"Disney films aren't known for their use of that term, no," I said to Zamek, who nodded as if given some incredibly sage information.

"Fucking weirdos," Remy said with a smile. "The whole bloody lot of you."

"So you finally able to answer questions, Nate?" Sky asked after several seconds of silence.

I nodded. "Just thinking about Atlas and sorting out the mass of information in his mind. About Hera and whether or not she's as safe in London as she thinks. The Aeneid isn't a fortress."

The Aeneid was one of the tallest buildings in London and had once been home to the king of London, Brutus, before he'd been brutally murdered by allies of Arthur and Hera. Hera had done well from his death and been given London to govern. London had been a neutral city, like most capital cities, ensuring that Avalon didn't control everything. That was before Arthur had taken control, and I wasn't sure what cities were still neutral. London certainly wasn't. For hundreds of years, Brutus as king had ensured that any nonhuman matters in London had been dealt with, allowing the humans to govern themselves without interference. I was pretty sure that was no longer the case.

"Hera has a cure," I said softly. "Atlas thought that War knew where it was. It's what he was looking into before . . . before they caught him. I also know that War is certainly working for Hera and that Rasputin knows about this poison. Hera was looking for it before the First World War, and Rasputin had something to do with it. He was working with War to find it or something. I just . . . it's all jumbled up in here." I tapped the side of my head. "They really screwed Atlas's mind up."

"And Rasputin?" Kase asked.

"I passed him over to Hades," I said. "He was talking about a War, but he was scared, and I didn't think he meant War as a person. I didn't want to be the one who took all of the information from him. I needed him to trust me, not confess to me. I was meant to go with him to New York, but I actually left him with Hades in London."

"And no one noticed that he was talking about a person called War?" Sky asked. "That sounds like something my dad would have looked into. I interviewed Rasputin myself. He never mentioned a person by that name."

"He clammed up," I said. "Don't know why, but he did. I wish I'd asked him more about War; I wish I'd been less concerned with my own life and where it was going."

"So Rasputin was useless?" Remy asked.

Sky shook her head. "He gave us information about the First World War, about Hera's plans for Europe. We managed to save lives, and the war ended a good five years before she wanted it to. But he never mentioned a person with the name of War. He also refused to be given a new identity and life."

"What?" I asked.

"I know. It's true, though," Sky said. "I was the one who spoke to him about it. He just said he wouldn't be safe anywhere except a secure facility. He said he'd ruined his life betraying Hera."

"So you locked him in a prison?" Remy asked.

"It is a *very* nice prison," Sky said. "But essentially, yes. You should know that Pandora, or should I say Hope, is in the same facility."

Fanfuckingtastic. "Anyone else there?" I asked.

"A few, but they're the two famous ones," Sky said. "Most of the others are nonvoluntary residents. There's a Gorgon who can't stop turning people to stone and a particularly nasty manticore. There are about three dozen residents in all, about three of which won't kill you on sight."

"How many guards?"

"Few dozen," Sky said. "Melinoe is in charge."

"And she is?" Zamek said.

"Melinoe is my sister," Sky said. "She's an earth elemental, with a little bit of necromancy thrown in for good measure. She can screw around with a person's spirit; it has some weird effects on people. Mostly nightmares or acting like they've had a stroke, but I once saw her turn someone into a drooling, gibbering wreck who tried to eat his own face."

"So she one of the good guys, or is she batshit crazy?" Remy asked.

"She's one of the good ones," Sky said. "She wanted to join in the war, but our parents told her she was better off staying here and keeping the people safe from a breakout of superpowered monsters."

"Smart move," Remy said. "So we're heading to this prison?"

"Yes," I said. "It's about two hours north of here in the middle of nowhere."

"Mum and Dad were concerned that Avalon would find it," Sky said. "But it's so far out of the way that they'd have to have an actual map to discover it. And even then it's pretty much invisible to anyone who isn't meant to find it. My dad paid enchanters a lot of money to ensure this place remained off the map. And just to make sure, he had telepaths remove the location from their minds."

"And we're going to get Rasputin out of it?" Kase asked.

"We're going to ask him very nicely if he'd like to help," Sky said.

"And if he says no?" Zamek asked.

"I don't plan on giving him the option to," I told him. "Rasputin knows more about War, so he's our next target. Atlas had a conversation with War about Rasputin, about how they worked together."

"Are we going to go to London?" Zamek asked.

"If that's where the cure is, yes," I said. "Hopefully Rasputin either knows where it is or can point us in the right direction."

"You know the second we step foot in that city, we're all dead?" Remy asked. "Hera will throw everything she has at you to make sure you don't leave in one piece."

"We need to make sure that we're going to the right place. Hera and I were going to clash at some point," I said. "Might as well make it over something worthwhile. Besides, I don't plan on just walking up to the Aeneid and knocking on the front door."

"You plan to get killed before that bit?" Remy asked with a smile.

"You perked up," I told him.

After a few more hours of driving, we reached the outskirts of Calgary, and everyone in the car became a little uneasy, as the obvious Avalon influence was clear as day. Among the police, there were also ITF vehicles. The Inter-species Task Force was essentially made up of humans who'd decided to help Avalon by unleashing their need to be complete assholes. They might as well have been wearing brown suits and goose-stepping. In fact, a few I'd met had actually had Nazi symbology emblazoned on their body. They'd made more than a few people disappear for being dissident voices. I would give exactly zero fucks if the entire ITF was shot into space.

Thankfully humanity as a whole was now on to Avalon and Arthur, seeing them for who they really were: an invading force. The ITF was still being forceful, but it couldn't be everywhere, so protests and riots still broke out.

There were checkpoints in the heart of the city, so Kase kept to the speed limits and went around the outside of Calgary, where the tension was still evident. Every time we drove past an ITF patrol, I saw her knuckles get whiter as she held the steering wheel harder.

Sky reached over and placed a hand on Kase's arm. "I know," she said.

"Why aren't there checkpoints between the US and Canada?" I asked. "I figured the ITF would be all over that. And I don't remember seeing any."

"And why would this prison still be here, so close to Avalon-controlled territory?" Zamek asked.

"The latter is because no one outside of a few people know it's there," Sky said. "It's protected by runes and illusion spells. Trust me—that prison would be safe if it was in the middle of the city."

"And the borders?" Remy asked again.

"We drove through a border checkpoint while you were asleep," Kase said to me. "The people there aren't ITF. They're just normal checkpoint patrols who happen to have worked for Hades for a long time. The ITF doesn't have the man power to take control of them all, so a lot of the border work is still done by people who used to do it. And my dad managed to put a few of his people in strategic points over the years."

"It meant going out of our way a little to get to the right checkpoint, but it was worth it," Sky said.

Once outside the city limits, Kase put her foot down. I'd asked why we hadn't just flown, but apparently we would have needed to wait a day for our Montana team to arrange a helicopter, and honestly, I'd have rather just taken the fifteen-hour drive.

Eventually, and after a lot of driving down dirt roads that did not look like they were made for the speed Kase drove, we arrived at a small stone beach. Kase parked the car, and we all got out.

"Wow," Zamek said as we surveyed the beauty that was Lake Louise and the surrounding forest and mountain range. The water was clear, and there was snow on the ground that crunched underfoot. Slightly farther up the river was a small red wooden hut.

"You ever been here before?" Remy asked me.

"No," I said. "I thought it best to stay away from the facility here. Just in case I piss off anyone I've actually put here."

"Like Rasputin?" Remy asked.

"Hera did not take his leaving well," Sky said. "She had hit squads after him. We moved him here because no one knows this place exists. It's not even on the list of official Avalon facilities. It's privately owned, privately funded, and safe."

"There's no one around here," Kase said, taking in deep breaths. "We weren't followed. That I can tell, anyway."

"Lead on," I said to Sky, who nodded and started walking across the beach to a section of bank that appeared to consist primarily of large gray rocks.

Zamek watched with interest as she placed a hand on one of the rocks, and the entire front of the sandbank moved aside, revealing a moving walkway beyond.

"That was different," Remy said as we stepped onto the walkway. The wall behind us closed.

"Impressive rune work," Zamek said.

"It's one of three entrances," Sky said. "One is on the other side of the lake and is similar to this. And the last one is in the mountains, and I'd rather not use it."

"Why?" Kase asked.

"It's a helicopter ride up there," Sky said. "Melinoe doesn't like people using it without forewarning. It's meant to be for emergencies only."

The journey took half an hour, but it was nice to know someone wasn't going to try to kill us all while we were unknown feet under a mountain range. The lighting was dim, and every few minutes we passed a small phone placed against the concrete wall of the tunnel. Presumably in case someone broke down. I quickly stopped thinking about it; breaking down under here would not be my idea of fun.

Eventually the walkway slowed, and the sounds of voices could be heard ahead.

"Do they know we're coming?" I asked.

"No," Sky said. "I don't know who is monitoring what messaging services, so I figured it best to not chance it."

"Do you and your sister get on?" Remy asked.

Sky smiled as the walkway came to a stop, and she talked to the four armed guards standing in front of a large metal-and-glass door.

I heard my name mentioned at least twice but didn't want to eavesdrop, so I took a seat on one of two orange sofas inside a waiting room adjacent to where Sky was. We'd all been in there for about a minute when she appeared in the doorway.

"Let's go," she said.

We followed her along a short corridor and into a lift. After a short wait, we were heading up.

The doors opened on a landing with domed windows in a semicircle all around it.

"Holy shit," Kase said.

"This is some James Bond–villain-level stuff," Remy said.

I couldn't disagree. The building was perched on the side of a mountain. The beach we'd arrived at couldn't even be seen in the distance. I wasn't sure how this was done, although sure enough Zamek wasted no time in examining every metal beam, pane of glass, and faintly glowing rune.

"We're invisible," he said excitedly.

"Yes," Melinoe said from the entrance to the landing. "This whole place is invisible to the outside. The facility uses similar technology to that of the rocks on the beach you used to enter. Hello, sister." Melinoe and Sky hugged. Melinoe was about my height, with olive skin and long black hair.

"Nate," Melinoe said, offering me a hand, which I shook.

"It's been a while," I said.

"I spoke to my mum. I'm sorry about your father. If there's anything we can do to help, we will."

"Rasputin," I said. "He has information we need. Or at least I hope he does."

"We'll prepare the facility for you to see him."

"How does this place work?" Zamek asked.

"Each resident here has their own quarters, depending on their needs. The humanoid members have a home, a garden, and even an artificial lake set within the mountain."

"How?" Kase asked.

"Dwarves," Remy said. "It has got to be dwarves."

Zamek looked very proud about that.

"Shadow elves and dwarves, we believe," Melinoe said. "The mountain range here is large, so the facility is able to spread out. We use walkways to get around. We can change the speed of them, so they can go as slow as the one you arrived on or faster than anyone could drive."

"And the nonhumanoids?" Remy asked.

"They are confined to their own quarters separate from the others," Melinoe said. "They require a more . . . *specialized* way of being dealt with. Some of them can be vicious even when perfectly calm."

"Shall we?" Kase asked.

Melinoe nodded. "You can't all come to see Rasputin at once. I would suggest that Remy, Zamek, and Sky stay with us, and we'll show you around the facility."

"Sounds good to me," Zamek said as we followed Melinoe outside the domed area and onto a large helipad.

"We're in a base in a mountain," Remy said. "I'm pretty sure Tommy would have a Star Wars reference right now."

I smiled. "We'll bring him back here when he's better. He can pretend he's on Hoth."

"You know the names of the planets?" Remy asked with a chuckle.

"I have seen those films a lot," I said. "I'm pretty sure Tommy quizzed me at one point. You might have noticed that he's a massive geek."

Remy chuckled and placed a paw-like hand on mine. "We'll get him back to his old self. Your dad too. And Frigg. Looks like there's a lot of people who need this cure. I'm sure we'll find it, Nate."

I looked up at the morning sky. It was overcast, and snow was beginning to fall, landing on the invisible dome high above us. "I really hope so," I said.

Chapter Twenty

Nate Garrett

While the facility itself was an incredible piece of technological and architectural genius, I wasn't there for a sightseeing tour, so Melinoe took Kase and me on another moving walkway farther into the facility.

The end of the walkway led to a bridge that sat between two mountain peaks over a fall of several hundred feet. I walked along it as quickly as possible without looking down. I might not have had the fear of heights I'd once had, but that didn't mean I enjoyed having nothing directly beneath my feet.

It wasn't long afterward that we left the walkway, walked through a guard checkpoint, and were taken to Rasputin's accommodation. Each resident had a glass front wall so that they could be seen, although it was usually activated from the inside so as to not disrupt their privacy. With the right combination on the keypad next to the door, the window was turned from a picture of a landscape to a view of the interior of the apartment.

Rasputin sat on a chair, watching TV. He wore a red silk dressing gown and was smoking a cigarette. His beard was now a neat goatee, and his hair had been cut shorter, but other than that he still looked the same. He glanced over at the now see-through window and then did a double take when he noticed me.

"Nate Garrett?" Rasputin asked, putting out his cigarette and getting to his feet. "As I live and breathe."

"Rasputin," I said. "We need to talk."

Rasputin laughed. "You had a chance to talk to me all those years ago. Instead, I was passed around and ended up here. Did you know they have to fly in prostitutes once a month? It's degrading."

"For them or you?" Kase asked.

"Who's the woman?" Rasputin asked.

"This is Thomas Carpenter's daughter," Melinoe said. "I suggest you be on your best behavior when they come in."

"I remember Thomas," Rasputin said. "I liked him. Come in."

He touched the panel on the wall, and the door slid open.

"I'll leave you to talk," Melinoe said. "If you need anything, the guards are close by. Hit one of the red buttons inside the house, and they'll come running."

"Exactly what am I going to do to Death himself?" Rasputin asked.

I didn't even try to hide the shock on my face.

"Yes, that's right, Nate: I know who you are. One of the Horsemen. I assume you've finally met War, and that's why you're back."

"Why didn't you say something?" I asked.

"I didn't know who to trust," Rasputin said.

"That's a lie," I said. "The real reason. I assume it's the same reason you didn't mention War to Sky and Hades and why you haven't spoken about this venom."

Rasputin motioned for me to take a seat. I sighed but took the offered chair.

"I guess the truth is needed here," Rasputin said. "I figured that eventually you'd be back here having met War, that you'd figure out that I was talking about a person and not an act. That I kept that information from everyone after you handed me over." He took a seat opposite me. "It's all linked to why I didn't want the new identity, to why I practically begged them to bring me here."

I waited for him to explain, and when he didn't, I said, "Okay, get on with it."

"Sorry," Rasputin said. "There's a lot to say."

"I don't have a lot of time to hear it all."

"When you passed me over to Hades in London, I was taken aboard a ship set for New York. On board that ship, I was attacked by a man who was pretending to work for Hades. Hades stopped him just when he was about to kill me, but before the man died, he whispered, 'No matter where you go, the Horsemen will find you.' Obviously it frightened me. I decided it best to keep my mouth shut about you and War and anything to do with the Horsemen. I spoke about Hera's plans for Europe, and I requested to be put here under twenty-four-hour protection."

"So you kept this information to yourself to save your own neck?"

"Of course," Rasputin said. "I figured if I didn't mention the Horsemen, didn't mention that you were Death, that War was . . . War, Mordred was Conquest . . . if I kept my goddamn mouth shut, maybe War wouldn't try to find me. Maybe Hera wouldn't try to find me."

"And the others?" I asked. "You know about all of the Horsemen?"

Rasputin nodded. "I know of them, but not necessarily where they are. I am sorry for not telling you. I considered it many times, but I guess I was afraid of what might happen next."

"And this venom that War used on my father?" I snapped. "On my best friend? Did you know about that?"

"What venom?"

Kase had been quiet for several seconds, and I felt the anger radiate off her. "The venom that almost killed my dad," she said.

Rasputin poured himself a large brandy. "Let's talk out back. It's more secluded."

We followed Rasputin to the rear of the apartment, where the lake sat. It wasn't really a lake. It was just another piece of domed glass over a cascading swimming pool, but with the mountains in the distance, it looked lakelike. Also, the swimming pool was about two hundred feet long. And separated at the end with a large wall that I assumed stopped neighbors from interacting.

"So you can't just mingle with your neighbors?" I asked.

"No, this part is mine and mine alone. Hope is around here somewhere. We all get together once a month to talk and not be so miserable. I see a few other residents on a weekly basis to play chess or cards and drink good wine. We are well treated here. And we cannot be overheard."

"My father has been poisoned by the same substance that hurt Frigg," I said. "It almost killed Tommy. Do you know what it is and where the cure is?"

Rasputin shook his head. "No, I'm sorry. I don't. Or rather, I know what was used on Frigg, and if it's the same stuff, you have a problem on your hands, but I do not know where exactly it is created or where a cure might be found."

"What *do* you know?" Kase asked.

Rasputin sat down on a wooden chair. "It's called Pestilence venom. Mostly because it literally comes from someone named Pestilence. A woman. Same as you and War and Mordred."

Kase breathed out slowly before walking to the edge of the garden and sitting down.

"You ever seen this venom in person?" I asked.

He nodded. "Once. It's bad, Nate. I know that during my time working for Hera, she spent an ungodly amount of time and effort to find Pestilence. She wanted to weaponize her. It had been done before, and Frigg had paid the price, but Pestilence vanished soon after, and from what I hear, Hera hadn't been happy about that at all."

"But you don't know where she is now?" Kase asked. "Or where Hera might have gotten the venom?"

Rasputin shook his head. "However, I do have a theory. And I know of someone who might be able to give you more information."

"Your theory?" I asked.

"Hera spent a lot of time and money trying to overthrow Brutus in London."

"I just thought she wanted London," I said. "I thought that was why she had involved herself in his murder."

"Hera is never that simple. She plays the long game. You know that."

"So Hera might really have this cure and Pestilence?" Kase asked.

"I believe that Hera succeeded in her aim to overthrow Brutus and now controls London, yes?" Rasputin said.

"You're kept informed."

Rasputin nodded. "It's one of the ways they like to ensure that no one feels like they've been left behind. Lots of socializing and reading. Keeps the mind stimulated."

"But not *too* stimulated."

He smiled. "Like I said, it's a theory, but I do know someone who might have more information about it. A few people, actually. Like the people who worked for Hades."

"Diana?" I asked. "She would have mentioned something."

"Or?" Rasputin asked.

"Pandora," I said, "sorry, Hope, is here."

"That's not a coincidence, is it?" Kase asked.

"Hope has a habit of being in the right place when she wants something," Rasputin said.

I really hadn't wanted to have a conversation with Hope, but it looked like I was out of options, although while I had Rasputin's attention, I figured I'd get some more information. "And War?" I asked. "What can you tell me about him?"

"He's a monster. A sorcerer of some kind or another, but he's also got the powers of an elemental."

That explained how he could use both air and earth. "I've seen his abilities up close."

"Well, he's also got a few powers close to what Ares had. Manipulation of anger and hate, the ability to feed off them to make himself stronger and heal faster. He's named War for a reason. A reason, I think, that Ares always resented. I think that's why Hera kept War in another realm for nearly his entire life."

Kase turned back to us. "That's a lie," she said.

"I assure you it is not," Rasputin said, unhappy that he'd been accused of something.

"There's some truth there," Kase said, getting to her feet. "But that's not the *whole* truth, is it? I can smell it on you. I can hear the subtle change of your heartbeat. You lied. I want to know why."

"Can you believe her?" Rasputin asked me.

"Yes," I said. "I would tell her the truth."

"You'd let her hurt me?" Rasputin asked as Kase took a step toward us.

I leaned in to him. "In a heartbeat," I whispered, never breaking eye contact.

"It's not relevant to your mission to get a cure," he stammered.

"The truth, Rasputin," I said. "Now."

"War was in the other realms, hunting down anyone who Zeus was the parent of. It took him a long time, seeing as how Zeus fathered about a hundred kids. Most no one knows about. Most didn't even know they were the child of Zeus. There's a daughter of Zeus and the Lady of the Lake. She's like you. Like War. Her name is Judgement. She might have an actual name, but that's how Hera spoke of her."

"And you didn't want to tell us this because . . . ?" Kase asked.

Rasputin sighed. "It was my job to help War find targets. Before I was sent to infiltrate Russian royalty, I helped War find people to murder. I traveled the realms to find them. With War. He was not a fun traveling partner. I am sorry that I didn't tell you about the Horsemen."

"You helped War murder people," Kase said with a shake of her head.

"I am not a saint, girl," Rasputin snapped, leaning forward toward Kase. "We've all done our share of bad things. We've all got blood on our hands. Maybe you haven't because you're a child, but I know Nate has."

I nodded. "Doesn't make it right, though."

Rasputin sighed again and sagged back into the chair. "No," he said. "No, it doesn't."

I looked over at Kase. "Don't kill him. I'll be back."

I walked to the door and tapped one of the buttons to alert the guard, and I was surprised to find that it was Melinoe who answered.

"You want to see Hope, don't you?" she asked.

"Yes."

"You want to take her out of this facility too."

"I'm leaning toward it."

"I contacted my father on the off chance you'd say that while you were here. He says you're a fucking idiot."

"I can't disagree."

"My mother used harsher language."

"Still not disagreeing," I said with a slight smile. "Hope might be able to help us get to the cure. Or at least she'll be a distraction so we can do so. And she wants Hera dead more than anyone I've ever met."

"I know," Melinoe said with a slight nod. "Doesn't mean it isn't stupid."

"Can I see her?"

"Yes," Melinoe said. "You know if I allow you to take her, I'll be aiding the release of someone who has tried to murder a vast number of people over the centuries."

"I never said it would be an easy choice. To be honest, I don't want her to come with us. I don't want her involved. But if Hope knows where the cure is—and from what Rasputin said, it's likely to be in London, and Hera has it—then this is our chance to get rid of Hera. To liberate London from her influence and to hopefully gain some ground against Avalon on the Earth realm. All three of those things need to happen if we're going to win."

"And you think that Hope is going to help you and not run off at the first chance she gets to kill Hera?"

"No idea," I admitted. "Honestly, neither option sounds all that bad at the moment. I literally only thought about talking to Hope when I arrived here. Thus ends the extent of my plans. So far I'm up to 'Find cure; heal Odin, Tommy, and Frigg.' Everything else is a bit hazy."

"You're going to go to war with Hera just to heal your dad."

"I would go to war with whatever god someone put in my way to save a person I loved," I told her. "Hera, Arthur, Merlin—I don't give a shit. They're in my way. They either move or die. And this is my father we're talking about. I would scorch the goddamn realms to save him."

"Will Kase be okay in there?"

I turned back and found that Kase was sitting next to Rasputin, talking. "She won't kill him if he behaves," I told Melinoe.

"That's good enough, I guess," Melinoe said before leading me to Hope's apartment, which was only a short walk from Rasputin's.

I tapped on the door, and the glass became translucent. Hope appeared on the other side of the glass wall. She'd cut her hair short and dyed it silver, but she still looked the same as when I'd last seen her. She wore a purple T-shirt with several Disney characters on it, a few of which I didn't recognize, and blue jeans. She was barefoot, and she sighed as she saw me.

Hope and I went back a long way together. She used to be Pandora, a demon who had been forced into her body by Zeus, Hera, and several of the other Olympians during the Titan Wars thousands of years ago. The demon, or whatever it really was, had taken control of Hope and decimated cities for the Titans. Hades had eventually stopped her, sealing her inside a prison and telling the other Olympians that they must never release her again. That had lasted a few hundred years before she'd escaped. And thus the cycle had repeated itself over and over again throughout the centuries. She'd escape, kill a lot of people, start a war or two, try to kill Hera or someone else involved with her, and then get caught.

The last time she'd escaped, Hope had finally revealed that she'd been in control of her own mind for a long time. Pandora was gone, but her power remained. And Hope was someone who had an even bigger grudge against the people who had destroyed her life than Pandora had.

"Nate," Hope said. "It's been a while."

"Hope," I said. "Pandora gone for good, then?"

Hope nodded. "Just me and my broken brain. You look tired."

"It's been a long few days. Can I come in and talk?"

Hope looked over at the door. "No. You put me in here. You stopped me from killing Hera and her cohorts. You stopped me from gaining vengeance."

"You would have killed a lot of innocent people," I said. "I couldn't let it happen. Hera's death would have started a civil war among her people. It would have spilled out into whole countries."

"So why are you here?" Hope asked. "You come to gloat?"

"No, I want to know about the Pestilence venom," I said. "Rasputin said you might know a few things. And I'm going to take a guess that you didn't end up here by accident, yes?"

Hope smiled. "I knew that at some point in the future you would want to discuss Hera with me. And I thought that being close to Rasputin would help. A touch here and there, and people just want to help me out."

"Why not escape?"

"Because if I escape, you track me down and stop me from killing Hera. Again. I thought it better to just sit this one out. And then Arthur woke up, and I *really* didn't want all of Avalon chasing me around, so here I am."

"Why not tell me about Pestilence?"

"Because information is leverage," Hope said. "And I thought that it would be better to keep that information to myself until needed."

"The Aeneid," I said. "Pestilence is there?"

Hope nodded. "There's a bit more to it than that."

"I would get on with it, then," I said.

"And what do I get out of divulging all of my secrets to you?" Hope asked. "A nicer prison? A massage once a week? You want to know what I know; I want to know what you're going to give me."

"People are hurt," I said.

"How sad," Hope said. "Now, what do I get out of helping you?"

"You get another shot at killing Hera," I said.

Hope's eyes widened in shock. "What?"

"Back then, killing Hera would have disabled countries; a lot of people would have died from the infighting of her family to take control. I want them all dead, Hope. Hera and anyone helping her stay in power. They broke the world. They lied and used everyone who trusted Avalon to be a beacon of good, and they fucked over everyone who ever stood against the darkness that Hera represented. The whole thing was one long con job. London is under Hera's control. I aim to correct that."

Hope's grin went from ear to ear. "You had me at 'killing Hera.'"

Chapter Twenty-One

Nate Garrett

Hope opened the door and motioned for me to come inside. The room looked very different from the lavish stylings of Rasputin's. Hope was clearly not someone who needed a lot of stuff. Apart from a table, a few sofas, and some almost overflowing bookshelves, she didn't have much in the way of clutter.

I took a seat, and Hope sat opposite me, the oak coffee table between us.

"Why do you need me?" Hope asked.

I explained about Tommy, Odin, and Frigg.

"I'm sorry for your friend and father," Hope said. "I am a little surprised that Odin turned out to be Daddy. Didn't see that one coming, to be honest."

"You and me both," I said.

"I'm also sorry I tried to kill the woman you love. I mean that. I was only interested in vengeance, and I'm sorry I put you in that position. I hope she's okay."

That was unexpected. "She's good, thank you," I said. "I've just become a dad for the first time."

Hope clapped her hands together. "Congratulations. I see why you want Hera and her people dealt with before they decide to get to you through your child. You know that Hera will come after it."

"Yes," I said darkly. "I know. But this is about the cure."

Hope nodded. "I was a guest of Brutus's for several decades, and in that time I lived alone in the Aeneid on the top floor."

"I was there," I said impatiently.

"Are you going to keep interrupting, or are you going to let me get on with it?"

"Sorry," I said.

"Thank you. Now, while I was there, Brutus used to come and see me. We used to talk. I got the feeling that I was one of the few people in the world he could talk to without fear of betrayal or judging. And he told me a story about Pestilence.

"Pestilence was not a cruel woman. She was not mean or vicious; she just wanted to live her life and be left alone. But she had this power to create poisons and venom from her body. She could decide whether or not to activate it, but essentially she was one walking, talking toxic disaster. Her blood could be used to create a potent venom called Pestilence venom. She allowed her blood to be taken by someone she trusted, namely Merlin. Pestilence was under the impression that the venom was to be examined and mixed with the blood of sorcerers to create something that could cure many illnesses. He lied to her. Mixing it with sorcerers' blood makes it exceptionally potent.

"I don't know if Merlin used it or it was stolen by Hera, but either way, it ended up on Baldr's knife and was used to try and kill Frigg. Pestilence found out and fled to Brutus, seeking shelter from the horrors that could be done in her name if more of her venom was created. No one in Brutus's employ knew of her existence. She was kept on a floor below mine, behind several doors locked with a variety of particularly nasty runes. Runes that only Brutus had the key to disarm."

"So Diana and the others didn't know?" I asked.

Hope shook her head. "No one knew. No one was allowed to know. Actually, that's not true—there were staff members who tended to Pestilence. Who brought her food and helped clean her apartment inside the Aeneid. But Brutus trusted them; I don't know why. I don't think it's important. They were human, I think. I think they believed that they were just doing a cleaning job once a week for a poor shut-in."

"Did you ever meet her?"

"Pestilence?" Hope asked. "Brutus brought her to me on several occasions. I tried my power on her once, to touch her and get her to do my bidding, but she laughed at me. She was a kind woman. I did not know until speaking to her that she was your sister. Of a kind, anyway. Rasputin knew. He knew about the Horsemen. Knew you were Death, which made sense when I thought about it."

"What happened to Pestilence?" I asked.

"Ah, well, I escaped before I could find out. But my guess is that she's still in that tower."

"Which Hera controls."

"Yes."

"Then why hasn't Hera just flooded her enemies with this venom? I've seen what this stuff does to the strongest of us; it would kill millions. Hera wouldn't bat an eye."

"She can't," Hope said. "It doesn't work like that. Either Pestilence has to want to turn her blood to poison, and the last I heard she wouldn't do that for Hera in a million years, or it has to be taken by force, and if that happens, then anyone in a certain radius of it being taken is going to die horribly."

"So Pestilence is in London? And whatever is happening, it's unlikely that she's a willing participant."

"Yes to both."

"If Hera has access to lots of this venom, then she's not done using it."

"Or she has access to very little, and that's why she hasn't used it as much as you'd expect. She needs time to get more."

I rubbed my eyes. Hera wouldn't mind waiting a long time if it meant getting more venom.

"You want me to assassinate Hera?" Hope asked. "I could see if I can find some explosives and level the whole building."

"No," I said. "There will be no innocent deaths. None, Hope. The ITF run London. I want you to put a dent in their control."

Hope laughed. "You want me to make them kill one another. Just the bad ones, I know. I can tell the difference just by touching someone, remember. I know all of their dirty little nasty secrets. Remember Germany?"

"Yes," I said. The memory was not a particularly good one.

"Why are you doing this?" Hope asked. "You can't possibly trust me. I know you want your father cured, but I don't exactly have a history of doing as I'm told."

"Hera and a lot of the other Olympians fucked you over all those millennia ago. You've spent your whole life seeking retribution for that. Maybe it's time to actually get it. And if you work with me, you'll get it. I trust that you want Hera's head. I trust that you're smart enough to know that if you rush her alone, you'll die. You work with me, she dies."

"Your plan needs some finessing," she said.

I nodded. "I know. I'm sort of doing this on the fly at the moment. I think there's a better chance of achieving our aims if we work together."

"And Hades has agreed?"

I shrugged. "Not asked him yet. Hope, I'm sorry that all of this happened to you. I'm sorry you got your life ruined because Zeus,

Hera, and the others wanted to create their very own weapon. I'm sorry you've spent your entire life full of rage and hate and that Pandora was in control for so much of it. I'm just sorry. You've lashed out at everyone and everything over the centuries. I'd like to think that actually giving you the chance to finally get your wish would mean that you'd work with me. I want to trust you on this. You're not Pandora. You're not some force of nature who only wants death and chaos."

"Although I do love chaos," Hope said with a small grin.

"Then aim it at the right people."

"If you can promise me I'll get to do that, I'll help you."

"Thank you," I said, getting to my feet. "One thing, though."

Hope nodded.

"I know you liked to play games in the past. I was never sure how much of it was Pandora and how much of it was you. I really hope this time you can see that playing games is a bad idea, but just in case you're thinking of it, let me spell something out for you. If you cost me the chance to get the cure, I will bury you in a pit so deep you'll have to evolve wings to get out."

"What a way with words," Hope said with a smile. "You know why I never killed you?"

"You tried to," I pointed out.

"No, I knew you'd survive. I just wanted you out of the way or busy with something else. No, I never actually tried to kill you. Not properly. I like you. That's why. Pandora did too. She thought you were kind to her when so many others were not, and I feel the same way. You don't have to threaten me to behave, Nate. We both know that you'd just kill me and be done with it. I'll behave because I don't really have many friends. I do have one request, though, if I do this."

"Name it."

"You visit me. You've been screwed over by as many people as I was. You and those like you were created to be weapons. To be a nuclear option when everything else goes to shit. We have that in common, Nate. You are one of the few people who understand what it's like to have no control over anything that's happened to you. That regaining some measure of control can be both infuriating and painful. I do this, you come visit and talk to me about your life, about the world out there. That's all I want."

I offered her my hand without needing to think for one second about the bargain I was making. "Deal," I said. "No more threats, no more lies and bullshit, from either of us. You say we're friends, then that's my price for friendship."

Hope nodded and shook my hand. "Also, I think Rasputin will want to come."

"What makes you say that?"

"Just a hunch. Go ask him."

"I'll talk to him."

"No matter, he'll agree."

"You already put the idea in his head?"

"About a year ago," she said with a smile. "Should he be asked to help kill Hera and leave this place to do so, his first request will be to get my help. Then he'll agree to help himself. His reasons will be real."

"I can't take someone who has been brainwashed into coming with me."

"Not brainwashed," Hope said. "I don't like that term. He wants to go; he just needed a shove in the right direction. He wants to make amends, to be free of the Sword of Damocles, but he's terrified of what happens to him when he gets back onto Hera's radar. Some people are incapable of being brave. I think Rasputin needs this as much as I do."

"I'll see what I can do," I told Hope and left the apartment. Outside I found Melinoe and three guards.

"She's going with you, then?" Melinoe asked.

"I need to ask Rasputin too," I said.

"Oh, he's already asked to leave with you. I granted it. He's not a prisoner here, except for his own safety. Hope, however, is one of the most dangerous people on the planet. Actually, on any realm. Ever. I hope you know what you're doing."

I nodded. "Me too. She needs closure."

"She wants Hera dead, and I'm pretty sure she'll be willing to do anything to get that result. I would not trust Pandora, but Hope? Well, Hope is a completely different beast. What did she want in return?"

"Me to visit her," I said.

Melinoe laughed. "You'll bring her back here, or you'll track her down when she escapes. Once she's out, she's your problem. I assume you'll be going to the UK now?"

I nodded. "Any idea how I can get there?"

"Helicopter from here to Vancouver. There will be a modified Black Hawk to take you to New York, where you'll get on a private jet to Southampton Airport in the UK."

"Your dad's, I assume?"

"I can still pull a few strings in his name." Melinoe turned to watch Hope as she poured herself a glass of wine and raised a toast to all of us outside. "I'll tell her, get her ready to leave, and meet you outside in an hour."

"Thank you for this."

"You really think you can save Odin?"

I nodded. "Frigg, Odin, and anyone else who Hera is planning to poison with her toxin. It sounds like she can't have access to a lot, but that's not something I'd bet much money on. She needs to be stopped. If she does have more and she's planning something with it, letting it out in a populated area could create an epidemic. Whether or not I was here to save my dad, this is no longer just about him. There's more at stake. Hera needs to be removed as a piece from Arthur's board."

"Not just Hera," Melinoe said. "If you get her, you've got to get Demeter, Aphrodite, Ares's living kids, Dionysus, and everyone else who is working with her. This will have to be a mass extermination. And there's not enough of you to do that alone."

"I know. We need help. I just don't know where I'm going to get it yet." I left Melinoe and her people to sort out Hope and made my way back to the main entrance of the facility, wondering if I'd made a huge mistake.

By the time I'd reached the entrance and rejoined Sky, Zamek, and Remy, I was working out how to tell them the news about our new allies. Kase and Rasputin joined us shortly after, which was when I started to tell everyone that Hope would be tagging along.

"We're doing what?" Remy asked when I was done. "Did you hit your head on the way there?"

"We need to take out Hera and everyone helping her," I said. "We can't do that with the five of us. Six, with Rasputin." I looked at him. "You sure you're okay coming? You weren't mad keen earlier."

"I want my freedom," Rasputin said. "I want out of having to always look over my shoulder. I want to atone for what I've done, and I hope that those two things are linked. Without Hera and her people around, I have no reason to be afraid that she'll find me. I don't want to live with that fear anymore."

"So we're going to England?" Zamek asked. "I assume we will be killed on sight."

"We're going to Southampton," I said. "I'm hoping there are some things at my old house that might be of use."

"The house that blew up?" Remy asked. "There wasn't a whole lot left when I last saw it."

"I'll just have to see when I get there," I said.

"Nate, you sure about this?" Sky asked as Melinoe and three armed guards brought Hope toward us.

"This is kind of like that bit in *Silence of the Lambs*," Kase said. "Except her face isn't covered because she doesn't eat people . . . that we know of."

"Nate, does she eat people?" Zamek asked.

"I have never known her to eat people," I said.

Melinoe stopped in front of us with Hope smiling alongside. "Here's your new terrible idea," Melinoe said.

"I will be back once this is done," Hope said with a smile. "Please do keep my apartment clean for me."

"I'm not your maid," Melinoe said.

"Yet here we are," Hope said as her smile grew.

"Oh, this is going to be awesome," Sky said with every piece of sarcasm that she could muster.

Melinoe raised one of Hope's hands, showing the small beaded bracelet on it. The runes carved into it ensured that she couldn't use her powers to influence or force people to do as she wished. They'd tried sorcerers' bands on her over the centuries, but she just wore them out. The beads were harder to make, but they worked for longer.

"I am fine with wearing these," Hope told me. "I would rather everyone be comfortable. But once we land in England, I want them removed."

"Sure," I said.

"You have a few hours to think of a plan," she told me.

"Storming the gates of Hera's hideout not the plan?" Remy asked. "I'm quite disappointed about that."

"I have missed you, foxman," Hope said.

"I would like to say the same, but frankly you scare the living piss out of me," Remy said.

Hope laughed, and the guards took her away to the helicopter.

"Do you actually have any idea what we're going to do next?" Sky asked me. "Once we get to England, I mean?"

"We're going to get help," I said. "I need to talk to a few people and put things in motion. That's what the flight is hopefully for. We can't just march into London, but we do have other ways to get in. We just need to make a few stops along the way."

"I hope whatever you have planned works, Nate," Melinoe said. "I hope you don't get yourself killed doing this."

"Thanks for your help," Sky said.

"You need to come by more often, sis," Melinoe said, giving her sister a hug. "We don't do family reunions, and I'm busy with this place, but it would be nice to see you once the war is done."

Everyone said their goodbyes, leaving me for last as they all went to get on the helicopter.

"Keep my sister safe," Melinoe said. "And the rest of you, but mostly her."

"She's one of the most powerful necromancers on the planet," I said. "I don't think she's the one you need to worry about."

"I know, but she's my little sister, so I worry nonetheless." Melinoe shook my hand. "Go kill that bitch, kill her friends, her family, and everyone else who helped to keep her in power. Everyone who turned a blind eye to her murders, her tortures, her utter fuckery. Sky said you were born to be Death. Well, I expect you to live up to that name. Salt the earth. Ensure nothing can grow there again."

"Hera's spent a lifetime coming for me," I said. "Coming for my family. My friends. The people I love. I know that Astrid will be next on her list, and Selene, and anyone else she can use to get to me. This is the last time she does any of that."

I left the facility and climbed into the Black Hawk, and we were soon away, soaring over the landscape at speeds a normal

Black Hawk couldn't hope to match. One of the benefits of giving humans the technology that Avalon had already achieved a generation ago.

After landing in New York, we switched to a private jet and took off again. A few hours later we landed in Southampton.

The desk at the airport passed me the keys for a Mustang that had been booked for me on the journey here and an SUV for everyone else.

"This where we split up?" Sky asked.

"I'll meet you at the village of Ellesborough in six hours," I said. "That should give us enough time to both get there. Hope, you're coming with me. I don't want you to run off. Rasputin, behave."

"Now, where am I going to run off to?" Rasputin asked with indignation.

"I'm coming with you," Kase said to me. "Don't argue."

"Sounds fair," I told her.

"You still haven't told us the plan," Remy pointed out. "I think that might help."

"I'll tell you all at Ellesborough," I said.

"Ellesborough is where the prime minister's country estate is," Sky said. "Or near it."

"We're going to pay her a visit," I said. "From what I understand, she's not too keen on Hera and Avalon either. But I need to go see an old friend first."

The group split up, and I drove the black Mustang to the New Forest, feeling strange as memories flickered into my mind. Memories of my living here, of having my home built here, of this place being important to me.

I pulled up in the driveway of my ruined home and felt a surge of anger and sadness at the destroyed and now overgrown building. It had been only a few years, but it was all it had needed. I parked the car and got out as the English weather welcomed me home by starting to rain heavily.

"Why are we here?" Kase asked.

"This was your home, Nathan?" Hope asked. "No one should lose their home like this."

"It wasn't my best day ever," I said. I walked over to the remains of my house and around to the rear of the property, where there had once been a garden, which had long since lost the war to the weeds.

A man sat on a chair in the middle of the garden. He had long dark hair, which matched his long beard. Scars covered his bare arms, which were each about the size of a tree trunk. He smoked a cigar, and the raindrops fizzled and turned to steam as they hit him.

"Nate Garrett," he said, getting to his feet. "You called. I guess you want information on Hera and her people."

"I know you," Kase said. "My dad met with you about a year ago to get information on Arthur."

"Hephaestus," Hope said, completely emotionless.

"Pandora," Hephaestus replied.

"Not anymore," Hope told him.

"You going to behave?" I asked her. "This is important."

"If it means killing Hera, I'll be as quiet as a mouse," she said. "Hephaestus wasn't involved in my creation; he gets to live."

"How gracious," Hephaestus said. "Is this going to be a problem?"

I looked back at Hope, who had taken a seat on a small mound of rubble. "I really hope not."

Hephaestus nodded. "Well, you need to talk to my associate here." He picked up a rock and threw it at a nearby tree.

A woman stepped out from behind the tree. She was, by anyone's standards, beautiful. Mostly because she was a succubus, and when she switched on her power, there were very few people who wouldn't fall for her charms.

She walked over, her gaze never leaving mine, letting me see the fear in her eyes. I wondered if she'd ever been afraid before. If she'd been afraid of Ares. I wondered when she'd decided to betray her entire way of life. And why she would ever want to do so. I wondered a lot of things, but none of them really mattered if she could get me what I wanted.

"Nate," she said, her voice almost musical.

I turned back to Hope to see her standing, rage radiating from her.

"Aphrodite," I said. "I killed your husband. And your son too."

Aphrodite nodded.

"I plan on killing anyone else who gets in my way," I said.

"I should kill you," Hope said.

"Not today," I told her. "You're here because if you want Hera, you leave Aphrodite be."

"That's the deal," Aphrodite said. "I don't want to be looking over my shoulder for the rest of my life."

"Hera needs to be stopped," Hope said, returning to her seat. "I shall play nice."

"Hera killed Phobos for disappointing her," Aphrodite said. "Made me watch because she feels I'm not as loyal as I could be. You killed Ares and Deimos in self-defense, or at least in combat. You killed them because of the awful things they'd done to you. I can understand that."

"You did a lot of awful things for Avalon," Kase said.

"Yes, I did," Aphrodite said. "I won't apologize for them. I just want out. Hera murdered her own grandson because of some perceived slight. She's losing her mind. I need you to stop her."

Hephaestus blew out a smoke ring. "I know what you're thinking," he said. "You're thinking this is bullshit, but it's not. Hera's paranoia is becoming stronger the longer she knows you're back. I've moved my family away. I'm not sure I'll ever see them again after this. You murdered Hera's favorite son and grandson, and she wants revenge above all else. She can't let it go. She can't understand how anyone she considered beneath her would be able to hurt her so badly. But if you kill her, there will be a power vacuum. The humans in charge need to be prepared to take back control of their country from the monsters who run it."

"The prime minister," I said. "I had planned to go see her and hopefully figure out if she can help."

"They have her family at Chequers," Aphrodite said. "She either obeys, or they kill her children. Hera has always been a big fan of that threat."

"Not just Hera," I said. "Demeter and Dionysus—neither of them can take over. This is a complete destruction of Hera's power structure."

"Dionysus is still there," Hephaestus said. "By his mother's side like a dutiful little suck-up. Demeter is in another realm. I have no idea where."

"Why not go to Arthur? Or Merlin?" Kase asked.

"They don't care about what Hera does," Hephaestus said. "They're too busy wanting to win this war against you people, and once they're done, Hera will be given more power, more control, and with it will come more paranoia. If we don't leave, eventually Hera will turn on us too. This is our only chance to escape."

I looked between the two of them. "This will leave you with nothing."

Aphrodite and Hephaestus shared a glance. "No, not nothing," Hephaestus said. "It will leave us alive."

Chapter Twenty-Two

Layla Cassidy

Realm of Valhalla

The war discussions had lasted long into the night, and more than once Layla had gotten into a shouting argument with a dwarf about how she was going to help the people of Valhalla with or without the dwarven military assistance. One young dwarf, who was probably a hundred years old, had called her a little girl, so she'd broken his nose.

She'd expected to be in trouble for that, but everyone had seemed genuinely happy about it, and after that, the talks had descended into celebratory drinking.

As the sunlight broke through the windows of the carriage she was in, Layla still wasn't entirely sure how the evening had gone from all of them arguing over every little thing to everyone sharpening their axes.

"I can't believe you broke that pompous little shit's nose," Jinayca said with a smile.

"You know him?"

"Knew his father. Also a pompous little shit."

Layla couldn't help but smile. "So we're really going to do this?" She looked out of the carriage window at the hundreds of identical carriages that stretched back beyond the horizon. Hundreds more dwarves continued on through the mountain itself, as apparently it was quicker for them to just dig their own tunnels, but it was too dangerous for nondwarves to be there. Layla thought that allowing only the dwarves to go on through their own tunnels had been a concession from the queen to her king and his allies, who still didn't seem happy about aiding the interlopers.

Layla was more surprised that the king and his allies seemed almost uninterested in helping the dwarven slaves being forced to work near the mountain. The queen had assured them that they were just concerned about leaving themselves and their people open to retaliation from Rela's Valkyries, but Layla thought there was more to it than that. She didn't trust, if not the king, then certainly his father and allies. And if the rumors were true that those within the dwarven hierarchy were helping Rela to keep slaves, then she expected some kind of betrayal before the fighting was done. A fact that she'd told Brynhildr.

"How long before we get there?" Brynhildr asked.

"Couple of hours now," Jinayca said.

"What happens when Rela finds out that we're doing this?" Layla asked. "Skost said that Rela would attack the human town if she thought she needed to."

"The humans will have to stand up for themselves if it comes to that," Jinayca said. "We can't be in two places at once."

"You think they will?" Layla asked. "Stand up for themselves, I mean?"

Brynhildr nodded. "I certainly hope so, but if not, Skost and the Valkyries loyal to her are still there. If Rela does try to do anything to the town in response, they'll hopefully give us the time we need to get there and help."

"That's a lot of 'hopefully,'" Layla said.

"Sometimes in war that's all you've got," Jinayca told her. "And it never stops being awful."

"Is this how it normally feels on the way to a war?" Ava asked.

"No, it's not normally done in such comfort," Brynhildr admitted.

"So what about the other problem?" Layla asked. "About a possible betrayal from the king?"

Brynhildr shook her head. "I expect something too. The king's people gave in too readily after holding out for so long. Some of the dwarves are still slaves, and the king's allies know this. Information kept from the dwarves at large and the queen in particular."

"Because she'd have gone to war to save them?" Ava asked.

"Yes," Brynhildr said.

"You think the queen knows?" Layla asked.

Brynhildr moved her hand from side to side. "I wouldn't put it past her. I don't think she believes the king will do anything. I think she genuinely believes he wants to do what's right for his people. I'm more pragmatic in my distrust of those in charge. Just keep an eye on those allied to the king, and we'll be fine. Should something happen, we'll deal with it, but no use in causing dissension before we have to."

Layla caught a glimpse of Tego sprinting between the trees. She'd stayed out of the dwarven city but had caught up with them the second they'd left. Layla wondered if Tego would be able to maintain that level of speed for the entire duration but quickly decided it was possible. She appeared to have boundless energy levels and could run for miles without rest. Layla had spent a few hours riding Tego around the forest that surrounded the village, just to get used to the idea. Tego hadn't been against it, and by the end Layla had enjoyed herself.

When they finally arrived, Layla got out of the carriage and was met by Irkalla, who looked tired. Chloe sat on top of a large boulder, looking peaceful, and Layla didn't want to disturb her, but Chloe spotted her and waved her over.

"So what happened?" Chloe asked.

"We found some dwarves," Layla said. "A lot of dwarves. They're going to help us. Most of them are, anyway. There are a few I don't trust. The king and his advisers, mostly. I get the feeling that they're less than thrilled about all of this. Everyone okay?"

Chloe nodded. "We managed to get about a tenth of the people from the woods here, but we marched all day and night to do it. The rest are still at the forest, after scouts said that there isn't a huge force here."

"We're going to scout," Irkalla said to Layla as she joined them. "Want to come?"

"You don't need rest?" Layla asked.

"I'm okay," Irkalla said. "I have enough spirits inside me that they're essentially the magical equivalent of shots of caffeine at the moment."

The trek through the dense forest took an hour, and Tego joined them after half of it.

Irkalla reached the edge of the forest and looked down on the massive operation happening in the distance. It was about a kilometer from where they stood to the huge crack in the mountain. A city of stone buildings sat on the opposite side of a stream that flowed down from the mountain range.

"The winter snow hasn't come this far yet," Irkalla said. "That should make things easier for us."

"What are they doing?" Layla asked.

"I don't know. I can't see anyone there," Irkalla said. "My concern is that the enemy is hiding in the houses of that village, waiting for us."

"That's a flying horse," Layla said. "They have Pegasus. Pegasuses. Whatever the plural of that particular type of flying horse is."

"I think they're just called flying horses," Irkalla said. "Pegasus was one particular horse."

Layla scanned the mountain but saw nothing particularly concerning. "I expected there to be more guards."

"They're probably inside. I think that over there is Empress Rela's personal carriage," said Irkalla.

"It's made of gold, I think, so probably," said Layla. "You think we can do this?"

"Take back a mountain? Sure. Overthrow a corrupt and evil government hell bent on subjugating its own people for nefarious purposes? Maybe. It's sort of what we're already trying to do."

"How long have you wanted to say 'nefarious purposes'?" Layla said.

Irkalla smiled. "It was fun to say, I'll admit."

Layla looked back over at the mountain but saw nothing happening. An uneasy feeling began in the pit of her stomach. "A lot of people are going to die here today."

"Watch your surroundings," Irkalla said. "Keep yourself safe. Keep those near you safe. We've been in bigger battles. We've won. We can win this too."

"You sure?"

Irkalla nodded. "We don't have a choice."

"And then when we're done, we get to go back to Asgard and do it all again."

Irkalla rested a hand on Layla's shoulder. "Some days are better than others. These are hard times, Layla. But once we're done, we can hopefully have some measure of peace."

Layla nodded. "I know. I don't mind the fighting. I don't mind the war. I just want it done. I just want to feel like I don't need to fight for my life every. Single. Day. It's exhausting."

"After a hundred years or so, you get used to it," Irkalla said.

"Really?"

Irkalla nodded. "Sadly, yes. The trick is to never give in to the baser instincts. We can win this war, but we need to be able to look at ourselves in the mirror when it's done. Or at least I do. But then, I have morals that are probably more skewed toward burning the whole lot of them to ash than most people."

The pair made their way back through the forest, only to find that the majority of the carriages had now arrived.

As the rest of the dwarves began to arrive, more and more of them took up residence in a nearby cave, although a number spilled out into the forest, where they made small camps. Layla walked around one of the small camps closest to the forest and found herself passing the king, the adviser whose finger Jinayca had broken, and the young dwarf whom Layla had punched.

"You're an umbra, yes?" the king asked before Layla could get away.

Layla nodded. "Yes."

"Your Majesty," the elderly dwarf said.

"Your Majesty," Layla repeated, managing not to add a few other words into the mix.

"When this is done and we have saved these people, what will happen to the dwarves who call this place home?" the king asked.

"I don't know. I assume you'll either stay here or go back to whatever realm you want to go to." Layla wasn't entirely sure where this was going.

"You know we created your kind," the elderly adviser said.

"Humans?" Layla asked. "Pretty sure you didn't."

"Umbra," the dwarf snapped.

"I know," Layla said. "One of the spirits bonded to me lived in Nidavellir. She saw the dwarves work with the sun elves to butcher her people."

The elderly dwarf went pink with anger. "Are you accusing dwarves of working with our enemies?" he demanded to know.

"Yes," Layla said. "I am one hundred percent saying that. I've seen it. I've had dwarves admit to me that it happened. Zamek was less than thrilled to discover that his own people were involved in what happened to the humans who lived there. And less than thrilled to discover that the sun elves were working with them. Apparently the sun elves were also instrumental in the fall of your realm. I think if we dug hard enough, we'd find that they were involved in a whole bunch of things that we're currently dealing with. Shame no one knows where they are. Honestly, I hope they stay missing; they're a complication we can deal with another time."

"They have much to answer for," the king said. "I will let my people go if they wish."

"Very generous of you," Layla said sarcastically. She'd been surprised that the king and his advisers had left the dwarven city at all, but they'd actually been quite keen to come. Layla presumed it was so that they could make out that the king was some big conquering hero who helped liberate any dwarven slaves from the empress.

"It is," the king said, having taken no notice of the tone Layla had used. "I am a generous king. I want for little, but when this is over, I think it will be time for me to talk to those in power of the other dwarven realms and stake my claim to rule them all. One king over all dwarves yet again."

"How very Sauron of you," Layla said.

"What does that mean?" the adviser asked.

"It means all-seeing," Layla said, trying not to smile at the lie.

"I am very Sauron," the king said.

"I have to prepare for battle," Layla said.

"You may leave," the king said with a wave of his hand.

Layla walked away, trying very hard not to laugh the whole time. She found Jinayca talking to Brynhildr.

"Your king is surrounded by fucking idiots," Layla said.

"You're not wrong," Brynhildr said as Tego padded out from behind a rock, wearing her full armor.

Layla was about to reply when there was a huge noise from over near the mountains. Layla climbed up onto Tego, and the panther took off at a full sprint.

Layla reached the edge of the forest and dismounted, only to find Chloe already there.

"The entire opening of the mountain collapsed," Chloe said. "My guess—and I've never met the man, so I'm not entirely sure, but—I doubt that Zeus's crypt is booby trap–free."

"Or someone else collapsed it to make sure people couldn't get inside," Layla said.

"That means someone is down there who is hopefully on our side."

It took a few hours to get everyone from the caves to the front of the forest. Large numbers were on horseback—or in Layla's case riding a half-ton saber-tooth panther. She wore her usual leather armor but had been given a matching helm, the top of which glowed deep green as the runes went to work. Jinayca had told her it would take one full shot from an ax or sword, but after that it wouldn't be able to deflect anything with so much power.

Orfeda rode up beside Layla on a massive white-and-gray horse. She wore silver-and-black battle armor that gleamed even in the darkness.

"You're going to be a target," Layla told her.

"Good," she said. "I am their queen. I will lead the way."

"And your king?"

Orfeda pointed farther down the line. He rode an equally large black horse, his metal armor matching it in color. "Snagnar is ready for war," she assured Layla. "He will not falter. He is not a coward, but more importantly, he would not wish for anyone to see him as a coward."

"Glad to hear it," Layla said. "You notice anything weird about what's down there now?"

Orfeda shook her head and then paused. "There are no more flying horses."

"There are no more anything," Layla said. "Something strange is happening."

Layla rode Tego along the tree line to where Irkalla, Chloe, and an exceptionally nervous-looking Ava sat.

"You see it too?" Irkalla asked.

"Ava, it'll be okay," Chloe told her. "You're doing exactly zero fighting. We're going to use the cover of battle to get you into that mountain. You will be safe. I promise."

"The front of the mountain fell down," Ava said, as if no one else had noticed it.

"We'll figure that bit out soon," Layla said. "You're staying here with Chloe until we can clear out whoever is down there. Like Chloe said, you'll be safe." Turning to Irkalla, Layla said, "I think the soldiers there have gone."

"Let's go find out," Irkalla said.

A few hundred dwarves and Valkyries rode out of the forest. It was tentative at first, and Brynhildr caught up with Layla to ride beside her. "Something is off here," she said. "I wasn't expecting tens of thousands of people, but I was expecting someone."

They reached the massive excavation site, where Layla climbed down from Tego and looked over the huge drop from where she stood to the makeshift village fifty feet below. There were bodies littered all over the ground. Hundreds of them.

Layla pulled the metal out of the ground around her, creating a platform that she stood on and used to lower herself to the ground. She walked among the dead as Irkalla and the others used the ramp a short distance away to join her. By the time they'd reached Layla, she stood atop a huge pit at the rear of the village, which had been concealed from view from the forest they'd been hiding in. There were many more bodies inside.

"Attacked and executed," Brynhildr said. "Most of these were humans who had gone missing over the last few years or had been conscripted to help with Rela's war effort. There are some Valkyries among their number, though."

"Not conscripted," Irkalla said. "Slaves. Prisoners used as slaves. They've all been dead for a few days now."

"Why kill them all?" one of the dwarves asked softly.

"They finished what they were brought here to do," Irkalla said.

"We will search for any survivors," Orfeda said. "Go to the mountain."

Layla and the others made their way to the mountain, where they met up with Chloe and Ava. The rockslide had all but covered the mouth that had been dug out.

Jinayca placed her hands against the mass of rock and tried to use her alchemy to move it aside, but nothing happened.

"There's no getting in there," Irkalla said.

Layla looked back at the loss of life. "All of this, for what? What were they searching for?"

"Hello?" someone shouted from inside the mountain, the sound traveling through the small gaps between the huge slabs of stone. "Can you hear us?"

"Who are you?" Jinayca asked.

"We're dwarves," they said. "There's a few dozen feet of rock blocking the entrance."

"Why is my alchemy not working?" Jinayca asked.

"This whole mountain is anathema to magic," the dwarf inside the mountain shouted.

"Who murdered everyone out here?" Chloe asked.

"What?" the dwarf asked. "We've been in here for two weeks without sunlight. We're forced to work further in the mountain, and we only came to the entrance when we felt it shaking. What do you mean? Everyone is dead?"

"At least two days," Irkalla said.

"We didn't know. I'm sorry. We were not permitted to leave the mountain, only to keep working. Our alchemy doesn't work, so it's all done by hand and pickax."

"Is there another way into the mountain?" Layla asked. "We need to know what Rela is searching for. We think it's Zeus's burial chamber. Have you found anything like that?"

"Why do you want Zeus's burial chamber?" the dwarf asked.

Layla moved away from the entrance, and Jinayca and Chloe followed. "Do we tell them about Zeus's child? They might trust us. They might know another entrance."

"We don't really have a lot to lose at the moment," Chloe said. "Whoever killed those people is going to come back when they discover the rockslide."

"Have you noticed that only part of the mountain fell down? And only on the inside, covering just enough to stop people getting in or out," Layla said.

"Someone did this by design," Jinayca said.

Layla walked back over to the mountain. "You still there?" she asked.

"Yes," the dwarf said.

"We're looking for Zeus's burial chamber because we think we can contact his spirit and find out where his daughter is. We need to find her before Hera does. Rela is working for or with Hera, and we think they're here to find his burial chamber too."

"They are," the voice said. "I'd step back a bit."

Everyone did as they were asked, and the rockslide moved aside, merging with the mountain once again. A dozen dwarves stood inside the mouth of the mountain, and behind them was a hooded figure, its arms stretched out to push the rock away.

"How'd you do that?" Jinayca asked. "I thought this place is anathema to magic."

"It is to most," the hooded figure said, throwing back the hood to reveal a woman with white hair and eyes that appeared to be pools of dark-blue water. They occasionally rippled from the middle outward, which Layla found to be both hypnotic and a little disconcerting.

"I'm Layla," she said, offering her hand to the young woman.

The woman looked at the outstretched hand and then back up to Layla. "You said you were looking for Zeus's child. Well, congratulations, you found me. My name is Judgement, I caused that rockslide, and you're all in deep shit."

Chapter Twenty-Three

Layla Cassidy

The dwarves all scattered back inside the mountain when Layla said that their people had come to rescue them.

"It was dwarves who betrayed them," Judgement said. "They sent their own people here as slaves to die for Rela. You can understand their distrust."

"Do you live in the mountain?" Irkalla asked as Jinayca walked away with murder on her face.

"Go after her," Layla said to Chloe, who nodded and rushed to stop Jinayca from doing anything rash.

"No," Judgement said. "I live *on* the mountain. I come and go as I please. I like to visit my father's tomb. I never really knew him when he was alive, and I came here looking for answers about a century ago and just decided to stay. I got to watch as Rela brought people here to excavate the mountain, but unless you're of Zeus's blood, your magic doesn't work in here."

"That would explain why you could do the rock-moving thing," Layla said.

"I'm a sorcerer," Judgement said. "I'm not really good with people, though, so this has all been a lot to take in. The dwarves knew I was here; I would occasionally remove someone who was cruel to them, have them die in an accident of some kind, but I just kept myself out of it. They dug in completely the wrong direction from where Zeus is buried, and everything was good."

"What changed?" Brynhildr asked.

"Hera turned up," Judgement said, with real hatred in her words. "The murderer of my father. It would be better if you spoke to him."

Jinayca returned with Chloe. "Where are the dwarven slaves?" Jinayca demanded to know.

"They went that way," Judgement said, pointing to a tunnel that led down beneath the mountain. "There are a few hundred down there. I assume the queen didn't believe you."

"She wants proof to show to her king," Jinayca said. "And when I have it, I'm going to cut his fucking head off."

"Never saw the king bring them," Judgement said. "I used to sit on top of the mountain—there's a pass up there—and watch as dwarves were brought here. Unconscious, shackled, and always brought by the same two dwarves. An older pair, both male, both paid well. The dwarves told me that one was an aide to the king's father."

"I need to free them," Jinayca said.

"Good, they deserve to be free. I know the queen helped break out several dozen humans over the years, but the dwarves were always kept inside the mountain. I don't even think anyone knew they were gone. Most were drunks, petty criminals, people who were too low class to be concerned with. Everyone should be concerned with."

"We were expecting a battle," Brynhildr said.

"Most of Rela's forces pulled out a few days ago," Judgement said. "Obviously, they butchered everyone first. I tracked them as far as I could without being seen, and it looks like they've set up a defense around the palace. I don't know what they're planning there, but if Rela is involved, it isn't good. On the plus side, it won't be long, and you'll get your war. So—you were looking for me because Hera wants to find me."

Irkalla nodded. "That's what we heard."

"I'm one of the Horsemen," Judgement said. "I assume you know of Mordred and Nate?"

"Yes," Layla said.

"Conquest and Death," Judgement continued. "War is out there somewhere; he was hunting me for a while. Pestilence, too, although I have no idea where she is. I think we're the only ones left. War killed at least one of us."

"Is Judgement your actual name?" Layla asked.

Judgement nodded. "Some got real names, because they had a real family. I was given to Athena and raised by her. Athena is an excellent warrior but not too great at the naming part of anything. She's not here, before you ask. I haven't seen her in a few centuries. Last I heard, she was searching for Atlantis for some reason."

"You can talk to spirits?" Irkalla asked.

"My dad," Judgement said. "That's it. I think it's a bloodline thing. Not really sure. You want to talk to him?"

Layla, Brynhildr, and Irkalla exchanged looks of trepidation.

"Hell yeah," Ava said enthusiastically.

"I like you," Judgement said with a laugh.

"The only reason I came to this place was to help find his burial site so we could find you," Ava said. "And you found us. Makes me feel like it was a little pointless coming here."

"Nothing is pointless," Judgement said. "You made friends; you learned things. And you got to meet me. I'd say you did quite well out of it."

"So what did you do for fun?" Ava asked.

"Before I came here, I killed things," Judgement said. "I hunted down monsters and ended them. Since I came here, I have remained at peace for the most part. I just wanted to know my father."

"My dad died when I was a little girl. My mom too. I don't really remember them."

"I am sorry for that," Judgement said. "My mother was murdered when I was but a child. She was the Lady of the Lake, or so I was told. I sometimes wonder how many siblings I have out there, especially seeing how Hera likes to hunt down Zeus's children and end them. I would like family one day, I think. I don't know."

"This is my family," Ava said. "They're not blood relations, but they do fight for one another. I think that's a kind of family."

"You are rich with knowledge," Judgement said. "And if these fine warriors are your family, you are rich with family too."

"And wouldn't Nate and Mordred be sort of family?" Ava asked, turning back to Irkalla. "Weren't you all born in the same way? Isn't that what people keep saying? You're Horsemen. Although you're not a man, so . . . Horseperson?"

Judgement shrugged. "I have no idea. I haven't met them. Athena told me stories of them, but she hadn't seen either of them in centuries."

"Nate is my son," Brynhildr said. "I haven't seen him in over a thousand years."

"Why?" Judgement asked, turning back to her.

"It's a long and unpleasant story," Brynhildr admitted.

"I hope when this is over, that changes," Judgement said. "I also hope to murder Hera and keep her heart as an ornament."

Judgement set off with Ava. They continued until they found a hole in a wall and rubble surrounding it.

"It's in here," Ava said, sounding excited.

Judgement and Ava went first, and everyone else followed them into the huge tomb beyond. It held golden statues, weaponry on the walls, a sarcophagus, and a huge mural of Zeus standing atop Mount Olympus throwing down lightning bolts on the horde below.

"Can you talk to him?" Layla asked Judgement and Ava.

"It's just power," Ava said.

"A shitload of power," Irkalla finished.

"This takes a lot more effort to do more than once a day," Zeus said as his spirit materialized in the middle of the room.

"How the fuck?" Ava asked.

Zeus was six feet tall and wore a white tunic. He had a long dark beard and matching plaited hair. He stood in front of his sarcophagus and looked around.

"Judgement," Zeus said. "Good to see you again. Brynhildr and Irkalla, you're both looking as lovely as ever."

"You know you're dead, right?" Irkalla said. "You can't hit on people."

Zeus laughed.

"How are you able to do this?" Ava asked. "I've never seen ghosts project themselves."

"Runes around the tomb," Zeus said. "It keeps my spirit linked to this world, should I wish to see it."

"Is there a heaven?" she asked.

Zeus shrugged. "No idea. Can't remember a thing from when I last appeared to now."

"Hera is looking for your spirit," Layla said. "We think she wanted to find it to hunt down Judgement."

"That does sound like Hera," Zeus said. "She and I weren't exactly a happy couple."

"I think I'm going to go with these people," Judgement said. "I wanted to come say goodbye. I don't think it's all that healthy to spend centuries just hanging around your father's tomb."

"Something I remember mentioning a few times," Zeus said.

"Is there anything else that Rela and her people are looking for?" Irkalla asked.

"No idea," Zeus said. "This chamber has more than its fair share of riches and powerful artifacts. I imagine they could do some damage to their enemies with them. I do not advise taking any, however. Most of them are powerful, but they are also cursed with blood magic. The power would be short lived. The consequences, possibly not so much."

"Can we risk leaving them here?" Layla asked.

"I'll reapply the runes," Judgement said. "No one will get in unless I allow them to."

"That's for the best," Zeus said. "Honestly, though, just collapse the tunnel beyond here. If you ever need me, you can come back and find me. Until then, farewell, Daughter."

"Farewell, Father."

Zeus vanished.

"I will stay behind and collapse the tunnels," Judgement said.

"We'll find the dwarves," Chloe said, motioning toward Ava. "We can collapse the whole damn mountain then."

"I think that's wise," Judgement said.

Layla and the rest of the group walked back to the mountain entrance, where she spotted the king and queen in discussion farther along the excavation.

"Where are your people?" Layla asked the king and queen as she reached them.

"We sent them home," the king's adviser said.

"Without my authority," the queen snapped.

"We left enough here to ensure that the mission is completed," the adviser began. "We assumed that you would not want our city to be bereft of defenders while Rela and her Valkyries are clearly not here."

"Does your father speak for you now?" Orfeda asked, with pure venom in her voice.

Layla ignored the dwarves for a moment and walked over to Jinayca, who was staring off into the distance.

"Something is wrong," Jinayca said. "We are surrounded by a mountain and several miles of nothing but open land. There is nothing anyone could do to get to us that we would not see."

Layla looked around at the few hundred dwarves who remained. They stood on the land between the excavation and the woodlands.

"I feel it too," Layla said. "Those dwarves are trying very hard not to look like a threat."

The ground rumbled and shook as the woodlands on the opposite side from where the rebellion had ridden burst into flames. Massive fire giants streamed out of the woodland, covering the distance between the two groups quickly. Layla changed her arm into a sword and spotted Surtr leading the charge.

The fire giants roared as Kara's squad of rebel Valkyries charged to attack before anyone could call them to stop. Kara was thrown from her horse and repeatedly stomped into the ground by Surtr as his army overtook him to battle the rest of the Valkyries.

Layla turned to check on the dwarves, only to see them all standing motionless, the king's father holding a sword against the queen's neck.

Layla and her team looked between the two groups, dismayed at the command to drop their weapons and surrender. The Valkyries who hadn't charged in with Kara's squad looked to Brynhildr, who nodded to comply.

The fire giants outnumbered the Valkyries ten to one, and the battle was quickly over. Many of their comrades were shouting in anger at the dwarves and giants alike.

"I will end you," Orfeda sneered at her king and his allies. "Your names will be removed from all records."

"Stop it," Snagnar snapped. "You should have just listened to me. We arranged to have peace with Rela. We arranged to live our lives apart."

"She's murdering her own people, you fucking idiot," Layla snapped. She felt heat from behind her and turned to look up at a smiling Surtr. "You smell like shit."

Surtr laughed. "I'm glad we get to meet again." He kicked Layla in the chest, sending her flying back across the excavation site and up toward the dwarves, who all moved away.

With the breath knocked out of her body and her head scrambled from the blow, Layla could only hear the shouts of her allies demanding that no more harm come to anyone. She looked up at Surtr as he walked calmly toward her, shrinking from twenty to seven feet tall in a few seconds.

"I thought you were in Asgard getting ready to die," Layla said, regaining her ability to talk.

"I was," Surtr said as he got nearer. "Now I'm doing a favor for Arthur. I remove the insects bothering Rela, and in return I get as much power as I want."

Layla cracked her knuckles and smiled as Surtr continued to walk toward the group, igniting the arrows that were fired in his direction before they hit him.

"This time won't be so easy for you," he bellowed.

Layla flipped him the middle finger and mounted Tego. "Let's show the big bastard what we do to bullies," Layla whispered to Tego, who growled long and low. They were on the move a second later, her sword arm cutting through anyone stupid enough to get close. She had eyes only for Surtr, who grew to over sixty feet tall, and judging from the pieces of rock he picked up, turned red hot, and flung at Layla, he disliked her just as much as she him.

Layla reached out with her power to control the metal inside Surtr, but for some reason she felt nothing to grab hold of. She regained her composure quickly enough to avoid one of his feet and sprang off Tego's back, stabbed her sword arm into his thigh, and cut through his side as she slid down several feet before launching herself off and rolling as she hit the ground. Layla's metal arm was destroyed, the heat inside Surtr's body too much for it to handle. Molten metal dripped from where her elbow had once been.

Surtr laughed and turned to face Layla. She caught sight of several runes that had been drawn around his stomach and back, each of them glowing the same color as his cracked skin. She had no idea who'd applied them, but she guessed that they were the reason she couldn't take control of the metal inside his body.

Layla dragged elements from the ground, reforming her arm, although the pain it caused was substantial. Tego darted between Surtr's feet, causing the sixty-foot-tall giant to try to stomp on her, but she was far too quick for him. Tego was unable to bite Surtr, though, as the heat would have been too much for her to withstand.

Layla picked up a bloody spear from the ground and threw it into the stomach of Surtr, right in the middle of the rune there. Surtr roared in pain, pulling the spear free and tossing it aside.

"You think that will be enough?" he bellowed as a barrage of arrows slammed into his back.

"I think you can only control that heat to stop something you can see," Layla said. "And I think your rune is broken."

Surtr looked at the rune on his stomach with fear on his face. Layla reached out to him but was still unable to get hold of the metals that made up his body. Instead, she took control of the metal in the ground beneath his feet, tearing it out and up toward Surtr's body like a thousand tiny darts. He stopped most of it from hitting him, but enough got through that more of the runes adorning his body were fractured in the onslaught.

A bolt of lightning hit Tego in the side, and while her armor stopped any damage, the impact caused her to pause for just a second. It was all that Surtr needed to kick Tego, sending her sailing through the air and into a nearby building with a horrifying crash.

Layla looked on in horror as her friend vanished from view.

Layla walked toward Surtr as he laughed at her. He moved to kick her, but she started sprinting and sliced up with her arm, cutting off his toes as she moved around the foot, using the discarded weapons of the dead to immediately remake her arm. Again it hurt like hell, but it was nothing compared to the rage that had erupted inside her.

Once behind Surtr's feet, she cut through his Achilles tendon, remade her arm, and leaped over to the second foot as the giant began to fall. She cut through the second Achilles and remade her arm once again, but this time more slowly, the pain and fatigue of having to remake it over and over beginning to tire her.

Surtr crashed to the ground, and Layla climbed up onto Surtr's legs and ran across his body, avoiding the larger cracks of molten skin, as she reached out to every piece of metal she could find around her. Hundreds of swords, knives, axes, and pieces of armor were flung into the air and melded above her head into one gigantic blade. She continued up toward Surtr's head as he rolled onto his back, trying to swat Layla off. She avoided his hands as they tried to take hold of her. The second she was close enough, she drove the giant blade into his skull without a word. She pushed the blade farther and farther into his head until what would have been the hilt touched what remained of his nose.

His arms dropped to his sides with a crash, and he began to shrink, but Layla was already jumping off him and running toward the ruined house, where she pulled apart the brick and wood to find an injured but alive Tego inside. She buried her face in Tego's fur.

"Thank you," she said softly. "I was so worried."

Tego nudged Layla with her paw and got to her feet.

The rest of her team was already fighting the combined might of the dwarves and flame giants, and while they were outnumbered, her side consisted of some of the most powerful beings in existence.

Layla turned her arm into a spear and threw it at a dwarf, catching him in the face. She exploded the steel in the spear, pushing each of the hundred razor-sharp points into the dwarf's head, killing him.

Orfeda dodged an attack by a charging dwarf and spun toward the king's father, slamming her sword up into his gut. She twisted it and dragged it out, and the older man dropped to his knees as blood soaked the ground.

A third dwarf turned and ran as the king dropped to his knees to cradle his dying father. Queen Orfeda was having none of that and chased after the fleeing dwarf. She tackled him to the ground before proceeding to beat the shit out of him. Layla left them to their own thing and helped her team defeat the giants and dwarves, but even with the power her friends and allies possessed, they were still outnumbered twenty to one at least, and there was only so much they could do.

When Irkalla took an arrow to the shoulder and was unable to avoid being punched by a fire giant soon after, Layla knew that they would just be worn down.

Her attention was taken for a moment, but a moment was all two dwarves needed to barrel into her, using their alchemy to tear the ground apart and wrap it around Layla, effectively keeping her in place as she struggled to get up.

One of the dwarves stood, drew her ax, and raised it high for a killing blow as the second continued to pile more and more mud and rock over Layla's arms to stop her from being able to fight back.

An arrow took the ax-wielding dwarf in the eye and exploded out the back of her head, taking the majority of her skull with it.

The dwarf who'd been keeping Layla in place stood to see where the arrow had come from and took one in the throat for his trouble. Three more arrows hit a giant in the chest and left an exit wound the size of Layla's head.

With the dwarf dead, Layla rolled away from the dirt that had been piled up onto her. She scrambled over to Irkalla, who was busy beating a seven-foot giant to death with her bare hands, the arrow still protruding from her shoulder.

"Who the fuck is that?" one of the dwarves shouted.

Layla looked over at the entrance of the mountain as Judgement walked out as calmly as if she were taking a pleasant stroll. She had created a bow and arrows out of thin air, the arrows themselves made of light.

The bow vanished from Judgement's hands, and two daggers of pure light replaced it. She screamed a cry of war before sprinting into the throng of fire giants and cutting through them like they were just weeds in a field.

As the giants began to fall, the dwarves and Valkyries who had been sent away returned in a massive swath of fury, and the tide of the battle swung against those who supported Rela. When it was done, bodies littered the ground.

"I think we won," Chloe said. She'd joined the fight with the dwarf slaves, while Ava had stayed inside the mountain.

"You don't look too much like you won anything," Layla said, exhausted.

"Battle chic," Chloe said. "It's all the rage these days."

"How's Ava?"

"Terrified," Irkalla said, slapping Layla on the back. "She has stayed in the mountain. She is a child, and none of this was meant to happen."

"Tell that to the twat who betrayed us," Chloe said angrily. "Where is the fucker anyway?"

Layla looked over at Orfeda, who was covered in the blood of the dwarves who had stood against her.

"Queen don't fuck about," Chloe said as she sat beside Layla. "Your arm okay?"

Layla nodded. "This didn't turn out how I'd expected," she said.

Brynhildr joined the pair, her face pained. "Friends of mine died here today. They died because the king's people set us up. I'm glad we didn't bring everyone in the rebellion here."

"We thought they might, though," Layla said.

"We didn't think that they would have an army of giants," Brynhildr replied. "Or that the king would send away his own people, leaving the queen vulnerable."

"We underestimated them," Layla said.

"And that is something we will not be doing again."

"I think we need to have a chat with the king," Layla said, feeling anger at what had happened and wanting to take it out on someone.

Judgement walked over to Queen Orfeda, who went to shake the sorcerer's hand.

"I don't do physical contact with people I just met," Judgement said. "It's not personal."

Orfeda lowered her hand. "My ex-king would like to say a few things," she said, pushing her husband over to the group.

"You've made a grave mistake fighting us," Snagnar said.

"Your father and his allies are dead," Layla told him. "You are next. You betrayed your own people; I'm pretty sure they're not going to be happy about that."

"Soon Rela will know what happened here," Snagnar said.

"How?" Orfeda asked.

"Valkyries on flying horses," he said. "They move fast."

"Were they just after me?" Judgement asked. "This is a lot of effort to find one tomb."

"Zeus's tomb was meant to be covered with riches and power," Snagnar said. "You unlock that, you find his spirit and the knowledge it contains. Hera just wanted to know where you were, but Rela wanted power."

"Hera told her there were weapons in there, yes?" Layla asked.

Snagnar nodded.

"What is Rela's plan?" Orfeda asked.

"Merge the realms," Snagnar said. "She merges the palace with Asgard; she attacks you from behind. Thousands of Valkyries pouring out of the palace grounds, slaughtering all in the city."

"Not possible without a huge amount of power," Jinayca said as she joined the conversation. Layla spotted Brynhildr going over to the mountain to get Ava.

Snagnar smiled.

Irkalla grabbed Snagnar's arm and wrenched it back, causing the king to cry out in pain. "Feel like telling us?" She forced him to the ground and twisted his arm into an unnatural position, just shy of snapping it at the elbow.

"The human city," Snagnar blurted. "She's going to use blood magic to do it."

"She would need someone on the other side to link the two realms," Irkalla said.

"Not if she used a realm gate as a link," Jinayca said. "She opens the realm gate that's linked to Asgard and then creates a merge."

"Is that possible?" Irkalla asked.

"Do you want to find out?" Orfeda asked. She turned to her king. "You have no place in dwarf society. You betrayed your own people for power and wealth. I sentence you to death when we return to the city."

Snagnar laughed. "By the time we make it back, you'll all be dead anyway."

“Then there’s little point in waiting,” Orfeda said. She drove a dagger into Snagnar’s heart and pushed his dying body to the ground.

“Congratulations on speeding things up,” Judgement said.

“We need to get to the palace,” Layla said as Tego arrived beside her and licked her hand. The massive cat was covered in the blood of those who had been stupid enough to get in her way. “Good to see you too.”

“Saddle up, people,” Jinayca shouted. “We’re not done yet.”

Chapter Twenty-Four

Mordred

Llyn Ogwen, Wales, Earth Realm

Mordred sat on the cold floor of the hidden temple beneath the lake. Excalibur was in his lap, and he couldn't stop staring at it, as if it were something cursed. Something he could send away with the power of wishful thinking.

"Mordred?" Viv asked from the archway to the dark room.

"I'm here," Mordred said, getting to his feet. "I'm okay. I guess. You ever sent anyone else through there?"

"No," Viv said.

"Probably for the best," Mordred said. "It's weird. And not the good kind of weird. More the 'really bad mushroom trip' kind of weird. How long was I gone?"

"About two days," Viv said.

"What? It felt like a few hours at most," Mordred said. He sighed. "So I got this piece of crap; what next?"

"Next, I guess I need to find a new vocation," Viv said. "I notice you haven't unsheathed the sword."

"Nor am I planning on doing that," Mordred said. "Not unless I have to."

Hel and Elaine left the room they'd been in, and the eyes of both moved from Mordred down to the sword in his hands.

"Is that Excalibur?" Hel asked.

Mordred nodded. "You want it?"

Hel shook her head. "Not a chance. No offense."

"No, join the club."

"Are you coming with us to Asgard?" Elaine asked Viv.

"Not at the moment," Viv said. "I have been here a long time, waiting for Mordred to come and reclaim what is his."

"Sorry about the wait," Mordred said. "I'll bring you my PlayStation if you like. Give you something to do."

"We're underwater," Viv said. "Not a lot of electricity here. Unless you can get it to run off these crystals."

"I'll ask around," Mordred said.

Guinevere and Lancelot both entered, the former rubbing her eyes as if she'd been asleep and the latter doing nothing but staring at Excalibur.

"Want something, Lancelot?" Mordred asked.

"I haven't seen it in a long time," Lancelot said softly. "It's as magnificent as I remember."

Mordred looked down at Excalibur and then back up at Lancelot. "It's okay," Mordred said. "I mean, it's just a sword. Nice hilt, though. Looks like it can take a whack without breaking. Good craftsmanship. The dwarves know their stuff."

"Yes," Lancelot said. "Yes, they do."

The group left soon after, Viv taking them back up to the land. She stood on the docks with Elaine and Mordred. "I will come help you when I can," Viv said. "I need to say goodbye to a few things first."

"Thank you for your help," Mordred said. "Or for putting me through hell. Whichever of those you're happier about."

Viv smiled. "You're a good man, Mordred. You'll make a fine king."

Mordred shrugged. "Everyone keeps telling me I'm a good man and will make a fine king. I'm beginning to think you all got a memo I didn't."

"Still not accepted it?" Elaine asked him.

"Nope," Mordred said. "I got the sword, I can use it to fight Arthur, but I'm not a king. I'm just someone with a pretty sword."

"You'll make a fine king indeed," Viv said and vanished back into the water.

"Back to Asgard, then?" Elaine asked.

"And what of those two?" Mordred asked her. Lancelot was sitting off to one side, seemingly staring into the lake, while Guinevere spoke to Hel.

"I don't know," Elaine said. "I guess they're going to have to come with us."

"You trust them?"

"You don't?"

"Not really," Mordred said. "I don't dislike Guinevere, but anyone that's off their tits is probably a liability. And my issues with Lancelot are documented."

"For now, I think that's our best choice. We can't just leave them here."

"I guess not," Mordred said. "Let's just get back to Asgard."

It didn't take long for everyone to make it back to Little Skellig and through the realm gate to Asgard. No one had been seriously hurt, and no one had been left behind—sadly, in Lancelot's case.

Once back in Asgard, everyone bar Mordred made their way down the cliff back to the city. Mordred sat alone atop the cliff as more tremors shook the ground. Whatever had been causing them was clearly not done.

Hel returned a short while later. "Elaine says you probably shouldn't just stay up here."

Mordred nodded. "I just needed some time. I go down there with this, and . . . well, I'm king, and various prophecies probably come true, and the whole thing is completely shit."

"I see those tremors are still happening," Hel said. "Any idea what they are?"

Mordred looked at the black smoke in the distance. "I remember Layla saying something about merging realms, about how there were tremors and pieces of one realm falling into another. This isn't that. I don't know what this is."

"Let's go get this over with," Hel said.

Mordred got to his feet and walked down the side of the cliff with Hel, having to stop every now and again because of the tremors. When they reached the ground, they were met by Hades and Persephone.

"Elaine took Lancelot and Guinevere to her house," Persephone said.

"Rather her than me," Mordred said.

"That Excalibur?" Hades asked.

Mordred nodded. "You want it?"

Hades shook his head. "Not even slightly. Sorry, I know this isn't easy. I wish I could help with the burden."

"People won't accept me as king," Mordred said. "I spent too long murdering people."

"People know that wasn't you," Persephone said. "People know you're a good man."

"Everyone keeps telling me that," Mordred said, feeling a bit like a broken record. "I'm not a good anything. I'm just a man who is trying to keep people alive. Nothing else. Every time I get told I'm a good man, I feel this twitch run up my spine."

"We won't tell anyone it's Excalibur," Persephone said. "That should give you some time to get used to the burden you've been given."

Mordred didn't feel like he was going to get a better offer. "How's Odin?"

"Still unconscious," Hades said.

"And Tommy?" Hel asked.

"He's still weak," Persephone said. "Still unable to change into his wolf form, still pissed off about it. He was meant to go to Shadow Falls, but he's making sure that any final evacuees go through the realm gate. He'll be going last. It was the only way to get him to actually promise to leave."

"That sounds about right," Mordred said.

"And these tremors?" Hel asked.

"We think they're trying to shake the walls down," Hades said. "Using earth elementals to cause the tremors. We've got our own elementals at the walls to repair any damage. We had some falling debris, but so far it's contained."

That was, at last, some good news. "And Nate?" Mordred asked, expecting to have any good news shattered.

"No idea," Hades said. "He's still on the Earth realm, and last we heard they were heading into England, but that's as far as it goes."

"Do they need help?" Mordred asked, hoping he could do something.

"We don't even know where they are in England," Persephone said. "Apparently, Nate didn't want that information getting out. Hera is still gunning for him, so that's probably wise."

"They'll come through," Mordred said.

"Yeah, if there's anyone who can out-stubborn Mordred, it's Nate," Hades said. "The man doesn't know how to quit, even after everyone tells him to."

"It's endearing," Mordred said.

"It's infuriating," Persephone corrected. "But in this instance, it's also exactly what they need."

"Oh, I forgot," Hades said, handing Mordred a bag. "It's a gift. Apparently, Zamek was working on it before he left and gave Loki a note to get it to you."

Mordred opened the bag to find a rune-scribed chain mail shirt. He thanked Hades and slipped the shirt on over the leather armor. It was surprisingly comfortable and weighed next to nothing. The glyphs adorning the fur-lined interior lit up, causing the chain mail itself to glow as if it contained a not-quite-extinguished fire.

Mordred started to hum the *Super Mario* theme. He didn't really care if anyone got annoyed with him; it helped him to take his mind off the fact that one of his friends was in another realm and couldn't be helped, another had been brought close to death, and another lay in a hospital near death. And there was absolutely nothing he could do to help any of them.

"So what do we do now we're back?" Hel asked, placing a hand on Mordred's shoulder.

"I need to actually do something and not just wait to be attacked," Mordred said. "You know what? How about we get a horse and go check the wall. Maybe there's another reason for these tremors. And before you say anything, at least then I'll feel useful."

"Sounds like a plan to me," Hades said. "There's a stable just over by the barracks."

Hel, Mordred, and Persephone all fetched horses and rode out into the city. Mordred hung the sword from his saddlebag, hoping it would be inconspicuous.

The drawbridge lowered, and the three of them rode off into the lands of Asgard as another tremor rocked them. This one was powerful enough to cause several of the uppermost bricks on the wall closest to the group to fall.

"That didn't take long," Hel said. "But if they're trying to knock the walls down, they're going to be a while."

Elementals moved the pieces of the wall back into position like they had never broken away.

"We should hurry," Persephone said. "I don't want to be away for long if Avalon forces have some sort of dastardly plan for everyone."

"It's Arthur," Mordred said. "Dastardly plans are pretty much all he has, I think. That and his golden armor. Does he still have that?"

"As far as we know, yes," Persephone said. "If nothing else, Arthur likes to be the center of attention."

"That was always the way," Mordred said. "He never could understand why anyone else would be considered interesting while he was in the same room."

"Who wears golden armor, anyway?" Hel asked.

"In my experience, assholes," Persephone said.

The group rode on for a few minutes until another tremor hit so hard that Mordred had to steady the horse so that it didn't throw him off in its fear.

"That looks bad," Hel said, pointing to the cliff pass that she'd walked down with Mordred not long ago. The pass was crumbling. Huge chunks of sand-colored stone fell from the cliff face, smashing into the wall of the city and tearing off chunks of it.

"I thought the runes would stop the wall from being easily destroyed," Hel said.

"I'm not sure several hundred tons of rock falling on something could be described as 'easy,'" Persephone said.

More of the cliff fell until the pass was no longer visible, and large parts of the wall had been destroyed while many of the guards had run for cover.

Mordred turned his horse back to the city and rode back as fast as the horse was safely capable of. All the while more and more tremors dropped more rock, as if someone were pushing it out of the cliff.

The group had to take a detour to the entrance to avoid buildings partially destroyed by continuously falling rubble. Mordred left his horse to be attended by a soldier, removed Excalibur, and set off at a dead sprint toward the cliff.

Hades, Olivia, Loki, and a dozen others were giving orders to the soldiers nearby.

"I think I preferred the constant drumming," Mordred said when Hades, Olivia, and Loki had finished ordering people around. "Anyone figured out what that was, by the way?"

"An air elemental," Olivia said. "He was killed before he could be asked questions."

"And then the tremors started at a faster pace," Loki said.

Hades nodded. "The military is ready for whatever Arthur is about to do. I think this is the beginning of the end of whatever stalemate he's had—"

"What the fuck is that?" Hel asked, pointing through the ruined wall to the outside.

Everyone turned to watch the ground outside break apart as if someone were pulling flowers down into the ground like in an old cartoon.

A lot happened in a very short period of time then. Soldiers flooded to the front of the city, climbing the already heavily occupied wall and waiting for whatever was about to happen next. The cliff face collapsed onto the wall closest to where Mordred and the others stood, creating a cloud of dust that was thrown up into the air.

Mordred used his air magic to disperse the dust only to witness the cliff face crack and pieces of rock explode out from it, landing on several nearby buildings and partially crushing them. People ran to help those trapped as panic and fear gripped the city.

More rock fell as a flame giant tore his way out of the cliff. At two hundred feet tall, with fire pouring out of its hands, it was the largest giant Mordred had ever seen. "Bollocks," he said with a slight sigh as everyone sprang into action to deal with the threat.

The giant threw pieces of rock at anyone who happened to get too close, kicking away those who attacked his feet and covering several soldiers in lava that erupted from the cracks on his legs.

"He's gotten too big," Loki said. "The power is pulling his body apart."

The ground in front of the group tore upward, making a shield that stopped another burst of magma from covering them.

Persephone, who had created the shield, turned back to everyone. "Don't stare; do something."

Everyone moved as one, throwing magic and power at the giant in an effort to bring it down before it could move closer to the more populated parts of the city. But every burst of power that hit tore away parts of the giant, allowing more magma-like blood to pour out of it. Mordred used his water magic to rapidly cool the magma before it became a danger, but he knew he was fighting a losing battle.

"We need to take the head and heart," Mordred shouted to Hel after she'd blasted the giant in the shoulder with pure necromantic power, rocking the enemy.

"Easier said than done," Loki said, pulling a seriously burned soldier past the group.

"I need to get up onto the cliff," Mordred said to Hades.

"The stables," Persephone shouted as the ground just outside the city erupted and blood elves flooded in through the broken wall.

"I thought we'd killed all of these," Hel shouted.

"Kill more," Olivia said, changing the target of her water elemental power from the giant to the mass of blood elves that scrambled over the remains of the wall like a swarm of insects.

Mordred sprinted into the stables and found the only winged horse there. Mordred approached the large animal calmly, seeing the distress it was already in from the noise of battle that raged not far from the safety of its stables.

"It's okay, boy," Mordred said, keeping his voice low. "I really could use your help, though."

Winged horses were known for being intelligent animals and completely loyal to their masters—it was one of the reasons that the Valkyries had used them for so long—but Mordred knew that if the animal didn't want to be ridden, he had no chance of making it happen.

The winged horse lowered his head so that Mordred could rub it. "You've already been saddled," he said. "Someone was going to take you out, and then you got stuck in here. You want to go for a ride?"

The winged horse snorted.

"You and Tego would get on really well," Mordred said. "If you get on with really big cats, that is."

The winged horse allowed itself to be led to the entrance of the stables and bucked when it saw the giant spew magma over a nearby building.

Mordred quickly soothed the animal. "It's okay; we're just going to go for a flying lesson. I need to get up to the top of the cliff, and then you're good to leave if you want."

The winged horse was obviously spooked by what it saw, but it allowed Mordred to mount it, and together they rode out of the stables, the winged horse gaining speed and taking off into the air.

The giant threw pieces of rock at those on the ground but mostly appeared to ignore Mordred and the winged horse as they reached the top of the cliff. Mordred climbed down and looked around at the ruined landscape. The realm gate was still there, but a lot of the surrounding area had fallen away or become unstable. Even with the damage, the cliff still rose sharply away from the city, and its highest point was easily twice that of where Mordred now stood, nearly four hundred feet above the ground.

"Thanks," Mordred said. "You can go to safety now."

The horse stared at Mordred for a few seconds and stamped its feet.

"Or stay here," Mordred said. He walked over to the edge of the cliff and looked down at the top of the giant's head. "That's pretty solid rock."

The winged horse nudged Mordred's arm with its nose.

"You think you can get his attention?" Mordred asked.

The horse took off and swooped down toward the giant, smashed its hooves into the back of the monster's head, and flew off at speed. The giant turned toward the cliff, and Mordred raised a hand of thanks toward the winged horse. He turned and ran the fifty feet back to the realm gate, took a deep breath, and sprinted toward the edge of the cliff.

The giant's expression was one of confusion as Mordred leaped off the cliff. He used air magic to push himself as far away from the edge as possible before he fell toward the giant, gaining speed with every foot.

Mordred created a shield of ice in front of him and pulled it down around his entire body, dropping his own temperature at the same time. It was something he'd been practicing for a while now, using his water magic on his own body, but he'd never tried anything like this before. He hummed the battle theme from *Final*

Fantasy IX. It comforted him as he hurtled toward the now-terrified giant, who tried to turn to get away.

A blast of energy from somewhere below forced the giant to look back at Mordred an instant before he smashed into the giant's eye like a frozen, nearly six-foot bullet.

All Mordred felt once inside the brain was speed and heat. He pumped more and more ice around his body, hoping to keep himself cold. The cold spread through the skull of the giant, who was already dead and was slowly folding from the knees like a large, fiery accordion.

Mordred shot out of the back of the giant's skull a second after entering, but to him it felt like hours. He removed the ice shield and braced for impact as he continued toward the ground at incredible speed. A blast of snow in front of him and a shield of air wrapped around him meant his landing was less painful than he'd expected it to be. Going headfirst into the ground at several hundred miles per hour was not something even a sorcerer wanted to do.

Mordred came to a stop next to a large building with several dozen people all standing outside it staring at him.

"And that, kids," Loki began, "is why you wear a seat belt."

Mordred was helped to his feet by several soldiers, all of whom tried to talk to him at once. They received nothing but blank stares in return.

It took Hel's appearance to shake Mordred loose enough to understand anything.

"That was bonkers," Hel said.

"Love you too," Mordred said with a smile. "Is it dead?"

"You blew half of its head off," Hel told him. "The giant is very dead. The blood elves have been pushed back, but I think this was all just a way to keep our attention."

"Why?"

Hel took Mordred to the ruined gate, littered with the bodies of the blood elves and more than a few who had fought them. Hades's arm hung loose, and he looked to be in pain.

"You need a hand?" Mordred asked him.

Hades waved him away. "I would rather my body healed me. It won't be long. Thank you, though."

"What you did was very stupid," Persephone said with a slight shake of her head.

"Yes, it was," Mordred agreed.

"It was cool, though," one of the soldiers said. "Like, 'holy shit, you're fucking mad' cool."

"I think the giant was meant to bring down a large part of the wall," Mordred said. "Looks like we stopped him before he could." He gave the soldier a thumbs-up before he reached the hole in the wall and climbed the ladder to the ramparts above, where he looked out across what was going to be a battlefield. There were hundreds of massive holes all across the plains directly in front of the city walls. And there were tens of thousands of enemies standing before the city, with more climbing out of the holes. Trolls, giants, blood elves, sorcerers, elementals, and more. All coming together to kill every living thing inside the city of Asgard.

"They tunneled here," Hel said. "We'd sent people to check out the tremors, and none came back. Looks like they were moving everyone up underground and then breaking through all at once."

A golden-armored warrior rode out to the front of the mass of Avalon allies. He wore a helmet in the shape of a dragon and carried a spear.

"Arthur," Mordred muttered, feeling anger the likes of which he hadn't felt for a long time.

"There will be no surrender," Arthur shouted, his voice bouncing off the walls all around the city. "I am here to watch everyone beyond this wall die. I am here to ensure it happens. You have all stood in my way for too long."

Mordred looked along the line and spotted a dozen air elementals using their power to ensure Arthur's words could be heard.

"Fuck off," Mordred shouted, using his own air magic to carry his words all around.

Arthur turned to look at Mordred. "I have a gift for you, Mordred." He motioned to two forty-foot giants, who carried a large box. They opened it and started throwing the contents over the wall with ease.

"The heads of the scouts," Hel said. "You bastard."

Mordred looked down at one of the heads that came to rest by his foot. "One chance, Arthur," Mordred shouted. "Take your friends and go home, or you all die."

The enemy's laughter reverberated through Mordred's chest.

"I will save you for last," Arthur shouted, pointing his spear at Mordred. "You will get to see your loved ones die first: your love, your friends, and . . . your aunt. Thank you for being so easily distracted."

"Everyone off the wall," Mordred shouted. He turned and dropped off the wall just before large parts of it exploded, raining huge chunks of stone down over the city. Avalon forces tore out of the enormous craters they'd made under the walls. The explosion caught Mordred, who'd already wrapped himself in dense air, and bounced him off the roof of a building, his ears still ringing even as he hit the ground. The ringing in his ears stopped, replaced with the screams of those who had been atop the walls and directly in the path of the murderous invaders.

Mordred saw Hades and Persephone engaged with the enemy. Hades turned to Mordred and waved him away.

Mordred sprinted through the city, Excalibur still clutched in his hand, as the city forces all raced toward the breached wall. He crashed through the door with a blast of air magic and found Elaine on the floor, covered in blood.

Mordred tossed Excalibur to one side and fell to his knees beside Elaine, his light magic igniting as he tried to heal his aunt.

"It's too late," she said. "The blade was coated in venom."

"You can be saved," Mordred said with tears in his eyes. "You don't have to die."

"Mordred," Elaine said softly, reaching out and placing one bloody hand against his cheek. "My nephew. You were like my son. I love you, but you can't save everyone."

"Who did this?" Mordred already knew. He just wanted to hear the name.

"Lancelot," Elaine said, her eyes closing and snapping open again. "I walked in on them fighting. I tried to stop them, and he stabbed me. He took Guinevere. He took her to Arthur. She'll be made an example of. He wanted Excalibur, too, but you took it with you."

"But Arthur hates Lancelot too." Mordred knew now was not the time, but he couldn't help it.

Hel entered the house and dropped down next to Mordred, a cry escaping her lips. "No," she said softly. "No, no, no, no."

"We all go sometime," Elaine said to Hel. "You love one another; be together. Be happy. Live. You're good together."

Hel placed a comforting hand on Mordred's shoulder.

"You're a good man, Mordred," Elaine said. "A great man. Believe in yourself. Believe in who you can be."

"Please don't," Mordred said.

"Show them all," Elaine said, her words barely a whisper. "Show them who you are. My nephew. My son . . . my king."

As Elaine took her last breath, Mordred's scream of pure, incandescent rage and pain crashed through the wall of the house, allowing it to be heard around the city.

Chapter Twenty-Five

Mordred

Part of Mordred wanted to find Lancelot and make him suffer. He wanted to take him somewhere quiet and ensure that Lancelot's pain would compare to his own. But that wasn't the man he wanted to be.

Elaine lay on the floor with Mordred kneeling beside her, weeping in pain. Elaine had been someone who had always stood beside Mordred. She had always seen something in him that no one else did. Not even his own mother. Not his friends. No one. When he was at his lowest, when everyone else had written him off as a murderous psychopath, Elaine had told him that she knew one day her nephew would return.

Mordred had been in prison at the time and had laughed at her, mocked her. Hated her. None of that had stopped the belief she had in him. And when he had become the man he was today, she had been the first one there. She had been the one to tell him he was better than he believed he was. That he was worthwhile. That he was capable of being good again.

Mordred had always thought that Elaine would go out fighting. That if she were to die, it would be on a battlefield surrounded by the bodies of her enemies. Instead, she'd died trying to protect Guinevere from Lancelot.

Mordred needed to clear his head. He knew that he couldn't fight angry. He knew that he couldn't fight Arthur with only rage and hate inside his head.

"Mordred," Lucifer said from the doorway. "Can I come in?"

Mordred nodded.

"We need your help out there," Lucifer said. "Huge parts of the wall have been torn apart, and the fighting has spilled into the city."

"Lancelot?" Hel asked.

"He was seen riding off with an unconscious Guinevere," Lucifer said. "No one could stop him."

Mordred continued to sit in mute pain.

"And Arthur?" Hel asked.

"Arthur isn't out there anymore," Lucifer said. "We don't know where he is."

Mordred looked up at Lucifer for the first time. "Arthur was never one to run from a fight."

"No, he wasn't," Lucifer said. He knelt beside Elaine and crossed her arms over her chest. He said something in a language Mordred didn't know.

"What was that?" he asked.

"It's an ancient language of people who lived far from here," Lucifer said. "It means *May you pass to a better place*. I was taught it as a child. Elaine deserves to be in a better place."

Mordred got to his feet. "I'm going to go find Guinevere."

"I'll join you," Hel said.

"You'll need this," Lucifer said, picking up Excalibur.

"No," Mordred said. "I can't risk it right now. I can't risk second-guessing myself about using it. And if I do run into Arthur, I can't let it fall into his hands. Just keep the sword safe. I'll deal with what it means when I return."

Mordred looked back at Elaine one last time. He would make her proud. He left the building and stepped out into the maelstrom of battle that raged throughout the city.

"We're going to need horses," Hel said.

Mordred nodded, feeling dazed. He felt like everything before him was unreal, as if he were separate from reality. He watched the battle unfolding before him with a quiet detachment. Griffins darted through the air, stabbing at the giants, who were far too slow to stop them. Tarron, the shadow elf, fought against blood elves who had at one time been his own people. Diana tore the head off an unlucky man and threw it at the person behind him. The second man recoiled in terror, but it was short lived, as he was soon turned to stone when Medusa walked by him. All of Mordred's friends were fighting for their lives, for the lives of their loved ones, and Mordred felt like he'd lost so much with one act of violence.

Violence perpetrated by Lancelot.

Lancelot.

A blood elf dodged past several of the Asgard soldiers and sprinted toward Mordred, who casually bisected it with a sword of pure light, stepped past the dead elf, and blasted the closest giant in the back of the head with more light magic. It punched through the skull of the giant and out just above its nose.

The rest of the blood elves stayed back, along with a troll and some humanoids. Everyone watched Mordred cautiously. He created two blades of light—one in each hand—and started to hum Ryu's theme from *Street Fighter II* before charging forward a second later.

He moved through the first group of enemies with a detached efficiency. They were not worth his time and effort to do more than to remove their lives and carry on. One sorcerer, a middle-aged man, threw a bolt of lightning at Mordred that forced him to dart aside, putting him closer to his attacker. The snarl on the sorcerer's face soon faded when the realization of exactly who he was fighting set in, and he died with a blade of light to the chest before Mordred decapitated him a moment later.

As the fighting went on, Mordred became more brutal in his methods of dispatching those standing in his way. He removed limbs, crippled people, and caused them to scream in pain and fear as his blood magic ran rampant, fueled by those already slain.

A blast of air smashed into Mordred's chest, picking him up off the floor and throwing him back twenty feet. He collided with a pile of bodies he'd created only a few minutes ago and pulled himself upright as two paladins, both in blood-splattered golden armor, walked toward him.

Mordred got to his feet, the tune on his lips forgotten. "Move," he said softly, his air magic carrying the words to the paladins, who laughed in response.

Mordred rolled his shoulders and sprinted forward, his light magic ignited. He avoided the swipe of a sword and used his light magic to phase through the paladin, ending up behind him. Mordred had been practicing with the technique for several months, and while it worked well, it had the unfortunate side effect of causing Mordred considerable pain. Pain he ignored as he turned and drove a blade of light into the exposed neck of the paladin.

Mordred detonated the part of the blade of light inside the paladin, removing the head and shoulders with one movement, and was already moving as fast as the eye could see to get to the second paladin. Light magic was powerful but exhausting to use, and he wouldn't have unlimited access to it before his body decided enough was enough.

The paladin turned to run, moving in slow motion as Mordred phased through him, but he moved slower this time, allowing the thousands of tiny light trails that the magic created to become a mass of hardened, sharp light. The paladin was cut to pieces inside his own armor, and blood poured out of the hundreds of tiny holes that Mordred's power had created. The paladin dropped to his knees, screaming in agony.

Mordred realized that there were dozens of enemy soldiers close by, but none of them wanted to come close enough to fight him. He turned and walked away toward the rear of the enemy line, blasting anyone who got in his way with magic.

Hel rode over on one horse with a second beside her. "Mordred, you ready?" she asked.

Mordred nodded and climbed up onto the horse.

As the pair rode through the city, they had to fight off the occasional blood elf or troll who decided they were easy targets, and they were soon riding flat out across the battlefield, but it was quickly apparent that the horses weren't going to make it through the mass of oncoming enemies.

Mordred got down from his horse, and Hel, having seen the same closing horde, did the same. They released the horses, and Mordred hoped they would be okay.

He created a sphere of light in his hands and stepped toward Hel. "Hit the ground. Cover yourself," he said, increasing the size of the sphere until it was nearly two meters in diameter.

Hel's eyes widened as she hit the earth, covering herself in a shield of her necromantic power, and Mordred threw the sphere into the air and detonated the magic inside.

The blast incinerated anything that was within a few meters of Mordred and blew back anything that was within ten meters of him, leaving only scorch marks. The battle still raged on, but for a brief moment, Hel and Mordred had some respite.

Hel stood and shook the earth off her. "That's new."

Mordred smiled. "I've been practicing."

They ran through the battlefield together and soon left the death and mayhem behind as they reached the forest. It didn't take long before they heard the sounds of voices talking.

Hel motioned for Mordred to stop, and together they moved toward the sounds as quietly as possible. Eventually the forest joined a large cliff face that Mordred knew stretched for miles to the west of the realm. There was a dip from where Hel and Mordred crouched to a less dense patch of forest, where trees met stone.

Arthur stood in the middle of the clearing, along with a dozen paladins, Lancelot, and Guinevere, who clearly wore a sorcerer's band and was gagged and bound. Arthur and two of the paladins laughed and joked at Guinevere's expense, and then Arthur turned to Lancelot.

Mordred used his air magic to try to listen to what was said, but he had to be subtle about its use so as to not alert anyone there.

Hel hung back too. Neither of them could fight off the power in the circle, not with Arthur there, and getting killed unnecessarily wasn't high on Mordred's list of things to do.

"What the fuck is this shit?" Arthur shouted, gesturing toward Guinevere.

"It's Guinevere," Lancelot said, his tone soft and weak.

Arthur leaned in toward Lancelot. "When I woke, you reached out to me. You *begged* me to allow you back into the fold. Do you remember what I said?"

"That I was to bring you Excalibur," Lancelot said.

Arthur clasped his hand around the back of Lancelot's neck. "Is this *fucking* Excalibur?" he shouted.

"Mordred has it," Lancelot blurted out. "The Lady of the Lake gave it to him."

"She's dead," Arthur said. "I know, because Merlin did it. And he's actually competent."

"Her daughter," Lancelot said. "She gave it to Mordred. Mordred has the sword."

"So why isn't Mordred dead?" Arthur asked.

"He's . . . he's not like he was," Lancelot said. "Before you sent him to the blood elves. He was powerful but nothing to be overly concerned about. Since he's recovered, he's grown strong."

"So I've heard," Arthur said, walking over to Guinevere and looking down at her with disdain. "I didn't ask for this one. So why did you bring her?"

"I killed Elaine," Lancelot said.

That got Arthur's attention. "You killed Elaine?"

Lancelot nodded enthusiastically. "I thought she had Excalibur, but she didn't. I took Guinevere because I wanted to show that I am going to continue. I will find Excalibur."

"Elaine was a powerful enemy," Arthur said. "How'd you kill her?"

Lancelot removed a black-bladed dagger from a sheath on his lower back and showed Arthur.

"A basilisk-tooth blade," Arthur said. "I am impressed. You know it will never work again, though."

Lancelot nodded. "I kept one just in case . . ." He stopped himself.

"In case what, Lancelot?" Arthur asked, his sharklike smile something that Mordred remembered well and wanted to remove permanently.

"In case . . ."

"In case I came to kill you?" Arthur asked.

Lancelot nodded.

Arthur laughed. "You have more intelligence than I give you credit for. I'm not going to be angry because you were prepared to kill me should you need to."

"I can go back and find Excalibur," Lancelot said. "If I can have some people, a small force, maybe . . ."

"No." Arthur cut him off. "We're going to take this realm from Odin and his scum allies, but if for some reason we don't, I have a backup plan. It's why I left the battlefield, Lancelot. I have to make sure it's all in order. I hate the idea of leaving the fighting, but needs must. I'm sure there will be plenty for me to kill once it's over. I've spread the word that Hades, Persephone, and the like are to be taken alive if possible. You, however, will take my wife through the realm gate to the north. You will take her to Avalon; you will place her in a cell for my return. You will not kill her. I may not give a shit about what happens to the bitch, but she betrayed *me*, and *I* will be the one to deal with her. Do. You. Understand?"

Lancelot nodded.

"I have to go back to the battlefield for now. I have to ensure that things are going smoothly." Arthur crouched by Guinevere and stroked her face with the back of his hand. She flinched away. "You really are too smart for your own good. If you'd only been the dumb bitch we all expected you to be, you might never have learned what I was; you might not have sought comfort in the arms of someone who was going to use you to keep himself alive."

Arthur laughed. "Fuck it, maybe you're not as smart as you think." He turned back to Lancelot. "You're sure that Mordred has Excalibur?"

Mordred inwardly cursed himself. He'd left the sword back at Elaine's in the care of Lucifer. He'd been rocked with fear that Elaine's last words would prove wrong should he use the sword, that everyone would see the man he was melt away to reveal the monster underneath, but now that he'd seen how much Arthur wanted it, he knew he should have brought it with him. It would have meant that Arthur's forces would have been interested in only him and not those he cared for. But there was nowhere near enough time to go back there, retrieve it, and return. *Well, that's just perfect.*

"He's scared of it," Lancelot said.

"That sounds about right," Arthur said. "He was always weak. You say he's powerful now. Well, that might be the case, but inside he's still the weak little nothing who got in my way. I will see you soon, Lancelot, and you, my lovely wife. Do not fail me."

"Yes, my king," Lancelot said, bowing his head slightly.

"Is that it?" Arthur asked. "Is that all I get? I think I deserve a somewhat greater reception."

Lancelot dropped to his knees and kissed Arthur's hand.

"Better," Arthur said. "You get what I need, you're forgiven. You don't, I'll make sure to end you this time, and you won't have Zeus to help hide you."

Lancelot nodded frantically as the ground beneath his feet lit up bright green. He darted back, to the amusement of the paladins and Arthur. There was a flash of light, and a few meters away from where Arthur stood were another man and more paladins.

Hel reached out and placed her hand on Mordred's shoulder as he tensed from the appearance of his father, Merlin.

"My lord," Merlin said.

"Is everything ready?" Arthur asked.

"Empress Rela is ready to begin her portion of the plan. She will attack from the rear of the city. After we breached the walls, we had several sorcerers avoid the fighting to place the correct runes in places they need to be. It is done."

"And the preparations for this realm?" Arthur asked.

"Should they be needed, they are ready," Merlin assured his king.

"Merlin, your son is here," Arthur said. "He fights in the battle against our forces."

"My son will be dealt with," Merlin said. "He has great power but a reluctance to use it. His mind is still broken by what was done to him."

"And Gawain?" Arthur asked.

"I left him in charge of Avalon. I assured him that he would be doing great things for our people."

"And so he will," Arthur said. "We will need fresh blood once this is all done. Gawain is a trusted general, and he should be rewarded as such. Maybe he could be emperor of North America."

"I believe he would enjoy that," Merlin said with a dip of his head before he, too, climbed onto a horse.

"Lancelot," Arthur said.

Lancelot almost snapped to attention.

"If you betray me again . . . well, have you ever heard of a brazen bull?"

The expression on Lancelot's face said he had.

"Imagine one, but activated only by magical power. I've been trying it out on people. I'm quite satisfied with the results." Arthur rode off, followed by Merlin and his paladins, leaving Lancelot alone with Guinevere. She seized her chance and headbutted Lancelot in the groin the second he came close enough.

Lancelot dropped to the ground, and Mordred took that moment to stand and head down the slope with Hel right behind him.

Lancelot spotted the two just as Guinevere got to her feet and planted a kick right between Lancelot's legs.

Mordred removed the tape from around Guinevere's mouth and cut through the bindings but only just managed to stop her from launching herself at a kneeling Lancelot.

"Hel, can you take her back to the battle?" Mordred asked.

Hel helped Guinevere up onto the horse that Lancelot had ridden to the meeting place, then got up herself.

"You going to get back to the fighting quickly?" Hel asked. "I'll try and find Hades or Persephone, someone who can hopefully do something about those runes. If they are trying to merge the realms, it would be a massacre."

Mordred nodded. "I'll be right behind you."

"Make him suffer," Guinevere snapped.

Mordred removed the sword belt that Lancelot wore with his two swords still sheathed and tossed it away. He grabbed the basilisk dagger and threw it into the nearest tree, embedding it up to the hilt.

"Please go," he said softly without turning back to Hel. A few seconds later he heard the horse gallop away.

"Hel not have the stomach for torture?" Lancelot said as Mordred walked away and took a seat at the edge of the clearing.

"She doesn't care for it, no," Mordred said. "Why'd you kill Elaine?"

"I knew how much Arthur would give for her death," Lancelot said. "I couldn't get that damn sword, but I thought Elaine might be the next best thing. And it had to be done before the wall came down."

"You were communicating with Arthur?"

"Sorcerer's circle with Gawain to begin with," Lancelot said. "I needed to stop running. It was nothing personal."

It felt pretty goddamn personal to Mordred, but he sucked the anger back down. "I loved Elaine."

"We all love someone."

"You only love yourself."

Lancelot shook his head. "I loved Guinevere once. Thought I did, anyway."

"So you're going to be one of his soldiers again?"

"I don't care about that," Lancelot said. "I just care about getting to live again. Not having to run. Not having to be afraid."

"And you'll murder Elaine and Guinevere to get it."

"I'll murder anyone I need to," Lancelot snapped. "I'm done living like this. Done living with a woman who detests me. Done fearing that if I leave her, she'll get caught and rat me out. I'm just done."

"Galahad would be disgusted with you."

"Galahad is *dead*," Lancelot said. "What he thinks matters exactly jack and shit."

Mordred got to his feet, walked over to Lancelot, and punched him in the jaw. "He's your son."

Lancelot spat blood onto the ground. "Galahad always hated me. He always looked down on me. He found out that his dad was a great swordsman but a lousy person. Boo. Fucking. Hoo."

"Speaking as someone who has a shit parent," Mordred said, "I have to say, you're certainly in the running for shittiest one."

"So is this how I die?" Lancelot asked.

Mordred picked up a sword and threw it over to Lancelot. It landed by his feet.

"You're going to let me fight for my life?" Lancelot said with a laugh. "You're a fucking idiot."

"You don't deserve it," Mordred said. "You deserve to be killed and left to rot in an unmarked grave. But Galahad was my friend. And he would want you to die with some honor. So here we are."

Lancelot picked up the sword and unsheathed it. "I am one of the finest swordsmen to ever wield a blade."

"I know," Mordred said, tossing his sheath aside and turning back to Lancelot.

"You can't win. I'm not even sure Arthur himself would be able to win against me." Lancelot smiled. "You'll die here. Guinevere will die soon after, and Hel, too, if she gets in my way. You'll have died for nothing. It'll be you in an unmarked grave."

"You talk a lot," Mordred said.

Lancelot shot forward, his blade tipped toward Mordred's chest, but Mordred easily pushed the sword aside and avoided the follow-up cut toward his neck. Lancelot didn't wait for a second, continuing to attack over and over again. He forced Mordred to parry and move aside but never gave him a chance to go on the offensive.

"You're better than I remember," Lancelot said after a few minutes of fighting.

Mordred had a cut on his cheek, but it didn't sting; he'd barely even known it had happened at the time.

"What do you have to say about that?" Lancelot said.

"One hundred and fifty," Mordred said.

Lancelot chuckled. "What?"

"One hundred and fifty," Mordred repeated. "I was counting to one hundred and fifty. I think that's all you're going to get."

Lancelot moved forward to attack in perfect formation, and Mordred slammed a spear of light into his chest, twisted it, and pulled it free. Lancelot dropped to his knees, blood pouring from the open wound.

"I figured that my love for your son bought you two and a half minutes of honor," Mordred said. He slammed the spear into Lancelot's temple and detonated the magic, killing him instantly.

Mordred took a deep breath. "Time to go win a war."

Chapter Twenty-Six

Nate Garrett

Ellesborough, United Kingdom, Earth Realm

I'd met up with the rest of the group in a small pub just outside Ellesborough, far enough from Chequers not to raise too much suspicion from locals when a group of strangers descended on the village.

The plan was simple. Hope was going to come with me, Kase, and Rasputin to Chequers. We had the codes for security from Aphrodite, who had decided that instead of involving herself physically, she would do better to help Hephaestus and the others plan a way to get into the Aeneid building without alerting the hundreds of guards who worked in and around it.

None of the others had been thrilled with the plan, and certainly none of them had been happy that Aphrodite was doing anything that didn't involve bleeding to death on the pavement. Sky in particular had had to be calmed from burying a dagger in Aphrodite's chest and calling it a day.

Rasputin was to be on lookout with Kase. The latter had been quite unhappy with their job. I'd picked Kase specifically for her werewolf powers but also because I wanted her to be away from anything inside the building. A fact that Remy had immediately picked up on.

"You can't keep giving her things to do that take her away from trouble," Remy said when we were about to get into the Jaguar XJs that Aphrodite had arranged for us.

"No idea what you're talking about," I said, opening the car door.

"Liar," he said, placing his hand on it to keep me from opening it farther. "Tommy got hurt. You tried to have him sent to Shadow Falls to keep him safe from further harm, and now you're sending his daughter away from things you're doing. You did it in Kilnhurst—you sent all of us in the opposite direction. And now you're doing it here."

"Kase is an excellent lookout," I said.

"She's also excellent at infiltration," Remy countered. "You're putting people away from danger because you're scared they'll get hurt. You can't protect everyone, Nate. You'll drive yourself barmy if you try."

"I can't have anyone else get hurt if I can stop it," I said, my voice barely above a whisper.

"You can't go through life like that," Remy said. "We're at war."

"I know, but Tommy and my dad got hurt, and I . . ." I stopped.

"You couldn't stop it?"

I nodded.

"You weren't there."

I nodded again. "I know."

"If you'd have been there, could you have stopped it?"

"I don't know," I said honestly. "Probably not."

"You'd be in a bed beside your dad," Remy said. "Or worse."

"Damn it," I said.

"Kase will do the job you assigned her," Remy said. "I don't think you need to change it now, but seriously, let people help you. Don't push them away to protect them; that might make things worse in the long run."

"I can't protect everyone," I said softly.

"A very smart person said that recently," Remy said with a smile.

"Who was that, then?" I asked him.

"I hope my new power, whatever it is, lets me hurt you."

I laughed. "We can all dream, Remy."

We both got into the car and set off.

Chequers was a fortress. There was a long driveway, giving the guards time to prepare for arrivals. The ground on two sides was flat and open with only a few trees for cover. One side of the large estate sat against a denser woodland, but it was also full of motion detectors and guards, neither of which I wanted to deal with if I had the choice.

The best way to get into the building was through the front. Unfortunately, that meant being spotted from some distance. It also meant trusting Hope to do the driving. We needed the guard to interact with her; we needed them to . . . well, basically, not see me. There was a pretty good chance that they'd open fire at me in seconds. Aphrodite had told me that my face was well known, thanks to my actions in Portland going viral, but that Hope could just be a maid or someone delivering instructions from Hera. Due to the fact that the main building had runes on it that stopped powers, the guards were mostly human, but there were a few non-humans there too. They'd be the ones that could cause a problem should anything go wrong, which, knowing our luck, was almost an inevitability at this point.

"You think Aphrodite was on the level?" Hope asked from the driver's seat of the Jaguar XJ, a large saloon car selected because it wouldn't look out of place among the usual cars driven by staff.

I was hidden in the rear passenger seat of the car, using my shadow magic to keep myself partially inside the shadows of the car while still not entirely in my shadow realm. It was hard work and took a lot of concentration, so of course Hope wanted to chat.

"Yes," I said. "She wants out. She wants safety. And I trust Hephaestus on this."

"Why?"

"He's been working for Hades for centuries," I said. "He wouldn't risk his family just to save Aphrodite. They don't exactly get on."

"Isn't she his ex-wife?"

"Are you going to chat the whole time?" I asked as we took the turn onto the long road that led to the large metal gates at the front of the estate.

Hope's smile could be seen in the rearview mirror. "Where are Kase and Rasputin?"

"Tree line," I said with a sigh. "About half a mile away. When we're done, we send the family out that way, through the back of the property."

"And the guards and motion detectors back there?"

"They won't be a problem when we're leaving."

"Aphrodite doesn't much care for the humans' survival, does she?"

"She might be betraying Hera, but that doesn't mean she's a nice person," I said.

"She was one of those who did this to me."

"You've mentioned it once or twice. You can't kill her."

Hope's eyes narrowed. "You gave your word to her?"

"I told her she'd be given safe passage if she helped."

Hope nodded as if she were fine with that. I imagined that once that safe passage was over and done with, Hope would have a new target to remove from whatever realm Aphrodite found herself in. I couldn't say I was overly sad about it. Aphrodite was a monster. She'd done horrific things in her life. She'd enjoyed hurting people for no other reason than that they'd offended her somehow. I was glad Medusa wasn't here; she'd have ripped Aphrodite's head off the second she'd laid eyes on her.

But Aphrodite was also terrified of Hera. And if Hera's behavior was becoming more erratic, if she was killing allies just as readily as enemies, I couldn't blame Aphrodite for wanting to leave. Hephaestus had been feeding Hades information about Hera for centuries, something I'd been sure not to mention to Aphrodite when we'd met. Despite all they'd been through, and despite Hephaestus's continued assurance of his disdain for his ex-wife, he still held a spark of flame for her.

"There are four guards," Hope said. "All with submachine guns."

"They can't use them. Too much noise."

"This isn't my first time," Hope said with more amusement in her voice than irritation.

"I wasn't telling you how to do it," I told her.

"I know. I just enjoy winding you up."

The car pulled up to the entrance of Chequers, where one guard stood in front and commanded Hope to switch off the engine. She did as she was told, but the man didn't lower his gun. They might have been assholes, but they were clearly not idiots.

A second guard walked around the car, looking in the windows but not actually touching any part of the vehicle. The third walked over to the driver's window and tapped on it, while the fourth stood behind her, gun casually aimed at the car.

Hope lowered the window and smiled her broadest smile. "Hera sent me," she said. "I'm to give the prime minister instructions." She removed a sealed letter from a purse on the passenger seat. Aphrodite had given it to us and said that if anyone opened it, the letter was on official stationery and in Hera's handwriting. Apparently, forgery was also one of Aphrodite's skills.

The guard reached over for the letter, and Hope touched the side of his face as she gave it to him. He blinked twice and leaned back into the car.

"Send me another," Hope whispered.

He nodded. "You," the guard barked as he stood upright. "Keep her company."

The guard who had been walking around the car nodded and moved over to the driver's window, while the one who had been there only a moment ago walked off to the small hut nearby as if to read the letter.

The other two guards stayed where they were as the second guard leaned into the car. Hope placed her hand on the bare skin around his fingerless gloves and smiled at him. He leaned toward her.

"Kill them. No noise," she whispered.

"Ma'am, can you get out of the car?" the second guard said, and for a moment, I thought it had all gone wrong.

Hope did as she was asked. She leaned up against the car, her arms crossed over her chest. She wore a black trouser suit and looked every inch the professional businesswoman she was meant to be imitating. I stayed hidden in the rear, my fingers beginning to tingle as what I was doing began to take its toll. Hope had to move quickly, or I was going to fall into the shadow realm, and then I wasn't entirely sure what light source would be safe to come out of.

Hope kept smiling as the guard she'd touched most recently walked over to the one in the hut, and they had a quick, whispered conversation.

The two guards moved back toward the car, taking different routes so that each of them would walk by one of their comrades.

When they were close enough, they sprang into action, driving knives into the throats of the two unsuspecting guards, and dragged their bodies away.

The first guard walked back to the hut, and the gate began to open. Once that was done, they both walked over to the car. "The gate is open," the first guard said.

"You were both excellent," Hope told them, much to their delight. They smiled and puffed out their chests.

"What else can we do?" the second guard asked.

"Number of nonhumans?" she said.

"Three—two inside, one out," one guard said.

"And they are?" Hope asked.

"Inside, sorcerer and elemental. The sorcerer wears a bracelet designed to let him use his magic."

That was useful information.

"The one outside is a werelion," the second guard said.

"Thank you so much for the information," Hope said, making both men beam with pride. "Go into the house and kill the lights. No deaths inside. We don't want to alert anyone. We also need the camera feed shut off and any alarms stopped. Return to me in the dining room when you're done."

Both guards ran into the estate as Hope climbed back into the car and drove through the gate. "They told their boss that we have access," she said.

"And what do you have planned for them next?" I asked, concerned she was going to start having them perform for her.

"You're worried I'm going to have them do stupid things," Hope said with a chuckle as she stopped the car next to a Range Rover. "I think I can control myself if it means getting to Hera."

"The werelion—you okay taking him out?" I asked.

"It would be my pleasure," Hope said.

The lights in the main courtyard died a second later, and I opened the car door, removed my shadows, and stepped out as several guards ran into the building.

"I'll see you in the dining room," Hope said. She bent down and placed a small explosive device under the car before throwing me the detonator and walking after the guards into the building.

The explosives were to ensure the guards had something else to concern themselves with when we were done. There were no runes outside the property that limited magic. The gates themselves were shields against such things, but inside was different, and I knew that once I was there, my magic was off the table.

I moved to the rear of the car and popped the boot, taking out the interior lining and tossing it aside as I removed the HK45. There were runes inscribed on the barrel that ensured it was completely silent, something Zamek was exceptionally proud of. I placed the gun in my hip holster and took four full magazines of ammo, putting them in my pockets. I'd prefer to use my magic, but I had no issues with using a gun should the need arise. Whatever the best tool for the job was.

I moved to the side of the massive building and placed a hand against a glass window, pouring air magic out of my palm to cover the entire pane. I hoped those two guards had finished their job, and I pushed slightly with the air. The glass cracked; the only thing keeping it together was the magic that covered it. I pushed the glass into the room, slowly placed it on a table, and removed the air magic as I climbed in.

I moved through the room to the door. I'd never been to Chequers before, but Aphrodite had drawn me a plan to show me where the hostages were kept and how to get there without needing to kill every single ITF agent inside the building. I was pretty sure that Hope wouldn't have minded the second part.

I opened the door and looked out into the corridor beyond. Two guards stood there, talking about the loss of power. Apparently, their boss was less than thrilled about it, and it should be back up and running shortly. Good to know. Neither guard wore visible armor, which made my life easier.

I moved out of the room and threw a blade of fire at the farthest guard, which hit him in the throat and sent him to the ground. The closer guard spun around, her gun already moving up toward me as I drove a blade of fire up under her chin and into her brain. Both guards dead in moments. The wraith in my shadow realm didn't like corpses, so I dragged them back into the room I'd just left and closed the door. Better to keep my presence unknown for now.

I moved through the house quickly and stopped at the staircase as I spotted another guard walking down toward the front door. Runes burned on his military-style armor, and I figured he was someone more important than the two I'd removed. He wore a small bracelet with even more runes on it. It was designed to let the wearer access their power in a place designed to limit it, which made him the sorcerer. I drew the gun and fired two bullets into his head as I stepped around the bottom of the stairs. Sorcerer or elemental, both died with silver shots to the head. He was dead before he hit the ground. I dragged his body up the stairs and into the first room, after checking it for people, and dumped it on the ground next to a bookcase.

I removed his bracelet and tried it on, hoping it might let me access my power, and a small sphere of air appeared in my hand.

The sorcerer's radio went off just as I was leaving. "We've got some issues with the power here—looks like it's been fucked with. You see anything, Dave?"

I turned and picked it up. "Well, shit," I said to myself. There was no point replying, as I almost certainly didn't sound like Dave, and there was a pretty good possibility that whoever was on the other end would notice. So I removed the power pack from the radio and tossed it across the room, where it slid under a leather chair.

I left the room, using my air magic in the keyhole to lock it behind me, and set off along the long upstairs corridor to where the prime minister and her family were being kept at the rear of the estate. I knew there would be guards outside the room and another two farther along the corridor, so I was prepared when I saw the first one walk out of a room, leaving the door open. He died with a bullet to the head a moment later, and I pushed him back into the room, where the remains of a meal sat on a wooden table.

I turned to leave and shot a guard who surprised me. He collapsed back onto the ground, and I left him there when I heard someone call a name from around the corner. I used the darkness to my advantage and looked around the corner. Two guards. A man and a woman. Both stood with guns aimed at the end of the hallway, both using torches that I only just managed to avoid. There was a staircase to the side of them that led down to the kitchen, where I was certain there would be more guards, so I didn't want to do anything that might bring an army upstairs and jeopardize the welfare of the family.

I reached out with my shadow, ready to take them both, but when it touched them, the shadow recoiled back to me. They were wearing runes designed to stop magic or at least make it have less of an effect on them. I stepped out and fired three times, catching the woman twice in the head and the man once just behind the eye.

I picked up both handguns, as well as the shotgun that was on a nearby side table, and removed the keys to the prime minister's room from the pocket of one of the guards. At the end of the hall, I opened the door, went inside without a word, and closed it behind me.

The prime minister, Eleanor Owino, stood with her husband and two young children. She'd been the first black woman to become prime minister and was one of the youngest to ever take the job. She'd run on a platform of progressivism and a determination to deal with the problems left by the previous government. Despite various media outlets portraying the married couple—both of whom had been born in the UK—in a light that didn't just border on racist but crossed that line in leaps and bounds, her party had won easily. Unfortunately, soon after, Arthur had woken up, and it had all gone to shit, but it had been a nice dream for about six months.

"Who are you?" the prime minister wanted to know. There was no fear in her voice, nothing but a demand for answers.

"Nate Garrett," I told her. "I'm here to get you and your family out of here."

"I know that name," her husband, Talib Owino, said. "Portland, yes?"

I nodded. "I'm famous. We need to leave."

"You're one of them," Eleanor said. "A sorcerer."

"I am," I said, looking at the two children—a boy of no more than five and a girl of about eight—both of whom had come out from behind their parents. "We're going to leave. We're going to get you somewhere safe."

"Why now?" Eleanor asked. "My family has been left in danger for a year."

"I'm sorry about that," I said. "But honestly, this is the first time I've been back in the UK for a few years, and we've been busy just trying to stay alive ourselves. None of us have been in a position to remove Hera or those who work for her. If you want to stay, you're more than welcome to, but Hera is about to fall from power in London. There needs to be someone to step into the vacuum she leaves and lead this country. There needs to be someone who will stand up to Avalon so when we defeat Hera, we don't have to worry about the ITF thugs murdering people on the streets. I think that would probably be you, yes?"

Eleanor Owino nodded. "There are many guards here," she said.

"Fewer than there were when I started," I pointed out.

"There's the big man too," the young girl said.

"Big man?" I asked.

"He scares us," the boy said.

"War?" I asked.

"That's what he calls himself," Talib said. "He seems to delight in terrorizing people."

"He'll be my problem," I told them.

"Are you really as powerful as the rumors suggest?" Eleanor asked. "Can you keep my family safe?"

I nodded. "We're going to get you all out of here, through the woods to my friends. One is a sorcerer, the other a werewolf. She's in charge."

"A werewolf?" the girl asked, sharing an expression of excitement with her younger brother.

I smiled. "Her name is Kase."

Gunfire could be heard outside, and I ran over to the window that overlooked the back of the house. I couldn't see anyone, but occasionally there were muzzle flashes. I guessed that the guards whom Hope had used had been given new orders.

"We have to go," I said. "Now."

I removed the holster and HK and gave them both to Talib. "You were in the Royal Marine Commandos, yes?"

He nodded. "Two tours of Afghanistan," he said, putting the holster on before checking the gun and taking the extra magazines.

"I wasn't planning on having you get into a firefight, but I figure you could use this more than I can." I looked beyond him at the prime minister and their two children. "You three keep back."

"I have been in firefights, Mr. Garrett," Prime Minister Owino said. "I will keep my children safe."

I'd read her file, and what she said was true. She'd been a part of Doctors Without Borders and more than once had come under fire from warlords or thugs looking to make a name for themselves. Even so, she wasn't a soldier, and I just needed to make sure she was aware of what was about to happen.

"We go out," I said. "Turn downstairs, through the kitchen to the dining room. There you will be met by my friend Hope. She will keep you safe while I make sure that everyone is more interested in me."

"There are guards in the woods," Talib said.

"Kase and Rasputin will have dealt with those," I told him, hoping that was true by now. I put my hand on the doorknob and turned back to the family. "Let's go," I said, opening the door and stepping out into the empty hallway.

I led the four of them downstairs and got them to wait against the wall as I stepped into the kitchen and moved around the large table in the middle of the cavernous room to the rear door, where a guard was looking outside, his gun ready. He didn't see me or the blade of fire. The first he knew of either was the instant it entered the base of his neck and killed him.

I moved his body and looked outside. A guard sprinted across the small courtyard and was riddled with bullets halfway across. The two soldiers Hope had touched walked across the courtyard and put another round in the head of their former comrade before walking over to me.

"We await Hope," one of them said. He had several nasty cuts on his face, while his partner had a bullet hole in his arm, although neither seemed to be bothered by their wounds. One of them stayed by the door while the other ran around to the side of the house, presumably to keep an eye out for future problems.

I went back to the family and told them to go into the kitchen and get down by the table while I fetched Hope from the room adjacent.

Hope actually met us in the kitchen just as I was leaving. "I got bored," she said by way of explanation.

There was a deep howl from somewhere in the woods, the sign that all was clear, followed by the guard poking his head through the door. "We have contact at the front of the property," he said. "We have eliminated several combatants, but there appear to be three Range Rovers arriving, all full of ITF. This house will have a dozen soldiers in it shortly."

"Get the family to Kase and Rasputin," I told Hope. "These two will help you."

The two brainwashed guards nodded.

The family exited the kitchen with the two soldiers and Hope behind them. She paused at the door of the kitchen. "When we're done, I'll deal with those two."

"Good," I said. "Make sure the kids don't see. They've been through enough."

Hope nodded. I watched them all vanish into the darkness of the woodlands as the front door to the house exploded.

I stepped out of the kitchen into the hallway and rolled my neck, looking out over the front of the building. I removed the detonator from my pocket, clicked it, waited until the first Range Rover entered the compound, and detonated it. I felt the rumble of the explosion as it tore the Jaguar we'd brought into the compound in half, along with anyone or anything near it.

A moment later, I was flat out running through the woods after everyone. I stopped only when I'd climbed into the back of an SUV driven by Kase, and we were soon driving away at speed.

"I dealt with them," Hope said.

"Good," I said as we drove past Chequers, and I saw War tear through the remains of the front gate. He looked over at the car I was in, and I knew there and then that this wasn't going to be it between us. Good.

"You know everyone will be waiting now," Hope said, turning around in the passenger seat to speak to me.

I nodded. "Let them wait," I said.

"Thank you for what you did tonight," Prime Minister Owino said, one of her children beside her in the seven-seater car. The rear two seats were taken up by her husband and other child. The only person who didn't have a seat was Rasputin, who had opted to sit on the floor, blatantly defying the law and obviously not caring. Couldn't say I blamed him for that. It had been a long night.

"The next few days will be long ones," I said. "They will be fraught, they will be dangerous, and Hera will not go easily."

"But you're still going to stop her, right?" Hope asked.

I nodded. "She stands between me and the cure," I said. "You're goddamn right I'm going to stop her."

Chapter Twenty-Seven

Nate Garrett

Later that night, after we'd dropped off the prime minister and her family at one of our safe houses, we met up with the rest of the group just outside London. The prime minister was going to have to arrange everything she needed to do to take control from her current location, and we all had to just hope that enough of the ministers in her party were loyal to her and their country, not to Avalon.

Zamek was certain that he could get us all into London without our being killed the second we stepped there.

"You okay?" Sky asked me as we drove toward an old and thankfully abandoned fort that had long ago fallen into disrepair. It was now apparently frequented by kids, who spray-painted graffiti and did whatever it was teenagers did in the twenty-first century, the whole time unaware of what sat under the centuries-old stone that they used as a playground.

"I guess when they made us, they really went all out. A few centuries ago, when Mordred was corrupted, we fought several times, and we were both closely matched, but our level of power has increased time and time again since then. Seeing War again made me realize that maybe we, too, are closely matched. Maybe this isn't a fight that can be won one-on-one."

"We'll figure something out about how to deal with him," Zamek said.

"I suggest stabbing him with something pointy," Remy said from the back seat of the SUV we were in.

"Thanks, Remy," I said.

Remy clicked his fingers and pointed at me. "You're welcome."

"What the hell was that?" I asked, shaking my head and smiling. "You figured out what you can do yet?"

Remy looked sad, and I felt bad for bringing it up. "Not yet," he said. "I'm not really sure how I'm meant to actually figure it out."

"How'd you figure it out last time?" I asked.

"I just kind of did it," he said. "Someone pushed me off a mountain. And then I just sort of figured out I could turn into smoke. Oh, and after that I had to fight a coven of witches. Sky was there."

"I remember that," Sky said. "Fun times."

"Did you get pushed off a mountain and fight the witches at the same time?" Zamek chimed in.

"No, not at the same time," Remy said, exasperated. "They were two very different occasions. It was back when everyone thought Nate was dead. I went on holiday to figure out what I was, and I ran into a coven of witches. They were not good people."

"That feels like a story worth telling," I said.

Remy shrugged. "Maybe one day it will be. In the meantime, we have far too many assholes shitting all over the country."

"And we're back to images I could have done without," Kase said from the driver's seat.

"You're welcome," Remy said again with a flourish.

"So, Zamek, once we get to this fort, what happens?" I asked, wanting to get answers before we reached our destination.

"Underneath the ruins is a crisscross of old dwarven tunnels," he said. "We've got to go pretty far down to get there, though."

"And what will an old tunnel do?" Remy asked. "Apart from probably contain giant rats."

"Apparently, back when London was little more than a massive bog, the leaders of several pantheons got together to get a series of tunnels built that travel from the Thames further inland. It was meant to be there just in case Merlin and Avalon turned from dream to massive disaster."

"And you know about this how?" Sky asked.

"While we were at the prison and Nate was talking to Hope and you were talking to your sister, I made a few calls," Zamek said. "I figured we were going to London at some point and wanted to figure out a way inside that wasn't going to get us all turned into paste."

"I'm already liking this plan," Remy said.

"I called Mac and Ellie," Zamek said. "They're part of a rebellion working inside London to stop Hera from being Hera."

"They're here?" I asked. Manannán mac Lir, or Mac, as he liked to be known, was a water elemental whose father used to calm the seas between the British mainland and Avalon Island, halfway between Britain and Ireland. His father had been murdered by people working for Avalon, and Mac was not one to just sit back without seeking some kind of justice for what had happened. I hadn't known he'd joined a rebellion, though.

Ellie was a werewolf, and at one point she had been high up in the pecking order for one of the most powerful packs in the country. That all felt like a long time ago, and I wondered if anyone would ever get to go back to their old lives even if we did win.

"They're in London," Zamek said. "They're going to arrange for us to have a little bit of cover while we try not to get killed."

"So they found some old dwarven ruins?" Sky asked.

Zamek nodded. "I'd theorized that there must have been some sort of underground system in the UK, simply because of the number of times dwarves had done work here with Merlin or Brutus hundreds of years before my people were scattered to the realms. I spoke to Mac a few years ago and asked him to look into anything in London that might look like a dwarven ruin. Took a while to find them, but eventually they got something."

"Are these rebels in London working with Hades?" Rasputin asked.

Zamek nodded. "They're on their own, but we all pool intel."

"So these people will help us?" Hope asked.

"Mac can be trusted," I said.

"What does this rebellion do?" Hope asked. "I assume they've been unsuccessful, as Hera is still alive."

"Mostly they help people get out of the city or country," Zamek said, ignoring Hope's tone.

"I had some dealings with them on missions," Kase said. "They're fighting a losing battle when it comes to Hera. And most of them are either human or not as powerful as those they fight, but they're smart, capable, and have connections to the government."

"The prime minister?" Rasputin asked.

Kase nodded.

"How capable are they, really?" Sky asked.

"They're a lot of ex-Avalon, ex-military, ex-police, doctors, teachers—people who just lived ordinary lives but know the reality of what Avalon is. Most of them have day jobs and do this on the side, helping where they can."

"But they're not Hera's level of power," Hope said.

"No," Kase told her. "She would kill them all in an instant. But they have stopped her from making as many people who disagree vanish as she'd like. A few journalists who got a bit too close to the truth for Hera's liking are alive because of them. Families haven't been torn apart. They do good work."

"Just not quite good enough," Hope said. There was no judgement in her voice; it was merely a statement of fact. Said in the rudest way possible.

A low growl emanated from the driver's seat.

"Maybe with a bit more tact next time," I said.

"What?" Hope asked. "What did I say?"

The conversation dropped off after that, and I lost track of where I was until we arrived at the old fort, long since left to ruin. There were no kids playing around the fallen masonry, but there were half a dozen heavily armed guards standing around the light-bathed patch of grass just next to the fort.

Zamek got out and walked over to the nearest guard, who waved us through. Zamek came back to the car. "We're to go around the corner and go down into the tunnels."

Kase followed Zamek's directions and parked the car before we all walked into the ruins, where one of dozens of armed soldiers opened a large metal door that led down underneath the ground. One of the soldiers came with us to show us the way. She took us through to the rooms beyond; they appeared to have been part of the original fort, but it was hard to tell. There was less graffiti here and no evidence of anyone using it as a play area.

"You know, Hera wants you to come to London," Rasputin said. "Arthur's plan is to unite the realms under his rule or burn those that resist, but Hera will just want revenge."

"You did kill her son and grandson," Hope said. "Which, by the way, if I haven't mentioned before, I wish I'd seen."

"I was there," I said. "It wasn't exactly a party."

"I would have had one anyway," Hope said with a smile.

"My point is that Hera will be expecting you," Rasputin said. "War saw you back at Chequers, and he will have relayed that to Hera."

"You sound afraid," Sky said.

"Of course I'm afraid," Rasputin said, sounding exasperated. "Hera will know we're coming for her. She's going to be ready. She's going to try and kill us."

"Lots of people have tried to kill us over the years," Remy said. "We've gotten good at avoiding it."

"Last we heard, Hera has her people preparing more of Pestilence's venom. I think she plans to unleash something in London itself," the soldier who'd been guiding us said.

"Any idea what?" I asked.

"Not completely," she said.

"Hera is more than capable of burning a whole city to ash just to ensure no one else can have it," Rasputin said.

"Are you saying she's going to plant bombs around London?" Kase asked.

"It's not exactly outside the realm of possibility," Hope said.

"Certainly sounds like a shitty act of Hera's," Remy said. "She's never been shy about murdering everyone and anyone who happens to be in her way. Forcing you to watch your friend die and then watch the city you called home for a decade burn is a very Hera thing to do."

"Neither of those things will happen," I said. "Odin doesn't have long. She'll make me choose. The city or the cure."

"That *really* is a Hera thing to do," Sky said.

"She doesn't know we have help," Zamek said. It was the first time he'd spoken since we'd started going under the ruins, and I got the impression he was more interested in the walls of the fort than in keeping up with the conversation.

"Okay, I know there's a lot going on, but did we just get lost?" Remy asked as we reached a dead end.

The soldier placed her hands against the wall, and the cracks in the stone glowed a brilliant blue before pulling apart to reveal a lift beyond.

The lift was large enough to take a helicopter and was made with a mixture of bronze, gold, and a black stone I couldn't identify.

"This is alchemy," Zamek said, almost pushing me aside in his rush to examine the stone.

Everyone else piled onto the lift, and the soldier pulled a lever, starting the descent.

"These are old," Zamek said.

"Dwarves can't resist making even the ordinary look ornate," Hope said.

"Why settle for anything that doesn't inspire?" Zamek asked. "Why settle for ordinary when you can make something special?"

"I'm sorry I said anything," Hope said, with just the glimmer of a smile.

It was strange seeing Hope interact with other people. For so long she'd spoken to as few people as possible without taking them into her power to control. Once it became apparent that Hope had been in a lot more control than anyone had anticipated, I'd wondered just how much of Pandora's personality was also Hope's. Apparently, Hope was more capable of talking to people without turning them into mindless objects. At least, I wanted that to be the case.

The descent took a while, and in the silence of most of the occupants of the lift, I heard Zamek muttering to himself as he found a part he recognized from a dwarf he'd heard of or indeed knew himself.

"This is my father," Zamek said as the lift stopped. He pointed to a griffin that had been made of gold and bronze and then placed inside some black stone, as if the creature were bursting out to be free.

"Do dwarves sign their work?" Kase asked.

"The swirl around the eye was my father's mark." Zamek knelt in front of the small object and placed his hands on it. When he stood and turned back to us, it was clear he'd been crying.

"They are tears of happiness," Zamek said before anyone could ask if he was good. "There is little that remains of the work of the royal family; it is a pleasure to see his work. Even more to know that it is part of something that helps people, even a small part."

Everyone stepped off the lift and followed the soldier down a tunnel that appeared to have been made entirely of bronze. The naked-flame lamps caused a cascade of color on the wall around them, and the smell of cooked food reached my nostrils.

The tunnel opened out to reveal the hundreds of people who lived down here. There were dozens of small makeshift huts, combining metal and wood into living accommodations. To the far left, a little away from the huts, were several large barbecue pits and stalls with vegetables and fruits on them.

"I'm going to go check out the meat," Remy said, wiping his mouth. "You know, just in case the sellers have information we need. Juicy information."

"I'll go with him," Kase said. "For the same reason."

"You've managed to keep all of these people safe from Hera?" Rasputin asked, seemingly impressed.

"She has death squads out searching for people," the soldier said.

"Death squads?" I asked.

"They may as well be," the soldier said. "The ITF are little more than thugs and assassins. They've killed a lot of people to keep them quiet. Made even more disappear."

"Also, how are we going to get into London?" Sky asked.

"This dwarven tunnel goes right into London," the soldier said. "It's like a sideways lift that moves really quickly."

I looked at Zamek. "Any ideas about this?"

"We had a few of those in Nidavellir. I had no idea there was one in the Earth realm."

Remy and Kase rejoined us, the latter wiping her mouth while the former continued to eat what looked like a chicken breast.

"This is great," Remy said. "Haven't had cooked chicken in ages."

"Okay, now that Remy and Kase are full, maybe you could tell us what we're going to do?" I asked.

"My orders are to take you to London," the soldier said. "The tunnel takes us to a disused entrance to an old ruin near Covent Garden. From there it's not a huge distance to the Aeneid. A lot of our people are going to meet us at Covent Garden. It'll be daylight by the time we get there, just after rush hour, and the place will be busy."

"We might be able to blend in a little better," I said. "What about the mass of CCTV cameras in London? If the ITF have access, we're going to get spotted quickly."

"We'll have vehicles ready to take us where we need to go," the soldier said. "And some of our people already have control of the cameras. It's how we get in and out without anyone knowing. Trust me, this isn't our first time."

"It's the first time we're going to assault Hera's property," Remy said.

"She will be waiting," Rasputin said. "She is always waiting. It's sort of what she does. Whether we go in with sirens or secrecy, she'll be ready. She was ready for this the day Nate was discovered alive."

"Keep out of War's way," I said as we continued on.

"I didn't plan on going up and saying hi," Remy said. "Does he happen to have a weakness? Bad ankles, or a particular love of drinking poison, or he has to believe in himself to stay powerful, or a weakness to the color yellow?"

"The poison one would come in handy," Zamek said.

"He was made to fight and kill," Rasputin said. "That is all he does. It's all he's capable of. You aim him at someone, and he doesn't stop until they're dead."

"Or he is," Sky said.

"Or he is," Rasputin repeated with a nod.

"I wonder if I could touch him and make him go after Hera?" Hope said, almost absentmindedly.

Rasputin considered this for a moment. "I don't know," he said finally.

"Maybe there's an idea, then," Hope said. "I touch War, get him to tear Hera's head off and use it as a football. Fun for the whole family."

Remy stared at Hope. "Your family is fucked up."

Hope nodded a little. "Can't disagree with that."

We continued on until we arrived at a large platform on rails that had been . . . tampered with. "That's an underground train," I said. "With no roof. Or walls."

"This looks wildly unsafe," Zamek said.

"We use it to ship supplies back and forth," the soldier said. "I assure you it's safe." She paused. "Mostly safe."

"I don't know about anyone else, but I'm very excited to ride the machine of death," Remy said, getting up onto it.

We waited for everyone to get on and sit on the seats where seat belts had been welded into the metal floor of the carriage.

"Before you go," the soldier said, "you should know we found another realm gate in London. The tower of Elsing Spital."

"I know where that is," Kase said. "Didn't know there was a gate there, though."

"Well, we can't get it to work," the soldier continued. "It's pretty deep underground, and I figured with a dwarf on your side, maybe you'd have better luck."

"Looks like we have an emergency exit," Zamek said.

"Best-laid plans of mice and men," Rasputin said.

"Everyone ready?" I asked.

Everyone nodded or said that they were. Hera and her people had caused enough misery, and I aimed to end that today.

Chapter Twenty-Eight

Nate Garrett

Covent Garden was as bustling and busy as usual. Even with the city under Hera's control and the threat of Avalon violence at any moment, people still wanted to come to London. To shop. To enjoy themselves.

We were all standing near the craft market when I realized that Zamek wasn't with us. I turned and spotted him running along after us, gaining more than a few glances from shoppers. Arthur putting the knowledge of the nonhuman world out for all humans to see had ensured that no one outright freaked out when they saw a dwarf running down the road, but he still got a few stares, much like Remy. While Zamek ignored the passersby, though, Remy waved or clicked his fingers and pointed at them.

"You want your own show?" Sky asked Remy after he high-fived a teenage boy who was walking past with his parents.

"Can't help it if I'm loved," Remy said. "This might be the only good thing to come out of Arthur waking up. We don't have to hide anymore. Well, we do, because Avalon wants us all dead, but we don't have to hide because I'm a talking fox. You get where I'm going with this, yes?"

Sky nodded.

Zamek caught up with us and passed several of us small bracelets. "The Aeneid. It'll be rune scribed to stop anyone using their powers. I'm pretty sure of that. Hera isn't an idiot. These should, in theory, stop or at least slow it down. If the runes are applied with exceptional power, the bracelets might not work all throughout the building, but they should make sure that we're not powerless when the fighting starts."

As we walked through the city, I spotted several dozen people joining us as we passed several alleyways and caught glimpses of large crowds of people on the other side of the alleys.

"This is where we part company," the soldier said. "We're going to take the fight to the ITF today. There's a branch close to the Aeneid that won't be expecting trouble."

"A pitched battle in the middle of London is a good way to get innocent people killed," I said.

"A lot of innocent people," Remy said, and I looked back at him and noticed Hope shrug.

"I don't much care one way or the other," Hope said. "I mean, I'd prefer not to have civilians in the way, but you can't win a war and always be the good guy."

"We're going to keep them occupied in their own place," a second soldier said, this one a large man with long red hair.

"And how do we get into the building?" Kase asked.

"Rear of the building there's a loading-and-unloading bay," the female soldier said.

"That will be guarded," Sky said.

"Actually, it isn't," the soldier said. "Not as securely as you think. The building is on lockdown; everyone has moved inside."

"So how do we get into the building?" Zamek asked.

The soldier removed a piece of paper from her pocket. "These are the runes used. When you told Mac and Ellie of your plans, they had a soldier of ours who had already infiltrated the ITF go to the Aeneid and find out what runes were used. He drew those."

"Thank him for us," Zamek said, taking the paper and looking over the runes.

"He died yesterday."

"I'm sorry," I said.

"If he was caught, they could have changed the runes," Hope said.

"He wasn't caught drawing the runes," the soldier said. "He was caught trying to access the main computer system of the Aeneid. They tracked him down and killed him at his home. He'd already sent me a picture with those runes on it."

"Thank you," I said.

"An SUV will take you as close as it can," the soldier said. "We will keep the ITF busy."

"This is feeling like Portland all over again," Remy said.

"Portland was innocent civilian protestors against Avalon," the soldier said. "We are not civilian protesters. I assure you, this will end very differently."

"Best of luck, and thank you," I said to the soldier when we stopped at the edge of Covent Garden.

"You want a vest?" the soldier asked me, opening the boot of the car and passing them around.

I took it from her hand and put it on, noticing the runes burning on the inside. "Impact absorption?" I asked.

The soldier nodded. "Won't help against magic, but the ITF won't be using magic. They use standard silver hollow-tipped rounds. Different calibers, depending on the weapon, but the same idea, nonetheless. They're magic killers. That's what they call them."

"That's very dismissive of everyone else," Remy said. "I feel a little offended."

Sky, sitting in the rear of the car, tried to cover her laugh by putting her hands over her mouth but failed in that particular endeavor.

"You help design these?" Kase asked Zamek.

"Leonardo, Antonio, and Jinayca," Zamek said. "They've saved lives, but they don't work well in the other realms, so they've had limited use."

"I get the feeling they'll be tested well today," Kase said, putting hers on.

"Make them pay," the soldier said when everyone was ready, and she walked off with the rest of her team.

"You think they'll be okay?" Sky asked as everyone else got into one of two black SUVs.

"I hope so," I said. "But there's going to be bloodshed today. People will die."

"Let's just hope it's the right people," Hope said from inside the car.

On the short journey, we drove past several streets where the ITF was out in force, dealing with troublemakers or anyone who happened to get in their way.

"Fuck me sideways," Remy whispered. "That's a legion."

"Let's not go that way," Kase said.

We stopped a five-minute walk from the Aeneid, and weapons were handed out to everyone inside the SUVs. I picked up an MP5 from the stash and grabbed a few extra magazines while I was at it.

The normally busy streets were deserted.

"I get the feeling this is Hera's doing," Kase said as we moved away from the cars and started our short journey toward the building.

"Maybe she's put some kind of curfew in effect," Remy said. "It wasn't on the news, though, so it must have been recent."

No one else spoke until we were all crouched down in an alleyway across from the rear of the Aeneid. The large metal shutters for the loading bay were down, and two ITF soldiers patrolled outside.

Somewhere in the distance was an almighty explosion, followed by the sounds of gunfire.

"War has come to London," Hope said.

"The person or the act?" Rasputin asked.

"Probably both," Hope told him with a smile.

The two guards were both clearly agitated by the noise of fighting, and one of them spoke into his wrist.

"We need to get that radio," Kase said.

"Hope, you think you can get them to help us out?" I asked.

Hope strode out from where we were hiding. She walked across the street as both guards raised their weapons toward her. I didn't hear what she said to them, but they seemed to know to keep her back. Hope shook her head from side to side.

"Bollocks," I said, raising my rifle but finding Hope in the way.

"On it," Sky said. She fired twice, once at each target, and caught them both in the head.

I rushed out of the alleyway over to Hope as Zamek ran over to the door next to the metal shutter.

"I couldn't get close enough to touch them," Hope said. "Apologies."

"It's fine—they're still dead," I said.

"Yes, but they could have been useful," Hope replied, bending down, picking up one of the radios, and passing it to me.

"Closed network," I said, tossing the radio to Kase. "Might come in handy to know where everyone is."

"Door is open," Zamek exclaimed. "No one inside."

Kase grabbed one guard and I the other. We carried them into the building and dropped them behind the metal shutter.

"That's a lot of runes," Remy said, pointing across the large loading area, where dozens of wooden crates were stacked floor to ceiling, at the runes that had been drawn across the far wall.

"What do they do?" Rasputin asked.

"I don't read runes," Kase said. "But I'm guessing explode."

"That's not far off," Zamek said, rushing toward it with everyone following behind. "It's complex. Seriously complex. The runes that are on this paper were correct, but they don't tell you just how much power is inside them."

"And this is a lot, yes?" Remy asked.

Zamek nodded. "The power needs to be redistributed."

"Meaning something else has to go boom?" Sky asked.

"Yeah, actually. Almost exactly that. Runes with this much energy can't just be disarmed; they need to be redirected. That power has to go somewhere. I think people died to make these runes."

"There's dried blood on the wall," Kase said, taking a sniff. "I would put money on blood magic being used to make this."

"Give me five minutes," Zamek said.

"You have three," I said. "Any longer than that, and those guards are going to have to radio in, or someone is going to radio them."

"Why put two lone guards outside the building?" Sky asked. "Doesn't make any sense."

"That is an excellent point," I said, sprinting back to the door we'd come through and opening it slightly, expecting to see a lot of guards out there. But it was empty, just as it had been when we'd entered.

"Something isn't right," I said, more to myself than anyone else.

"Nathan," the radio in my hand said. "Oh, Nathan."

I sighed and answered it. "Hello, Hera. Any chance you could save us some trouble and just die?"

"You killed those two guards," she said, her voice almost sickly sweet.

"Are you high?" I asked as I walked back to my friends.

"I'm waiting to show you what I've done," she said. "I've waited so long for you to come to me. Those guards were the alarm system. They die, I get notified. I assume you're stuck inside the loading area. Shame. I'd hoped to kill you myself, but this will have to do."

"Everyone down," I shouted, pushing out a huge amount of air to create a shield between my friends and the wall of runes. The shield covered us all just as the wall exploded. The sound bounced around inside the dome of dense air, causing my ears to ring for several seconds.

Part of the ceiling above us collapsed, and Kase turned into her werebeast form, pouring ice from her mouth into the air above us to help strengthen the shield.

"We can't stay here," Sky said.

The final pieces of rubble fell onto the shield, which I charged with more magic and then cast out, throwing everything that had fallen onto it to the sides of the loading bay. The wall in front of us was gone, and a quick blast of air removed all of the dust, revealing the huge reception area in front.

"Stay down," I said, noticing several armed guards ahead. I picked up the debris with a gust of air and began to spin it around me in a whirlwind of shrapnel, smashing through the huge windows in the lobby and adding the glass to the mass around me.

Several guards popped up and fired at me, but the whirlwind that surrounded me acted as a shield. I aimed the power back across the reception area, cutting the guards to pieces and destroying everything in its path.

"Anyone who wants to live, run like fuck," I said, using my air magic to carry my words through the broken windows of the building and to the street around me.

Someone took a shot at me. My shield of air stopped the bullet, and the hand of my wraith emerged from the shadows next to the soldier and dragged him down into the depths a moment later, to the terror of everyone close by. The death of the ITF agent fueled my power soon after.

"My power still works," Sky said as the now utterly ruined reception area cleared.

I took the soul of one of the dead soldiers inside the reception. He was human; therefore, I didn't need to worry about absorbing his power, but he had died fighting, so I hoped he would be helpful. He had known nothing.

I took the souls of four more soldiers before I found what I wanted. Each soul came with the memories of the person I'd killed. Their lives, their loved ones, their families, and the evil acts they'd carried out in the name of Avalon justice. They would not be missed by many, and they'd deserved worse than I'd given them.

"Two floors down," I said, removing a key card from the guard.

We all went to the lifts as the sounds of the fighting continued outside, and I hoped that my friends would be okay. After using the key card to activate the lift, we were going down to the correct floor. The doors opened to a corridor with glass walls on both sides, showing the laboratories beyond. Several people in lab coats were cowering behind desks and benches.

I took a step forward. "The cure to the Pestilence venom. You bring it to me. Now."

No one moved.

"Now," I shouted, my air magic tearing the glass walls aside and throwing them all to the end of the corridor.

"You will not threaten us," a large man said, stepping out of one of the laboratories. "You don't scare me."

"I don't?" I asked.

The man smiled and shook his head.

"How about her?" I asked, pointing to Kase, who took a step forward, still in her werebeast form, and let out a low rumble of anger that caused him to take a step back.

A man at the end of the corridor between labs turned, ran into a see-through room, and locked it behind him.

"The cure," I said. "It's in there, isn't it?"

The large man shrugged.

I sighed. "What's in that room?"

Hope touched the man on the hand. "Please do tell," she said.

"Blood samples," the man said. "Blood samples of creatures we've taken. It's rune scribed."

"So he locked himself away to save himself and let you all die?" Remy asked. "He your boss, by any chance?"

The man nodded.

Remy laughed.

"And what are you doing with the venom?" Sky asked.

"What venom?"

"The one you used to try and kill my father," Kase said with a low growl. "The one you used on Odin. Pestilence's venom."

"There isn't any," the man said. "You can't get it out of her."

I looked around the room. "Right, someone here better actually explain what's going on."

A middle-aged man stood up from behind a desk.

"Right, everyone else, into one of the labs at the far end," Zamek said, corralling everyone with a little help from a growling Kase.

When everyone else was gone, a woman stood up beside the man. She was a decade younger, but both of them looked terrified.

"I'm not going to hurt you," I told them.

"But you work for Hera," Hope said. "So I have very little interest in being nice."

"She forces us," the woman blurted out. "I worked for Brutus and tried to leave when Hera came, but she uses threats, blackmail, anything she can use to get us to work for her."

"We would like answers now," Rasputin said. "We can keep you safe. We can get you away from Hera, War, and anyone else who works for her. We just need your help. Please."

"After Brutus was killed, I went to see Pestilence, to tell her to leave," the woman said. "She refused. She drew runes all over her apartment and door, the corridor outside—hundreds of them. It must have taken her days. She was exhausted when I found her, before she'd activated them. She told me to go. To run. But I couldn't. I couldn't leave her to Hera. I had to do what I could to slow down whatever Hera had planned, and I knew that at least part of that involved Pestilence's blood. I knew if I worked here, I could slow down turning the blood into a viable weapon."

"It's already a weapon," Sky said.

The woman shook her head. "Only for one attack, and then it's worthless. Hera wants it to be used as a bomb or gas, something she can cause maximum damage with."

"What floor is Pestilence on?" Hope asked.

"Twenty-nine," the man said.

"What did Pestilence do?" I asked.

"She activated the runes," the woman said. "It's taken Hera and her people years to get rid of them. Without dwarves to read them, no one knew what they said. Hera threw hundreds of people at the problem. Most of them died. The runes in the corridor were linked to the ones inside the apartment, and they were all individual at the same time. It was a work of art."

"And now they've got to Pestilence?" Rasputin asked.

"About three months ago," the middle-aged man said. "They got through the corridor and into the room and found that Pestilence had placed herself in a coma. She's drawn runes on her body and used the power of the dissipating runes outside her apartment. Hera got into the apartment and found her unconscious, alive only because she wasn't human. Unfortunately, those same runes on her body created a cloud of toxic gas that killed everyone who tried to retrieve any blood."

"Hera had the medical staff here place Pestilence in a specially designed cell inside her apartment," the woman said. "It was meant to keep her alive so that we could get to the blood without having to go inside the cell. But it didn't quite work, and more people died. The problem is that taking the blood out of the body is fine, but the second you remove the syringe, the toxic vapor is released."

"How did you get the venom?" I asked, feeling irritated.

"Hera's sorcerer lackey found a way to use runes to shift her power back into the prison Pestilence was in. It lets us take blood without fear of dying."

"So why isn't there loads of this venom?"

"The stuff War took was a trial run," the man said. "The rest is locked away inside that vault. The sorcerer changed the runes to stop us dying, but more than one vial a week, and the runes burn out and someone dies."

"I'm surprised Hera cares," Hope said.

"She doesn't," the man said. "But she doesn't want to have to find new people every time."

"You're all human?" Sky asked.

The man showed the sorcerer's band on his wrist. "No, we're not," he said. "Hera just doesn't like anyone to have power that she can't control."

"Can you destroy it?" I asked. "The venom? All of it."

The woman nodded. "But our boss won't let you get to it."

"Zamek, get that door open," I shouted.

"On it," Zamek said, running over to the far end of the floor.

"And the cure is with Hera?" I asked.

"There's two vials of cure," the woman said. "It's all we've been able to make." She went to a nearby number pad on the wall and entered a code, opened the door, and removed a small vial of blue liquid. "This is all we're allowed to have on us to try and create more. The second vial is with Hera at all times."

"We have to destroy the venom," Rasputin said. "It can't be allowed out of this place."

The female scientist passed me the vial. "I never wanted it to be used on anyone. I hope whoever was infected can be cured in time."

I walked after Zamek and came face-to-face with the man inside the vault. "Open the door," I said.

"Hera will not allow it," he said, puffing out his chest.

"Zamek, can you redirect the power in the runes to go back inside this vault?"

"It would turn him into soup," Zamek said.

I looked behind the man at the stack of vials of dark-green liquid. "Is that the venom?" I shouted back to those at the front of the floor.

The man and woman nodded in unison. "We were about to run experiments on it," the man said after I'd run back over.

"What happens to the venom if it's exposed to air?" Sky asked.

"The compound stays in a gas form until Pestilence uses her power. If those vials break, the gas will fill the chamber, but it dissipates after about twenty minutes."

"So he will need to hold his breath for twenty minutes, and then it's okay?" Kase asked.

"If it touches skin or gets in pores or anything, it's lethal. It eats through masks and suits. It will rip his body to shreds."

"Excellent," I said, walking back over to Zamek. "Open the fucking door," I said to the supervisor. "Last chance."

"Hera is with me," the man said. "She will protect me."

"Good luck with that," Zamek said, slamming his hands against the runes.

The supervisor inside the room was thrown back into the vials of venom, which shattered from the impact. Blood poured from his eyes an instant later, and he was on his knees throwing up blood after five seconds. Ten seconds later, his entire body began to fall apart.

"Fucking hell," Remy whispered.

I gave the vial of cure to Zamek. "Get this back to Asgard."

"Nothing will stop me," he told me, taking the cure. "You know that once we're through the realm gate, there's no way for you to follow us, right? I can't stay here and keep it open indefinitely; it's too dangerous."

"I know," I said. "I'll figure something out."

"Best of luck, my friend," Zamek said.

"Kase, Remy, Rasputin, go with him."

"But what about you?" Kase said.

"I'm not done here. I can't risk Hera keeping that cure; she might have more venom too."

"And I still need to kill her," Hope said.

"And we're going to let her, right?" Sky asked.

"You're goddamn right we are," I said.

Chapter Twenty-Nine

Nate Garrett

The scientists who wanted to get away from Hera, which was most of them, went with Zamek and the others to the realm gate. Hope touched the hand of each and every one of them, and those who were completely loyal to Hera were locked in one of the laboratories.

"What do we do with Licinius?" Sky asked.

Licinius was a sorcerer who had once worked for Brutus but, after his old master's death, had been quite happy to continue working for Hera. He'd told everyone that he was doing it to keep her in check, but it was pretty apparent that he just liked wealth and power and wasn't too fussed where it came from.

"We find him, we'll see," I said. The scientists had mentioned that he'd been working for Hera, basically in charge of the venom program. Personally, I didn't much care what happened to him, but he might be useful, so I didn't want to make any rash decisions.

We took the lift up as far as it went—the twenty-seventh floor—and then we took the stairs. The previous owner had been fairly paranoid about people trying to kill him, so the top ten floors were accessible only by private lift. Unfortunately, his paranoia had turned out to be justified, seeing as he'd gotten eaten by a dragon.

We reached the twenty-ninth floor and exited the stairwell to find only a white door that was wide open, revealing the corridor beyond, which was covered in runes. Each rune had a small amount of burn damage surrounding it.

"Pestilence," I said.

The door at the far end opened, and Licinius stepped out. He spotted Sky, Hope, and me and froze, the expression on his face one of surprise, but it was quickly replaced by the usual arrogance.

"Nathaniel," he said in mocking tones.

"Just couldn't stay away from all the money, right?" I asked.

"Sky," Licinius said, ignoring my gibe.

"You always were a weasel," Sky said. "You really going to stand there and protect Hera?"

Licinius shook his head. "I'm hoping that you manage to kill her. That would be nice, I think. To be in charge of all that Hera owns."

"There are a lot of Hera's family out there that would get to name themselves in charge before you," I pointed out.

"Yes, but they're not here," Licinius snapped.

"You don't have your magic, do you?" I asked, noticing the sorcerer's band on his wrist. "Clearly Hera doesn't trust you that much. Which, in hindsight, is probably a good thing for her."

"Hera is lost in her own paranoia," Licinius said, drawing a gun from behind him and keeping it by his hip.

"What if we fail?" Hope asked. "What happens then?"

"Then I've apprehended those who would be the next to try. I can't lose."

"And what about Pestilence?" I asked.

"She's a weapon," Licinius said. "She needs to be kept alive to ensure that no one comes after me. I can't have that, Nathaniel. I certainly can't have the son of Odin come for me. Yes, I know. Hera told me. She's always known. She doesn't like you much."

"Feeling is mutual," I said.

Licinius swung the gun toward Sky and back to me, taking his eyes off Sky for a second, which was all she needed to throw a blade into Licinius's hand. He screamed in pain, dropping the gun to the floor. I quickly kicked it aside before punching the little weasel in the jaw and knocking him to the floor.

"I'll keep him company," Sky said. "You go see to Pestilence."

Hope and I stepped past Licinius and into Pestilence's apartment. It looked pretty much like every hotel suite I'd ever been in, but with its own kitchen. The biggest difference was the large transparent prison cube in the middle of what had once been a living room. It was big enough for a bed, which contained Pestilence, and various machines that monitored her vitals. Two gloves had been attached to one wall, and there was a drawer next to them that could be slid in and out of the prison to remove the syringes.

"Fucking hell," Hope said. She took a step forward, and the ground beneath her feet tore open, a half dozen small blades flying up into the ceiling. Several of them hit Hope in the legs and stomach.

Hope collapsed to the floor with a cry.

"Licinius," I shouted, and the door opened, Sky pushing Licinius into the apartment and knocking him to the floor. "What the fuck did you do?"

"Oh, I forgot about the traps," Licinius said with a smug grin. "Small silver blades hidden under the rug. Bet they hurt."

"I'm going to remove your eyes," Hope said through gritted teeth.

"Any more traps?" I asked.

"Who knows," Licinius said.

Sky dragged him to his feet and pushed him forward. "Let's play 'watch where Licinius walks,'" she said.

"There aren't any more," Licinius shouted as Sky pushed him ever closer to the prison. "It was just the one. I heard you; I didn't have time."

"I'll find something to tie him up with and come help," Sky said, dragging Licinius off toward the open door of a bedroom.

I removed my vest, tore my jumper off, and wrapped it tightly around Hope's waist.

"I'll be fine," Hope said, resting her hand on me and standing. "I've had worse. It just hurts like hell. We need to deal with Pestilence."

"You need a doctor," I said.

"Nate, just once, listen to me. We need to deal with Pestilence. She can't wait." Hope got to her feet, removed the silver blades in her stomach, and tossed them aside. Blood poured freely from the wounds. "Silver hurts like an absolute bitch."

I went to help her, and she motioned for me to stay. "Look, Nate, I can do this."

"I can do this alone," I said. "You just stay there."

"I heard what Remy said, Nate," Hope said. "You keep pushing people away because you think it's safer. Maybe it's not up to you."

"You're hurt."

"You'll want to save her or figure out a way to stop her from being used, but she's in agony. Constant agony. That doctor I had enthralled—he told me as you were all leaving. They did a telepathic link, and the feedback fried the brains of three people in the room."

I looked through the wall to Pestilence. She had olive skin and dark hair, but her skin was cracked and sore and looked painful. "Neither of us can go in, remember? She's toxic just by being in the same room. We'll have to figure out a way to stop whatever is keeping her alive."

Hope nodded. "You're right. Let's see if we can find something to shut the runes in the room down. They're keeping her alive. These runes have a lot of power added to them, but it's too dangerous to shut them down inside there, so maybe it's feeding to another rune in the apartment."

"Stay here; I'll be back," I told her. I checked the nearest room, hoping to find something that might help, but when I looked back, I found Hope inside the room with her.

I sprinted over and tried the door. "Hope, what the hell are you doing?"

"What needs to be done," Hope said.

"No, there's another way," I said, trying to pry the doors apart. "Hope, there's another way."

Hope turned back to me. "Nate, just once, stop trying to save everyone. Please. Just let this happen." She looked back at Pestilence and turned off the beeping machines before drawing a dagger and cutting through the runes on the floor. There was a burst of power, and Pestilence gasped. A moment later, Hope touched Pestilence's bare arm and whispered something, and Pestilence calmed.

"Hope," I said.

Hope plunged the dagger into Pestilence's heart. The comatose woman opened her eyes in shock and looked over at Hope and me. She raised a hand; then it fell, and she died.

"She said thank you," Hope said, turning back to me.

"You didn't have to do this," I said, placing my hands against the cool glass window. "Damn you."

"You are a good man, Nathan Garrett," Hope said. Her eyes started to bleed, and I noticed that the knife in Pestilence had melted, along with her bed and the floor beneath it. "A good man," Hope repeated.

"I'm sorry it ended like this," I told her.

Hope shook her head. "It ended right. It ended with me doing the right thing." She slumped to her knees. "Make sure someone kills Hera. Make sure she can never create anything like me again. Promise me."

"I promise," I told her.

Hope smiled. "I had fun over the centuries, Nate. I'm glad I met you."

"Me too," I said.

Hope placed her hands in the same places as mine on the opposite side of the glass. "Monsters need to die, Nate. But sometimes they get to choose the time and place. Sometimes they get to do one good thing before they die. Goodbye."

I nodded as Hope fell back to the floor and convulsed for a few seconds before going still. "Goodbye," I whispered, looking up and noticing that I'd left melted handprints on the glass walls.

Sky burst through the bedroom door a moment later and saw me on my knees.

"Pestilence and Hope are gone," I said. "Hope sacrificed herself to end her. Pestilence wanted to die."

Sky looked through the glass door behind me. "I'm sorry."

I nodded. "I know she was a monster to a lot of people, but I always had a soft spot for her. She did a lot of nasty stuff to people who probably deserved it, and I get why."

"There's a helicopter on the roof. Licinius told me."

I walked into the bedroom and picked up Licinius, who didn't struggle. Sky had tied his hands with an electrical cord. "You're coming with us," I said.

"You promise not to kill me, I'll tell you where Hera and War went. I'll show you how to get to the roof," Licinius said in one long stream of desperate confession.

"Sure," I said, unfastening his legs and pushing him toward the door. "Show us."

Licinius led Sky and me up to the top floor. We opened the door to Hera's office and found Hera sitting behind her desk.

I threw a ball of fire at her, but it smashed into an invisible force between us and harmlessly vanished.

"Nate," Hera said. "It's the same stuff used in Pestilence's cage. Pretty much immune to magic. It's rune-scribed glass, essentially, but it's exceptionally powerful stuff."

"Lucky you," I said.

"Licinius," Hera said. "I thought you'd betray me."

A door behind Hera opened, and War stepped through. He threw something at the wall; it bounced off and landed on the floor with an awful wet noise. I looked down at the head of Aphrodite. A second wet sound was Hephaestus's head.

War laughed, and the rage inside me built.

"You did that, War?" I asked.

"No, I did," Hera said. "I've been looking to remove them both for a long time. Their betrayal was just the reason I needed. How long was Hephaestus working for you traitorous little curs? Decades? Centuries?"

"I'm going to kill you both," I said.

"You will kneel before you die," Hera shouted at me.

"I will not," I said calmly.

Hera's face went bright red with rage. "Licinius, I will make your death last."

Licinius's face paled.

"You have always been nothing but a pain in my life," Hera seethed at me. "You have interfered in my plans, time and time again. And for centuries, no one was allowed to touch you. I had to go behind the backs of Arthur and Merlin to try and kill you, because they wanted you to eventually join their cause. Well, that ship has sailed, and now I can unleash my fury upon you."

"Go on, then," I shouted. "You don't half fucking posture. That's all it ever is with you—backstabbing, murdering, and posturing. You were gifted with incredible power, and all you use it for is to hurt others. You're afraid of me, Hera. You've always been afraid of me; that's why you screwed around with the ceremony to give me my blood curse marks. That's why you constantly went behind your master's back to have me killed. That's why you're standing there right now, behind this shield, instead of actually wanting to end this."

"I am standing here because we don't have time to kill you," she said.

"Can I tell you a story?" I asked softly. "Ever since Odin got hurt, I've been bottling up my rage. I've been making sure to keep myself together. I didn't want to do anything that might jeopardize why I'm here. But now I'm here. And I'm going to find you, and I'm going to kill you, Hera. And anyone between me and you is going to die a horrible death. You have my word on that."

Hera laughed until a bolt of lightning struck the shield between us, leaving a scorched mark that, from the look of surprise on Hera's face, wasn't meant to happen.

Hera showed me a vial of blue liquid. "The last known cure," she said.

"Pestilence is dead," I said. "I don't think it'll make much difference now."

"Oh no? What about Frigg? Doesn't she need saving?"

War laughed before walking over to the barrier. "I'll be seeing you in Asgard, little man. That's where you're going to die."

I smiled. "Good luck."

Hera got to her feet. "We must dash—helicopter waiting for us. Do give my best to your father when you see him next. And to Hope." She smiled. "Oh, no Hope? Is poor little Hope dead?" She laughed. "About damn time."

I placed my hands against the shield, and heat poured out of them, turning it bright red in seconds.

War and Hera left the room, and the bookcase wall closed behind them. A few seconds later the shield rose up into the ceiling.

"It only comes down when she's in here," Licinius said. He walked over to the bookcase and pulled a lever before pushing the hidden door open.

"I guess your life is not forfeit," I said.

"You get us out of here, and I promise I'll tell you everything about Hera's operation," Licinius said.

"Sky, keep an eye on him," I said.

Sky smiled and smashed Licinius's head into the bookshelf. "Damn, slipped," she said.

I left them to it, ascended the stairs, and arrived on the roof to find a helicopter and pilot. A second helicopter was in the air some distance away, too far to throw a lightning bolt at. The pilot aimed a gun at me. A shadow leaped out of the ground, wrapping around the man's arm.

I walked over to the pilot and crouched beside him. "You're going to take me and my friend to Little Skellig. If you refuse, you die, clear?"

"You can pilot this thing without me?" he asked. "I think I'm safe."

I turned to Sky, who had arrived on the roof with Licinius. "You pilot one of these things?" I shouted to her over the strong winds.

She nodded. "Can't land very well, but I can get it in the air and keep it there." She sat Licinius down and walked over to the pilot. "Let me have a look."

Licinius, seemingly believing himself free of our gaze, leaped to his feet to run off, but I'd been watching him out of the corner of my eye and wrapped air around him, dragged him over to the edge of the roof, and held him over it, his shoes dangling hundreds of feet off the ground.

"Why?" I asked him. "Why join Hera? Was it the money?"

"Partly," he said. "The power was good too."

"You knew about Hephaestus working for us, yes?" I loosened the air before he said anything. "Don't lie to me."

"How are you able to use magic up here?"

"Apparently, the runes aren't as strong as Hera believed. Answer the goddamn question."

"Yes," Licinius shouted. "Atlas too. I needed to keep the information to myself until I needed to spend it."

"You betrayed them to Hera for what?"

"For Hephaestus, I got New York. When this is all done, it was to be mine."

"And Atlas?"

"That was just because I hated the smug prick. I'd been looking for a reason to give him up, and Hera was in one of her rages after discovering you'd killed Baldr. Seemed like as good a time as any."

"You're a nasty little shit," I told him.

"You promised me you wouldn't kill me," Licinius said, looking down at the ground.

"I did, and I won't," I said, bringing him back onto the roof. "The impact should do that." I kicked him off the roof and walked away as his screams were lost in the sudden gusts of wind.

Chapter Thirty

Layla Cassidy

Realm of Valhalla

The remaining army of the dwarves and Valkyrie rebels rode across the realm of Valhalla to the palace and its grounds. Layla hoped they'd get there in time. She'd been warned that at the first sign of trouble, Empress Rela would sacrifice the humans that lived in the nearby town of Fólkvangr. She knew that it had been a risk to involve the dwarves and publicly go after Rela's people at the mountain, but it was one that had needed to be taken.

The hundreds of anti-Rela troops were soon bolstered by more Valkyrie rebels and dwarves. Layla knew that the reinforcements would be the difference between victory and defeat, but she tried to push it from her mind.

Layla looked over at Ava, who was riding beside Jinayca and Judgement. The latter were going to get the teenager to the realm gate and through to somewhere that wasn't a battleground, preferably Shadow Falls, but that depended on how much time Judgement could give Jinayca to alter the destination on the realm gate.

Brynhildr rode up beside Layla. "You ready for this?" she asked as the palace came into view in the distance, along with hundreds of Valkyries standing between the palace and the rebels.

"Any chance these people will surrender?" Layla asked.

Brynhildr shook her head and pointed her spear forward, roaring a battle cry. Arrows came over the field toward them, and more than one of her Valkyries fell before they reached the enemy line, but Brynhildr was in the front of the first wave that smashed into the enemy Valkyries with horrific force.

Layla and Tego were close behind as arrows from the dwarves sought out the flying horses that would have otherwise been a danger to everyone. Irkalla used her necromancy to blast any Valkyrie unfortunate enough to get close to her.

Layla took Tego over toward Judgement and Jinayca, the latter of whom was protecting a terrified Ava, while Judgement cut through anything in her path with a detached efficiency that both scared and impressed Layla.

A blast of energy smashed into a Valkyrie that got too close to Ava, sending her careering into a nearby tree. Layla searched for the blast's origin and saw Chloe, who was fighting off three more Valkyries. Layla reached out, took hold of the metal in the nearest Valkyrie's armor, and tore it from her body. She threw it back at her as a spear, taking her through the heart.

Chloe killed the others and joined her as Judgement stopped killing anything that moved and looked back. "This is fun," she said.

"Not the word I'd use," Jinayca said.

The group moved through the enemy-strewed palace grounds, with Tego ahead to check for anyone who might be waiting, although Layla began to see more and more of Rela's guards retreating into the palace itself.

Layla and her team reached the realm gate with little in the way of trouble.

"Anyone else have a bad feeling?" Chloe asked.

"Yep," Layla said. "Judgement, you okay keeping Ava and Jinayca company?"

Judgement nodded. "Don't see why not."

Layla ran around the corner of the realm gate and took the stairs two at a time to the lower garden, with Chloe right after her.

Tego joined them, her maw covered in blood.

"Glad to have you with me," Layla said.

Tego purred.

"Oh shit," Chloe said as the three reached the top of the cliff above the city.

The town had already been put to the sword. The dead littered the streets, blood covered every surface, and runes were drawn across every building that Layla could see.

"This wasn't done in one night," Chloe said.

Layla rushed down the stairs to the city itself, stepping over bodies left in the street. She ran as best she could through the city to the guardhouse where she'd last seen Skost. She gasped in horror, and a small cry left her throat as she spotted Skost and her guards nailed to the entrance of the city, twenty feet in the air. Their heads were piled on the ground beneath their feet.

Chloe placed a hand on Layla's shoulder and squeezed. "My God," she whispered.

Layla shook her head. "This was pointless slaughter," she said.

"These runes," Chloe said. "You recognize them?"

Layla nodded. "They look similar to the ones used in Jotunheim to merge the realms. We need to get to the others."

The pair sprinted back through the city and found Tego sitting at the bottom of the steps of the realm gate next to several dead bodies. The large cat made a soft sound as Layla approached her.

"I know," Layla said. "We'll stop her."

A deep, dangerous growl left Tego's throat, and she bounded back up the stairs with Chloe and Layla right behind.

The ground beneath their feet lit up dark red, and all three stopped.

"What the fuck is this?" Chloe asked as Judgement ran toward them.

"Snagnar was either wrong or lying," Judgement said. "They're not merging the realms."

"Last time huge chunks of the realm were being thrown around," Layla said. "Nothing like that here."

"What is this, then?" Chloe asked.

"Honestly, I don't know, but this isn't a merge," Jinayca said from the top of the stairs.

"Ava?" Layla asked.

"Ava went to Shadow Falls," Jinayca said. "She's safe, although shaken. We need to get into that palace."

The four of them raced back through the palace grounds, to be met by Brynhildr and her Valkyries along with Irkalla, Queen Orfeda, and her dwarves.

"They all ran into the palace," Irkalla said. "I think they were meant to keep us busy."

"The town of Fólkvangr is gone," Layla said. "All of it. The people there have been slaughtered. I'm sorry, Brynhildr—Skost and her guard are among the dead. I'm so sorry."

The look on Brynhildr's face told Layla that anyone between her and Rela was going to die. There were no questions about it.

"Why?" Orfeda asked.

Layla told them about the runes. "We need to get in there," she said, pointing at the palace.

"There are runes all over it," Irkalla said.

"I have people on it," Orfeda said. "But it won't be easy."

There was a huge shake of the ground, and several of the rebels fell over, reaching to hold on to something to stay upright. An instant later, a deafening explosion came from the direction of Fólkvangr. A large contingent of the group ran back through the grounds toward the town and found that the entire place had collapsed into the ground, leaving nothing but an enormous crater.

"Oh shit," Jinayca said. "They had a realm gate under the town."

"And it did that?" Chloe asked.

"If the realm gate isn't properly closed, the energy has to go somewhere," Orfeda said.

"Someone needs to go down there and check," Jinayca said. "If it's still open, it'll be pouring power into this realm. That's an 'everyone dies' kind of problem."

"How do we get down there?" Layla asked. "I imagine there were tunnels beneath the palace, hence the reason we weren't allowed to stay in the palace. Who would have created this?"

"I can't say for certain," Orfeda said. "Snagnar's father had been studying them for years. He always told us to try to find a way to get us back to our home realm. It could have been him; he's certainly arrogant enough to do it. I didn't think anyone would be stupid enough to actually try and create a new realm gate."

"And I assume if Snagnar's father was involved, so was the king," Layla said.

"It's a good assumption," Orfeda said.

"If I don't mention it again, the king was quite a catch," Irkalla said.

"Either way, why make one under the city?" Layla asked.

No one had a good answer.

"There are a few flying horses left," Brynhildr said. "I'll take you down. Jinayca, you come with us."

"I'm coming too," Irkalla said.

"I changed the realm gate here to Asgard before I left," Jinayca said. "I don't advise using it until we've sorted out whatever mess is down there. It might blow up or something."

"We will wait for your return," Orfeda said.

They found several horses from the Valkyries who had abandoned them midbattle and rushed into the palace before it had been locked down.

Layla climbed up behind Brynhildr, and they flew down into the crater that used to be a town. Layla knew that at any other point in her life, she'd have enjoyed flying around on the back of a horse, but the sight of the bodies that were scattered around the rubble at the bottom of the crater was something she was unlikely to ever forget. Or forgive.

The group dismounted and followed a large tunnel to a chamber where the realm gate was. It pulsated bright green.

"Those fucking idiots," Jinayca said. "Snagnar, or whatever idiot did this, didn't get it right. It took everyone who was inside this chamber or immediately outside it to their destination, but it needed blood magic to work. Essentially, they tried to create a realm gate with a massive radius so that they could take an entire army through here to another place without adjusting the realm gate on the other side, and they royally fucked it up."

A crack of power whipped out into the rock nearby, causing it to be torn apart.

"Can you fix it?" Irkalla asked.

"It's not taking power anymore," Jinayca said. "So that's something. The explosion must have severed the links to the blood runes inside the town. But to shut it down for good . . . I don't know. This is a magical Chernobyl."

"I don't know that reference," Brynhildr said.

"Imagine an accident so bad that it's the worst thing you can think of in terms of what it could do to every living thing within hundreds of miles of it," Irkalla said. "Now make it worse."

"This will keep leaking magic," Jinayca said. "Eventually it'll either burn itself out, or it'll crack open the realm like an egg and kill every living thing. And I do mean *every* living thing."

There was a noise from a large hole in the side of the chamber, and everyone immediately readied themselves for battle.

Brynhildr walked over to the hole and looked inside. She reached in, dragged out Empress Rela, and threw her across the chamber.

Rela hit the ground hard and let out a gasp of pain. Her arm was twisted in the wrong direction, and she'd lost several fingers on the other hand. Part of her face had been blasted off, and Layla wondered how she was even capable of being alive, let alone conscious.

"Hold her down," Jinayca said.

Everyone else did as they were told, and Jinayca used Rela's own blood to draw a rune on the empress's forehead.

Rela gasped.

"Pain gone?" Jinayca asked. "Won't last long. I would use your time to tell me what happened so I can fix it, and maybe you don't die."

"Fucking dwarves," Rela said.

"I can remove the mark," Jinayca said, her eyes narrowing in anger.

"No," Rela said. "It wasn't right. It exploded. I only lived because the First Consul shielded me. I was thrown into that wall. I think I'm dying."

"Good. Hope it hurts," Irkalla said.

"What *happened*?" Jinayca asked.

"They activated the realm gate, used the blood of those above," Rela said. "Too much power, too little control. How many of my Valkyries survived?"

"How many were down here?" Brynhildr asked.

"A few thousand."

"None," Layla said. "There are no survivors. Because if there had been, I'd have executed them myself. You murdered tens of thousands of people to power this heap of shit."

"Why not use the normal realm gate?" Jinayca asked.

"By the time the last of us are through the gate, we're already exposed to Asgard's army. We needed to all go through at once. We needed to get behind the Asgard army; we needed to launch a surprise attack. This was decided to be the best way of achieving that aim."

"And none of the Valkyries said no to the murder of thousands of innocent people?" Layla asked.

"I have cultivated the Valkyries over a long time to believe that those humans were worthless. Anyone who thought otherwise was given other duties or disposed of. I demanded total obedience."

"Who did this?" Jinayca asked.

"Snagnar and his father said they could do it," Rela said, wincing. She coughed up blood. "Hera gave us the instructions. Apparently, Merlin found them and said they should work."

"Yeah, wonderfully," Irkalla snapped.

"How was it meant to shut off?" Jinayca asked.

"Onetime use," Rela said. "Takes everyone in the tunnels down here. There's a second gate under the palace. They were used in conjunction."

"That would have been useful information to have started with," Brynhildr said.

"I'll go with Brynhildr," Irkalla said. "You two try to stop this one."

"No use," Rela said. "It was overheating and exploded first."

"So either everyone out there went to another realm," Jinayca said, "or you atomized thousands of your loyal people."

"We were in a hurry," Rela said.

"No excuse for being incompetent," Jinayca said.

"Why didn't the people fight you?" Layla asked.

Rela tried to laugh, but the expression was quickly replaced with pain. "By the time they knew what was happening, it was too late. They tried to escape, but my Valkyries were waiting. That traitor Skost got what she deserved too. The humans relied on us. Needed us. They had no idea what to do when we turned on them."

Layla bent down, licked her thumb, and wiped off the rune on Rela's forehead.

Rela cried out in pain.

"You want the rune back?" Jinayca asked.

Rela nodded as much as she could.

"How do we stop this?"

It took Rela several seconds to be able to speak. "I don't know."

"Then what use are you to us?" Brynhildr asked, drawing a knife.

"Both of you go check that she's not lying about the other realm gate," Jinayca said. "Vengeance can wait."

Irkalla and Brynhildr left as requested, and Jinayca knelt down beside Rela. "You're going to die here, Empress," she said. "You want to actually do the right thing before that happens?"

"Go fuck yourself," Rela said softly, her eyes flickering.

Jinayca walked over to the realm gate. It had settled since the last whip of energy, but Layla knew it could do it again at any time.

"There's metal inside it," Layla said.

Jinayca turned back to her. "It should be a ring."

"It might have been at one point; now it's just bits."

"You think you can control it?"

Layla reached out. "Yes. But not in the same way you would a normal piece of metal. It's hot and cold at the same time, and there's power in it. I've never felt anything like it."

"If you can move the metal to realign it properly, I should be able to change the runes."

"And if this doesn't work?" Layla asked.

"We have two options here," Jinayca said. "We fix it, or we die trying. There's no third option."

"Okay," Layla said. "You're going to need to go get the queen and as many dwarves as you can. I don't think just the two of us will cut it."

"The other gate is whole," Brynhildr said as she returned. "Mostly. There are chunks missing, but there's no power leaking out of it. Lots of dead Valkyries around it, though."

"All of this death for nothing," Jinayca said. "What do you hope to gain?"

"I might die here," Rela said. "But I die the empress. You are traitors to my crown. I hoped you'd go look at the other real gate and get killed if it exploded."

"I like her less and less every time she opens her mouth," Irkalla said.

Layla remained with Rela, who was no threat to anyone, while Brynhildr, Jinayca, and Irkalla went to retrieve more help.

A second whip of power smashed into the floor not too far from Rela's head, clearly scaring her, but other than that it was uneventful.

"You know you haven't won here, right?" Layla asked.

"I am still empress," she said. "I win."

Jinayca arrived with Orfeda and several more dwarves. "I have sent more to the other gate," Orfeda said. "It might not be working now, but let's keep it that way."

"Okay," Layla said. "What's the plan?"

"You will alter the metal inside the gate," Jinayca said. "The dwarves will use their alchemy to do the same with the stone and wood that makes up the rest of the gate."

Layla reached out and felt for the metal inside the realm gate, sensing the hot and cold of it as she touched it with her power.

"Anything I can do?" Irkalla asked from the door.

"If you start to see the magic whip out, try to stop us dying," Jinayca said.

Irkalla gave her the thumbs-up as Judgement walked into the room. "Right, what do I do?"

"What can you do?" Jinayca asked.

"I can use matter magic," she said. "That has to count for something, yes?"

"You can help me adjust the metal," Layla said. "I get the feeling this isn't going to be as easy as it sounds."

"You're all going to die here," Rela said from the floor.

"Hey, Brynhildr," Judgement shouted. "You want to be empress?"

Brynhildr shook her head.

"Too bad," Judgement said with a chuckle. "You're now empress. Congratulations."

She bent down and thrust a knife through Rela's heart, then looked at the others. "Well—just doing what my name says," she said.

"Ready?" Jinayca asked.

Layla nodded and reached out to take hold of the metal inside the realm gate. What should have been a ring was in five pieces, with a dozen more fragments that were scattered around inside the wood and stone of the gate.

Layla took the right-hand side of the gate, Judgement the left, and together they pulled pieces back together into the jigsaw that was the metal ring. It caused Layla considerable pain, and sweat poured down her face as the ring flickered between freezing and burning. Her hands hurt, and more than once she had to take a breath; she noticed that Judgement was in exactly the same position she was.

"This sucks," Layla said. "It sucks so badly."

"I'm beginning to regret leaving the mountain," Judgement said.

"How many are left?" Jinayca asked. The dwarves all looked to be in agony or exhausted from trying to fix something that was never meant to exist. Several of them had passed out and had to be replaced by others. Orfeda, however, remained defiant and refused to give in, her face a mass of concentration and exhaustion.

"Round what, eight?" Layla said.

"See you on the other side," Judgement said with a smile.

If placing the larger pieces back together and joining them with their power was hard, picking out the tiny pieces from the stone and wood and working them back into the metal was like trying to do open-heart surgery while standing twenty feet away wearing mittens.

Layla allowed her instincts to take over, her mind operating without conscious thought. Each tiny metal shard moving back into the whole brought them a step closer to fixing the problem. So many people had died, and Layla was determined to ensure that no one else did.

When she was done, she found herself on all fours, sweat dripping off her as if someone had just sprayed her with a power wash. Judgement was on her knees, sucking in air.

"That was shit," Judgement said. "Really, really shit."

"Did it work?" Irkalla asked from the entrance. She, too, looked exhausted.

"What did I miss?" Layla asked.

"Had to stop that whip thing from killing you about a dozen times," Irkalla said. "Shields of necromancy around other people aren't exactly easy to make."

"Thank you," Layla said.

Jinayca stepped away from the gate. "It worked," she said. "But at a cost."

Several dwarves lay dead on the ground.

"Damn it," Layla said softly. "I'm so sorry."

"They died heroes," Orfeda said. "They will be remembered."

"So it's safe?" Layla asked.

"It won't explode," Jinayca said. "We still need to figure out how to get to Asgard. The battle must have started by now."

"Can we use this?" Orfeda asked, tapping the realm gate.

"As a normal realm gate, yes," Jinayca said. "So long as the other gate remains inactive, neither can overload."

Everyone climbed up the staircase that the dwarves had hastily built out of the very rock of the crater.

"I never cease to be amazed at what dwarves can do," Layla said.

Jinayca took Layla's hand in hers and squeezed it slightly. "Thank you for what you did back there." She turned to Judgement. "Both of you."

They reached the top in silence, where Queen Orfeda had joined her dwarves, the remaining Valkyries, and Chloe, who was sitting next to Tego and scratching her behind the ears.

Brynhildr and Irkalla approached the group, along with Judgement.

Orfeda walked over to Layla. "My people and I are with you until the end."

"We go where you go, Layla," Jinayca said. "Tell them what you need."

"We're not done here," Layla said. "We need to go to Asgard and defend the city. If you don't want to come, I understand, but I hope we can do this together."

There was a loud cheer, and Layla ran over to the realm gate with Jinayca, who activated it.

Layla waited in Valhalla as hundreds of dwarves and Valkyries walked through, until only she, Brynhildr, Chloe, Tego, Irkalla, and Jinayca remained.

"Be safe; kick ass; take names," Layla said.

Everyone walked through as one and came out into a war zone.

The walls of Asgard were no more. Smoke rose all around the city as fires took hold. The dead littered the ground, and large parts of the city appeared to be overrun.

The dwarves and Queen Orfeda had gone through first and had taken up a defensive position around the realm gate to protect everyone coming through. "May this battle be sung about through the ages," Queen Orfeda shouted, leading the charge of the dwarves into an advancing group of blood elves.

The Valkyries stood watching the battle and continued to protect the realm gate from anyone who got too close. Layla, Irkalla, Chloe, Jinayca, and Brynhildr moved to the front of the hundred-strong army of Valkyries.

"Valkyries," Brynhildr shouted. "We will win this. We will be victorious."

Layla climbed atop Tego as Brynhildr motioned for her to speak. "Let them know what you want," she whispered.

"Ladies," Layla shouted, pointing her sword arm toward the enemy in the distance as Tego roared. "Make Avalon fear you."

The Valkyries charged forward into the battle, cutting a path through anything that dared get close enough to them.

"You think we can win?" Chloe asked.

Layla turned to her best friend and smiled. "You're goddamn right I do," she said, and she charged into battle.

Chapter Thirty-One

Mordred

Realm of Asgard

Mordred left Lancelot's body where it fell. He wasn't interested in burying it or honoring the dead. Instead, he rode on toward the battle that raged all around the city. He wasn't entirely sure what he was going to do when he got there, but he imagined that it would involve killing anyone who stopped him from getting to Arthur and his father.

The sounds of fighting could be heard from several miles away, and as he reached the battle, he saw Hel fighting furiously in the midst of several enemies.

He rode as fast as he could toward the fighting, and on more than one occasion he had to use his magic to snap arrows out of the air as they aimed for him.

Suddenly, the earth beneath Mordred's horse erupted, throwing him back off the animal and swallowing the horse up before he was able to stop it. A paladin walked toward him, his shiny golden armor smeared with blood.

"I have longed for this day," the paladin said, creating a massive war hammer of rock that he brought down where he thought Mordred might be.

Mordred was already on his feet when the war hammer hit the ground with a deafening thud. He moved back quickly, putting some distance between him and the paladin, and judged his options, quickly deciding that they weren't exactly great.

"I will be a hero for your death," the paladin said. "Arthur will give me my own country."

"Cool," Mordred said. "If you live through this, get your eyes tested."

"What?" the paladin asked, clearly confused.

Hades charged into the paladin at full speed, picking the smaller man off his feet and spiking him on the ground with enough force to almost embed the paladin in the earth itself.

"Get going," Hades said. "This one is mine." He stomped down on the paladin's exposed head, and Mordred ran past, moving as quickly as his light magic would allow so as to reach Hel, who had killed two paladins and was now engaged with Arthur himself.

The king parried every attack, either necromantic or physical, that Hel threw at him, and he looked over at an oncoming Mordred and smiled. Hel used the moment to try to catch Arthur out with a silver sword, but Arthur easily dodged it, moved around to her side, and drove a sword of fire through her.

Mordred stopped running as Arthur casually threw Hel aside.

"Sorry you made it all this way for nothing," Arthur said.

Mordred's rage exploded inside him, and he moved toward Arthur faster than he ever had before. Arthur swiped at him with another blade of flame, but Mordred slammed into him, picked him off his feet, and ran with him at full speed into the cliff behind him.

Mordred released Arthur and headbutted him over and over again, raining down punches on him in an effort to hurt him as much as possible.

Mordred went for one more punch, and Arthur caught Mordred's fist in the palm of his hand. He shot up from his half-buried position, causing more rock to fall all around them as he headbutted Mordred, then slammed his open palm into Mordred's chest, sending him flying back thirty feet.

Arthur got to his feet and dusted off his armor, the purple matter-magic glyphs on his hands dying away. "This is the finest piece of elven and dwarven craftsmanship that was ever created," Arthur said, waving off the paladins that went to attack Mordred, who was getting back to his feet. "Magic bounces off it. It's why Hel there used a sword."

Mordred looked over at the woman he loved, who was bleeding profusely but still breathing. He wanted to help her, wanted to heal her, but so long as Arthur was there, that was never going to happen.

"She's not dead, I guess," Arthur said. "That'll be nice for her to watch you die, then."

"You are not better than me," Mordred said, spitting blood onto the ground. Despite the rune-warded chain mail he wore, he'd still been hurt by Arthur's attack.

"I should have just killed you all those centuries ago," Arthur said. "Guess it's time for me to correct that mistake."

Mordred knew how good Arthur was at fighting. It was the one thing everyone agreed on. So it was no surprise that when Arthur came toward Mordred, he blocked or countered everything that Mordred threw at him.

"Come on," Arthur said with a chuckle after catching Mordred in the jaw with an elbow. "Is this too hard for you?"

Arthur stepped back and unhooked the breastplate of his golden armor before dropping it to the dirty ground. A multitude of colored glyphs exploded over his arms. "How about now? Is this fair now?"

Mordred wasn't about to remove his own chain mail; that was pretty much suicide. He touched his bleeding nose and smiled as he activated his blood magic. He shot several tendrils of blood magic back toward the paladins behind him, each one snaking around a different paladin. The screams were all he could hear as he walked toward Arthur. Mordred needed to get to Hel. He knew he could heal her; he just needed to get Arthur to move away.

Mordred wrapped blood magic around his fists, and Arthur darted toward him, his own fists wrapped in the same blood magic. The pair connected with punch after punch, the blood magic–wrapped fists causing the pain of the blows to amplify tenfold.

Arthur fell to one knee, and Mordred was tackled from behind by one of the paladins. Mordred punched the paladin in the face with the blood magic–wrapped fist, knocking him away. But Mordred's craving for more blood magic began to take control of his mind, and he immediately switched off the magic, rushed over to Hel, and placed his hands on her wound, flooding her body with his healing light magic.

"Stay with me," Mordred said softly.

"I'm fine," Hel said, her voice weak. "Why is it that wherever we go, someone always tries to kill us?"

"Luck," Mordred said with a smile.

The paladin kicked Mordred in the side of the head, and he was unable to defend himself in time. Mordred ended up in the dirt, trying to roll away from any more blows.

Arthur screamed in rage and rushed toward the paladin, grabbed him by the back of his armor, and threw him back toward the others. Blood streamed from Arthur's broken nose as he reached down for Mordred, grabbing hold of his neck and lifting him up until his feet dangled above the ground.

"Who is the weapon now?" Arthur screamed. "You were made to kill me, and look at where you are!" Arthur threw Mordred back toward the cliff, and Mordred used his air magic to shield himself from the impact.

He turned back to Arthur, who sprinted over to him and tried to drive a blade of fire into his stomach, but Mordred avoided it and smashed his ice-covered fist into Arthur's jaw, knocking him to the ground.

"You know about that, eh?" Mordred asked, planting his foot on the side of Arthur's head, shoving his face into the dirt. "Yeah, I only heard today. So you hate me because I'm someone who can actually kill you. That's it, isn't it? That's why you hate Nate too. We can kill you. We can stop you."

A sword of light appeared in Mordred's hand, and Arthur blasted him in the chest with a torrent of flame that Mordred barely had time to get away from. He wrapped himself in dense air, feeding it with the freezing-cold ice, and even then he could feel the heat. It forced him to his feet.

When the fire had gone, Arthur was back on his feet, standing above Mordred, power radiating from him. He kicked Mordred in the face, walked over to his breastplate, and put it back on.

"I'm done with this," Arthur said, kicking Mordred in the head again. "Are we ready?" he barked to Merlin as the older-looking man joined them.

"Yes," Merlin said.

Mordred looked up at his father atop the silver horse he rode.

"Your son will die now," Arthur told Merlin, punching Mordred in the face as he tried to get up. "His magic will no longer affect me."

"He is a waste," Merlin said. "I regret ever giving my seed for his birth."

Mordred laughed. "Fuck you too, Dad," he shouted out.

Arthur kicked out at Mordred again, but Mordred grabbed the limb, dragging the king over him onto the mud.

Before Mordred could continue, he was encased in earth, his father ensuring that no harm befell his king.

"Don't know when to give up, do you?" Arthur said.

"We don't have time for this," Merlin said softly. "Rela has failed. We must move to our contingency plan."

"It's a shame," Arthur said. "She was to help crush Asgard between her Valkyries and our army, but I guess she wasn't up to the task. I was sort of looking forward to having her as my queen too. Oh well."

Mordred tried to break free, but it took all of his strength just to ensure the earth didn't crush him.

"You won't merge Asgard and Avalon," Mordred managed through gritted teeth.

Arthur looked down at his helpless opponent and laughed. He slapped Mordred across the face and punched him in the eye, and then, with an evil smirk on his face, Arthur tore out Mordred's eye as the helpless sorcerer bucked and twisted.

"You should see yourself," Arthur said, showing Mordred his own eye and laughing as if he'd just said the funniest thing he'd heard in years.

"I'm going to kill you," Mordred said through clenched teeth.

Arthur dropped Mordred's eye to the dirt and destroyed it under his boot. "Tens of thousands of troops came here today to crush you, but if it didn't work out, we needed a backup plan. An underground tunnel system that doubles as a massive elven realm gate. Yep, we have elves on our side too. We have our way out, but you're all going to die here in the dirt. I cannot leave any of you alive. If I can't take you prisoner and I can't rule this realm, I shall remove it from existence."

He stood and walked over to Merlin, drew a gleaming spear from a sheath that Merlin carried, and walked back to Mordred to hold the sword above his exposed chest. "You should have died long ago, you pathetic little ant."

Mordred wished he'd brought Excalibur. Wished he hadn't thrown it aside. Maybe then he'd have had a chance. Maybe.

Arthur raised the spear above his head, but before he could bring it down, Tommy smashed into him, picking him up off his feet and throwing him twenty feet back toward Merlin. The two collided, but Arthur was the first to rise, his spear left on the ground as he ran back toward Tommy, who changed into his werebeast form and screamed in pain.

"You're still hurt," Mordred whispered as he tried to get to his feet, only to be blasted in the chest with a battering ram of air by Merlin.

Mordred flew back over toward Hel and landed in a heap. He could do nothing but watch as Tommy attacked Arthur, who dodged the blows of the weakened werewolf. Tommy punched Arthur in the chest, denting the armor, which, judging from the look on Arthur's face, was a huge shock, but when Tommy tried to follow up, Arthur threw himself to the side, rolled away, and picked up the spear.

"No," Mordred shouted, but Tommy didn't hear him, and Arthur drove the spear into Tommy's stomach.

The werewolf roared in pain as Arthur twisted the blade before pulling it out and kicking Tommy back toward Merlin. Mordred forced himself back to his feet and charged forward, but Merlin and Arthur blasted him with magic and forced Mordred to wrap himself in a shield of air. The shield cracked, and in his weakened state, Mordred was unable to stop two of the paladins from dragging Tommy's unconscious body away, placing it on a horse, and riding off with it.

"No," Mordred shouted again, but the shield broke, and Merlin threw a spear of air at him that slammed into his chain mail, throwing him back.

Arthur took a step toward Mordred, and the world around them shimmered slightly. Mordred noticed the look of fear on Merlin's face, followed quickly by one of surprise on Arthur's.

"You brought an army," Hades said as he walked toward them.

Merlin's concentration on the magic covering Mordred evaporated, as he had more immediate concerns, and Mordred scrambled out of the hole, ran over to Hel, and placed his hands on her wound once again, pouring every little bit of magical power he could into her.

Hades placed his hand on Mordred's shoulder as he walked past him.

"No wife to back you up?" Arthur asked with a laugh.

"She's busy killing all of your people," Hades said. "I didn't want to take her away from the job she loves."

"I always wondered why anyone would fear you," Arthur snarled. "You were always too calm, too willing to make peace. There's no war in you. Not anymore."

Hades nodded. "Thousands of years ago people tried to get me to fight in a war I didn't believe in. I gave in to their requests. And when I'd finished fighting, they begged me to never fight again. I have lived my life ensuring I don't have to do what I did that day."

The air around Mordred became treacle-like, and the ground began to shake. "My king, we need to leave," Merlin said. "Now." It was the first time Mordred had ever heard his father afraid.

"I will kill him," Arthur said, his purple pure magic flowing up around his hands.

"It's too risky," Merlin said, almost pleading with his king.

"Thousands of people died here today," Hades said as he continued to walk toward the rapidly retreating paladins, along with Merlin and Arthur, the latter of whom was now bellowing for a horse.

"They'd like to have a word," Hades continued.

Mordred had never seen anything like it. Hundreds, maybe thousands of souls lifted up from the ground. An army of ghosts.

"I guess my *Lord of the Rings* comment earlier wasn't so off the mark," Mordred said with a smile, which was returned by Hel.

The army of souls marched through Mordred and Hel as if they weren't there. Mordred recognized some of the soldiers as being Avalon guards, but most were a mass of blues and greens that were barely even shapes for more than a second at a time.

The army of souls crashed into the dozen paladins as Merlin rode off at high speed. With his spear in hand, Arthur stood there like a statue, his arms out to the sides as if embracing the souls that swirled around his body, while his paladins were torn apart. Their screams of horror and pain were something that Mordred was sure would stay with him. After a few seconds, Arthur lowered his hands, winked, turned, and walked away to his waiting horse. He climbed up and rode off to join Merlin as the rest of his paladins died. When the paladins were dead, all that remained were the bloodstained weapons and rune-marked armor.

Hades waved a hand toward an approaching group of creatures, and the army of souls took off at high speed toward them.

"That would have come in handy earlier," Hel said.

"Don't like to do it," Hades said. "Promised people I wouldn't. I have to wait for the dead to be ready before it can be done too. And they don't last long when killing people with rune-scribed armor."

"Merlin was scared of you," Mordred said, slumping to the ground, exhausted from healing Hel and his fight with Arthur.

"Merlin knows what I am capable of," Hades said.

Mordred watched the fog of green and blue evaporate after killing the group of enemies. Hades walked over and helped Mordred to his feet.

"Tunnels are an elven realm gate," Mordred said.

"We'll check on it," Hades said. He whistled, and two horses moved slowly over to them. "Get back to the city; help there."

"You going after Merlin and Arthur?" Hel asked.

Hades shook his head. "Not today. The fighting is fierce closer to the city, much of which has been lost. We need everyone we can spare. We had no idea of just how many more enemies Avalon could bring. Thankfully it looks like help arrived."

Hades pointed off into the distance as hundreds of dwarves charged into the fray outside the city walls, and behind them were hundreds more Valkyries, with Layla riding Tego into battle.

"You mean we might actually win this?" Mordred asked.

"No," Hades said. "But we might survive it. I think right now that's all we can ask for."

"They took Tommy," Mordred said. "I couldn't help him. I couldn't stop them. I didn't have Excalibur. I left it in Elaine's hut . . . I . . . I failed. We need to track them down, need to find Tommy." Mordred took a step forward, and Hel stopped him.

"You're hurt," she said. "I'm hurt. Everyone is hurt. We go after Tommy like this, and Arthur and Merlin will kill us. We need to regroup, we need to find people who haven't just had the shit kicked out of them, and then we find Tommy."

"We will find him," Hades said. "But right now, we need to save everyone else. As harsh as that sounds, Hel is right—going after Tommy might get him and everyone who goes after him killed."

"Why not kill him?" Hel asked. "Why take him?"

"We will find out," Hades said. "But for now, we fight."

Mordred noticed someone atop the partially destroyed cliff where the giant had emerged.

"Is someone going to copy my plan?" Mordred asked. He got his answer a second later when the figure jumped off the cliff.

"Whoever it is, is crazier than you," Hel said.

"Crazy like a fox," Mordred said.

"Having met Remy, I would agree with that statement," Hades said.

The explosion of power from the ruined wall could be felt even from the distance at which the three were riding.

"What the hell was that?" Hel asked.

"I have an idea," Mordred said. "And if I'm right, I'm just really glad they're on our side."

Chapter Thirty-Two

Nate Garrett

Realm of Asgard

Turns out that when you dropped someone off the roof of a building several hundred feet tall, anyone remaining on the roof was really keen on helping out to ensure they didn't meet a similar fate.

That meant we had a lift to Little Skellig, although once there, the pilot quickly took off again. Couldn't blame him—I was pretty sure that either myself or Sky would have killed him if he'd tried something.

The realm gate activated for me on touch, so we stepped through into Asgard, only to be hit with the sounds of war.

I walked over to the now-much-shorter edge of the cliff. "Where'd the rest of it go?" I asked, looking down on the fighting below.

"The wall is ruined," a griffin said as it landed beside us. "I was asked to come here should anyone use the realm gate. To help you get down."

"I'll get down my way," I told him, noticing the gathering crowd of Avalon forces pushing their way through a huge gap in the wall. "Tell Selene I'll be there soon."

"Don't jump off the cliff," Sky said as I walked back to the realm gate and turned to face the edge once again. She vanished up into the sky, carried by the griffin.

"Race you to the bottom," I whispered and sprinted toward the edge of the cliff, launching myself off it and blasting my air magic behind me like a jet pack to get me far enough away.

I positioned myself so I was pointed head down and built up my pure magic. The crackling black power encircled my body, with tiny spots of white and purple sparking all around me. Pure magic might not have any defensive use, but that didn't mean I couldn't gather as much of it as possible to use in one hit. I just hoped that I wouldn't *mistime* it and crash into the ground with a splat. And as I'd never tried this before, that was always a possibility.

I pushed my magic out in front of me, continuing to build it, hoping that I didn't reach a point when it had to be unleashed whether I wanted it to or not. The pure magic sparked and crackled as my body began to feel the strain of what I was doing, my hands, arms, and shoulders crying out for me to not be an idiot.

I'd picked a spot just outside the city wall on purpose, ensuring that it was only the enemy forces coming into the city and not the defenders trying to stop them.

I saw arrows fly toward me, but the magic turned them to dust upon contact, and more than one enemy looked up and pointed at me. *What's that big ball of death?* I liked to believe they were thinking. Unfortunately for them, I'd never find out for sure.

The second before I slammed into the earth with all the style and panache of a piece of toast, I detonated my magic.

Short version: everything within a fifty-foot radius of me died.

I stood in the center of absolute death. The charred—and in some cases partially missing—remains of anything stupid or unlucky enough to have been anywhere near me were the only things that remained. More of the wall had been destroyed in the blast, too, although I wasn't too concerned about that, considering so much of it had already been gone.

The enemies outside the wall scattered, presumably to find something else to do that didn't involve being torn asunder. The enemies inside the city that were just outside the blast radius turned to me en masse, and anything with an IQ higher than that of a pine cone looked like it'd rather be somewhere else.

I couldn't use my pure magic for a while now. It was a finite resource, and once exhausted it needed time to recharge, but I figured I'd make do killing stuff without it for a while. I noticed the rune-scribed armor. Magic would be less effective against it. Pure magic cut through it like . . . well, like pure magic through rune-scribed armor, but normal magic would be easier for them to shield against. I needed a weapon.

Most of the weapons used by those I'd incinerated had been turned to little more than molten slag in the blast, but I noticed a partially mud-covered black blade that would have been used by a blood elf and picked it up.

"Very kind of you guys to just wait for me," I said to the crowd, which still hadn't quite decided whether I was someone to attack or run away from.

I tested the sword in my hand. It felt pretty good—a little weighty toward the tip of the blade, maybe, but it was usable. And usable was all I needed. I took a step toward the crowd, whose members had apparently regathered their strength and started to shout at me.

I took another step, and a lot of the shouting turned into a dull, almost apologetic roar. A few of those in front—mostly blood elves—turned to see what was behind them and found no way out.

Three of them rushed toward me. I parried the first sword and spun around its user to plant a foot on the side of the head of the second blood elf, swiping up with my sword and removing the hand of blood elf one. Blood elf three pounced at me, but a tendril of shadow leaped out of the ground and dragged the screaming blood elf into the realm to be devoured.

"So the runes don't stop my wraith," I said. "Good to know."

I was about to show them how much my wraith enjoyed feasting when there was a howl from nearby. That was the last straw for many of the group, who simply turned tail and fled into the city. I killed the two remaining blood elves and set off at a run toward the hospital, wondering what had made the howl and hoping—just for an instant—that my father was better.

I reached the hospital doors and found Selene, who had several bodies at her feet and a spear in one hand and sword in the other. She'd turned into dragon-kin form, and her huge silver wings were splattered with blood.

"Kase brought the cure," Selene said, hugging me. "Are you okay?"

I nodded, feeling the relief flood through me. "Astrid?"

"Shadow Falls. She's safe. Lucifer told me to head there, but I told him I was waiting for you. That we'd go together."

"I need to stop Arthur," I said. "War and Hera are here too. Left to their own devices, this whole realm will be destroyed."

"Who's War?" Selene asked, her wings vanishing as she pushed open the hospital door.

"A big dickhead," I said. "Made in the same way as Mordred and me. He's on Team Hera. Get everyone out of this realm any way you can. Tell my dad I'll be on the battlefield."

"I'm coming with you," she said.

I kissed her on the lips. "I would love you to, but we need to make sure the realm gate is clear."

"The Valkyries did that," she said. "The dwarves too."

"I've missed a lot," I said.

"Your mum came here looking for you. She's out there killing people at the moment. She's an interesting lady; she reminds me of you."

"I'm sure at some point I'll actually meet her," I said with a slight smile, feeling more than a little nervous about the possibility of finally meeting her. The nerves could wait, though.

A dozen soldiers ran out of a nearby building and off into the city. Something was coming. I turned to see Hera in the distance. Selene made a growl of anger low in her throat.

"Shall we?" I asked.

Selene and I walked through the group of soldiers toward Hera, who had an entire horde behind her. The remains of several buildings separated the two groups, and a howl broke out from somewhere in the distance.

"I have come to kill you, your father, your mother, your love, and your child," Hera said. "Not necessarily in that order."

"All this for revenge?" I asked, using my own air magic to carry the words to her.

She shook her head. "The child of a Horseman," she said. "We made sure to kill Mordred's all those centuries ago, and now we need to kill yours. The thing can't be allowed to live. It's simply too dangerous for our plans. Everyone else you love—they're revenge."

"You will never get close to my *child*," Selene said.

"You came to kill a helpless child," I said, my words carried to those who followed her. "And instead, you've found an incredibly pissed-off dragon-kin and me. For those who don't know, I was meant to be a Horseman. I was meant to be Death. You are all about to have a really shitty day."

There was another howl from behind me, closer this time. It was followed soon after by Kase, Olivia, Persephone, Zamek, Sky, Remy, Lucifer, and a dozen others. All of them were armed to the teeth and, judging from the expressions on their faces, looking for a fight.

Hera stopped walking. "Kill them all," she commanded, and her horde ran toward us.

They were fifty feet away when Odin slammed into the ground in front of me, a massive battle-ax in one hand and a whip of flame in the other.

Kase squeezed my hand. "He's *really* pissed off."

I smiled. "Excellent."

Odin turned back to me and gave me the thumbs-up. I nodded in return. It made me happy to see him up. I'd thought I'd lost my father after having only just found him. But now was not the time for reunions. Now was the time for fighting.

Hera's horde clashed with our much smaller group like two out-of-control freight trains. Magic and shows of power were thrown around as if in one of Mordred's video games. The rune-scribed armor everyone wore was soon rendered almost pointless, considering the amount of power in the air.

Three balls of lightning spun around me, blocking anyone from getting close, killing more than a few, while the hand of a wraith snatched those unfortunate enough to be in striking distance. It was a constant use and refilling of power that I knew couldn't last forever, but it would last long enough. I only had eyes for Hera.

Hera, who had tried to kill me at every opportunity. Who had messed with the ritual to block my powers, ensuring they didn't appear for centuries. Who had murdered my friends, who had been responsible for the torture of even more. Who had caused wars and strife just to further her own delusional ambitions. Today was going to be her last day alive. And there was no force on any realm that would ensure her safety.

I spotted Hera as she killed guard after guard who tried to get close to her. She held a short sword in one hand and a spear in the other and killed with grace and speed. She spied me as I got close and almost absentmindedly plunged the spear through the next of the enemies attacking her, dragged it out in a shower of blood, and walked on as if nothing had happened. She was powerful. I knew that. I knew that she'd killed Zeus and countless others and that she hadn't gotten to sit in the throne of her power base for as long as she had without being able to back up her words with action.

I blasted her in the chest with a torrent of air that picked her up and threw her back across what had once been a street. She bounced once and ended up in a building that exploded a second later, showering pieces of brick and mortar down all around her as she emerged without a scratch.

She placed a hand to her breastplate, and the runes that adorned her silver-and-black armor burned bright red. "Try that again, mongrel," she snarled.

I was nothing if not hospitable, so I blasted her in the chest with the full force of my air magic. She moved back six feet, but she never left the ground.

She smiled at me, a wicked, cruel expression that I'd seen countless times over the years. There had been a time when I'd had a measure of sympathy for Hera, a strong, powerful, smart woman who had been in a relationship that had made both people miserable. Any sympathy had long since turned to dust.

I was only a few feet from her when she rolled her shoulders and readied for battle. "You going to give me a chance to surrender?" she asked, her voice meek and playful.

I shook my head. "No. You die here. Today. I just wanted to tell you that. No sympathy. No quarter asked or given. Your empire is dust. London is no longer yours. Pestilence is dead. Licinius is dead."

"I'm going to kill you, your bitch, and your bastard offspring," Hera said with a smile. "I was going to keep you alive to see me skin them, but I'm not sure I can be bothered."

I swiped up with my sword, which she quickly parried with her own before thrusting her spear at my chest, forcing me to move back. She used the sword and spear like the expert I'd always assumed she would be, giving me little chance to do anything but make an occasional attack. She cut me across the arm twice, and I managed to cut her cheek, which only seemed to enrage her more for a moment before she regained her composure and settled back into her calm, methodical fighting style.

"You murdered my son," she said eventually.

"He deserved it," I told her, using a jet of air to push her spear thrust aside. I stepped inside her attack, aiming for her heart with my sword. She avoided the blow by moving to the side, the blade cutting under her arm, but it gave her the opportunity to headbutt me and kick me in the chest, sending me to the ground.

I blasted her with a jet of fire, which drove her back, just as the runes on her armor failed. She looked down to see that I'd cut through them with the sword.

"Very smart," she said, although she sounded like she was implying the opposite. She hit me with a fist of rock, which sent me flying back. I was plucked out of the air by several dozen hands of rock, all of which held me in place.

Unfortunately for Hera, I wasn't exactly a "let her kill me" kind of person. My hands were encased in thick rock, and I heated it quickly with my fire magic. The rock turned to lava enough that I pulled my hands free and blasted a plume of flame at her, which she avoided by dropping down into the rock beneath her feet.

A sphere of air spun in my hand, moving faster and faster as the earth beneath my feet began to crack. The second it tore open, spikes of rock moving toward me at speed, I drove the sphere into the ground and detonated the magic.

The crater it created was twenty feet in diameter and almost that deep. And in the center was me. Hera lay against the side of the crater, her face bloody.

"You're more powerful than you were last time we met," Hera said, pushing herself upright.

I took a step toward her, but a torrent of water slammed into me from beneath the ground, throwing me into the air. I wrapped myself in a shield of air, but the water encircled me, crushing against the shield, threatening to break it.

I looked down at a smiling Hera and plunged a marble-size ball of lightning into the water, then detonated the magic. The feedback to Hera was almost instantaneous, as she was launched back into the wall of the crater, vanishing from view as she allowed the earth to take her once again.

I fell thirty feet to the ground and landed on my feet, my air magic ensuring I didn't hurt myself. I doubted Hera would let me have a moment to recover should I land badly.

Six stone golems—each ten feet tall—burst out of the wall of the crater and ran toward me. A sphere of lightning plunged into the chest of the first and detonated, destroying it and the two directly behind it. I couldn't move in time to avoid the crushing embrace of one stone golem, who grew in size as the remains of its kin were absorbed into it.

It drove me into the ground, and all three golems brought down their fists onto my air-shield-covered body, forcing me into the earth as Hera's laughter echoed in my ears. I looked up as the largest of the three golems spewed ice all over my body except for my head, keeping me in place as it raised its now ice-covered fists to drive into me once more. It paused. Hera stood over me, pouring more and more power into the ice that kept me in place, ensuring that even with my fire magic activated, I was at best going to manage a draw.

"They won't kill you," she said. "I'll be doing that myself."

I'd known that Hera would come over to gloat. Thunder rolled high above, and electricity crackled all around. Hera's eyes opened wide in surprise, and I smiled just the tiniest bit. She'd always thought herself someone who played a great game of chess, always thinking three moves ahead. But she hadn't expected me to allow myself to be driven into the ground, to just lie there while she walked over to mock.

A blast of something slammed into the two smallest golems, disintegrating them and hitting Hera square in the chest, throwing her back from me. "Get away from him, you bitch," a woman I couldn't see said as she walked toward me.

The largest golem turned to greet the newcomer, and I noticed a griffin hovering high above. Several hundred feet at best guess. It dropped something, and I couldn't quite make out what it was with the Asgard sun and my current position.

The golem looked up just as the falling thing impacted with its head. The golem's head simply vanished. Everything from the neck down collapsed in on itself as I freed myself from the icy prison. I looked over at the woman who had blasted Hera—whom I couldn't see anywhere—and I knew her name.

"Mum," I said.

My mother—Brynhildr—stared back at me with tears in her eyes. "My son," she said, placing a hand against my cheek.

"I'm fine, thanks," Remy said, extricating himself from the ruins of the golem. "Just fell a few hundred feet and demolished a golem."

A lot of questions buzzed around my mind, but the most important one was, "How?"

"New power," Remy said. "I can increase and decrease my density. I'm essentially invulnerable to external damage while using it. Also, that was fucking cool."

"It was indeed," I said.

"I'll kill Hera, and then we'll talk," my mum said.

"It'll have to wait a bit longer than that," I said. "War is out there. Hera is out there. Innocent people are being hurt. Once those things are dealt with, we'll talk. I'll go after Hera."

"I don't think you need to," Remy said, pointing to Hera, who was running across the top of the crater.

"I surrender," she screamed as she dropped down into the muddy hole we'd created with our battle.

"You what?" I asked.

"I surrender," Hera said. "I won't fight. I'm done. I'll tell you everything you want to know."

I was about to open my mouth to speak when a bolt of light slammed into the back of Hera's head, and in an instant a young woman stood behind her, driving a dagger of white light into Hera's head, taking the onetime goddess to the ground. The younger sorcerer—which she clearly was—detonated the magic in the blade, and Hera's head vanished in a puff of gore.

The young woman stood up and dusted herself off. She walked over to me and offered me her hand. "Sorry, was that bitch yours to kill?"

"I'm not really bothered who did it," I said.

"Nate, right?" she asked.

I nodded. "And you are?"

"Your sister," she exclaimed.

"My what?" I asked, looking at both my mum and Remy, the latter of whom was staring at the young woman with his mouth agape.

"Well, not blood relations so much as blood magic related," the woman said. "My name is Judgement. You're Death. We're siblings by blood curse magic. The bitch without the head murdered my father, and maybe my mother too."

"And they were?"

"Zeus and the Lady of the Lake," Judgement said.

"It sounds like I've missed quite a lot," I said.

"Long story short," Judgement said, "yes. Yes, you have."

"I'll explain," my mum said.

"Anyway," Judgement said with a smile, "I'm going to go kill some more people, so I'll see you later." She ran off, the smile still on her face.

"I think I'm in love," Remy said.

I watched Judgement vanish into the city.

"Thanks for the assist, by the way," I said to Remy.

"No problem. What's the plan?"

"I'm going to go see if I can help end this war," I said. "And then I'm going to find War and kill him."

"He was on the battlefield last I saw," my mum said. "He has killed many."

"Then those will be his last," I said, looking down at Hera's corpse and feeling my pure magic ignite inside me. "Time to go end this."

Chapter Thirty-Three

Nate Garrett

My mum and Remy came with me to the battlefield, fighting several enemies on the way, although most saw me and ran. Both Brynhildr and Remy stopped to help injured soldiers as I spotted my father battling against several enemies at once.

"Nate, I forgot to mention," Remy said, "Hera dropped this." He showed me the vial of cure.

"Get it to Lucifer or anyone who can give it to Frigg. It's the only thing that will cure her."

"Be careful," my mum said.

I nodded, left my mother and friend to help the soldiers to safety, and ran across the battlefield toward my father.

Odin looked over at me and pointed away from him, toward a small group of boulders. Turning, I set off toward them and found many dead around them and Rasputin leaning up against them, his face and upper torso covered in blood.

"Nate," he wheezed.

I knelt beside him. "What happened?"

"War happened," he said. "Silver blade. I'm not going to make it, am I?"

I shook my head. His skin was waxy and pale, and he looked like he'd lost a huge amount of blood.

"The armor is keeping my organs inside me," Rasputin said. "I wanted to live up to how Hope made me feel. She made me feel like a warrior, like I was the bravest man on earth. And when she died and that left me, I was just the same man I'd always been. Someone who ran when it got hard or who helped bad people because I was too scared to even run. Leaving Hera was the hardest thing I'd ever done."

The more he spoke, the weaker he sounded, but he clearly had things he wanted to say, and it wasn't my job to stop him. It was my job to listen.

I looked over at my dad, who was busy killing anything and everything in sight. He had half a dozen soldiers with him, and together they'd created quite the team. I figured he'd be okay.

"I always wanted to be a warrior," Rasputin said. "I wish I had been able to stop Hera all those years ago. I wish I'd been brave enough. But here I am, dying on a battlefield because I'd wanted to prove to myself that I could do something. I saw War over here. He was just butchering people who were trying to surrender. I couldn't just let that go. Those with me felt the same way."

"Do you know where War is?"

Rasputin shook his head. "He ran off into the trees when Odin and his people showed up."

"Warriors are not people who go to war, Rasputin," I told him. "Warriors are people who are afraid to do something and do it anyway. People who know their fear and say, 'No, that won't stop me.'"

A flying horse dropped to the ground beside me and trotted over. The Valkyrie on its back looked down on us.

"He will die," she said.

I nodded.

"Will he die a warrior's death?" she asked, removing her helmet to reveal long dark hair that fell over her silver armor.

I nodded again. "He fought War. Tried to stop him murdering surrendering soldiers."

The Valkyrie looked impressed. "Then his soul will be taken to Valhalla. He will be remembered for what he did here today."

Rasputin smiled. "You're going to kill War, aren't you?"

I nodded. "That's the plan."

"You think you can?"

I shrugged. "Only one way to find out."

"You're a strange man, Nathan Garrett," Rasputin said.

"Brynhildr's son?" the Valkyrie asked.

"Nice to meet you," I said.

Rasputin took his last breath a moment later. I stood and placed a hand on his head. "Go well," I said softly.

"I've been sent to find anyone this far out," the Valkyrie said. "Word has gone out about an evacuation. Runes have been found all around the realm that are to destroy it. There are tunnels beneath the city; they're an elven realm gate. Get as many as you can to them before it's too late."

I sighed. "Of course it is. Good luck with your mission. I'm going to find War and end him in the most violent way I can find."

"Too late," she said, pointing over to where my father and his soldiers had been fighting. War and several soldiers had arrived at the battle, and it appeared that it was not going all that well for the rebellion forces.

I sprinted toward the group as War avoided a blade of flame from Odin's hand. He moved around my father and drove a dagger into his side, pulled it up, and kicked Odin square in the chest, sending him flying back toward me as he laughed.

I used air magic to catch Odin out of the sky. The majority of War's people were dead, and he made no movement to come to me. He beat his chest and laughed.

"That does not feel good," Odin said. "Silver blade. And I might be healed, but I'm nowhere near full power."

"Sit this one out," I said.

Odin sat down. "Good idea."

"This realm will burn soon," War said as I walked toward him. He showed me a rune on his forearm. "I have the power to say when it happens."

I remained silent as the soldiers with him, who all appeared to be sorcerers, cackled and made what I was sure they thought were hysterical jokes.

I glanced down at the leather armor I wore. The runes that had been scribed on it had been worn away, meaning it was about as protective in a magical battle as a packet of crisps. I unfastened the top part and tossed it aside, leaving me in the armored trousers and black T-shirt.

"You expect me to do the same?" War bellowed. His own armor was covered in blood, and the runes had long since been worn away to nothing. He'd drawn a skull in the blood on his metal breastplate, which was honestly quite impressive if he'd done it upside down while still wearing it.

I shrugged. "I don't much care what you do," I said.

One of the sorcerers threw a plume of fire at me. I wrapped myself in a shield of air and shadow, the fire doing nothing more than warm me up. When he'd finished using his magic, the look of surprise and horror on his face was almost worth not killing him where he stood. But not quite, as I threw a blade of fire toward him. I knew he'd block it or at least shield himself from it, but what he hadn't counted on was the fact that I threw twelve blades one after the other, the last one a silver dagger I'd picked up from near Rasputin. He hadn't anticipated the nonmagical attack, which cut through his shield and embedded itself in his forehead.

War laughed.

The other three sorcerers attacked me and died in quick succession. Blades of lightning and fire cut through the defenses of two of them, and a marble-size sphere of magical power detonated in the other's mouth, taking half of her head with it.

It left just me and War, who clapped at me. "This is how it should be," he said. "Is there anything you'd like to say before we start?"

"A few years ago, I started to use this," I said, creating a sphere of air in my hand. "Tommy told me that it was like something from an anime he watched. It was called a rasengan. They're not exactly the same, but he had a point. I like to call it a spinning sphere of death, but that's a little bit of a mouthful."

I walked toward War as the sphere grew in size, lightning and fire pouring into it, until it was the same size as my head, spinning at a speed that made it little more than a blur.

"You can't kill me with that," War said with a laugh.

The wraith hand left the shadow realm, and darkness encircled the sphere, dragging it down into the realm. "You tried to murder my friend, but he's better now. Our reunion will have to wait until we're done here, but in honor of Tommy, I would like to say just one thing to you."

War crossed his arms over his chest. "And what would that be?"

The wraith appeared behind War, screaming in rage, forcing War to turn to see the new threat, which allowed the shadows at my feet to open and the sphere to reappear. It was larger now and had combined with the power of my shadow magic.

I took it in my hand and darted toward War. "Eat rasengan, motherfucker."

War turned at the last second, unable to defend himself as I drove the sphere into his chest and detonated the magic.

I stood in the third crater of the day. The power of the sphere had destroyed everything around me and behind War. The crater was ten feet deep and a hundred feet in diameter. While my pure magic had exploded outward like a nuclear shock wave, the magic from the sphere had gone in every single direction all at once.

War was on his knees next to what had once been dense forest. The armor on his body had all but melted to nothing, his skin raw and painful.

"You can't kill me," he said.

"We have already fought," I told him. "But I was trying to keep my temper, or at least trying to make sure no one else got caught in the cross fire. I don't need to try to do anything but kill you now. You should have given up long ago."

He blasted a torrent of air, inside of which were thousands of razor-sharp shards of ice. I dropped into my shadow realm and appeared behind him, driving a blade of fire into his back.

"I don't have anything to be scared about," I whispered in his ear. "My friend is saved. My love is safe. My child is safe. My mind is no longer worried about the people I love." I drew the sword out, ignited a sphere of lightning, and drove it into the wound at War's back.

War bounced a hundred feet over the ground, his magic all that kept him from being torn apart by the force.

I dropped into the shadow realm and appeared beside War once again, driving a fist into his jaw. "I am not playing anymore," I said to him. "I'm not trying to give you a chance to atone. You hurt my friends. You killed my friends. You threatened those I love. Hera is dead. You will join her."

The air around War shimmered, and a torrent of power left his body. It smashed into me, lifting me up and throwing me back, the wind knocked out of me.

"Neat little trick, isn't it?" War said, getting to his feet. "Using my magic to push out as a physical force without having to tap into the elements. It took a long time to learn."

I remained seated on the ground as War walked toward me, his skin already starting to heal. He stopped after a few seconds and turned to meet Odin's charge. War avoided the battle-ax that my dad used. He rolled back and picked up a sword from the ground, then knocked away the blow from the ax and twisted away before darting forward and punching my father in the face, spinning him to the side.

I was on my feet and running toward them as War drove his sword through the back of my father and out the front where his heart was. Odin blinked and dropped to his knees as I screamed in rage, throwing bolts of lightning and fire at War, who lifted my father up with one hand to use as a shield before driving the sword through him again and throwing him at me.

Before my dad reached me, War threw a dozen razor-sharp blades of ice that cut through his arms and legs. I caught my dad in my arms, both of us tumbling to the ground as it began to rain.

"No, no, no, no, no," I said over and over again as I tried to stop the bleeding. So much bleeding. It was all over my hands, my arms, my face. I rubbed my eyes and tried to figure out a way to keep the blood from coming.

"Nate," Odin said softly. "Stop."

War's laughter reverberated around my brain. "No, I just found you," I said, feeling a pit of emptiness inside me. "I can't lose you already. I just found you. I can't."

"Make sure that daughter of yours grows up knowing her granddad was a badass," he said with a smile. He placed a hand against my face. "I love you, son. Always remember that."

"I love you too," I said as my father died in my arms.

The rain intensified, turning the battlefield to nothing more than mud. I laid Odin's body on the ground and stood, looking at a grinning War.

"Just us now," he said. "You think you can beat me?"

I looked down at my bloody hands and felt the pain and cold rage inside me.

"I can't die," he screamed. "Not by you, not by anyone. I am a god."

"I've killed my share of those," I said softly as thunder rolled up above.

War moved faster than I expected, and while I managed to switch on my matter magic and avoid the first blow to my jaw, the second to my gut lifted me off my feet. War kicked me in the chest and followed up with a roundhouse kick that sent me spinning before I hit the ground hard. My matter magic had kept me from being badly injured.

War laughed. "I did wonder if the rain was your doing," he said.

I stood and cracked my knuckles. "It was," I said.

Lightning streaked down from the sky, slamming into War's back and punching through his body into my outstretched hand. I held it inside me, mixing it over and over with magic, until my body hurt from the strain of keeping so much power inside.

"I want to beat you to death with my own hands," I said. "I want you to know the loss I feel. To know the pain I feel."

War was on his knees, gasping for breath, as the rain became harder. Lightning struck the ground all around us, my power almost out of control, as if it were calling out for even more.

I stood in front of War and looked down at him. "Die screaming, you son of a bitch," I said and unleashed the magic and lightning inside me directly into War's face. His screams of pain were soon muffled by a wet sound, and then there was nothing as his charred remains fell to the ground.

My body was ruined. Everything hurt.

I fell to the mud. My clothes had all but disintegrated from the power I'd used. My hands were a broken and burned mess, my chest and legs the same. I couldn't see clearly out of one eye, and what I could see out of the other was darkness and mud. And my father's body.

My magic would not respond to me as it tried to heal the horrific wounds I'd inflicted on myself. I hadn't been sure I could use my lightning magic in such a way, to absorb so much power and release it all at once. Not even my pure magic had such an impact on my body.

After a few seconds I thought I could smell burning, although there was a chance that was just me. My eyes were healed, and I managed to get to my feet. I looked down at War and tore the remains of his head off his body before tossing the head aside as the smell of fire became ever stronger.

I moved as quickly as I was able to the side of the crater and climbed out, looking back at the inferno that was engulfing the forest. War's rune had clearly activated when he'd died.

I turned back to the city, and an explosion tore part of it asunder. A mushroom cloud moved high into the sky, signaling the power of the devastation that had been caused.

A wall of fire spread out through the city like a tsunami, consuming all. I was in between two walls of magical flame. I sighed. "Bollocks to the fucking lot of you."

I caught sight of something—a small dot amid the devastation of Asgard—racing out of the broken wall toward me. The fires loomed and continued to move toward each other at a quick pace, and I hoped that whatever was racing toward me was something I could use to not be in the middle of two flame tsunamis.

It didn't take long for the saber-tooth panther to reach me as I ran toward her. She wore some kind of armor and had a saddle on her back.

"Tego," I said. "We getting out of here?"

Tego nodded.

I looked down at my father and knew that we'd be faster without him. "Go in peace, Dad," I whispered as I mounted the panther. "Lead the way, my friend."

As we raced along the battlefield to wherever Tego knew was safety, I looked back at the destruction, the loss, the devastation that had befallen Asgard. We had turned back Avalon; we had stopped them from taking us all. We had done it. But we had lost a lot to achieve that aim. Arthur and those who supported him would feel that pain back on them tenfold. In that moment, as the flames consumed all that had been, I swore that everyone responsible would receive no mercy from me.

Tego sprinted into a cave, taking turn after turn in the maze of passages that she ran into, never once slowing. The walls glowed with elven and dwarven runes. Eventually we reached the center of a large room, where Tarron the shadow elf activated the realm gate.

I found myself in Shadow Falls. I climbed down off Tego and thanked her for her help. Before I'd even left the cave, I was engulfed in a hug by Selene.

"My dad," I said. "War killed him."

Selene held me tightly as I wept.

Chapter Thirty-Four

Nate Garrett

Realm of Shadow Falls

Elaine was dead. That was the first thing I was told once I'd entered the city of Solomon, the capital of Shadow Falls. Hades, Persephone, and several others took me aside and told me about her. They told me that Mordred had been seriously injured in a fight with Arthur and that no one knew where Arthur was.

And then they told me that Tommy had been taken.

I sat there, dumbfounded. "What do you mean, 'taken'?" I asked, feeling angry.

"He stopped Mordred from being killed," Hades said. "But Mordred couldn't stop Arthur from hurting him and the paladins from dragging him away. I arrived soon after, but there was no time to go after Tommy. Not while so many other lives needed saving too."

I nodded. I understood that. I would have done the same if it had been anyone but Tommy. "Do we know where he is?" I asked.

No one did. I got up and walked over to Olivia and Kase before hugging them each in turn. "We will find him," I told them.

They both nodded. There was no other option. We found Tommy, or we died trying.

"I'm going for a walk," I told everyone. "Does anyone know where Mordred is now?"

"We haven't seen him in hours," Persephone said. "We need to find him, though."

"I gave him Excalibur," Hel said. "But he said he needed some time to himself."

I pushed the anger and hurt at having lost so many aside, and I left the building. I knew that I couldn't rush off to find Tommy. Not just because it was tantamount to suicide but because we had no idea where he was. Also, I couldn't just leave Selene and Astrid. I couldn't leave Mordred and my friends to pick up the pieces alone. Tommy was one of the toughest people I'd ever met. He would be okay. I had to believe that.

I found Selene and Astrid sitting beneath a large tree just outside the city. There was a small pond nearby, and dragonflies buzzed across it.

"Astrid was hungry," Selene said. "I didn't think feeding her while you were being given bad news was the best idea."

"Elaine is dead," I said as I sat beside her. "She was like a parent to me. She backed me up; she helped me when I left Avalon. When I left Merlin. But I can't begin to imagine how that's crushed Mordred. She loved him like a son."

Selene rested her head on my shoulder as Astrid lay in her carry cot, fast asleep, oblivious to what was going on around her.

"Tommy was taken," I said softly.

"We'll find him," she said with complete certainty.

"I know," I said. "But damn it, I told him to get out of the realm. I told him to stay somewhere safe. What the hell was he doing fighting? What the hell was he doing fighting Arthur?" Tears fell as I said the last sentence. "Damn you, Tommy. Why didn't you fucking well listen to me?"

"Because he's a hero," Selene said. "He did exactly what you would have done. Or Hades, or Mordred, or Diana, or any of us. He stayed and saved lives. Dozens of lives, Nate. He got people to the realm gate; he held off blood elves and creatures he had no business fighting in his shape. He didn't falter; he didn't back down; he just did what was right. He stopped Arthur from killing Mordred. And you know damn well that if the roles were reversed, you'd have stayed too."

I nodded. "I know. I know it's irrational to be angry at him. I just . . . I can't imagine the horrors that Arthur will inflict. The damage he will do. 'You can't save everyone.' That's what Hope told me. I pushed it aside because you're damn right I'll try to, but I can't. I couldn't save my father or Rasputin or Hope or Pestilence or Tommy or Elaine. I couldn't save any of them. So I'm going to utterly fucking destroy those responsible."

"Good," Selene said. "Go find Mordred. Tell him what you need. Tell him he needs to step up and be a king. He got Excalibur. Now is the time to rally the troops. Now is the time to stop reacting and take the fight to Arthur."

I leaned over and kissed her. "I'll be back, and then we end this."

Selene nodded. "You're goddamn right we do. You know where Mordred is?"

I nodded. "I have a pretty good idea, yes."

"You going to tell anyone?"

I shook my head. "Not yet. I'll give him some time."

"You haven't seen him since we arrived, have you?" Selene asked.

I shook my head. "No, why?"

"He lost an eye in the fight with Arthur," she said. "Arthur nearly killed him and Hel. Tommy and Hades saved their lives, but Mordred will never again have both eyes."

"I'll go find him now," I said. "Mordred has had it tougher than most, and honestly, I'm not even sure how he hasn't reached a breaking point yet."

"He's a good man."

"He is," I said, and I left Selene to her moment of peace and quiet while I hunted for Mordred.

I found Layla, Chloe, Piper, and Ava first, though; all of them were sitting on the steps to the palace. I spotted Tego lying over by the side of the building, sunning herself.

"You okay?" Chloe asked me with a hug.

I nodded. "You all seem to be okay, too; that's good to see."

Tego snorted in my direction.

"I'm obviously happy that you're okay," I shouted over to her.

"You too," Layla said. "We're not done here, are we?"

"Arthur is still out there. Avalon is still powerful. No, we're not done."

"More people are going to die," Chloe said, more of a statement of fact than a question.

I nodded. "Yes. A lot more. Arthur and his people won't go easily into the night."

I patted Chloe on the shoulder when she looked downhearted. "We'll do this," I told her.

"I never doubted it," Layla said.

"Take some time and rest," I said. "We need to figure out how we're going to take the fight to Avalon."

Ava looked down at the ground. "I'm not sure I'm cut out for this," she whispered.

"You're sixteen," I said. "No one is expecting you to be the next Captain Marvel."

"That's because I already have that job," Chloe said with a smile that earned her a shake of the head from Piper.

"I want to help," Ava said, more forceful now. "But how? What do I do? I talk to ghosts occasionally. I know when people are going to die. But I don't know exactly what people or where. I just . . . I didn't expect to be in a war zone."

"None of us did," Layla said. "And no one is expecting you to do anything. You've done more than anyone could ever have expected of you. You should be proud of yourself."

Ava nodded.

"We'll keep an eye on her," Piper said to me. "It wasn't that long ago that none of us had gone to war. That none of us had seen death and destruction on the scale we've seen recently. It's a learning curve for us all, and whether you choose to help fight with a sword or you help fight in another way, we're all helping the same cause."

I left them to their conversation and ascended the steps to the magnificent palace above. The last time I'd been in Shadow Falls hadn't been a fun experience. I'd lost friends then too. It felt like a long time ago, although in reality it had been only a few years.

I entered the palace and, after walking through the many busy corridors, found my mum, Brynhildr. She sat at a table along with a dozen other Valkyries, who all turned to look at me.

"My boy," Brynhildr said, rushing over to hug me.

"Odin died," I said. "He died fighting War."

"I heard; I'm sorry," Brynhildr said. "He was someone I liked and admired, if not always agreed with."

The Valkyries all filed out of the room.

"Did Frigg get the cure?" I asked.

My mum nodded. "She's upset and finding things hard to understand, but she'll be okay."

"You tell her Baldr is dead?" I asked.

She nodded. "She wanted me to say sorry for what he tried to do. He was her son, but she knew what he was."

"We have a lot to catch up on," I told her. "But right now, I need to find Mordred."

"You think Mordred can do it?" Brynhildr asked. "He seems . . . fragile."

"He's probably the strongest person I've ever met," I said. "He might be a bit all over the place, but there aren't many I'd stand beside as quickly as I would him. He's a good man. Probably better than any of us."

"You've grown into a good man," Brynhildr said.

"Thank you," I said. "Although I'm not sure that good or bad come into it. I just try to be the person I need to be. And sometimes that means doing bad things to help good people."

"Like killing War and Hera?" Brynhildr asked.

"I didn't kill Hera, although I was going to," I said. "And War . . . well, War got what he wanted all along. To face me in open combat with no limits. I imagine he regretted that decision about two seconds after he realized what I am."

"And what's that?" Brynhildr asked.

"You know what I am," I said. "I was born to kill gods. That's what it says up here." I tapped my head. "Mordred, War, Judgement, Pestilence, myself—all of us born to make sure that if anyone stepped out of line, we could kill them."

"Not just gods," Brynhildr said, "but devils too. Should they reappear, you were the first line of defense."

"So we were born to kill Arthur. I assume he knows this."

"I would think so, yes."

"Good," I said. "Then he knows what's coming."

I said my goodbyes and found Mordred exactly where I'd expected him to be. Sitting on the steps at the rear of the palace by himself, with a bottle of whiskey in one hand and a sheathed

Excalibur in the other. I sat beside him, and he passed me the bottle of drink.

"I couldn't save him," he said softly. "I wanted to, but I'd left Excalibur behind. I couldn't save Tommy. I couldn't stop them taking him."

I reached over and pulled Mordred into a hug. "It's not your fault," I said.

"I couldn't save Elaine either," he snapped, throwing Excalibur down the steps and taking back the bottle of whiskey. "I had the sword on me then. And I still couldn't do a goddamn thing."

"You weren't in the room when it happened," I said. "You can't be in two places at once. Elaine's death, Tommy's kidnapping, the death of my father, and any others you care to worry about. They're not on you."

"All I want to do is keep people safe. I tried to come out here and get drunk off my ass, but my damn magic makes it impossible. Even so, I needed to come talk to Galahad."

"You killed his father, yes?"

Mordred nodded. "Lancelot murdered Elaine."

I took the bottle of twenty-one-year-old whiskey and had a swig, feeling the warmth trickle down my throat. I made a contented sound.

"Good stuff, isn't it?" Mordred said. "Galahad has a whole cellar full of it. Figured he wouldn't mind."

"Galahad hated Lancelot," I said. "Everyone hated Lancelot. He was a prick."

"Guinevere hated him too," Mordred said. "Still sucks that it came to that."

"Where is Guinevere now?"

"She's resting, I think," Mordred said. "She took a lot of cave troll bone and is currently high as a kite."

"Cave troll bone? She's taking troll bone?" I couldn't help it; I just started laughing.

"Oh, bloody hell, Nate, grow up," Mordred said with a giant smirk on his face.

"Troll bone," I said, almost wheezing. "I know it's very serious, but even so, damn it, I was not prepared to hear those words today."

Mordred shook his head. "Guinevere is a fucking mess, Nate. She's been on the run for centuries, lied to, used as a pawn, threatened, addicted to drugs, and almost killed. She's still not safe. Arthur is still out there. No one is safe while Arthur is still out there."

I stopped laughing. It didn't feel so funny now. "Sorry," I said.

"It's okay," Mordred said. "I just can't believe how many lives Arthur has managed to fuck up over the years. And I couldn't kill him."

"It's Arthur," I said.

"I almost killed him last time," Mordred said.

"Last time was over a thousand years ago," I said. "And there were a lot of differences."

"Bastard took my eye."

I nodded. "Yes, I sort of noticed that. It looks like you've had it cleaned up. And you're wearing a patch."

"Hel made me," he said, smiling for the first time.

"It looks jaunty," I said.

"I look like a pirate," he told me, then sighed. "That's all he does. Take. I saw Hades hit him with enough power to tear paladins to shreds, and Arthur just stood there and mocked it. What's it going to take to stop him? A nuclear bomb?"

"I really hope not," I said. "Maybe we can shoot him into the sun?"

Mordred stared at me for several seconds, before I noticed him shifting focus to someone walking behind me. I turned to see Judgement walking along the lawn.

"Hey," Judgement said, waving. She had a bottle of whiskey of her own and, judging from the smell, a massive spliff.

"Feeling pretty good?" I asked Judgement.

"I like whiskey; I like cannabis," Judgement said. "I make no apologies for either."

"You don't need to," Mordred said. "Enjoy the fleeting moments of tranquility."

I turned to Mordred. "You high too?"

Mordred laughed.

"War is dead, I take it," Judgement said.

I nodded.

"You kill him?" she asked.

I nodded again.

"Good," Judgement said with a swig of whiskey. "He was a cunt."

She stopped by Excalibur, picked it up, and passed it to Mordred. "This belongs to you, I believe."

Mordred stared at the sword for several seconds.

"You unsheathed it yet?" I asked.

Mordred shook his head. "I'm sort of scared to see what happens."

"Well, my friends, I'm going to go get drunk, get high, and sleep," Judgement said. "Later, people!"

"I like her," I said. "She'll fit in great around here."

"She doesn't hum enough theme tunes," Mordred said with a smile.

"Speaking earlier of Hel, how is she?"

"I love her so much, Nate. I'm not sure what happens if I take the job of king of Avalon. Fuck Avalon. Fuck it all."

I stood and placed a hand on his shoulder. "You'll figure it out. It starts with you unsheathing that sword."

Mordred stood and, with one quick motion, unsheathed Excalibur. Nothing happened.

"I was expecting a lightning bolt or something," he said.

"I'd provide one, but you know, magic in Shadow Falls doesn't work right."

"Yeah, let's not blow anything up," Mordred said. "Maybe that's why it's not working."

"Are there any magic words you need to utter?"

"It's a sword, Nate; it doesn't have ears."

Mordred tightened his grip and concentrated for a second. My magic vanished.

"Whoa, what happened?" I asked.

"This sword lets me stop all magic from a certain distance. It also lets me enhance my own magic, and it makes you tell the truth."

"I'm terrified that I'm not good enough to do this," I said. "Shit . . . it appears to be working."

"Not good enough?" Mordred asked. "Seriously?"

I nodded. "I'm meant to be Death incarnate. You're Conquest. We were designed to kill people like Arthur. But Arthur is . . . Arthur. He's so far beyond anything any of us have fought. And we don't know where he is."

"We'll find him." He sheathed the sword. "I need to do this in front of everyone, don't I?"

I nodded.

"Bollocks," he said, walking off around the side of the palace.

I followed Mordred at a distance, picking up several different tunes that he hummed on the way. People stopped him and said hello, and his walking became more and more purposeful until we reached the fort, where a makeshift camp was in the process of being set up. They'd done a lot of work since I'd left, the benefit of having alchemists and dwarves working for you. Thousands of people were going to be living here, I assumed until houses could be made or properties could be made larger. It wasn't the most comfortable of lifestyles, but everyone was safe. For now, anyway.

Mordred walked up to a large number of people that included Lucifer, Hades, Persephone, and Hel. He drew Excalibur and tossed the sheath onto the ground, holding the sword up above him. "You want me to be your king, I shall be your king," he said before muttering, "like I have a fucking choice."

Because not everyone was listening, I threw a small bolt of lightning at the tip of the blade. Unfortunately, because as I'd said to Mordred, magic was unpredictable in Shadow Falls, the tiny amount of magic I'd used touched the sword and exploded in a shock wave of power that rushed over everyone. It didn't hurt anyone, but it sure as hell got their attention.

"People of the rebellion," I shouted. "Do you swear fealty to our king? To King Mordred?"

The shout of "Yes!" was deafening.

Mordred turned back to me and walked over. He whispered, "What if I can't do this?"

"You are my friend," I said. "You are better than you know. You will be able to do this."

"And you know that how?"

"Because Elaine believed you could. Because all these people believe you can. And because"—I dropped to one knee—"you are my king."

"What if I'm not ready?" he whispered.

"I will have your back, always," I told him. "There is no force on any realm that will change that. We will see this to the end—together."

Mordred stared at me for several seconds. His mouth moved, but no words left.

There was an almighty cheer from the crowd, and Mordred turned to them, doing his best not to look like a rabbit in the headlights. He smiled and raised Excalibur once again. He'd never wanted any of this. He'd never wanted to be king. He'd never wanted the responsibility.

He was going to be a great king.

Mordred lowered the sword and turned back to me. "On one condition," he said. "If I have to do this, if I have to be a king, then I'm going to need people who I can trust at my side." He held Excalibur, which glowed with power, and placed the tip against each of my shoulders in turn. "Sir Nate."

"Are you sure?" I whispered.

He offered me his hand, which I took as I got back to my feet. "My friend, I have never been surer about anything in this world. You are now and forever a knight. We'll figure out what that means later, but for now, it means you're going to help me win this war."

"I was always going to do that," I explained.

"I know, but if I have to be a fucking king, you can be a knight," Mordred whispered to me, making us both laugh.

People got back to their feet and began to chant for King Mordred. I looked at my friend with pride and happiness.

Arthur had tried to kill Mordred. He'd broken him, destroyed his mind, done horrific things to him. But after a thousand years of being someone he wasn't, he'd come back to us. He'd come back to us better than he'd ever been. A wrong had been righted. Mordred was king. Arthur had failed in his mission to destroy a man who was better than him. And if I had my way, Arthur would soon discover that was going to be his downfall.

Epilogue

King Arthur

Realm of Atlantis
One Week Later

It hadn't exactly gone to plan, but it hadn't been a disaster either. War was dead, yes, and the realm of Asgard was destroyed, which wasn't brilliant. But on the plus side, he'd kicked the shit out of Mordred, which was something he'd been looking forward to for a long time. Elaine was dead; that was a wonderful thing, as she'd been a thorn in his side for too long, and he'd heard that Odin was no more. That really was quite the result.

Arthur imagined Nate deep in mourning as he walked along the prison corridor. The walls and floor were metal. They'd once been a light-blue color, but time and wear had made them more rust colored than anything else.

Occasionally the screams of prisoners could be heard, and Arthur would wonder which one was being tortured. They weren't after information; they just wanted to know how long they could torture someone. Merlin found it distasteful, even with Gawain there twisting his brain if he needed to.

Arthur had come to Atlantis for a few reasons. Primarily because there were things he'd put into motion here that he needed to oversee, but also because if the rebellion decided to attack Avalon, they would find it empty of Arthur's presence, giving him time to launch a counterattack.

Hopefully it wouldn't come to that and his people on the Earth realm would keep those ungrateful wretches busy, but he had to make sure. He stood by a prison door and turned the handle before pushing it open.

Inside Tommy sat naked on a chair, his wrists cuffed with extra-long chains to metal hoops attached to the floor. The wounds he had suffered in Asgard had mostly healed, and the venom Arthur had commanded be used on him was nearly out of his system entirely. The torture hadn't started yet. Gawain had been impatient; he'd wanted to rip pieces off Tommy, but Arthur hadn't brought him here for that.

"Hello, Tommy," Arthur said, taking a second chair from the corner of the room and placing it in front of him.

"Go fuck yourself, Arthur," Tommy said.

Arthur smiled. "Seeing how you're still alive, maybe you should be nicer. Do you know why you're alive?"

"I'm not going to tell you anything."

"Oh, no, I don't care about that. You see, I have this plan for you. You're going to be here awhile as my esteemed guest."

"What do you want?"

Arthur had allowed Tommy to keep his powers so that he might heal, but the cuffs on his wrists were silver, as were the chain and the loops in the floor. Tommy was no threat to him. Although he hadn't been even before he'd become a prisoner.

Arthur stood up and knocked on the door. A paladin opened it and stepped inside, followed by three more. They all stood at the corner of the hundred-square-foot cell.

Arthur turned back to Tommy, who eyed the paladins with a mixture of anger, hate, and confusion.

"Tommy, I assure you, when we're done, you're going to be a whole new man." Arthur chuckled to himself as he left the cell, and the sounds of screams followed him down the corridor a moment later. Arthur smiled. *Come find me, Nate. We're not done by a long shot.*

ACKNOWLEDGMENTS

We're at the halfway point of the Rebellion Chronicles, and if you've stayed with me this long, I thank you for that. It's been quite the ride.

Like every book I write, there are a host of people to thank for it ever getting to the point of being written, then readable, and finally in your hands.

My wife and children will always be the first people to thank. They're the reason I first started to write seriously all those years ago, and they're always there to support and push me to be better.

My parents have supported me from the first word I ever wrote, and I probably wouldn't be here writing these acknowledgments without their influence. I will always thank them for that.

To my family and friends who support and read my work, to those who ask me when the next book will be out and who wanted to make sure that Nate was actually coming back, it's always good to know that people have your back. Thank you for that.

A massive thank-you to my agent, Paul Lucas, for his advice and friendship, and generally for just being awesome.

To Julie Crisp, my editor who helped turn my jumbled mass of words into something readable, thank you. The book is considerably better for having had you work on it.

And last but by no means least, to everyone at 47North for their support, friendship, and just being fantastic to work with over the years: thank you.

ABOUT THE AUTHOR

Photo © 2013 Sally Beard

Steve McHugh is the author of the bestselling Hellequin and Avalon Chronicles. He lives in Southampton, on the south coast of England, with his wife and three young daughters. When not writing or spending time with his kids, he enjoys watching movies, reading books and comics, and playing video games.